I0631581

THE
JUDGEMENT
OF
OSCAR
KINGMAN

Christopher J. Smith

First published in 2017 by Meredith-Smith Pty Limited

National Library of Australia
Cataloguing-in-Publication entry

Smith, Christopher J.

The Judgement of Oscar Kingman / Christopher J. Smith.

ISBN 978-0-9874633-6-4 (pbk.)

A823.4

First Edition 2017

The characters in this book are fictitious and any resemblance to real persons, living or dead is purely coincidental.

www.christopherjsmith.com.au

Christopher J. Smith lives on Australia's Gold Coast and
is married with two adult sons. As well as being a novelist,
he has written and composed almost two hundred songs
and produced two commercial albums...
Cold Outside and *Missing Chapters from the Book of Blues.*

Other books by Christopher J. Smith

GHOSTS OF TOKYO

WASTELAND

Acknowledgements

I wish to express my gratitude to
the alliance of boarders.

Author's Note

The Judgement of Oscar Kingman is set in the United
States of America. Many locations are real and based
on geographical accuracy... many are not.
For example, the town of Tyrells Inlet is entirely
fictitious. As stated elsewhere in this book, all
characters are fictitious and any resemblance to
real persons living or dead is purely coincidental.
The law enforcement practices and pathology present
in this book are not necessarily anchored in fact.

This is a work of fiction.

FOREWORD

What you are about to read is a work of fiction. It may well be a patchwork, or a montage of truths woven together, but it remains a fiction nonetheless. I am not Oscar Kingman and Oscar Kingman is not me, however, parts of Oscar Kingman's life are drawn directly from my own experiences.

The narrative seeks to understand how today's world functions and why. How we disenfranchise the different and then demonise the disenfranchised. This is not a book about the black holes that exist in cyber-land or the advent of modern terrorism. It is not a book about war, drugs, political or corporate greed, pollution or climate change and all those other fears real or imagined that we face in today's world. Neither is it about the appalling violence that we witness daily on our streets and pipe into our homes as entertainment. It is not even a book about child abuse or organised religion.

It is a book about people or, more specifically, each individual person on this planet and how we all interact, because mankind is the sum of all parts and it is mankind to be held accountable. All those things I have mentioned above don't just occur on their own, they are mankind's doing.

And so I created the fictional Oscar Kingman because in truth, mankind has created millions like him and worse, and whilst I do not judge Oscar Kingman and all those like him, I want to know why. I want to understand how mankind can be so stupid.

While writing this book I was constantly aware of how the parents of the 1950's and 1960's saw the advent of flower power, the pill, sex, drugs and rock & roll as the beginning of the end. Could there be anything more evil than a teenager in tight jeans with a 'Beatle' cut?

I came to question what right today's parents might have to assume that things are far worse now than they were back then, that this might truly be the beginning of the end.

But then like I said at the outset…. it's only fiction right?

BOOK ONE

FAMILY

'Honour thy father and thy mother,

that thou mayst be longlived upon the land

which the Lord thy God will give thee.'

Exodus 20,12

WAKE TO A NIGHTMARE

Today Oscar Kingman would kill his boss.

Top, terminate, snuff, croak, butcher, whack, waste, ice, rub out and just plain murder the fucker.

Of course Oscar didn't know that yet. The day started like most every other day in Oscar's life and therein lay the problem.

He woke lying on his right side, eyes still closed. There was that moment, that tiny delicious moment of first consciousness where anything was possible. He might not be bald, might be rich, married to a smart and beautiful woman. He might drive a Ferrari. But no, in half the time it takes a thought to form, reality comes crashing in. So yesterday and all the yesterdays before that come cramming into his head. The reasons why he never wants to get up again are the very reasons he has to get up. Up out of his bed. The mounting bills, the speeding charge, the mole on his back that needs checking, the mistake he covered up at the office at risk of being discovered, unearthed. His whole miserable goddam life playing past his closed eyelids like some private viewing.

He tried to open his eyes, but they were crusted shut with old tears and bad dreams. Did he cry last night? Probably. He heard strange noises from the other side of the bed. Fat cow farts and scratches and starts up snoring again just like that. Probably dreaming of the next trip to the hairdressers or what colour to paint her fucking nails in case she crosses paths with Robert Redford. Oscar allowed himself the small pleasure of imagining the movie star running into his wife somewhere, Redford clutching his chest in fright and looking round for someplace to run. '*Ha!*'

Enough of life's small pleasures. Sharon had about as much chance of running into Redford in Walmart as *he* did of divorcing her and marrying a smart and beautiful woman. He jammed his fingers in his eyes, clawed out the sleep and rolled on his back. Oscar Kingman thirty six years old, soft, balding, lousy end-of-the-line job, married to Attila the Hun and the proud father of two of the most obnoxious teenage girls a loser could hope to sire. And a coward, scared of the wife, the kids, the boss. Yeah, pretty much scared of everyone. *'Don't let him talk to you like that you spineless jerk, do something.' 'Yes dear.'* But of course he never did do anything and she was right, he was a spineless jerk. *Probably be on his headstone one day 'here lies Oscar Kingman, spineless jerk, loved by... well loved by nobody really.'*

He tilted his head to look at the white heaving shoulder of the lovely Sharon. It sent a shudder through him, motivated him right out of that bed. Sat there on the edge coming to life, scratching at the scar that ran across his left palm. 6.38 and into the shower. He spent five minutes battling with the limp shower fitting until he finally got it to stay pointed at him, then someone, probably Sharon, came in and flushed the toilet, scalded his arse. He pushed himself back to the tiled wall while the water sorted. He wasn't sure, but he thought he might have been crying. Hard to tell.

Out of the shower he towelled off and wiped a clear space across the steamed-up mirror... and there he was, Oscar Kingman thirty six years of age. Soft, balding and... well that was it really. Put that on his headstone as well if anyone bothered enough to buy one. He combed the last of his hair over and wiped more of the mirror clear. Stepped back, maybe not so bad, just a bit flabby round the edges. Could always tighten up a bit, exercise, maybe run a bit. He looked up at his head, the Oscar staring back at him. *'Who you fooling?'*

He pulled open the mirror cabinet and took out his razor, no blade, *'you're kidding me.'* Oscar's one masculine act was to shave with a blade, not one of those pussy electric things.

Sharon's thing was to use his blades to shave her fat hairy legs. She'd probably use it to slice off his balls if she hadn't been chewing 'em off bit by bit since the day they got married. He groped around amongst the hideous mess of shampoos, creams, conditioners, pads, mascaras, deodorants and product, whatever the hell that was. *'Christ it's like a trashed laboratory in here,'* thought Oscar. He knew none of this shit was going to help Sharon, and the hideous gum chewing she-devils were looking more like their mother each day, so no luck there either. They were on holidays now, probably sleep till noon, but at least he could get in the bathroom.

Five minutes looking and he gave up, dug out a clean shirt (*not ironed of course*) and brown striped tie. In the kitchen he got a bowl from the pile on the drainer and a cereal pack from the cupboard. Empty. The last three flakes fluttered into his bowl. Oscar stood there fully two minutes. *'Who did this kind of shit?'* Who put an empty cereal pack back in the cupboard? Same dick as puts a dead milk container back in the fridge, the rubbish bin back with no liner that's who, take your pick. He dropped the cereal pack in the liner-less bin and went and pulled on his suit coat. Dark sweat stains creeping out under the armpits permanent now. Only one he had, have to do.

Oscar Kingman pulled the front door closed behind him and went down the steps to the drive, the empty drive. *'Shit, this can't be happening,'* the car gone. The car stolen. *'The goddamned car, stolen.'* He stood there keys in hand staring at the empty drive, oily cracked concrete and carless. Oily cracked concrete with weeds coming through and carless. *'I'll call Sharon from the office, she can deal with it,'* thought Oscar as he dragged his tired soft body down the drive, his tired soft body with its unshaven head and its rank brown suit coat complete with the giant underarm sweat stains shaped kinda like the great state of Texas.

First bus drove clean past him. He looked down and patted himself to make sure he wasn't invisible. Twenty minutes the next bus pulls in on squeaky brakes. Stink of fifty people smacks him in the face. He treads on toes, sticks his briefcase into people and finds a tiny slot to stand where he can't do any harm, much. He looks around furtive, young girl there chewing gum, punching phone, ears trailing a couple of wires, short skirt, bad makeup. She sees him looking at her legs, up her skirt, spits her gum at him. Could be his daughter, *'isn't is it?'* Can't risk another look. Thirty three minutes on the bus into the city with the words to Chris Rea's 'Road to Hell' going round and round in his head.

Thirty five minutes later and Oscar is at the office, outside anyway. Oscar Kingman, junior estimator at Loughrans Loss Adjusters. Oldest junior estimator in the history of the firm. The oldest junior estimator in the history of the firm turned and wandered across to Top Shot Coffee, strong black, heaps of sugar and a breakfast bagel. He juggles coffee, bagel and briefcase out the door then spies a place on the edge of the fountain and beats the next contender into the spot. *First win of the day.* Been sitting maybe thirty seconds, unwrapped the bagel and he feels the water soaking through to his arse. Stands up quick into the path of a jogger cutting through the mall, and it's a shit shower of hot coffee and bagel stuffing all down his front. Oscar Kingman, thirty six, standing by a fountain downtown in the morning rush holding his sopping shirt out wide against the scalding. Watching a fucking jogger in red and black checkered stretchy shorts, with a green backpack disappear into the morning crowd. Dead bagel on the granite pavers between his feet. *The harlequin fucking jogger strikes again.*

Today Oscar Kingman would kill his boss. Of course he didn't know that yet.

WHAT'S IN A NAME?

Oscar's father had been some kind of salesman. Had one of those forestry type names, Chip or Buzz or something. His mother's name was Lorrie, short for Loretta. Lorrie fresh out of high school working a diner out on the interstate near Huntersville. Smart enough to want out of there but stupid enough to wind up in a cheap motel room with the sweet talking Buzz, Woody, Chip or whatever he called himself. Woke up at 7.30 in the morning to find the bill paid and the salesman gone, back to New York or wherever he came from. Never saw him again old Chip or Buzz or Woody or whatever his name was.

Of course a couple of months later she's head down arse up in a toilet bowl out back of the diner thinking '*somethings not right here*' and she was on the money, right, correct, unusually perceptive, spot on. Another seven months and she's lying on her back in a hospital somewhere doing the breathing and the pushing thing textbook like. Lorrie was alone except for her Granny Molly. Molly was pretty pissed that her daughter had abandoned Lorrie in this time of need. It was particularly galling since this was exactly how Lorrie was born, out of wedlock and with only Molly there to support her daughter. Short memory. Of course her daughter, name of Glenda by the way, got lucky. Along came her very own white knight and married her, kid and all.

Not so lucky Lorrie though. When her parents kicked her out she moved in with Granny Molly and that's where she'd end up raising the baby. The baby that was born at 3.10 in the morning November first 1971. Granny Molly had gone to bat for her against her parents and the dreaded nuns that ran the hospital and, she had won. No adoption, she wanted Lorrie to keep the baby and Lorrie wanted to keep the baby, so it was a battle fought and well won.

It was 2.30 in the afternoon, November first 1971 and Lorrie was propped up in bed, Granny Molly right there holding her hand.

"You did great Loretta, I knew you would and he sure is a beautiful little boy. It's been a long time since we've had a baby in the house. Seventeen years to be exact," said Granny Molly squeezing Loretta's hand. "I've got everything ready at home for when you come out. I've seen Father Bresnahan at the church and we're all pencilled in for the baptism."

"Will my mum and dad be there?"

"I don't think so child. Your mum's pretty damned stubborn and your dad will just do what he's told, but don't worry, I'm sure they'll come around eventually," replied Granny Molly. "Now, have you thought about what you are going to call your lovely little boy?"

"I have Granny, I've thought about it a lot and I want to give him a smart name, you know intelligent like. Give him a head start maybe. You remember when I was ten or eleven you took me to see that movie Sound of Music? Well the name Oscar stuck in my mind right back then. He was one of the guys wrote the music, you know Oscar Hammerstein."

Granny Molly shrugged, raised her eyebrows, shrugged again then sat more upright and said, "Oscar... Oscar Kingman. You know sweetheart I think I like it."

And just like that little Oscar's troubles began. Right there.

What's in a name you say... pfffh!

OSCAR MEETS MISS ELAINE

Oscar used his empty paper coffee cup to scrape up the mortal remains of what might once have been a reasonable breakfast bagel, delicious even, but dead now and laid out on its own granite slab. He held the soggy mess in both hands and walked to the nearest bin, unloading the lot and after looking around for something to wipe his hands on he gave up shrugged, slid them up and down his shirt front. He looked at his hands and realised they were empty. *'Briefcase, shit, left over there by the fountain.'* Too late Oscar... gone, nicked, lifted, pinched. Right about now Oscar, a thirteen year old street kid is rifling through your valuables. Keys to a stolen car, old chocolate bar, blank assessment forms, dog-eared copy of Philip Roth's *My Life As A Man*, black banana and a grimy copy of *Bra-Busters* jammed in the expander flap. Treasures of a lifetime. Chance of a lifetime this fortune. The cardboard constructed, fake leather briefcase sailed off empty into a hedge like some geometric crow, there to lie and rot all dignity done.

Ego in the bin with his breakfast, Oscar Kingman wandered deeper into the mall like some coffee and bagel coated zombie. The mall, that place anyway of zombies, the undead and the only partly living. He recalled a clothing store, off the rack, off the rack and live to fight another day, torture done. Inside he found row after row of Chinese made garments. *The Art of Mediocrity sewn by Sun Tzu or Tzu's son. Stop thinking, head hurting.* A sales attendant, with a smile wide enough for two heads, made towards him, then dived off on important business elsewhere; anywhere at all after seeing the full framed Oscar hanging there off his own shoulders like some cheap stained scarecrow. He spotted a mature female attendant over by the shirt racks.

"Excuse me, but I wonder if you could help me?" said Oscar from about three paces.

"Oh you poor man, been in the wars it looks," replied the tagged Miss Elaine, accomplishing an astounding recovery considering how the poor man she confronted looked like he'd been hung upside down during a severe bout of diarrhoea. But he smelt like coffee and in that same split second she spied traces of foodstuffs, solids, maybe an ex-breakfast. Behind all that he actually wasn't that bad looking, bit soft round the edges, shave and a haircut maybe.

"Yes, I guess so," offered Oscar. "I was ploughed into by a hit run jogger before I even got to the first bite... black coffee and bagel."

"So you'll need..."

"Just a shirt and tie will be fine. I'll have to wear them away, but I'll need a bag for this lot," interrupted Oscar.

"You sure you don't need trousers?" said Miss Elaine, moving in close and laying her hand square on Oscar's crotch. "These feel a little damp honey." Squeezing now.

In spite of himself Oscar responded to her touch. Been a while. She moved in real close, smell of lavender and he felt it go all to pieces.

Miss Elaine stepped back.

"Er I'm sorry..." said Oscar. "Maybe another time... different circumstances."

"I don't think so sweetie, I prefer my men alive," said Miss Elaine, fifteen years his senior, dark rooted peroxide blond, desperate and reeking of lavender. "I'll get you some shirts to try."

All business, she circled a round clothing rack and arrived back at go with a pale yellow, a pale green and a white shirt.

"Ties?" ventured Oscar apologetically.

Miss Elaine of the lavender soft-on fame glared, stared at him for just a few seconds more than was decent and then wandered off in search of some kind of tie.

In the change cubicle he knotted the cheap nylon tie up under the collar of the pale green shirt and looked himself up and down in the mirror. He'd do, late and damp in spots, but he'd do, he would have to. He bundled his old shirt, tie and suit coat under his arm and checked his hair in the mirror. Was that a tear, christ have I been crying? Oscar slid down the wall to sit on the little ledge. He put his head in his hands and wept, really wept. Tears, snot, the works.

"You stay in here any longer you'll pay rent or I'll call security."

Oscar looked up to see the hostile Miss Elaine. Fifteen years his senior, dark rooted peroxide blond, her of the lavender soft-on fame. '*Ten minutes ago she's squeezing my balls, now she's bustin`em,*' he thought, through a veil of tears.

He took a deep shuddering breath and dragged himself out to the cashier, escape imminent. Finally safe, on the street.

He made his way, just him and his big white shopping bag of tragedy, back up the mall toward the offices of Loughrans Loss Adjusters.

THE GOOD LIFE

The first few years were pretty good for Oscar. Of course he was a baby, infant, kid, so didn't know what was going on and wouldn't remember if you asked him. Just the usual eat sleep shit thing that babies do. But they start figuring the angles pretty quick. Some of `em could be reading the New York Times, but they pretend they aren't up to more than a few gurgling noises and a blank stare from a jerky head. Getting away with it for as long as they could. Couldn't blame `em, once they got you up and walking it was pretty much all downhill. Was for Oscar anyway. Of course he wasn't one of those smart babies, no New York Times baby our Oscar. The most Oscar managed was to suck lead paint off the iron cot, first tooth he bit himself.

So he's about three when his cozy little existence got less cozy and shifted toward the more fundamental meaning of the word existence. Granny Molly was getting old, old and tired, tired and old. Too old and too tired to put up with the crap that Loretta was dishing out. Out drinking most nights, never a finger lifted to help, never a word of thanks, and the language! As far as Loretta was concerned, it had become Molly's solemn duty to raise Oscar while she raised hell. As far as Loretta was concerned, Granny Molly had ceased to be called Granny Molly. Oscar started thinking her name was *'you stupid old bitch'* because that's what Loretta called her when she spoke, shouted, yelled at or abused her in the context of *'why don't you mind your own business you stupid old bitch, I'll sleep with whoever I like.'*

So the stupid old bitch, Granny Molly that is, threw her out. Kept the kid and threw Loretta out. Loretta was pretty pissed about having to find somewhere to live, but didn't seem too upset about being parted from young Oscar. Things settled down for a few weeks at least, right up until our mother-of-the-year figured she could score a half decent welfare payment if she dragged young Oscar along with her on the squalid mess that was her life. So in under a month Loretta was back at Granny Molly's, Oscar in danger of being ripped in half while they pulled on an arm each. Finally Granny Molly tired of the contest and flopped down on a dining chair. She was beaten, done, exhausted and just plain too old to win against this hyped up drugged out thing that used to be Loretta, sweet little Lorrie with the cute ringlets and the pink blanket always wrapped round her arm. Gone the little girl, gone the ringlets gone the pink blanket. Just tracks round her arm now, festering tracks caused by dumb choice.

After Loretta and Oscar had gone, Granny Molly sat there at the kitchen table for a long time. Finally she sniffed up and dragged the phone off the bench beside her.

"Hello."

"Hello er Glenda, it's me, your mother."

"What do you want?"

"I'm just ringing to say Loretta has taken Oscar…"

"Who, taken who?"

"Taken Oscar," Molly fought back the tears. "Taken Oscar, your grandson Glenda. I need your help."

"And why do you think this is anything to do with me, with us?"

"Glenda, she's your daughter. She's off the rails, drinking and who knows what else. I'm scared for Oscar, for your grandchild Oscar."

"Look mother, she burnt those bridges with us a long time ago. We haven't seen or heard from her for years, then you call up and say we should help."

"Burned her bridges… Glenda you threw her out, she was just a kid, she was pregnant and needed your help."

"That's right," said Glenda, "she got pregnant. How do you think that made me, made us feel?"

"Don't know Glenda. Probably the same way I felt when you got pregnant."

"That was different," spat Glenda.

"Yes it was," replied Molly. "I took care of you, never threw you out when you needed me most. She's your daughter. How could you do that to your own daughter?"

Click

"Hello, hello. Hello Glenda!"

Granny Molly looked at the phone like it was haemorrhaging scorpions. She hung it up and pushed it away from her. Then she laid her head in her arms on the table and wept, cried like a baby, cried for Oscar, cried for Oscar for maybe the last time anybody would ever cry for Oscar.

• • •

Sweet Lorrie Kingman, her of the ringlets and pink blanket past. Now gone down with the faces and the names of the past, gone now, well down that road to perdition. Just a matter of time, just a matter of fate. Just a matter of time and fate. Sweet Lorrie Kingman, somebody's daughter, nobody's child. Sweet Lorrie Kingman just an occasional thought in a weak and pathetic father's darkest moments of contrition. Sweet Lorrie Kingman never a thought from a fine upstanding catholic mother. That model of upstanding christian citizenry. *'So Glenda, whatever happened to that lovely daughter of yours?'* *'Oh she still lives out in California, doing great.'* Sweet Lorrie Kingman gone now and switched for someone else. Switched for

Loretta Kingman, switched for Loretta (*ten bucks a blowjob in an alley*) Kingman. Cute ringlets gone for filthy lank hair smelling of cigarettes. Loretta (*just ignore the kid*) Kingman, '*he won't bite.*' Loretta Kingman dragging a poor boy child named Oscar from dump to flop, one night a fat john rolled on him, nearly squashed him. '*Ignore the kid.*' Loretta Kingman fault of the world, shame of the world, fault of the sins, the sins of the mothers and fathers. Someone made it happen, didn't just happen on its own, someone made it happen.

So for almost three years, Loretta Kingman dragged her sorry arse, her sorry arse and her innocent wide-eyed son, up and down the west coast. The city alleys, the ditches, the drains, the bridges and freeway pylons. Here and there a squat, few days maybe a week passed out on someone's couch while the guardians of the children doled out dry cereal, chocolate milk and looked the other way. Looked the other way, looked the other way while she did what she did. Did what she did for money and life, the next hit, the next needle, the next filthy needle, the last filthy needle.

Never even came out her arm that last needle, that last filthy needle just hanging there like a fucking leech. What it was, what it was. Kid named Oscar out on the street lifting oranges, lifting Hersheys. Mother in the flop lifting nothing, never lift again. Oscar sat there for near two days. Seen her like this before, once went a day and a half. Oscar sat there near two days. First night he tried to jam a piece of orange between those rictus lips, chocolate between those rictus teeth. Tried to pour water down that rictus throat, but it pooled between her legs along with that foul smelling stain of dead voided bowels. He gave up, slid onto the floor and slept. In the morning, in the morning. In the morning she was just as dead as the night before, maybe more and finally Oscar realised. He'd shaken her, yelled, shaken and finally slapped her. Sometime in the late afternoon he finally realised. Finally realised... stood up and looked down at her. Little Oscar Kingman just six damned tragic years old and stood there now in the scummy last light that forced through the filthy windows. *'You can't do this, can't do this. You can't leave me here.'* Oscar Kingman stood there looking down at the damp crumpled thing that was all that was left of Sweet Lorrie Kingman, all that was left of Loretta Kingman, and he cried. Then he stopped crying and he kicked her, kicked her hard, kicked her hard enough to knock the needle out of her arm. Kicked her again *'stupid fucking bitch'*. Kicked her again then cried and went out on the street.

Six year old Oscar Kingman went out onto the street and grabbed at passers-by. Took ten or twelve grabs before anyone took this grubby little kid, this grubby scrawny filthy little kid seriously, and went in with him to find the corpse. The corpse that was once sweet Lorrie Kingman. Sweet Lorrie Kingman dead at twenty three, dead eyes open and soon to be staring at the inside of a black plastic bag. Nobody's fault but ours.

WENDY LEGGET

Oscar Kingman stood on the pavement outside the offices of Loughrans Loss Adjusters. The building housing a mix of business, Loughrans on five. The clock by the lift in the foyer read 9.34 a.m. and that made Oscar late, made him nervous. Made for the promise of another unpleasant episode in what had so far been a pretty shitty morning.

The lift doors opened on five and Oscar peered out into the wood panelled foyer, double glass doors to Loughrans on the left, toilets and lunchroom on the right. He took a right and stuffed the white plastic bag full of dead clothes in one of the old metal lockers nobody used anymore. Felt a little safer and turned straight into the scornful gaze of Edmund Llewellyn. Mr. Edmund Llewellyn, Edmund to his senior staff, Eddie to his mates, but Mr. Llewellyn to Oscar Kingman because Oscar Kingman was the oldest junior estimator in the history of the firm and Edmund Llewellyn was the boss. The big cheese, branch principal, chief executive, number one, kingpin, top dog, bigwig, head honcho, big kahuna.

Oscar felt the weight drag on his shoulders.

"You... main office now."

Oscar knew where this was going. Edmund Llewellyn, who claimed he was descended from some kind of Welsh warlord, whatever that was, liked to get his jollies picking on people. People like Oscar. Llewellyn was a bully of the first order, reminded Oscar of a kid at school, 'Piggy' Banks. Couldn't remember his real name just his nickname. Fat kid, big for his age. School photos looked like he'd been sent down from three grades up. Used to pick on everyone in the class who was smaller, who was everyone. Picked on everyone did Piggy. Picked on Oscar most days, most days most days. '*One of these days, one of these days,'* thought Oscar almost every day. *'One of these days I'll do for you Piggy Banks.'* Never did of course, never ever gonna happen.

So Edmund Llewellyn herded Oscar in through the double glass doors and hooked a finger at the receptionist to follow him into the general office, the killing field.

"Everybody out here now!" sounded the Welsh knight or whatever he claimed he was, and out they came. Accountants, salespeople, senior estimators, junior estimators, assessors, typists, general clerks, filing clerks, managers, assistant managers and secretaries to the managers… the whole tribe.

Llewellyn pointed to a spot on the floor like some Hollywood director, some ballet school dilettante, some nazi directing queues at the ovens, some bully. He got on the spot. X marks the spot. Oscar got on and waited for the axe to fall.

Oscar looked around the room which was equally divided, well almost equally, into those who loved this type of entertainment, some of the managers, all the sales guys, some of the secretaries. Those hostile faces all glowing and glaring back at him. *'Give it to him Eddie, go for it.'* And then there were those who didn't like it at all. Those who didn't because it could easily be them up there. Was yesterday, might be tomorrow, inwardly relieved outwardly quiet, sad with eyes downcast. But one set of eyes met Oscar's square and true. Wendy Legget. Wendy Legget square and true. Wendy Legget, filing clerk and aspiring receptionist. *'Loughrans how may I direct your call.'* Wendy whose glasses were too thick and whose skirts were too long. A mousey little thing, quiet and efficient, but mousey just the same. She'd been up there, X marks the spot and all. She'd been up there and she knew how it felt, smiled in support now for Oscar, because it was Oscar she loved.

Wendy Legget jumped as Edmund Llewellyn slammed the flat of his hand down on a desk to demand their attention.

"So, here we are again then," he said menacingly as he consulted a file, Oscar's file. "Here we are for the third time in what… seven weeks, wondering why you are late Kingman. Wondering why you think you are somehow exempt from the rules of the office and the requirement to abide the terms of your employment contract."

Now brandishing the apparently superfluous file above his head, Llewellyn picked up the pace.

"You're not only late, you are unkempt and you stink. Your pants are wet, you smell like a damp dog and you have a price tag hanging off the back of your hideous shirt," he said turning to his audience, some of whom acknowledged his cruel thrusts and parries with a laugh.

He stepped in even closer, almost nose to nose with Oscar now. *'Pickles, Llewellyn ate pickles for breakfast. Who ate pickles for breakfast?'*

"And to top it all off you can't even be bothered to shave before you turn up."

Oscar felt his bowels clench. His fingers twitched, clenching now as well. He looked past Edmund Llewellyn, skirted round that pickle breath to make eye contact with Wendy Legget.

"Perhaps," said Edmund Llewellyn more softly now, theatrically weary with the strain of it all and turning away to spread his arms and embrace his audience. "Perhaps Mr. Kingman you might share with us today's particular excuse so that we might enter it into your file. Your file, which I hasten to add will be marked final warning and forwarded on to head office."

Oscar felt the eyes on him. Some burning like hot pokers and others soothing like soft balm. He took a deep resigned breath, beyond caring now, past hurt.

"Of course you won't believe me so is there any point Mr. Llewellyn?"

The Welsh knight spun back to face Oscar.

"Don't presume to tell me what I may or may not believe Mr. Kingman."

"My car was stolen. My car was stolen and I had to take the bus. I arrived in the city with enough time to grab some breakfast which I did. I was run into by a jogger and was scalded by hot coffee. While I was cleaning up the mess, my briefcase was also stolen."

Here the tale was interrupted by laughter, snickers and a varied assortment of oohs and aahs. Oscar carried on.

"I had to go and buy a new shirt and tie," he paused, "all of this is true and can be verified by calling my wife and the clothing store in the mall, the one where, as you so kindly pointed out Mr. Llewellyn, they let me walk out with the price tag still hanging off the shirt."

"Don't play with me Kingman," spat Llewellyn.

"I'm not playing with you," replied Oscar. "I would never presume to do that."

Raised eyebrows and teeth sucking around the room.

"You asked me so I was simply giving you the honest facts about why I was late sir."

He felt a little stronger did Oscar. A little less frightened, scared, harassed, exploited, less bullied. Less bullied by Edmund Llewellyn and all the other bullies, all the other 'Piggy' Banks of this world. And Oscar knew they were out there waiting. Out there queueing up to take their shot at him, but he felt a little stronger. Why was that, wondered Oscar, why did he feel less vulnerable? Was it strength gained from the kind smile of Wendy Legget?

'Thank you for calling Loughrans - how may I direct your call?'

LOST AND FOUND

Mesmerising! Coloured strobes bounced and fluttered on the wet stone wall. Dusk now and a light rain falling. Light rain to mute the barked orders and the murmured asides. Light rain to wash away the sins. Wash away the sins and cover the tracks of another wasted life, trail ended in a dirty alley in a black plastic bag.

Six year old Oscar strained up in his seat in the back of the squad car. Pretty lights, blue red orange. He learned their pattern. Noises, different noises behind him, *'watch it there'* and Oscar stood himself up on the seat, twisted round and looked out the back window. Through the myriad of stars that slid down that rear window, through the flashing bouncing fluttering lights, Oscar watched men manoeuvre a black bag on a tall wheeled bed out onto the street and he knew what was in that bag. He cried again, out loud this time, loud enough to send a chill through the bones of the not so innocent, those not so innocent. Could she hear him, there in that bag?

It took the police three days to track down Loretta Kingman's parents in North Carolina, fine upstanding christians both. It took Loretta Kingman's mother Glenda, less than three minutes to write down Granny Molly's phone number on a scrap of paper and pass it out through the half open door. The door that closed with a soft ecumenical thud.

'Bless me father for I have sinned, but I didn't want that little bastard in my house. Whatever would people think?'

Indeed indeed, what would they think? All good, all good. Light a candle say ten Hail Marys. All good, absolution a divine right, an alibi for blind faith, a balm for the soul of the blessed.

Granny Molly, well Granny Molly slumped against the door frame, not surprised but wounded. First question out of that poor old lady's mouth…

"The child, Oscar? The child, where is he, is he okay?"

"He's fine," said the officer softly. "A little quiet and he was a bit undernourished, but he's fine. The doctors have had a look at him and say all he needs is a bit of love and attention."

"I never stopped," whispered Molly. "I never stopped loving him, loving them both, it's just…"

"I understand," said the officer.

She leaned forward and placed her hand on Granny Molly's arm.

"Molly… can I call you Molly? Molly, If I can come in we can sit and talk for a bit while you absorb all this. Then we can see you and Oscar reunited."

Molly was a tea drinker and two strong black cups with a heap of sugar can do wonders for a woman. In twenty minutes she was fussing about loading herself into her best blue twinset. Primped and preened she arrived back in the lounge, a soft smile painted across that wrinkly old face. Somehow younger. Last three years of hell over now, the waiting, the waiting.

"I think Oscar is a lucky little boy, lucky to have you," said officer McKenzie.

"She was a sweet girl, Lorrie, Loretta, his mother. She came here with Oscar when her own mother, my daughter Glenda, turned her out on the street. Never understood that. Never understood what happened to Glenda… why. Anyway Loretta came here and Oscar was born and for a while it was wonderful."

Officer McKenzie let her talk, let her remember, let her feel it all over again.

"Then she seemed to become bitter, talk bitter. Bitter about what her mother and father had done, bitter about missing out on her teenage years maybe, I don't know. But it all changed. I knew sooner or later, knew it in these old bones that sooner or later the police, you, would knock at my door." She looked up at officer McKenzie. "I prayed that it would be Loretta, you know, the knock. Not Oscar. I prayed that it would be Loretta you were knocking about. Is that a bad thing? Does that make me a bad person?"

Granny Molly never waited for an answer. She took hold of officer McKenzie's arm and headed for the front door.

Molly sat as if in a trance, watching the world go by outside. Watching the world pass by outside the police car. A police car on a rescue mission, but no markings, no sirens, no lights. The green of the outer suburbs turning to the dun of the inner suburbs and finally giving way to the twisted industrial shambles of the outer city where the wind blew frantic trash halfway up chain wire. There where the red brick crumbled, forgotten iron sheets rusted and the gangs got their start.

"…and the social worker."

Molly heard a voice in the distance, came back to reality, found herself back in that car. Officer McKenzie saying something.

"I'm sorry," said Molly. "I was miles away."

"That's okay," said officer McKenzie. "I was just saying that I've spoken to the office and the social worker is bringing Oscar downtown. Just a few more hours and this will all be over."

"She named him after Oscar Hammerstein, you know, Rogers and Hammerstein. Lorrie, Loretta. She said she wanted to give him a good name, an intelligent name, a good start in life, like that."

TINY STEPS

Edmund Llewellyn stood there unsure. Unsure what had changed, but something had. Up there on level five in the offices of Loughrans Loss Adjusters, some little thing, some tiny almost imperceptible thing had changed. Almost imperceptible except he had perceived it. Edmund Llewellyn, Knight of the Welsh Realm, master of battle, big kahuna at the smallest of seven branches of Loughrans Loss Adjusters. Something, the air had shifted a little sideways, something. Time stood still for him, gave him the opportunity to look around the faces gathered before him, his minions assembled. All the time in the world to take stock, to judge for himself, to count up the numbers. And there it was, the numbers, the numbers. The numbers had shifted against him. He had to concede to himself that he might have gone too far, pushed this placid little fucker too far. Far enough to give him balls enough to swing the vote, stack the numbers. There it was, there it was and it was called sympathy. It shall come forth and it shall be known as sympathy. *'Too far.'*

He turned and strode into his office.

"Back to work!" as the door slammed behind him.

The crowd lingered, murmurs ensued. Oscar had felt it also. The numbers, the numbers. He saw the tiny thin slit appear in Llewellyn's blinds, Llewellyn watching, Llewellyn spying, Llewellyn wondering.

Oscar went to his desk and got to looking busy. One of the sub managers, maybe a swinging voter, came by his desk.

"Car stolen eh? Good one Oscar."

'Shit.' He got on the phone.

"Hello Sharon. It's me look, I think the car has been stolen. I had to take the bus. Sorry I haven't had a chance to call till now but can you call the police and report it?"

"Why me?" she whined.

"Because I'm at work. I'm at work trying to keep this miserable job that pays for you to sit at home all day, that's why."

"Don't you dare snap at me."

"Just do it please Sharon, and do it now, thank you."

'Damned fat cow Jesus what is wrong with her?' thought Oscar.

'Little bastard,' thought Edmund Llewellyn steaming away in his office.

'It's now or never,' thought Wendy Legget, that familiar tingling feeling back in her pants.

Wendy Legget was a quiet little thing, a mousey little thing, quiet and efficient, but mousey just the same. Glasses a little too thick, skirts a little too long and hormones a little too rampant, little askew there. Wendy Legget, who earned a monthly discount on the rent from her landlord for doing what she liked doing most, what she needed to do most. Wendy Legget, who paid for her fruit and veg each week with ten minutes of painful, essential relief in the back of the greengrocers. Wendy Legget, the clinically diagnosed sex addict. When Wendy had an itch, she got it scratched, had to, and Wendy always had an itch. What Wendy never had was love. Never loved anyone except maybe Randall Lynch. The Randall Lynch who turned up at her window one night after he'd lucked out with his sweet little girlfriend. The Randall Lynch that climbed into her warm bed and lit that fire for the first time, sent her to the moon. Randall Lynch, back secretly three or four nights a week for eight months until his parents moved to London. But was that love, was that lust? Love and lust, lust and love. Maybe because he was just the first, but was that love?

But now she loved someone, loved Oscar. Loved Oscar Kingman and thought of nobody else when she writhed around her bed at night with her hand jammed down her damp panties, paid the rent, bought her fruit and vegetables. Every time he came to the filing room, which was often, she tried to get up the nerve to tell him and every time she failed. She thought there might be something. She'd caught him furtively looking down her blouse, leaned over further, tried to help him, but he caught her eye and blushed. She thought there might be something.

And now this morning. This morning she sensed it stronger, stronger when their eyes met, when she helped carry his cross on the way up the mountain. When she tried to send him her strength against Llewellyn. Yes, it was now.

She walked to Oscar's desk, dizzy with the act of it, what she would do, was about to do. She smiled down at him, shy now. Oscar felt her there, looked up.

"Wendy, what can I do for you?" he said self consciously.

"Ah… I was wondering if you could help me with something? Something in the filing room."

Oscar looked at her uncertainly.

"Sure, sure in a minute okay?"

He watched her go, through the office and down the corridor. Waited a few minutes then made a show of searching around for some file or other, gave up, referred to his notes, made a new note. Seems old Oscar knew how the world turned after all. Six months since him and Sharon had attempted sex. Six months and then it had been spectacularly absurd. Her drunk and only half conscious, him sober and hating himself, doing it anyway, make a change from Bra-Busters, change from any of that. But no, not in the end. In the end he was disgusted with himself, taken hostage he felt. And this morning, that woman in the shop, *'what was her name? Elaine, yes that's right, Elaine. Miss Elaine with her hand on his cock and all. If it wasn't for the lavender maybe.'*

Suitable time elapsed, he stood up and tore the page off his notepad, headed for the filing room. Headed for the filing room shaky like a kid on his first date, excited, scared, like a kid on his first date. No sign of her.

"I'm round here Oscar."

He walked around the small metal desk where she normally sat surrounded by files, sticky notes and strange soft toys. Around behind the tall filing shelves and there she was. Wendy Legget, undeniably mousey, glasses a little too thick, skirts a little too long, there she was looking somehow different, different somehow. More than the average buttons on her blouse undone, pink bra on display. Oscar stood there, clearly visible from the corridor, rooted to the spot, wanting to go to her, not wanting to go to her, bits of him stirring, growing.

Smiling she reached down and took hold of the hem of her skirt, hiked it up to her waist. Flushed, Oscar matched the pink bra to the pink panties. He took a step forward, involuntary, machine-like. She hooked her right thumb in the band of her panties and peeled them down slowly. They dropped below her knees and she stepped out of them one foot then the other, still holding the skirt aloft. She reached out a hand to Oscar.

"Come here Oscar, come to me."

"But, but the door," spluttered Oscar peering around the filing shelves and out at the corridor.

He went anyway, took that outstretched hand, that bridge across the ages, that shelter from the storm, that promise of love, even illicit love, sex, happiness. He took that hand and she drew him in. She placed his hand between her legs, that damp place between her legs. That damp place of promise and sex and happiness. And she sighed. It was done, he knew, she knew. She had made him hers, but to be sure, she forced her hand down inside the waistband of his trousers, took hold of him and felt her own power growing there in him. She moved her hand back and forth goading, caressing teasing. Oscar was washed over with the sweet relief, sweet rescue of someone who can be loved after all, *was* loved after all. He felt her hair against his cheek, not mousey but sweet smelling and all silk. All sweet smelling silk and promise and for the first time in a long while, Oscar Kingman felt happy. He kissed her hair. She felt him twitch, pulled her hand out.

"Not yet Oscar, not yet. Tonight. Tonight at my place, now you should go."

She reached up and kissed him lightly on the cheek. Felt the wetness, felt the tears, now saw the tears. Oscar knew he was crying, didn't care.

He nodded. Wendy bent down and picked up the pink panties. She walked around to her desk and took a felt pen, wrote something on them, then stuffed them in his trouser pocket.

"Tonight," she said and turned back to her work without even the slightest inclination to rush off to her favourite cubicle in the ladies toilets.

"Tonight," responded Oscar and turned and strode off down the corridor.

A colossus, striding down the corridor, adjusting himself as he went.

At his desk, Oscar carefully took the pink panties from his pocket and spread them on his knee under the desk. There, there it was. The address, her address. Oscar Kingman felt he had found sanctuary.

He started as his phone rang. Picked it up.

"Mr. Kingman, it's your wife."

"Tell her I'm busy please."

"She says it's very important."

"Let me guess," said Oscar, "television's gone dead in the middle of some awful soap, or maybe a broken nail... sorry, sorry about that," said Oscar. "Okay, put her through."

"What?" he said when she came on the line.

"What do you mean *what*? Don't talk to me like that."

"What do you want Sharon, I'm busy?"

"The police have just been here. They've found the car. All smashed up about four blocks from here."

"Okay so deal with it Sharon."

"But there's more," said Sharon, with a suitable pause for drama. "They also caught the car thief."

"Well that's good news I suppose,"

"No it's not. It's not good news at all," said Sharon starting to cry now. "It was Margie."

"What?"

"Margie, our daughter Margie, your daughter."

"Oh shit,"

"Yeah shit. They arrived here with her like some common criminal. Said she'd been out with friends all night, joyriding that sort of thing, boys in the car and all."

"And you didn't even miss her this morning, not till the police arrived with her? Didn't think to wonder why she never showed up for breakfast? Christ Sharon, what the hell is wrong with you? What about the other one?" yelled Oscar.

"Carol, she's got a name right, Carol. Says she knows nothing about it. Police spoke to her but they think she's lying, so do I."

"So where are they now?" asked Oscar not sure if he really cared.

"Grounded. In their rooms," said Sharon. "You'll have to deal with this when you get home tonight."

Oscar held the phone away from his face and looked at it like it was some nasty thing to be avoided. He pulled it a little closer.

"I suggest you deal with it. They have no respect for me and that's your doing, so you deal with it. I'll be home late tonight, very late."

"Whaddya mean my doing? Whaddya mean home late?" she yelled.

"Keep it up Sharon, the more you shriek at me the later I'll be."

And he put the phone down and went out to the reception desk. Nothing would spoil the rest of this day. This day that had started so badly and now held the promise of salvation.

"Moira, if Sharon, Mrs. Kingman calls again tell her I'm busy. Tell her I'm busy, tell her I'm out, tell her I've died for all I care, but under no circumstances do I want to talk with that woman."

Moira looked up at him, the tiniest smile right there on her face.

"Yes Mr. Kingman."

"Oscar. Call me Oscar, please."

"Yes Mr. Kingma... Oscar."

He turned to leave.

"And Oscar," said Moira.

"Yes Moira?" he said turning back.

"Well done. Nice one Oscar, you rattled him, Llewellyn I mean. It's about time someone did." said Moira, the smile definitely there now.

GRANNY MOLLY

Molly's heart nearly broke.

There he was. There was Oscar standing right there in the doorway holding hands with a kindly looking woman, social worker guessed Molly. My goodness how he'd grown, how big he looked since that last time she'd seen him, surrendered him to the screaming and bellowing Loretta. Watched him dragged out the door crying and yelling and looking back at her, reaching out with that one free arm, tiny hand grasping. Nearly broke her heart that time. Doing it again now. Standing there looking around till he finally spotted her, broke loose from the social worker and ran to Molly crying.

"Granny Molly, oh Granny Molly."

And just like that Molly, Molly for the past three horrible years, Molly was Granny Molly again. It felt good, felt better than good, felt like life had begun again. She hugged her great-grandson to her bosom and smiled up at officer McKenzie, waiting there, her own heart a little swollen.

"It's all sorted. Just your daughter to sign over guardianship, but she agrees so that's a formality," said the social worker about an hour later.

Granny Molly had sat with Oscar in an interview room while plans were made, wheels turned, decisions taken. Occasionally they had swapped her out for officer McKenzie while Granny Molly provided some detail or other, signed some paper or other. Now it was done.

"Officer McKenzie will take you home now and good luck," said the social worker to Granny Molly. She bent down and kissed Oscar. Oscar, still young enough to be a heartbreaker.

"And good luck to you too Oscar. I'd love to come and visit with you some time."

Oscar looked down shy like, but nodded.

Back in the police car and it was a full rewind of the trip in earlier. Out of the city, through the urban wasteland, inner suburbs with their brown dead lawns and shitty concrete statues and finally the leafy green of the outer suburbs. Refuge of Granny Molly and her damaged little man, great grandson Oscar.

Granny Molly had been quiet right up until they turned into her driveway. As they sat there now, Granny Molly turned to officer McKenzie.

"You know, my daughter's husband, my son-in-law Richard, well he's not all bad. He's weak, can't stand up to my daughter, won't stand up to her, but he's done things. Things to help. A few months after Glenda threw Lorrie out on the street, Richard turned up here. He had a pile of bonds and share certificates, signed over to me. Said I was to have them, the income and all, to help raise Oscar, see him through college and all. Swore me never to tell anyone especially Glenda." Her eyes took on a faraway look and she shook it off.

"It'll help. The money I mean. It'll help. I don't know whether to be angry with him or pity him, but at least he did something. He's more scared of Glenda than he is of her god, who he doesn't seem to care for much. Said he never was much of a catholic, just born one and didn't really buy into the faith thing, but it's hard for him married to Glenda. Her whole life revolves round the church. She's on all the committees, pillar of the community. More concerned about what the parish might think of her, that's what caused all this I think. Sorry, I'm rambling. I just wanted to tell you about Richard, something good. You've been very kind to me."

She climbed out of the car and gathered Oscar and his meagre belongings from the back seat.

"Thank you again," she said. "And please visit with me anytime you are in the area… anytime at all."

Officer McKenzie watched Granny Molly and Oscar walk up the path to the door. Granny Molly turned and waved. Then they were gone.

EDMUND LLEWELLYN

Edmund Llewellyn sat in his office blinds drawn, pushing a big slate ashtray around his desk. He didn't smoke, but it was a reminder to everyone who entered that he was a man of substance, a Welshman, descended from Welsh nobles or so his father claimed. Llewellyn had been born in North Carolina, but as his father was proud of telling him, he shared his Welsh ancestry with a number of great American presidents including Thomas Jefferson, John Adams, James A. Garfield, Calvin Coolidge and Richard Nixon.

Of course he'd been to Wales. Only place he'd ever been outside the USA other than England in transit. Hated the place, backward, funny language. Whole time there he was proudly and fiercely American, no connection at all with these Welsh. Very uncomfortable, couldn't wait to get out of there, didn't know why he'd come. He'd made a cursory attempt to verify some of the things his father had claimed, had told him, but couldn't find anything. Found a heap of Llewellyns of course, but that was to be expected. Search over and abandoned, he bought the big ashtray from the souvenir shop at a slate mine. Someplace called Blaenau Ffestiniog. Had to write the damned stupid name down, couldn't remember it. Why would you... remember it that is, in a land of hicks and hillbillies everything done over in black smudges. Blaenau Ffestiniog, *'Blaenau Ffucking Ffestiniog.'* Full of funny scary little people. Couldn't wait to be gone.

So what was bugging him? What was bothering him? What had brought on these feelings of unquiet, concern, mild upset verging on micro panic? Llewellyn hadn't felt like this since last year, that filing clerk, Wendy, Wendy Legget that's right. Heard rumours and took a chance, kept her back late on overtime one night and made his move. Welsh knight takes pawn. Only he ended up feeling that pawn took knight. She was up for it all right, rumours founded. She never spoke, not a word, but came at him for a second bout and poor old Edmund Llewellyn Welsh knight couldn't get it up, not that quick, gone soft in the jousting stick. Finished herself off with blank eyes that never left his while he fumbled to get zipped up and out of there.

He showed her though. The very next day she got a turn in front of the class. Careless filing, untidy workplace, shabby dress, bad attitude. It was worth the risk to get his balls back. If she objected it was her word against his. Filing clerk versus big cheese. She never kicked back so he refused her overtime claim and still she never kicked back. Time passed and she was back where she belonged, back room filing. But this Kingman, that was different. Kingman was his favourite target, great sport that jerk, a sitting duck. So what was wrong this time?

He replayed Kingman's words over and over in his head.

'I'm not playing with you. I would never presume to do that. I was simply giving you the honest facts about why I was late sir.'

No it wasn't in the words. Maybe a little bit in the words, but more in the eyes. Was it the beginnings of defiance, seeds in and watering? Was it the start of a line in the sand?

'And who was he looking at over there behind me? Maybe playing to the audience,' thought Llewellyn.

'Dangerous shit,' he thought.

Dangerous dangerous. He knew nobody could hurt him individually. He'd screwed them all one way or another, some figuratively, some actually and he felt safe against individual attacks. But a group attack was another thing entirely. If enough people spoke up there could be problems. No smoke without fire. *'Vigilance, vigilance, need to be vigilant.'* He would need to watch that Kingman, grind the little shit down again. Start right away.

He stood up and opened the blinds to his office. Went back and pulled a file from his in-tray.

"Kingman. In here now."

Oscar looked up to see Edmund Llewellyn standing in his office doorway. He reached into his pocket and felt the thrill of Wendy's pink panties in his pocket. Wendy's magic pink panties. Popeye had spinach, but Oscar had Wendy's magic panties. Made him strong, bulletproof, made him canny.

"Yes Mr. Llewellyn, coming right away sir."

Made him self effacing, pliant even. Showtime!

Oscar walked into Llewellyn's office, brushed past that death stare, right at the extreme end of the junkyard dog's chain. He pulled out a visitor's chair.

"Don't sit down Kingman, you're not going to be here long."

Llewellyn walked to his chair, dropped in it. Slung his feet up on the desk. *'Confidence confidence.'*

Oscar felt the fire in the back of his eyes, fought it back, hosed it down. He pulled a mantra from off the top of his head.

'Every doggy has his day, every doggy has his day, live to fight another day, every doggy has his day.'

Not much of a mantra sure, but enough to keep him in check, take the shit.

Every doggy has his day.

"Headquarters want to pull the schedule up on the Chivers case. Need it tomorrow. I want the full costings on my desk nine o'clock tomorrow."

'Look at that,' thought Oscar, *'every doggy really does have his day.'* He had finished the costings on the Chivers case three days ago. It had given him an excuse not to go home. But he wasn't telling Llewellyn that.

"But Mr. Llewellyn, that's maybe two days work. I can't stay late tonight, I have a family emergency at home, to do with the stolen car and all."

"Well, you could always resign Kingman. Otherwise get on with it. 9 o'clock in the morning."

Oscar fingered the magic panties, Wendy's magic panties.

"Yes of course Mr. Llewellyn, first thing. I'll stay all night if I have to."

'Like candy from a baby,' thought Edmund Llewellyn as Oscar slouched out of his office.

'Looked like he might burst into tears,' thought the Welsh knight, *'don't know what I was worried about.'*

Oscar walked back to his desk, his step in time with his new mantra.

'Every doggy has his day, every doggy has his day, live to fight another day, every doggy has his day.'

Llewellyn watched him as he flopped down in his seat apparently broken.

And the Oscar goes to... Oscar!

Oscar scurried about the office looking busy, checking dates, adding figures, going over testimonies, checking reports, pulling files and taking notes. If you had to describe him you would say he was a man hurrying to finish the Chivers file costings, checking and re-checking until he was confident he had got it right. Dot the i's, cross the t's, all that stuff and more. At around

12.30 Edmund Llewellyn, Welsh knight, captain of industry, Big Kahuna at Loughrans Loss Adjusters, stepped out of his office and locked the door. Lunch.

Oscar Kingman looked around the office, the whole place relaxing, breathing out and relaxing. An hours grace. Still, thought Oscar, there were spies afoot. Llewellyn's trained bullies.

'Look busy,' said Oscar to himself. *'The game is afoot, the spies are about, every doggy has his day.'*

A shadow fell over him and Oscar turned to find Wendy Legget, Wendy Legget of the magic panties fame, right there beside him.

"I just heard," she said. "He's making you work the costings on a case, making you stay all night."

"No," said Oscar quietly, "he just thinks he is."

She looked puzzled.

Oscar pulled his second drawer open and poked a thumb at the pile of papers that lay there. Lay there complicit in his deception, not just paper, but paper aiding and abetting him.

"Finished?" said Wendy, her eyes lighting up.

Oscar looked around the room conspiratorially, put a finger to his lips.

"All costed and done," he whispered, tapping the side of his nose.

Mum's the word, say no more, between you and me.

Wendy bent further across his desk.

"A little something to keep you going," she said seductively.

Her breasts hung free, the pink bra gone. Erect nipples standing to attention, begging for attention. Oscar blushed, still not used to it, to this.

"Tonight," said Wendy. "7.30 good for you?"

THE WORLD OF WOMEN

Funny how things change.

Out on the street with his mom, with Loretta, Oscar was quiet. Quiet like a mouse but canny, street smart. He knew how to duck and weave, how to steal to eat, that stuff. Now that he was living with Granny Molly he was still quiet but he'd lost his smarts. He wasn't stupid or anything, just way out of his depth. Three years on the streets, three years on the lam, three years in the jungle then landed on a soft pillow in suburbia. It was the school. School was the big problem. Never done any of that stuff and arrived late. Couple of years late. Oscar was big for the first grade, too big, too big and apparently too stupid. Couldn't read, couldn't write, couldn't spell. No grounding there, no sweet bedtime stories, no kiddies television to get a boy ready for academia. Went into first grade too old, too late, too big and too stupid looking. *Looking, looking.* Stupid looking but not actually stupid. And that was the problem. Sitting up there, sticking out four inches taller than everyone like a target. Not just a target for the kids, target for the new age bolsheviks up there at the blackboard as well.

Oscar wasn't stupid, never stupid. He was actually very bright, just out of his depth like a fish out of water. And he wasn't big for his age, but kids didn't know that, thought he was the same age as them. No time at all kids are calling him Stupid Oscar. Stupid Oscar the big giant dummy. So Oscar grew smaller to fit in. Bent over, crouched and hung low to fit in. Tried not to be seen, tried not to be heard. Six months in and Oscar was smaller and smarter. Well maybe not really smaller, but less visible and he was a fast learner, so he was catching up, catching up fast. Didn't matter though, he was always going to be Stupid Oscar to these kids. First impressions count, damage done.

Then there was the problem of Granny Molly. Over protective, over indulgent. Thought she was doing the right thing, but she'd pulled up the damned drawbridge without realising. Cut poor Oscar off from the world of men, built a wall around him. Big soft cuddly wall, Oscar inside getting soft, soft and vulnerable. Soft vulnerable and growing a target on his head, on his back. Oscar becoming a target. Wasn't really Granny Molly's fault, she was just doing her best.

Granny Molly took Oscar out on weekends. Took him to the park, the zoo, bought him ice cream. Did everything she could for Oscar, everything possible for a woman in the world of women. Wasn't really her fault. Wasn't Granny Molly's fault, she was just protecting him, loving him.

By second grade, Oscar had caught up to all the other kids in the class, was even closer to their size, some of them spurting up and all. But he was still Stupid Oscar, always would be. No reason for it now, no basis in fact, was just the way it was, would always be. Way it would always be if Oscar didn't stand up for himself. Trouble was they didn't teach that stuff in the world of women. Well not in the part that Granny Molly lived anyway. How to stand up for yourself.

They taught how to eat ice cream, how to make tea, bake cakes, knit scarves and stuff. But speak up for yourself? Not in that part of the world of women where Granny Molly lived. Granny Molly knew it was happening, saw it happening, talked to Oscar about it, but just plain lacked the necessary skills required. It wasn't that Granny Molly wasn't worldly, it was just that she'd built these walls for herself, long before Oscar arrived on the planet. She'd laid the foundations nearly thirty years back when her own husband Norm had met his end in an upstairs poker den. Norm's luckiest night ever, won bigger than any other night, real big. It would make Molly happy. Norm's unluckiest night ever, then accused of cheating by some down-on-his-luck grifter losing his last dime. Accused of cheating but wasn't, never did. Straight-up guy was Norm, all his friends knew that but not the grifter, not the sleazy low life, down-on-his-luck grifter who sat there red eyed and white knuckled looking for someone to blame. Sure, Norm liked to gamble, horses, cards and stuff and sure he loved a drink, but he loved Molly more. Promised her that was his last night and he meant it. Promised he would be a good husband and a good father.

Norm was sat there thinking *'how lucky am I?'*

Keep his promise to Molly and take home a big pile of cash for her and young Glenda. Was sitting there thinking all this when that desperate grifter came up out of his seat like some demon, like some fucking banshee. Came across that table shrieking like a bad wind and stuck that dinky little knife in Norm's neck faster than lightning, faster than anyone could stop him. It was just a tiny knife, but big enough to pop Norm's jugular. While the rest of the table wrestled the grifter away, Norm collapsed on the floor clutching his throat, blood squirting further than a man would think possible. Before anything could be done for Norm, it was all gone, the blood, the life, everything. All gone. Norm, twitching, twitching… gone.

Molly had sat in that cold church and thought about the world of men, the world that had taken her sweet Norman. Norman, was a good man, another good man gone into the world of men never to return. The world of strip clubs, plastic mini skirts in highway motels, back rooms, thick smoke, sour beer and whisky stink. The world of blood and spit, boxing rings horse tracks and lost dreams. Molly sat in that church holding hands with her little daughter Glenda and she cried for good sweet Norman. When she stopped crying about three days later she laid the foundations. First brick in the wall that would eventually surround Oscar.

OUT TO LUNCH

12.45 p.m. and the office was quiet, everyone out to lunch but reception and a few die-hards. Oscar Kingman almost all alone on level five, Loughrans Loss Adjusters. He felt the need for fresh air, the need to clear his head, so he took himself out. Out past reception where some pointy faced girl covered lunch for Moira, out through the double glass doors, down and out into the street. Over to Top Shot Coffee, past that fountain of despair, past the site of the breakfast bagel incident and over to Top Shot Coffee. It felt different out there, he felt lighter. Not quite a spring in his step, but lighter, somehow lighter. He emerged from Top Shot Coffee a few minutes later with sandwiches and orange juice and went toward the park. He checked his watch, could afford fifteen minutes. Llewellyn was always gone an hour for lunch and Oscar would make sure he was busy beavering away at the Chivers file when Lewellyn returned.

He found a spot on the end of a bench just inside the entrance. As he sat, the pretty girl on the other end shouted body language at him. The legs swung away, shoulder went up, head turned. '*Fuck off creep*' said the body language.

Oscar ignored her, ignored the body, ignored the girl wrapped in the body. Would have cared yesterday, maybe got up and left. But not today, not today.

He sat there watching the passing parade, eating his sandwiches, drinking his juice. Invisible to everyone but the girl on the other end of the bench and he seemed to be fading to her as well, body language less hostile now. He sat there and watched them come and go, shopgirls, office workers. Three girls in beauty brand uniforms from the perfume counter of some department store or other, teetered past on stilettos. Teetered past bound inevitably for the chiropractor, the podiatrist. Teetered past in their own personal cloud of sweet, sickening perfume overload. Women smelled them, looked up and frowned. Envied them, hated them. Men smelled them, looked up, kept looking up, further away they got harder they strained to look, imagining.

"Hi Oscar." He looked up to see one of his fellow workers, an office clerk, walk by.

"Er hi," returned Oscar rather surprised.

This was turning out to be a day of firsts. Oscar Kingman was becoming visible, finding substance, appearing solid.

He sat and watched as a couple came into the park, her a sweet looking girl in a plaid skirt and cardigan, him in a shirt and tie, coat over his arm. As they walked they whispered, whispered and walked, made plans for the future.

The future.

'Was there a future?' thought Oscar. *'Was there a future for me? Was there air somewhere out there for me, somewhere I could breathe?'*

He sat there watching the couple pass, imagining him and Wendy Legget, lovers and partners, saw himself walk past with her. *'But what about Sharon? What about Sharon and the she-devils? What about Sharon and Margie and Carol? Margie the car thief, Carol the accomplice, the alleged accomplice. What would happen to them, all three of them? Did it matter, did he care?'*

Even though Oscar was growing more substantial by the minute, even though he seemed somehow more solid, less transparent, even with all that, could he face Sharon? Could he possibly get up the courage to have it out with Sharon, to tell her he was leaving? Doubtful, scary. It was one thing to yell at her on the phone, another thing entirely to stand in front of her and speak his mind. Even the thought of it sent shudders through him. But he could work on it. Gradually tip the balance on the teeter totter. On one end Wendy Legget, on the other Sharon. The daughters, his daughters, weren't even on this ride. He'd never participated in their upbringing, was never allowed. There never was a father-daughter thing, never long talks, smothering daddy kisses, trips to Disneyland, read me a story daddy. There was never any of that. They probably didn't even know his name, thought it was *man with the wallet* or something. No forget them, they were Sharon's creation and they were Sharon's problem.

But Sharon, well Sharon was Oscar's problem. All two hundred and forty pounds of her. Oscar could imagine it, the rage. The rage and derision.

'Keep working on the derision angle,' he told himself. *'Man up Oscar, you can do this,'* he said to himself screwing his eyes shut.

But when he opened them again on the cold hard light of day, right there in the park, he wasn't so sure. He would work on it. He would leave Sharon and the girls and live with Wendy. He would live with Wendy if she would have him, if that was what she really wanted. Could he have got it wrong, misread the signals? *'Oh dear!'*

He looked down at his hands, could he see through them, just a bit? Could he have imagined it, got it wrong the Wendy thing? *'Did she really want him? And if she wanted him was it just for fun, just for a night, just for sex? Or did she want him for more than that? Do you take this man...'*

Oscar shook his head.

'Stop this,' he said to himself but out loud.

The girl on the other end of the bench gave him a sideways glance, furtive, renewed judgement, revised conclusion. She dropped what was left of her lunch back in the bag and was gone, looking back over her shoulder at Oscar like he was dog shit on her shoes. Oscar sank.

He sat there for a few minutes enveloped in a cloud of self doubt so thick he was visible only from the waist down. Felt like that anyway. He checked his watch. Time to go. As he stood up he was brushed aside by a jogger, a flash of red and black checkered stretchy shorts, the harlequin fucking jogger. It was the same guy, the guy from breakfast. The harlequin jogger carried on unconcerned and pulled up just outside the park gates. There he leapt up and down, flexed, stretched, harlequin body screaming '*look at me, look at how fucking healthy and fit I am.*'

On an impulse Oscar went out of the park and stood right in front of the guy.

"What?" said the jogger.

"You don't remember me?" said Oscar, not believing he was actually doing this, not able to stop doing it. "I'm the guy you ran into in the mall this morning. You spilt my breakfast, ruined my clothes, no apologies, nothing."

"Fuck off," said the erudite harlequin jogger, holding Oscar in a steady threatening gaze just a little too long for comfort.

Oscar's left leg began wobbling uncontrollably. The jogger spat on the pavement at Oscar's feet and walked away. Oscar spent the next few seconds getting his leg under control, getting it useable, then he followed the jogger down the block. Followed him at a distance. The jogger went into a glass front office building and across the spacious foyer. Oscar waited then followed him in. From his vantage point beside a granite pillar, he watched the jogger enter a lift. He moved in closer. The lift pulled up on four. Oscar hit the lift button, got in the next lift and hit four, not believing he was actually doing this, not able to stop doing it.

The lift stopped on four, doors opened. He stayed where he was, unsure what to do next. Holding the doors open and peering out to the right, Oscar could see male and female restrooms and the emergency stair entrance. To the left was the entrance to Garvie Symmons Stockbrokers, big tinted glass doors. A sudden movement behind the glass caught Oscar's attention. There he was, the jogger, coming through the foyer with a sports bag and towel.

'*I know where you're going you bastard*,' said Oscar to himself.

He pulled his head back in the lift and hit the close button. The doors closed with a soft sigh and the lift started down to street level. The lift opened in the foyer and Oscar Kingman walked briskly, head down through the front door and was gone.

SHARON

Sharon Kingman nee Wilson sat at the kitchen dining table staring at the phone. Six times, six times she'd rung her husband's office, Oscar's office and six times she'd been fobbed off by some secretary or other. The last time she had got abusive and had sensed barely controlled hostility in return.

"I'm sorry you feel that way Mrs. Kingman, but I can only tell you what I have told you five other times this morning. Mr. Kingman is not here. If he was here I would put you through but he is not. I will leave another message for him, tell him you phoned... again."

"Don't take that tone with me young lady," blustered Sharon, not used to not getting her own way.

"I'm sorry Mrs. Kingman but I am employed to answer the phone, not to be abused by you. I am hanging up now." Click!

"Don't y..."

Sharon stared at the phone for fully ten seconds. With the handset gripped between her pudgy fingers, she started slamming it down on the table, frustration and rage visited on the handset, the innocent handset. When the wooden dining table was well dented and the handset was in about ten pieces and was by then just wires, speakers and various bits of plastic, she stopped. Blood pressure threatening to blow the top off her pointy little head, heart racing fit to burst, she slumped back in the chair. *'Bastard, when that little bastard gets home I'll kill him.'*

She sat there planning her speech, big bully girl speech. She'd make him pay. First the car, then the police, uncontrollable daughters now this. Oscar hiding from her. She knew he was hiding from her, the little weasel, little bastard.

Oscar was a wimp, always been a wimp, from the moment she laid eyes on him. She knew all that, knew it from the start. She wasn't that smart, but she knew the way the world worked, in her little corner anyway. People didn't much like Sharon, even as a little girl. Even as a little girl she was overweight and low on confidence. To compensate, she ate too much and pushed people around. Like Oscar, Sharon was the biggest kid in her class. Not because she was a few years older like Oscar was, but because she ate so much. Put it away like a damned machine she did. Just got bigger and bigger. By the time she met Oscar at some Saturday night dance, she was a big girl and getting bigger. Had all the excuses though. Runs in the family, heavy bones, mum's a big lady, it's in the genes, maybe medical.

'I diet and I diet and I get lots of exercise, but I just put it straight back on.' Sure, put it back on right after she drank a family sized soda or ate a couple of burgers with sides. Cakes, cookies, soda, fries, ribs, flavoured milk, potato chips, all the healthy stuff, all the main five food groups. Like a damn food orgy... like that. Only exercise she ever got was hefting overloaded fast food trays.

After standing around at dances for six months being ignored by everybody, first the boys and then even by the few friends she had left, she came to the conclusion that she would have to lower her sights if she hoped to attract a boyfriend, husband, mate for life or any of the above. So she lowered her sights and there was Oscar. It's completely unfair to say that she used him because he used her just as much if not more.

Oscar was out of high school and had got a job in the mailroom at a Loss Adjusters. Before then Oscar didn't even know what a loss adjuster was, but the job was a favour done for him by one of his teachers at boarding school. One of the humans. He'd had the job three months and he found a room in a boarding house in the city. It had been a tough transition for Oscar. Off the streets at six years of age, straight into the world of women and from there straight to hell, do not pass go. But he survived, made it, pulled through intact, got out of there in one piece. Now for the first time in his life he was on his own, responsible for his own actions and survival.

After he paid his board there was hardly any money left for entertainment, so nights and weekends he wandered around the city streets looking for something to do. Not far from where he lived he found a community centre, a hall, loud rock music peaking and ebbing as the door opened and closed. He stood outside for an hour, imagining what it was like in there. Saw girls go in huddled in packs laughing and he finally went closer. Five dollars, right up there on the tatty sign. That's all that stood between him and the mystery, five dollars. Oscar was petrified, more scared of the girls than the boys, but he braced up and went in. The guys saw him, saw he was no threat, no competition, ignored him for now. Girls never saw him at all, Oscar Kingman invisible man. The music was hypnotic and in spite of himself he found his foot tapping. Then the band played a slow number. It cleared the dance floor but for a few steady couples, young lovers wrapped around each other like snakes round a pole, tongues halfway down each other's throats. As the floor cleared he saw her, all on her own on the other side of the room. Sly, furtive, nervous, he watched her. Unaware that she was watching him, sly and furtive but not nervous… sizing him up.

For three Saturday nights in a row he'd gone there and watched her get left on the shelf. He'd devise a plan of attack. Old lingerie catalogues and girlie mags just weren't cutting it anymore. His hormones were raging. Got on the bus, boner. Went to the movies, boner, went to the store, boner. He was a walking boner, something had to be done, an urgent plan formulated, wheels set in motion.

The fat girl at the dance, well not really fat, more plump, she had an all-right face. She was alone, she seemed desperate and she had big tits. All things that were highly attractive qualities to a boy who found himself in a constant state of arousal. Of course Oscar had no friends, no confidants with whom to discuss the matter, compare notes. If he had, he might have understood that most boys felt the same at that stage in their life. But then maybe knowing it might not have helped much anyway. So Oscar gleaned his sex education from the reader's letters pages of the girlie magazines. Got the actual physical mechanics sorted. Next a plan of attack was needed. *Operation 'get the girl.'* Get the courage, get the girl.

Get drunk maybe. Not smashed, sozzled, legless, pissed, just enough courage to speak to the girl. Of course it wasn't much of a plan but then he wasn't much of a drinker. He'd barely ever touched the stuff, was a bit scared of it after what had happened with his mother. So it wasn't much of a plan, but it was all he had and desperate days called for desperate measures.

He knew where to find some alcohol, booze. The boardroom at the office had a few bottles in the cupboard. Plan was to get to work early, get in the boardroom with some sort of empty bottle and fill it with whatever he could lay his hands on, bit from each maybe, that way no suspicion. On the day the plan went smooth as clockwork, hardly a soul about when he arrived. He crept into the boardroom and took a little off the top off each of the five bottles in there. By the time he crept out he had a quart or more of vodka, gin, whisky, rum and something that he'd never even heard of called vermouth. The elixir of life and love right there in his hand.

Saturday night he arrived early at the community hall, hung in the shadows across the street. He didn't have to wait long and there she was coming down the street, target sighted. There she was with two other girls, one plain and thin, one shapely and pretty. Once inside Sharon was left to her own devices. Outside, in the shadows across the street from the community hall, Oscar took the lid off his bottle. His lethal cocktail was heavy on the vermouth and he gagged and spluttered on the first tug. He calmed down, slowed down, took a few tentative sips. It felt better, warmer down there. Nothing yet though. How long would it take, how much did he need? All interesting questions as yet unanswered, so he braced himself and in one chug, emptied half the bottle down his throat. Jesus, he felt sick, stomach rolling up toward his throat. His eyes were watering and there was a funny tingling sensation at the hinges of his jaw. He was going to throw up. Fought it. Fought it because there was no plan B, no turning back. Deep breaths, deep breaths and the feeling started to subside. He took another tug at the bottle, then planted it behind a garbage can there in the shadows. When he straightened up he was feeling okay. Bit wobbly but okay. Look sober, look sober, up the stairs, out with the five and he was inside.

"Dansh?" said Oscar to the plump girl.

"What?" said the plump girl looking annoyed but secretly excited. Here he was and not too bad up close. Have to do.

And with that she pushed the button on her own plan.

"Shorry, sorry I said would you like to dance?"

"With you?"

Oscar looked around, nearly fell over with the vertigo of it all.

"Well I'm the only one here, so yesh, with me."

He put out his hand like he'd seen in the movies and after a surprised pause she took it and he led her onto the dance floor, her hand hot and wet, his head hot and wet, spinning.

They bounced about out there on the dance floor, Oscar like some demented jackrabbit and Sharon more reserved, small movements, making judgements. He was drunk, oiled up, boozed out of his brain. The smell of him up close made her eyes water. He might not stay upright for much longer, she had to act fast, strike while the iron was hot as they say. Might not get a chance like this again, a patsy like this. She took his hand and half led, half carried him to the door, made it outside. He was confused, felt dizzy, but kept moving, let himself be led into an alleyway beside the hall. She unbuttoned her blouse and pulled her bra up.

There they were Oscar. Real live tits and big. He put his face in them, trying to sing something while she unbuttoned his fly, held him pushed against the wall with one hand while she pulled his jeans down with the other. She let him slide down the wall and when he was all but flat on the ground, she pulled her panties aside and sat on him. Of course that was all she did. Oscar was so far gone by then that her theatrically enhanced cries of *'yes, yes, oh yes!'* could have been coming from another alley, another world, another planet. Sharon bent down and bit into his throat hard, branded, hickied, she had him, owned him. Then she got up straightened her clothes and went home. Mission accomplished. Oscar Kingman out cold, branded and hickied and left there with his jeans down around his ankles in some dirty alley beside the community hall. He woke at about 3.00 a.m. and threw up. Then he rolled the other way and went back to sleep with a big smile on his face dreaming of sex in an alley, with a real live flesh and blood girl. He dreamed he was in love.

Sunday morning he woke again, this time to a gentle rain that fell on his naked legs, soaked his shirt and jeans. He tried to open his eyes, it hurt too much. He rested for a bit then tried to lift his head off the ground. It felt like his head had been nailed down. Serious big spike right through the middle and into the pavement. He panicked as he heard the sounds of the city waking around him, realised his pants were down around his ankles, Christ. He hiked them up best he could, scraped his arse on the concrete, whimpered a bit, head throbbing, throbbing throbbing. Brain trying to get out through the front somehow. Sick, he felt sick, just wanted to be in his own room in his own bed with his own pain. He rolled over onto his stomach and pushed himself up into a crawl position, a few steps back along the evolutionary track. Tried to stand, dialled up a whole new level of throbbing. He felt something sticky, something foul under his right hand. Vodka, gin, whisky, rum and vermouth all recycled at 3 o'clock that morning. Welcome Oscar, welcome to the delights of alcohol. Mind you, it's nothing a bit of training and common sense might not fix.

He got himself upright with the help of the wall and made his way like some broken bendy man out into the street. Three blocks home. *'Shit, three blocks home,'* but he made it. It was still early. He got up the stairs, stripped off and fell exhausted into his bed. His head span, the room span. He dreamt his head span and the room span, then he opened his eyes and everything stopped spinning. He suddenly remembered it all. He remembered it all. The girl, the alley, the sex and then, sick, hungover, soaking wet and, unbeknownst to himself still a virgin, he slept.

PHONE HOME

Oscar stood outside the big glass fronted office building and wondered briefly what the hell he was doing there. He cleared his mind and tried to focus. In the rare moment of calm that followed he deduced that at some point, all of this would come together, everything would fall into place, be revealed. He made it back to the office a little after 1.15 p.m. and Moira was back at her post. She smiled.

"Is the boss back yet? Mr. Llewellyn I mean," he asked.

"Not yet," answered Moira. "By the way Mr. Kingma... sorry, Oscar, I think you are in all sorts of trouble. Sounds like your wife will kill you when you get home."

"Who said I'm ever going home?" said Oscar smiling as he went through to his office.

By the time Edmund Llewellyn got back ten minutes later, Oscar looked suitably stressed, strung out, overworked, underpaid and hang dog. Llewellyn was pleased, the genie was back in the bottle. *'Let this lot know who they were messing with.'* Oscar watched him go into his office. He kept up the charade thinking maybe Llewellyn would crack the blinds and spy on him, but not Llewellyn, not Edmund Llewellyn, Welsh knight and jouster extraordinaire. As far as he was concerned it was problem solved, business as usual. There were losses to be adjusted, claims to be checked and rechecked, staff to be pushed around. What point was there in being the boss if you couldn't push people around?

At 1.30 p.m. Wendy Legget came through from reception and walked past Oscar as if he didn't exist. For a moment, Oscar panicked, was confused, doubted himself, but then she turned in the corridor where nobody else could see her and blew him a kiss. Oscar started breathing again, took a couple of deep ones, in out in out, like that. It was okay. Don't panic Oscar everything is okay. He felt good. He felt so good that he actually felt a little bad for Sharon. Not guilt, *'shit definitely not guilt.'* Just a little bad that the poor sad fat cow was going to have to look after herself from now on, look after the she-devils all alone from now on. He was out of there. He spent a few minutes debating with himself. *'Should I ring her, yes no, yes no?'* Then he realised he was past it now. Too far down the track that led away from all those years of bullying and bad marriage. All those years of putting up with the derision and the dance of the harpies. They couldn't hurt him now.

He picked up the phone and dialled his home number. It rang out.

On a table in the suburbs a taped up piece of crap on a dented kitchen dining table spluttered and gurgled and did its best to ring, tried hard, but couldn't be heard over the daytime television drama playing out in the lounge room.

PENGUINS

Living with Granny Molly was a giant leap forward for Oscar. He'd remembered Granny Molly well enough, but he couldn't really remember too much about living there before, in that house. Because his very last memory of that house had been a bad one and he'd pushed it deep, ever so deep down into that place where you stored the unbearable, to bear the unthinkable. Now the memory was coming back, creeping back up into his conscious mind like rising damp up a soft plaster wall. He remembered little grabs, snippets. By the time he was eight, at the end of second grade, he remembered it all. He remembered grabbing at door posts, anything solid to latch on to. Remembered screaming, screaming for Granny Molly and even though he was then just three, he remembered thinking, *'if we leave here bad things will happen,'* and they did. After dragging him halfway round the country his mother had died, left him alone there in that place. That place where they found him. Of course he had never forgotten his mother's leaving, his mother in the giant black plastic bag on that trolley, would never forget that.

But there's lots of truth to the old saying that kids are resilient. Kids will bounce back. Hide nothing, get it out in the open, talk about it. Kids will heal, kids will surprise you.

So now, two years after he had moved back in with Granny Molly, two years since he came back, he was starting to breath easier. After school and on weekends they did things together, Oscar and Granny Molly. They went to the park, baked cakes, watched television, went to the movies. And every night before he went to bed, he would talk with Granny Molly about his mother, his mum Lorrie. Gradually the anger melted away, gradually he understood, the way children do if you can just deliver the messages in simple parables. Mummy was a little bird with a broken wing, mummy's gone to live with the angels etcetera etcetera. So gradually Oscar learnt trust, knew someone loved him. Knew that Granny Molly would always be there for him.

Then she died!

If Oscar had been older, maybe twenty years old or more he would have said something like *'you have got to be fucking kidding me. What again?'* but he didn't. He just stood there and wet himself. Because he knew she was dead, he knew what dead looked like and worse, he knew nothing good would come of this.

They were having breakfast, Saturday morning. Oscar opened the fridge to put away the milk and when he closed the fridge door and turned back Granny Molly was face down in her cereal bowl, death by rice krispies.

Oscar tapped her on the shoulder, poked her sallow cheek and said, "You're dead aren't you Granny Molly? They're going to pack you up in a big black plastic bag and take you away aren't they Granny Molly?"

He'd seen it all before, so now he just stood there and wet himself a lot, cried just a little, then went and picked up the telephone. While he waited for them to come he went to Granny Molly's wardrobe. He took down all her dresses and lay on her bed hugging them. The scent of dried lavender strong and sweet in his nostrils, the scent of Granny Molly.

Stroke they said, died of a massive stroke, so sudden. They didn't tell Oscar this of course, he just overheard it. Had no idea what it even meant. And suddenly there was that lady again, the social worker, Mrs. Garcia. This time Oscar went straight into a big old house, it was called an orphanage they said. They explained that he'd be there maybe a month or so while they decided his future. Decided what was best for little Oscar Kingman, where to file him, where to hide him.

The orphanage was run by strange people called nuns. Oscar thought they might have been ladies like his mother only older, or like Granny Molly only younger, but it was hard to say. They wore funny costumes that made them look like the penguins he'd seen at the zoo. The difference was the penguins were friendly, ate fish, played around. Not these people, these *maybe* ladies. These penguins were cruel.

He had to call them all sister something, sister this, sister that. Oscar was at least smart enough to know they weren't his sisters, but that didn't help with his confusion. These penguins were cruel. Some of the penguins had boy's names. One particularly scary one with a sharp red face called itself sister Michael. Even Stupid Oscar knew that Michael was a boy's name. And it wasn't just the penguins, not just the nun people that were cruel in that place, some of the other children were too. Some of them had been there a long time and it seemed the longer they were there the nastier they became.

The second week he was there, Oscar had a visit from the social worker lady. She took him to a little room off the front hall.

"How are you doing Oscar?"

Silence. Pin drop silence. Oscar's bottom lip twitching, curling a little. Just silence.

She moved closer and took his hand, sat beside him on the big old couch.

"I asked you how you are doing Oscar. Now I know that orphanages aren't the best places in the world but, the nuns are kind and I'm sure they are looking after you well."

Oscar looked up at her puzzled, confused, uncertain.

"Oscar I know it's sad that your Grandma died but…"

"They're not kind." Spoken so softly, his tiny voice pointed at the floor.

"Bu... what? What did you say Oscar?"

"I said they are not kind."

"Oh Oscar, why would you say such a thing? These are kind ladies Oscar. They do god's work here. They have dedicated their lives to looking after children like you," said the social worker.

Oscar considered what she had said, of course he wouldn't have known what analyse meant, but that's what he was doing, analysing it. Picking it apart, mouthing each bit back to himself. He looked up at her, a spark of defiance.

"I don't know what dedicated means," said Oscar. "And I don't know what god's work is other than when they punish me they say things like '*god is watching*'. Only thing I know is they hit me. They are cruel and they hit me."

The social worker raised her eyebrows, leaned back a little as if to take it all in.

"Oscar, you mustn't say things like that. You mustn't tell lies. The nuns would never hit you, they would never hit a child."

"Take me home. I want to go home."

Angry now, abandoned unbelieved unloved.

"I'm sorry Oscar sweetheart, this is your home for now and..."

"Take me home!" yelled Oscar, kicking out at her, betrayed.

"I'm sorry Oscar," she said standing up. "I'm sorry that your mummy died and your granny died, but you need to buck up your ideas young man. Until things are sorted out, this is where you are and this is where you'll stay. This is your home for now. If you behave yourself and do as you're told I'm sure it will be fine."

She went to the door, opened it.

"Goodbye Oscar," she said and was gone.

Oscar sat there on that oversized couch still trying to figure what it was she had said. '*Buck up your ideas, buck up your ideas*' what did that mean?

Suddenly the door crashed open, slammed back against the wall and in raged a nun person. The one who called herself sister Michael. She was across the room in a blur of black, white and Irish rage and she took hold of Oscar's ear and pulled him off the couch. She took hold of eight year old Oscar Kingman's ear and pulled him off the couch before he could get his feet planted under himself. He hit the ground sideways and was dragged up onto his feet again, all by his ear.

"Cruel are we? Hit you do we?" snarled the nun, the bride of christ, the doer of kind deeds, the bringer of succour and mercy. "Cruel are we? We'll see about that!"

And she hauled him out of the room. She hauled poor lost lonely eight year old Oscar Kingman out of the room by his ear, smashing his head against the door frame as she went. She dragged him up the hallway, dragged him past the tapestry on the wall. The tapestry on the wall that read...

But when Jesus saw this he was indignant and said to them, 'Let the little children come to me; do not stop them; for it is to such as these that the kingdom of God belongs. Mark 10:14.

In her little office, the nun person sister Michael could barely contain her rage.

"You ungrateful little savage," she spat, flecks of spittle playing around the corners of her harsh mouth.

Oscar stood there resolute, maybe a little more than resolute, resigned, maybe a little defiant even. Oscar Kingman now knew he was alone in this world, this nasty world that took everything from him and gave him back nothing but hurt. Oscar Kingman, eight years old and four foot two inches high, stood there in front of Aileen Coughlan, now disguised as sister Michael, bride of christ, bringer of succour and mercy. Sister Michael, Irish nun, recruiter of Irish nuns and demander of respect as one of the holy chosen. Sister Michael, five foot seven inches, bully.

"Hands!" she spat.

Oscar slowly raised them palms up. He knew. He'd been here twice before in the short space of time since his arrival. Palms up those little hands shook and quivered. He wouldn't cry, never cry. He'd been through worse, nose broken by a whack from one of his mother's boyfriends, her many boyfriends. He'd been through worse, wouldn't cry.

Thwack!!

The cane came down in a wide sudden arc. That cane, shaped, honed and designed to hurt. That cane wielded with such professional malice, that cane came down across Oscar Kingman's tiny pink hands, tiny pink innocent hands, and that sound reverberated around the world and out into the depths of space itself.

'I will not cry.'

It came down again and again. It came down again, again and again. *'I will not cry.'* Even though the souls of Loretta Kingman and Granny Molly cried out in anguish, felt his pain, felt his suffering, even then Oscar did not cry.

The vicious Irish nun, wimple askew, right sleeve of her black habit, her black disguise, hoisted up above her elbow, counted six strokes and looked down at the sinner below, hands still raised, palms up. *For mine is the kingdom of god.* And she brought that cane down again, again again and again, until inevitably, the sinuous weapon broke through the skin and welt became cut and cut became gash and gash became wound and wound became blood. And the blood of Oscar Kingman flew up from the cane and mixed with the spittle on the face of Aileen Coughlan, the face of sister Michael, Irish nun person and defender of the children, of all that is right. And finally Oscar cried, and the souls of all the lost children cried with him and their hideous wailing could be heard echoing through the universe. Every dead soul heard that wailing, every dead soul… but certainly not that Irish nun.

In the little infirmary another nun, this one younger and kinder, took Oscar's hands and bathed them in warm water. She poured antiseptic on the open wounds that ran diagonally across his left palm and held tight to his hand as poor Oscar flinched back with this new torture. He screamed with this new torture and that scream saved a soul. That kind young nun, that kind young nun would be gone tomorrow. Gone out from her hiding place in the black habit, gone out from this hateful order. Gone. Faith no more. Faith no longer an excuse.

But now as she dried his hands, applied lotion to his wound and bound it, Oscar collapsed into retching sobs. It could have gone either way, but it didn't, it went that way. Oscar Kingman was broken.

DO YOU OSCAR, TAKE SHARON?

Oscar put the handset back on the hook, unperturbed. He actually thought that word *unperturbed*. That's what he was, unperturbed, imperturbable, might never be perturbed again. He allowed himself the smallest of chuckles as he thought of Sharon. Imagined the steam coming out of her ears like in some kid's cartoon. Pointy little head on that big round body, steam coming out the ears. *'Priceless!'*

He doodled on a blank file page, looking busy but now deep in thought, mapping backwards, remembering, counting the miseries. Were there any good memories, any good bits? Thinking back now Oscar realised that there really weren't any good bits at all. There was only not-quite-so-bad bits. Not quite so bad, verging on the good bits. Maybe that's all there ever was, all anyone ever had. Who knows?

The wedding hadn't been too bad. Sharon's mother hated him and her father couldn't care either way as long as she was gone. Her father made some crack about halving the household budget with her gone, Sharon gone. But Sharon's mother hated Oscar even after the truth came out. One of those women, just needed something to hate and apparently Oscar was a soft target, low hanging fruit. But regardless of how she felt about him she insisted it was done right, done properly in a church and all. So they had gathered in that little city chapel, a crowd of around twenty, a few aunts and uncles, and had done it properly. Oscar felt strange in that church. That church belonged to another god, not the catholic god he knew about.

Oscar's best man was his only friend Peter Miller. Oscar had met Peter in the boarding house. Oscar and Peter, Peter and Oscar, two peas from the same pod, barely tell them apart. Not physically mind. So Peter was Oscar's best man, stood by him in that little city church, said all the right things, nervously, haltingly said all the right things. Handed over the cheap ring, stepped aside and let it happen. Afterwards they all went back to Sharon's parents apartment and pretended they were happy. Pretended they were enjoying themselves. Oscar and Peter parked on a couch in the sitting room while Sharon made her way around the little table all laid out with cheap packet snacks and frozen pastry treats from the microwave, picking here picking there.

Her uncle Clive had come up to him, given him a glass, poured him a beer. Ignored Peter but poured Oscar a beer.

"Good luck son. You're sure gonna need it," he'd said laughing, walking away.

He remembered Sharon watching him from the other side of the table, other side of the marriage feast, cream and chocolate icing smeared on her top lip, down the front of her. Oscar remembered the wedding night. Sure he was exited. Exited about the sex, that part anyway. Didn't want the wedding but had no choice, no options, no escape. But the wedding night was okay. One of those not-quite-so-bad bits. Sharon took control, took control then and forever after it seemed to Oscar. She took control and made it all happen. Made it happen then rolled off him and reached for the plate on the sideboard.

"Want some more wedding cake?" she had said around a gob full of chocolate cream cake.

They didn't communicate much, not then not now, thought Oscar, checking that Llewellyn wasn't lurking about. They didn't communicate much, but the sex was okay once in a while. He figured life could be worse. Better than hell anyway.

Oscar toiled away in the mailroom at Loughrans and Sharon worked in a deli. Of course she pilfered, stole, lifted and misappropriated tons of food, but it got them through on their crap wages. Friday nights, Oscar would meet up with Peter

Miller and they'd go to a cafe, always the same one, have a soda, maybe a coffee. Peter was an only child. He was a sickly boy born late, born a mistake to a mother thirty nine and a father forty four. Never had much of a relationship with his parents. They treated him okay, but by the time he was fifteen they were already getting old, father almost sixty. They both died in his final year of high school and Peter had been moved in with his aunty. It was an unhappy arrangement and when he graduated she turned him out and he found work in a bookstore, got a room at Oscar's boarding house.

Out there the world went on around them. Wars fought won and lost, fortunes made and squandered. People died, more were born to take their place. It didn't matter, none of this affected Oscar and Peter much. Didn't affect them much until Peter was one of the ones who died. Friday night came around and Oscar had sat alone in his usual seat in the cafe, Peter's seat vacant. Saturday morning he'd phoned his old boarding house. The landlady said Peter was in the hospital. She'd found him coughing up blood in the bathroom, called an ambulance and got him off to hospital. He was always coughing, always coughing and hacking, never thought too much about it. Oscar had gone down to see him in hospital but they wouldn't let him in to see his friend. Five or six days later the landlady called Oscar at work, told him Peter had died. Leukaemia they thought. Peter died of leukaemia.

Oscar got time off from Loughrans. Back then his boss was a nice person, a concerned person. Mr. Alperstein. Old Mr. Alperstein was a gentleman. Loughrans was different back then.

"Sure Oscar," he'd said. "How long do you need?"

"Just a day sir."

"You sure that's enough? The mailroom will survive without you for a couple of days if you need a bit more time."

Oscar remembered old Mr. Alpenstein's kind face. He remembered how Loughrans Loss Adjusters had been back then. Far cry from now. Back then they were spread over two floors of the building and had more staff, no computers back then, more paperwork. Mr. Alpenstein had taken him under his wing, taught him, promoted him out of the mailroom, moved him up the ladder. In six years, Oscar had made junior estimator. About a year before Edmund Llewellyn in fact. About a year after that old Mr. Alpenstein retired. The battle for senior estimator was joined about two years after that. Just one position available, just Oscar and Edmund battling it out.

Oscar played it straight, worked hard, checked rechecked, did it right, did it fair. Edmund Llewellyn cheated, lied, undermined. Edmund Llewellyn, Knight of the Brown Noses. Llewellyn won, been working on the new boss since the day he arrived.

'Yes sir, no sir, anything else sir? I would have had it earlier sir but Kingman held us up. Not really Oscar's fault sir, he's just a little slow. Means well, but a little slow.'

That was when life at Loughrans had changed. Oscar was working directly for Llewellyn who now held Oscar's fate in his grubby hands. Moved up, moved on, but kept his foot firmly on Oscar's throat from that day forward.

Oscar looked up now at Llewellyn's door, shivered, felt the pain of it all over again. Felt the blood roaring in his head, heard it. Fought it down, calmed himself.

'Stay calm, stay calm Oscar,' he told himself. *'Look busy, look busy.'*

He thought back to Peter Miller's funeral. He'd gone out on the train to that little church and graveyard and he'd stood there with Peter Miller's aunty and uncle and a handful of other people he didn't know. He'd listened to a eulogy from a priest who had probably never even met Peter Miller. Oscar listened to that unremarkable priest talk bullshit, talk about Peter the boy, Peter the man. Talk about how god would make a place for Peter at his table, how there would be a place for Peter in the house of the lord. Theatre, all theatre. Peter had known there was no god the same as Oscar. So they lowered Peter into the ground in a cheap pine coffin and they all said amen and left, got out of there as quick as they could. Poor Peter Miller, in the ground at 2.00 o'clock, forgotten by 2.30. Oscar stayed a little longer. He had stayed to say his own goodbye to his best friend Peter Miller. He didn't need any help from some god. Then he'd walked to the station and he'd gone back, back into the city.

Oscar took a deep breath and looked around the office, the remembering of it was hard. All those years ago, still painful.

He remembered the tiny top floor walk-up that served as their first home together, him and Sharon. He remembered asking her how come?

'What's going on Sharon?'

He remembered that huge argument. No, not argument, fight. That huge fight when she'd come round the table at him, pummelling him, Chinese take-out going everywhere, up the walls.

"So what!" she screamed. "So fucking what, you never tell a lie Oscar?"

"Lie… lie! That what you call it? My life Sharon, my fucking life. How could you do that, how?"

Oscar looked down at his hands clenched on the desk, felt the rage growing in him again. Calmed himself, tried to stop thinking… couldn't.

He remembered that other night, the *next* time she had told him she was pregnant. Pizza this time, stayed on the plate this time. She had no reason to lie this time. Oscar had imagined himself with a son. A son for Oscar Kingman. He was almost happy. He'd imagined life with a son, all the things they could do together, father and son things. He'd imagined that he might be happy. This misguided euphoria went on for months until early one morning Margie had been born. Came into the world screaming and was still doing it now pretty much. No son for Oscar Kingman. Just the first of the harpies.

Oscar thought back to that event, the birth of his first daughter, and he realised he had to take some responsibility for the outcome. He should have been stronger, should have pushed harder, never accepted Sharon's dominance. Sharon took that baby, that pure unsullied infant in her arms, in her plump arms and moulded her into an ally. Her tiny little innocent ally in her daily harassment of Oscar. He tried to reach the child but was granted no time alone with her, access denied. Tried to love her but failed. On the day she was brought into the apartment, on that very first day, Sharon spoke to the infant in a sickly baby voice, denouncing Margie's father as a fool, a failure, a wimp. Conditioning, conditioning, brainwashing. Oscar stood by and let it happen, stood by and let it happen because after one or two attempts to stop it he figured it was easier to ignore it. Outnumbered, he'd retreated.

The next one to arrive, the next little soldier to arrive, to swell the ranks, was Carol. Oscar had once more dared to hope. A boy child, grant me a boy child, a son, but it was just another harpy. And worse, it was someone else's harpy. The child to be named Carol arrived with a shock of red hair and features somehow foreign to the Kingman household.

"She's not mine is she Sharon? This baby is not mine."

Sharon just smiled at him, never answered. Oscar left the hospital with mixed emotions. It would be easier this time, not to be allowed to love this one. It would be easier not to love this one.

So that's how it was, from then on. Sharon issued orders, barked bellowed screamed orders and Oscar complied. Paid the bills, kept the peace. He'd been broken years ago, so now he was easy, compliant.

A door slammed. Oscar snapped back to the present, stood up from his desk, scratched the ugly scar on his left palm and looked around straight into the malevolent glare, the ray gun eyes of Edmund Llewellyn.

"You asleep Kingman? You asleep or just daydreaming?"

"No Mr. Llewellyn, I was just... I guess I'm a little tired," replied Oscar with the proscribed dose of humility.

"Tired. Poor old Oscar's a little tired," said Llewellyn in a childish sing-song voice. "Would poor widdle Oscar like a lie down?"

"I... I..."

"You what? I'm warning you Kingman. You had better pull your finger out and get that report finished because if I don't have it on my desk 9 o'clock in the morning you're finished. Hear me Kingman? Finished!"

And he was gone. Out through reception and gone.

Oscar looked around the room. Some fear, some scorn, some sympathy, all mixed in together there in that office. He looked at his watch 2.05pm. He sat back down and for the benefit of the spies in the room, the brown nose brigade, he shuffled some papers around, made notes, looked busy until everyone lost interest in him. His hand slid into his pocket and he toyed with the panties, Wendy Legget's magic pink panties.

'So tonight,' thought Oscar.

He decided he wouldn't go home. After he left the office he'd stop and buy whatever he needed to stay over at Wendy's.

He was excited, nervous. Oscar was excited and nervous at the prospect of a first date, first night with someone he might love, someone who might love him. He stacked that up against all the years of loveless marriage, abuse both mental and physical. She could pack a punch that Sharon. Two forty pounds with an arm like a ham hock. Heard a lot these days about men abusing women, not so much about women abusing men. *'Arm like a ham hock.'* Oscar laughed to himself, laughed at the thought, the image. Enjoyed himself a little. *'Can't hurt me anymore.'*

THE COURTSHIP

Despite himself, Oscar had gone back. He said he wouldn't but went anyway. He'd stayed away three weeks and spent his Saturday nights somewhere else or with Peter Miller. Peter wouldn't go near the dance anyway, but on that fourth Saturday night the lure of the flesh got to Oscar, ground him down, ground him down. Peter was working late at the bookstore, stocktake or something. Oscar sat about fidgeting and browsing through his magazines until he could stand it no longer. He went, tried not to but he went. And having gone, he stood in the shadows opposite the community hall, wondering if the girl was in there, would she talk to him, dance with him. Could he do it? Could he go in there and do any of that without a drink?

Inside the hall, Sharon was up and dancing, doing the cool thing. Dancing with the plain thin girl. Sharon thought she was a pretty cool dancer. Head held high and arms twirling this way and that. Looked like a goony bird trying to take off. She put in a creative flourish and span a full three sixty degrees, arriving back at start point in time to see a pimply faced guy asking her plain thin friend for a dance. She was left there alone, fuming with rage, burning with embarrassment, did the best she could to dance off un-noticed to the safety of the wall, there to avoid the spotlight, simmering, simpering.

'I'll fix that bitch,' she thought. *'Do that to me again. Who was that guy? Who'd want to dance with her anyway, scrawny boney bitch?'*

Things weren't working out the way she had planned, something had gone wrong. Where was the guy she had dragged outside. She was sure he'd be back, back for more, sniff sniffing about. Sure he'd be back, then she would spring her trap. But he hadn't come back, she'd scared him off maybe, the little runt. And just like that, as if summoned up by magic and malice, he appeared in front of her on the other side of the dance floor. Sharon straightened herself up, limbered up, flexed and warmed, ready to go. Got herself role ready.

Oscar arrived the long way around, went right round the edge of the dance floor, hands in pockets looking totally composed, feeling like a jigsaw ready to fall apart.

"Wondering when you'd be back... sniffing around for more," she said with a sneer.

"Ah, well, would you like to dance?" asked Oscar.

"No, I don't want to dance. We need to talk. What's your name anyway?"

"I'm Oscar. Oscar Kingman."

"Oscar. Gees are you for real. What sort of name is Oscar?"

"What's yours, your name?" said Oscar ignoring her taunts.

"My name's Sharon." A pause. "You're in deep shit Oscar Kingman."

Oscar stepped back with the sting of it, puzzled. *Deep shit, deep shit*!

"What are you talking about?"

"Jesus Oscar, you stupid or something? I'm pregnant you moron."

Oscar felt the air choked out of him, couldn't breathe. He bent over and sucked in air from closer to the floor, like it might be thicker down there, less people using it.

"But, but... how, I mean?" he stammered looking up at her sideways, still struggling.

"The usual way moron."

She made a circle with her thumb and forefinger, jabbed her other finger in and out the circle. Obscene gesture, *jiggy jiggy!*

Oscar felt his life slipping away. This new life he was just getting started on, ripped from his grasp. He straightened up.

"How do you know it's mine? How would…"

The slap caught him off guard, nearly knocked him sideways, lot of weight behind it. His face stung. People were looking over now.

She moved in close. He smelt tuna on her breath, smelt the sour sweat from under her arms.

"You think I go around sleeping with just anybody?"

That very thought had occurred to Oscar.

"You're the first," she continued, "you're the only one. Of course it's yours. Man… my parents are gonna kill you."

"And you're sure? Sure you're really pregnant I mean?"

"Duh! Of course I'm sure."

"So what now?" said Oscar. "What are we going to do?"

"What are we going to do now? Shit I can hardly believe you, what are we gonna do now? We're going to get married. That's what we're going to do. Have to."

Again with the choking. Oscar thought he was going to die right there. But he didn't die right there. That would have been too easy. No it looked like being a long slow painful death.

The following night, Sunday, with the trap now closed, Sharon delivered the news to her parents. Her mother suffered mild apoplexy and her father let loose with a creative selection of words to describe his daughter.

He stomped around the room muttering…

"My daughter, my own fucking daughter a whore. Fucking floozy… a tramp, a slag, a loose slut. This is your fault you know," he said stopping to point an accusatory finger at his wife. "You raised a trollop, I warned you. Can't keep her damn legs together."

Sharon's mother was regaining her colour. The look she gave her husband stopped him in his tracks.

"What," he said pouting, "what did I do?"

Silence, thoughts gathered. When Sharon's mother spoke it was with authority. She who would be obeyed.

"I presume you know who the father is?"

Sharon nodded

"And what exactly do you plan to do about it?" asked Sharon's mother evenly.

More silence.

"We love each other. We love each other and we want to get married," she said with a straight face.

Would have been news to Oscar of course, poor old Oscar, him like a rabbit caught in the headlights and all.

"Sweet Jesus!" said Sharon's father, suddenly barely able to contain his joy, fighting the urge to fist pump.

'Yes! Every cloud really does have a silver lining. Never thought I'd see the day.'

Another withering look from Sharon's mother left him looking suitably contrite.

WHATEVER WILL BECOME OF ME?

Sharon Kingman sat in front of the television. It banged away in the corner but she saw nothing, stared right through the thing to some time in the past. Sharon Kingman was scared, well maybe not scared but certainly concerned.

'What the hell was Oscar up to?'

Her eyes snapped back into focus and she looked up at the mantle, mostly a shrine to the harpies, but there, up there half hidden, mostly forgotten and gathering more dust than memories, was a photo of her and Oscar on their wedding day. The colour was old and faded, everything more brown, more beige, more like real life now. With some effort, she pushed herself up out of her chair and went to the mantle, reached down the photo. The top of the frame was thick with dust, on her hands now like the dust from the wings of a wounded moth. She dragged the frame down the front of her housecoat, happy trails, and stood looking at that picture, that photograph, that record of what was. A younger Sharon and Oscar stared back at her, but spoke not of promise or happiness.

She tried to understand the look on her own face, but failed to recognise it for what it was. Failed to recognise it as smug triumph. She was the victim now, *'maybe always had been,'* she thought.

She looked at the young Oscar, struggled a bit with his expression as well. What was that, apprehension, fear, resignation, nervousness, misgiving, trepidation, dread, foreboding… butterflies, jitters, the willies, the creeps, the shivers, the heebie-jeebies? It was all of them, the lot, the lot and more besides, so what was going on now? What was happening now?

Only once or twice in all the years they had been together had Oscar bucked the system, her system. Only once or twice, like when he came to figure that she wasn't pregnant, that she'd lied to him that night in the dance hall. When he realised she'd trapped him, baited, snared and reeled him in. He got over it, took a few days, but he got over it like she knew he would. Over it because he was a wimp, scared of life, scared of her but more scared to be alone out there in that big wide world. Who else would have him? So he came back and he settled down and he went to work and he paid the bills and balance was restored. Her balance.

"So what are you up to?" she said aloud to young Oscar, that nervous young Oscar there behind the dusty glass.

Sharon Kingman wandered into the kitchen. She dropped that photograph, frame and all, memories and all, dust and all into the trash can. Prophesy, see the future. She flopped down at the table and stared at the telephone, the handset all bound up with christmas tape, bright jolly christmas tape, all she could find. Merry Christmas, Merry Christmas, Merry Christmas it said. The tape said. The phone said nothing, stayed silent. She reached out and carefully lifted the handset. Maybe it was past it, too badly busted to do its job. She lifted it to her ear, heard the ringtone, maybe a little fainter than usual, less urgent, but still there. She checked the clock on the wall... 2.10 p.m. She dialled Oscar's office, heard the ring, panicked, jammed a pudgy finger down to break the connection, stop the call, avoid the inevitable.

'He'd be back. He'd be back with his tail between his legs, simpering and whimpering like always. But what if he didn't come back, what then?'

Sharon felt a mild flutter in her chest, somewhere down in that ample chest, as she fleetingly considered the possibility that Oscar might have finally cracked, might never come back.

'Stupid,' she thought. *'Of course he'll be back.'*

But something chewed away at her. *'What if, what if?'*

What if he didn't come back, what would that mean? How would she manage, cope, exist? She wouldn't miss him, wouldn't miss Oscar, could replace Oscar with battery operated realism, already had in fact. It wasn't the no-Oscar thing that worried her, it was the no-Oscar benefits. The money, the household chores. The house was in her name, she'd seen to that, but who would mow the lawn, pay the bills? Insurance, light and power, food and booze. Food and booze.

'Jesus where was the little creep, what was he up to?'

He was up to something, she could feel it.

When he came back, if he came back... when he came back she would ease up a little, be nice to him a bit. Tell the girls to be nicer to him. Didn't ever think this might happen. Hadn't happened before, but couldn't be too careful. The girls, the girls. Awfully quiet up there. She got up and went to the stairs, called them.

"Carol, Margie!"

"Carol, Margie?" Louder.

"Margie, Carol, come down here now... please." Louder still.

"I said get down here now!" Screamed.

Silence, silence above. Getting angry now Sharon hauled herself up the stairs, the balustrade flexing with the weight, the urgency. She went first to Carol's room, empty. She went next to Margie's room, empty. Empty, nobody there. Absconded, done a bunk, gone on the lam, *'shit can this day get any worse?'*

She went back down the stairs and into the kitchen, picked up the wounded handset and called Oscar's office.

"Loughrans Loss Adjusters, how may I direct your call?"

"Yes it's Sharon Kingman and before you hang up or give me some excuse, this is urgent. Tell him he needs to speak to me now. Tell him his daughters are missing," said Sharon, keeping a level tone, struggling to stay calm.

"I'll see if I can locate him for you Mrs. Kingman. I'm not sure if he is back in the office."

Breathing, just breathing, nothing more to add. Waiting.

"Mrs. Kingman, are you there?"

"Yes I'm here." Staying level, staying calm, being calm.

"I have located Mr. Kingman. Putting you through now."

Oscar came on the line.

"Oscar, finally, why aren't you taking my calls? But but.. I realise that, but all day Oscar? Listen to me. Margie and Carol are gone. I don't know how they got out, how long they've been gone but, well they're gone. You need to come home right now. What, what did you say? What did you say to me? Don't you talk to me like that, how fucking dare you. Did you... Oscar, Oscar. Don't you dare hang up on me, don't you dare..."

"Fuck fuck fuck!"

Sharon slammed the handset down against the phone again and again. The jolly tape burst, Merry Christmas, Merry Christmas, bits of phone exploded around the room. She caught her finger in the flex, tore a nail.

"Fuck, fuck, fuck!" screamed Sharon.

Crash, smash splinter went the phone, dead now these past twenty seconds. The rage went on another twenty or thirty seconds, paroxysm, before her body, her fluttering heart, told her to stop, knock it off. Rage subsiding, violent shudders, tears now as she sank down onto the kitchen floor. She noticed her nail, torn sideways, blood forming around the quick, felt it finally. A new bout of self pity left her shaking, wobbling even, there on the kitchen floor like some giant spoilt baby.

"Why?" she wailed. "Why is he doing this to me?"

ON THE ROAD AGAIN

Eight year old Oscar Kingman lay in his bed that night weeping, more than weeping, sobbing his poor heart out. He had been led out of the little infirmary straight into the custody of the Irish nun Michael. The kindly nun, the other one, the one who had dressed his wounds paused, put a hand on his shoulder when she saw the sister Michael nun waiting there.

"Is there a problem?" said sister Michael.

"No sister, no problem. I just thought I'd…"

"I really don't care what you thought sister. You're young. You'll soon come to realise these little sinners, these children need strong discipline, need to be punished. Need the fear of the lord knocked into them. This one, this one I fear will face eternal hellfire and damnation, this one is already lost. This one will burn in hell! He's going to hell."

She stepped forward and grabbed Oscar by his bandaged hand. Oscar cried out in pain, pulled back. Sister Michael, Irish nun, bride of christ, defender of the faith and protecter of little children hauled off and whacked him around the head, knocking him senseless, nearly knocking him down. His head span and his ears rang, a noise like an approaching train travelled up through his head, blood rush, blacking out, hanging on. Oscar was dragged off down the hall, looking back over his shoulder at the kindly young nun, eyes askew, eyes pleading. There was nothing to be done, nothing to be done.

And so Oscar had been locked in the dormitory, locked all alone in that dormitory, left alone all day to stew over his sins. *'I am made of sin, all sin.'* Left alone all day to stew over his sins, no lunch, no dinner no salvation. He lay there hungry and weeping and he wondered how it was that he had become such a sinner, such a foul and stinking sinner and at such an early age. *'How come I am made of sin?'*

The following day the orphanage was a place of whispers, the morning a time of whispers.

'Sister Bernadette has gone, Sister Bernadette has gone. Pssst! Did you hear about Sister Bernadette?'

The building seemed empty, distracted. People came and went, penguins, nuns, staff came and went almost as if the children weren't there, had ceased to exist. In the afternoon, Oscar was pulling duty, doing punishment, happy to atone for his sins, eager to please, eager to stay safe and be invisible, trying. Oscar Kingman, invisible boy. He was sweeping the long wooden hallway, when the big heavy front door opened and there stood a man, a big man, seeming all square with a big square head. He wore a black suit and black shiny vest and it appeared to Oscar that he might have had his white shirt on backwards or something. He had short spiky grey hair and questing eyes, eyes that searched out sinners, a hunter of sinners. Those eyes came to rest now on Oscar for a few long seconds. Oscar recoiled against the wall as if he might pass through it, avoid the hunter, be anywhere but there in his path, then the man brushed past him and strode up the hall toward the office. As the big square man disappeared into the office Oscar heard a voice say…

"Oh, Father Flynn, how good it is to see you."

Father Flynn, crusader and searcher-out of sinners, slammed the office door heavily behind him. As Oscar looked along the hall, he noticed a head peering back at him, beady little eyes watching. Eddie Moran, bully in training, just ten years old and learning fast. Suddenly Eddie jumped out into the middle of the hallway.

"That's about you, that in there," he said, giving Oscar the rabbit ears with both hands. "That's about you creepy Kingman. Father Flynn's here to take you away. You're going to hell Oscar Kingman you sinner. Oscar's going to hell, Oscar's going to hell, Oscar's going to hell…"

And he was gone, off down the hall and around the corner.

Oscar panicked, heard voices raised in the office, thought he heard his own name mentioned, raised voices mentioning his name, Oscar, Oscar Kingman. He stood there petrified, little eight year old boy forced to weigh up the options. Options, options. Not necessarily voluntary options. Cry, piss the pants, hide or make a run for it. Oscar Kingman made his choice, only choice really. He turned and bolted for the front door. He was down the front steps and gone up the street before anyone knew. He ran two blocks along quiet back streets before coming out onto a shopping street. Cafes, fruit shop, dress shop, barber, couple of bars.

Back on the street, the long way round via Granny Molly's and the orphanage, but back on the street again. Not better than Granny Molly's but certainly better than the orphanage, much better than the orphanage. Back on the street.

It had been a couple of years, but Oscar remembered. Oscar remembered how to lift an apple, chocolate bar, grab a loaf of bread, all that. Pick someone looks like they'd have kids and walk behind them, be family, trail along bored like. Follow mummy into the shops as if you're invisible. Not hard for little Oscar Kingman, only half visible to begin with.

It wasn't until the sun got low in the sky that Oscar realised what was different this time, out there on the street. Used to always have some place to go at the end of the day. His mother, went back to his mother wherever she was. Down an alley, under a bridge, cheap hotel room, squat, always somewhere, but not tonight. No mother around tonight to make that choice, to be close to no matter how wasted she was. He was afraid, lonely and afraid. As the streets got darker every man in a suit looked like the Father Flynn person, hunter-of-sinners person. He went deeper into the cold dirty city and found an alley. He crawled into the space between the wall and a dumpster and cried. Cried and cried and cried. He cried for his mother Loretta, cried for Granny Molly, but mostly he cried for Oscar Kingman, sinner on the run, hunted.

It took them five days to find him. Five days, four cold lonely scary nights behind that dumpster, venturing out only for food and sunlight. Each night a little better than the last, a little worse than the one before. Where to go, what to do, marking time. On the afternoon of the fifth day he had been in the park. There were toilets there, he came here every day. He knew to be careful round toilets, one of Loretta's lessons. He'd come out of the toilets and was sitting on the grass by the little ornamental lake, people nearby having a picnic, sandwiches, soda. Oscar was hungry. He went out of the park and along the street toward the convenience store, hung out a little way down the street looking out for a surrogate mother. Gave up, too hungry to wait, so he went in alone. Oscar broke his own street rules. Went in alone and got caught soon as he got his hand on the fruit.

"Little bastard, gotcha!"

Oscar struggled, but that big hand had hold of his arm like in a vise. The shopkeeper held a struggling Oscar with one hand, phoned the cops with the other and then went on serving customers just like Oscar wasn't there. Wasn't there struggling at the end of his arm like some damn fish on a hook, rabbit in a snare. But he was there, and he was there a quarter hour later when a lady cop came in and took over. Once more, Oscar Kingman found himself locked in the back of a police car. Oscar Kingman, escaped sinner captured.

• • •

"This the one?"

"Looks like it."

"Jesus what a mess. He stinks."

"Been out there four five days sarge, not surprised."

"Oscar? Oscar is that you?"

Oscar turned to see a lady looking at him. As she walked towards him he thought she looked familiar.

"Oscar it's me, det... Officer McKenzie. You remember me Oscar?"

Oscar stared, still not sure. Then it came to him, the police lady who had helped him and Granny Molly. He looked at her clothes and she realised what was going on.

"Yes, it's me Oscar, you remember me?"

"You not in the police anymore?" he asked a little uncertain.

"Yes I am," she replied. "I am but I don't wear a uniform anymore Oscar. I'm a detective now."

McKenzie looked around at the watching faces. The Desk Sergeant, policewoman who'd brought him in, couple of other cops, just standing there watching.

"You know this kid Detective?"

"Sure do. We're old friends aren't we Oscar?" she raid ruffling his filthy hair.

She knelt down in front of him, looked at the bruise on his face.

"Oh dear, what happened here sweetheart?"

Oscar recoiled when she touched his cheekbone, tender.

"And your hand, what happened to your hand?"

"I fell over that's all?" said Oscar almost in a whisper.

"Okay well let's take a quick look shall we, then we can get you cleaned up."

McKenzie started to unwrap the filthy smelly bandage, once white, grey now and stained black in parts with dried blood. The final wrap delivered a foul pus stench and brought a sharp intake of breath from McKenzie.

"Jesus!" somewhere behind Oscar.

McKenzie took his other hand and turned it over palm up. Through the grime she could clearly make out the angry red welts. The light pressure of her thumb evidence of the pain, the tenderness.

"Oscar I need to ask you again sweetheart. What happened, who did this to you?"

"Told you, I fell over," said a tiny voice.

"Okay Oscar, we'll worry about that later, right now let's get you cleaned up and then we'll get a doctor to look at this lot."

She stood up, the detective detecting, already at the deducing stage maybe. She shook her head, angry now.

"Suppose someone tells me what the hell is going on here?" she said looking at the Desk Sergeant.

"Seems he escaped from some orphanage," shrugged the sergeant, referring to his notes.

"Escaped, escaped! Look at him for christ sakes. He's what, eight, nine years old." She reached over, gathered the sergeant's notes off the desk and turned to the female officer. "You bring him in?"

"Yes Detective. I'm Hicks."

"Good, come with me Hicks."

McKenzie took Oscar gently by the elbow and helped him down off the seat. As they went down the corridor she turned to the other woman.

"Hicks, I want sandwiches, juice, a full set of clothes and a doctor here in that order. About two years ago this boy's mother died and he went to live with his great grandmother. State made her legal guardian. There was a social worker on the case name of Garcia I think. I want you to find her and get her over here now. You manage that?"

A nod from Hicks.

"Good. I'm taking him down to the showers, clean him up. I'll see you down there okay?"

McKenzie took Oscar into the female locker rooms. She taped a plastic bag over the mess that was his hand. He stood there meekly while she stripped him off and wrapped him in a towel. He wasn't embarrassed, he was defeated, a boy made of sin.

"Can you manage okay in the shower Oscar honey? You need a hand or will you be okay?"

"I'm old enough to shower myself," said Oscar quiet like.

"I know you are Oscar, just checking. Round there to the left, scrub yourself well and be careful of that hand."

Oscar started to walk towards the showers. He stopped and turned.

"Where will you be?" he said with the saddest, loneliest, tiniest voice McKenzie had ever heard.

"I'll be right here Oscar. Right here sweetheart."

McKenzie sat there on the wooden bench and went through the pockets of his filthy pants. Nothing there, couple of old chocolate bar wrappers, bit of orange peel. She shook her head, then picked up the notes she'd taken from the desk sergeant.

The city desk was holding a missing persons notice. One Oscar Kingman, eight years old absconded from a catholic orphanage on the east side. *'Orphanage, what the hell was he doing in an orphanage?'*

She looked at the date of the report, shook her head. He'd been out there on the street five days. Tag note showed he'd been grabbed by a storekeeper while trying to steal oranges.

Ten minutes in she went and checked on Oscar. Steam pouring out of the cubicle and over the noise of the water she could make out the sobbing. Break a hardened detective's heart that sound. She went back to the lockers in time to see Hicks arrive with a bag of clothes in one hand and a deli bag in the other.

"That was quick."

Hicks smiled.

"They said the doctor is upstairs and the social worker Garcia, she's on her way over now."

"Good, thank you Hicks."

"That's okay. Look I'm sorry about what happened up there, the sergeant and all, I should have said something."

"That's all right," said McKenzie. "You weren't to know. This poor little kid. He's been through the wringer. Since the day he was born he's had nothing but grief. Single mother, father unknown. The mother's parents threw her out. We plucked him off the street the night his mother died... overdose. He'd sat there with her, trying to feed her, wake her up for nearly two days. Last I saw him he was living with his great grandmother. Dear old thing. Lost track, don't know what happened after that. Guess we'll find out soon enough."

Hicks raised her eyebrows and McKenzie turned to see Oscar standing there wrapped in the towel, looking small, so small.

• • •

"So what do you think doctor?"

"Well on its own, I mean just looking at that one injury on his left hand, nasty as it is, I would be hard pressed to make the call. But the other welts on the hand, and the clear welts on the other hand lead me to conclude that the boy has been viscously caned. The force behind those blows, to bust the boy's hand open like that, jesus. Then there's his face. Injury consistent with a serious blow. Punch, open hand, who knows?" said the doctor. "Probably open hand but an adult."

"Mrs. Garcia the social worker, has told me that Oscar's great grandmother died a couple of weeks ago. He was put into that orphanage while the state sorted out what to do with him. What kind of people run that place? Who treats a child that way?" said McKenzie.

She tapped a folder that was on the desk. "The Garcia woman brought in this file. Says here she is Oscar's case worker. Says she interviewed him at the orphanage about a week ago to see how he had settled in. According to her file he was doing fine."

"You'd be amazed detective. I see a lot of this sort of thing working for the department. As a matter of fact I contacted the church diocese about a year back concerning another child from this very same orphanage and there have been other stories floating about. Certain claims were made by a child, who was around ten or eleven years old if I remember correctly. She claimed a nun had burned her with a hot clothes iron because she had ironed her skirt badly, something like that."

"What happened?" asked McKenzie.

"Well as I say I contacted the diocese. A priest, very unsavoury character, came to see me. Told me the child was disturbed, had self inflicted, you know, burned herself. He asked me for any evidence I had to suggest otherwise. I had nothing, just the girl's word and a gut feeling. He made it clear that the church was not happy with my suggestion. Told me the church and the department, church and the city, for that matter, were well connected. Friends in high places. Implied that I should be a little more careful, more circumspect. As I say a very unsavoury type, scary. I have no proof of course, but I know when I'm being threatened."

"Will you stay while we talk to him, to this child?" asked McKenzie.

"Detective McKenzie, I've got a seven year old son of my own and I've felt bad about that little girl ever since. Of course I'll stay."

"I'll bring them in then," said McKenzie opening the door to the outer office.

"Mrs. Garcia, Oscar, you can come in now please."

"Okay," said McKenzie when they were seated, "Mrs. Garcia, why don't you fill us in on what is going on."

"I would prefer to talk without the child in the room," said Mrs. Garcia.

"I beg your pardon?"

This from McKenzie.

"I said I'd prefer to talk without the child in the room."

"Mrs. Garcia, this is not about you, what you may or may not prefer. It's about a child who has clearly been physically and mentally abused. A child in your care apparently, one of your cases," said McKenzie.

"Just the same…"

"Just the same nothing Mrs. Garcia," said McKenzie, all bad cop suddenly.

Bad cop bad cop.

"Based on what I have just learned, a crime has been committed, a serious crime, so this is now an official police investigation. The child stays, you talk. If you don't tell me everything you know then it will be construed as obstruction of justice. I can arrest you, do it that way if you wish?"

Bad cop bad cop.

McKenzie let this all soak in. She knew she was on shaky ground, thin ice, working without a net, but what the hell. She watched Garcia. Garcia not so cocky now, rattled.

"So it says in your file that you went and interviewed Oscar here just a week back, that correct?"

"Yes."

"And how was he?" asked McKenzie, watching Oscar and taking his hand.

"He was fine."

McKenzie saw the look in Oscar's eyes as he tried to pull his hand away. Betrayal. She turned her best bad-cop stare on Garcia.

"Okay Mrs. Garcia. I'm done playing twenty questions with you. I'm going to ask you one more time what happened when you interviewed Oscar last week and I want details. You understand me Mrs. Garcia?"

Little less cocky, little more rattled.

"Look, I went there as a matter of routine. It's what I always do when a child has been in an institution, any institution for a few days. I find out how they are settling in, if there's anything they need. I update them on any progress in their case if it's, you know, that type of case."

"And Oscar, I'll ask you again, how was Oscar."

"Oscar was... Oscar was fine. He complained a bit, but they all do."

McKenzie held up her hand, made a note.

"Okay, continue.

"I was saying that he complained a bit, said he wanted to go home. A typical reaction from a newly orphaned child," concluded Garcia.

"That's all, nothing more?" asked McKenzie.

Garcia shook her head. McKenzie looked at her, could see it written all over her face, *carved across her fucking forehead.*

"I don't think you're being totally honest with me Mrs. Garcia, I don't think you are telling me everything," said bad cop McKenzie.

She turned to Oscar.

"Oscar honey now, I want you to tell me what happened when this lady came to see you in the orphanage. There's no need to be frightened, just tell me what you remember."

"But you can't do this. He's just a child, clearly disturbed," said Garcia.

"Excuse me Mrs. Garcia, but you've had your opportunity to speak, told me you had nothing more to add. So for the moment I would appreciate if you just sat there quietly while we hear what Oscar has to say. As to whether the boy is disturbed, well it certainly isn't clear to *me*. He doesn't appear disturbed. He does seem injured, betrayed, frightened half out of his wits and it was your job to find out why, help him. You don't seem to have done your job and so now it's time for me to do my job."

"How dare you…" Garcia affronted, Garcia maligned.

"Shut the fuck up Mrs. Garcia. Sit there and shut up!"

More notes from McKenzie.

Oscar felt a little less afraid, uncertain, but a little more sheltered.

"Now Oscar," said McKenzie softly, "just tell us what happened when Mrs. Garcia came to visit you in the orphanage."

Oscar looked down, sniffed, rubbed his eyes. He stared down at the fresh bandage on his hand and then looked at Garcia. He looked at the doctor, looked down again, picked at the bandage. Then he looked up and spoke directly to McKenzie. When it came, it came like a landslide, like an avalanche, words tumbling over words.

"I told her I was afraid, told her they were cruel to me and they hit me. They punished me for nothing. They were cruel. I never did anything wrong," he said, eyes wide now appealing, needing to be believed, now more than ever before. "I told her they were cruel and they hit me but she didn't believe me. Told me I was a liar. She told me I was a liar and that the nun people were good and that I was a liar. But they're not good, they're not good they are cruel. They hit everybody, they hit me."

The avalanche settled, last rock rested, last word settled over the one below. Silence. Oscar looked down petrified, maybe gone too far. Didn't mean to.

McKenzie slid off her chair and knelt in front of Oscar, gently took both his hands.

"I know they hit you and I believe you said those things to Mrs. Garcia Oscar. I believe you."

Oscar looked at McKenzie, turned to look at the doctor, head shaky, jerky like a chicken. The doctor nodded and smiled at him.

"And then what happened Oscar?" said McKenzie.

"The lady went out," said Oscar, less shaky, more visible now. "She went out and talked to sister Michael."

Big gulp of breath, McKenzie scribbling notes.

"Then sister Michael came and pulled me out of the room, pulled me along by my ear."

Hand going there now remembering.

"She took me to a room sister Michael, she took me to a room and she hit me and hit me with a stick, on my hands."

Landslide starting again, words like rocks tumbling out into the void, rolling one over the other, tumbling out.

"She hit me and hit me with a stick and my hands were all bleeding and then a kind lady helped me, put a bandage on my hand, a bandage on my hand and helped me and I was crying and she was crying and the pain was so bad I couldn't stop crying and the kind lady was crying. Then she took me out and the other one, the cruel one grabbed me and hit me again. She hit me here, on my face and everything went black and I was scared she wouldn't stop hitting me."

He stopped, stopped so sudden you could hear those words settling one on the other, coming to rest.

"Oscar sweetheart," whispered McKenzie, "Oscar sweetheart, who was the other lady, the kind lady that helped you?"

"Her name. I think she was Berny... det, sister Bernydet, something."

McKenzie leaned forward and hugged him, wrapped her arms around him and hugged him, as much to hide her own tears, cover her own emotion.

"The other one, the sister Michael one," sobbed a tiny voice, "she said I was going to burn. She said I was going to hell, She said I was going to hell. I'm scared. I don't even know where that is."

McKenzie clutched him tighter and looked over his shoulder at Mrs. Garcia sitting there now white faced and shaken. Oscar was less invisible.

OSCAR HANGS UP

Anyone watching Oscar Kingman could see that he was hard at work and hard at work he was. Oscar Kingman was hard at work looking hard at work. The junior estimators sat out in the general office like they were just ordinary clerks. There were three junior estimators now with growth and all and the other two were in their twenties, barely swaddled thought Oscar, fumed Oscar. But there they sat, middle row with the ordinary clerks. Anyone watching those three junior estimators would have clearly seen that Oscar Kingman was the busiest by far, oldest and busiest by far. Weighed down by it, rushed off his feet, can't talk now, busy busy busy, all those things, because Oscar knew how to blend in, just another dancer in the chorus line.

Oscar was so busy looking busy that he didn't even see Moira standing there close enough to cast a shadow.

"Mr. Kingman, Oscar." He looked up.

"Yes Moira?"

"Er look I'm sorry, but your wife is on the phone and she insists that it is very urgent, something about your daughters going missing. I know you said not to put her through but…" she shrugged and opened her arms like the messiah.

"Okay," said Oscar. "Okay. Thanks Moira, I'll take it, put her through."

The phone rang, he picked it up.

"Yes."

"Oscar, finally, why aren't you taking my calls?"

"Because I told you I'm busy that's why," replied Oscar levelly.

"But but.."

"And when I say I'm busy I mean I'm busy and can't be disturbed." Patience wearing thin now.

"I realise that, but all day Oscar? Look, listen to me. Margie and Carol are gone. I don't know how they got out, how long they've been gone but, well they're gone. You need to come home right now."

"Are your ears painted on Sharon, I mean are you deaf or just plain stupid?"

"What, what did you say? What did you say to me?"

"You heard me Sharon and hear me now when I say fuck off you fat cow and leave me alone. I don't care about you *or* your daughters. Hear me, I don't fucking care."

"Don't you talk to me like that, how fucking dare you…"

Click!

"Did you… Oscar, Oscar. Don't you dare hang up on me, don't you dare."

BOOK TWO

HELL AND HOW TO GET THERE

'And the smoke of their torment goes up

for ever and ever; and they have no rest,

day or night, these worshipers

of the beast and its image, and whoever

receives the mark of its name.'

Revelation 14:11

THE ROAD TO HELL

"We think it's best Oscar, the best thing for you. Your grandmother and I well, we both work and... you know, we're too old to be trying to raise children, so we think this is the best thing."

Oscar looked up at the man speaking to him. The man said his name was Richard. He said he was Oscar's grandfather. Oscar remembered Granny Molly talked about Richard, said he was kind but weak.

'Didn't want to make waves,' was what Granny Molly had said.

So he sat there, Oscar sat there now, eyes flickering between the man's head and the shopfronts that sped past behind the man's head. Dry cleaner, gas station, florist, grocery, butcher.

"Besides," continued the man, "you can come and stay with us for the holidays. Well part of the holidays at least."

Shoe repair, bike shop, baker.

"Where are you taking me?" said Oscar, first words since he'd got in the car.

"We spoke about this," said Richard. "Your Granny Molly wanted you to go to a good school and we think, your grandmother Glenda and I that is, we think this is a good school. This school is run by good people and you'll live there with lots of other boys, boys your age. You'll have lots of fun I'm sure."

"Like the orphanage, that's what they said about the orphanage," said Oscar, defiant.

Fruit shop, bank, insurance agent, sandwich bar.

"No, not like the orphanage Oscar. We're looking after you now. We wouldn't let anything like that happen to you again."

Nursery, scrap metal, woodyard, hardware, carpark, trees.

"Then why can't I live with you, why do I have to live at this boarding school?"

Trees, trees, trees.

"I just told you why Oscar. It will be fine, you'll see."

Trees, trees, brick entrance way, trees, flowers.

The car crunched up the long gravel driveway and turned round a big circular garden bed to face back the way it had come, parked beside a wide concrete stairway that led up to the entrance of an imposing three storey red brick building. Looked like a prison, tower like a prison.

"Here we are then," said the man called Richard, climbing out.

The man called Richard who said he was Oscar's grandfather. He went to the trunk.

Oscar sat there looking up the stairs.

'Up those stairs, what lay up those stairs?'

The big brown door at the top of the stairs opened and out stepped a man. Oscar suddenly knew where he was, what he suspected all along, what Eddie Moran had known for sure.

'Oscar's going to hell, Oscar's going to hell, Oscar's going to hell, Oscar's going to hell...'

Oscar stared up at the man on the top step, smiling down. Smiling down and wearing black, all black like a long dress. All black like a long dress, all black except for a big cross hanging on a chain. A cross hanging on a chain and a white collar. Oscar had seen such a man before and he knew. He knew, he knew he knew. This was hell.

'Oscar's going to hell, Oscar's going to hell...'

The man called Richard came around to Oscar's side of the car, a small bag in his hand. He opened the door.

"Come on Oscar, it'll be fine, you'll like it here. If there's any problems you can telephone me... okay."

But Oscar just shook his head, eyes locked on the smiling man above. He scuttled across to the other side of the car, got smaller, less visible, felt the tears coming. Oscar Kingman, boy made of tears.

The man called Richard turned to the man on the stairs, coming down now, closer and closer. Turned to him and shrugged.

"Sorry, he's been through a lot. He's pretty upset."

Suddenly the car doorway was filled with black, big cross hanging down lower as the man leaned in. He was older than Oscar first thought, maybe even older than Granny Molly. Up close Oscar could see that the man's clothes were shiny black and worn in places. He had tired eyes, weary eyes that smiled somehow kindly, somehow suspiciously, from behind little frameless eyeglasses. He was big, big and wide and the remnants of his hair stood spiky on a pale pink scalp. He looked at Oscar, looked at Oscar and held out his hand. When he spoke it was with a thick accent.

"Come Oscar, there's nothing for it but you're here now. Let's you and I have a talk, then we'll get you all settled in, okay?"

And so Oscar found himself led up those stairs, surrendered, the old man in black carrying his little bag, his worldly possessions, led up those stairs into the flames. He knew. Vaguely aware of a voice below.

"We'll see you in the holidays Oscar."

The car pulling out, crunching off down that gravel drive.

Oscar was led in through the big door, portal to hell.

Abandon hope all you who enter here.

He found himself in a big room, a big room hung all around with strange paintings, stood all around with strange statues. Like the paintings and statues at the orphanage. Strange people standing on clouds, arms open, hearts shining on the outside. Almost naked, hanging from crosses.

"Come Oscar, this way."

He let himself be led up three steps to a small passage, and along this to a tiny office near the end.

"Please Oscar. Sit down boy."

Oscar was in a state of confusion. '*When did it start, was this how it started?*' He sat where the old man pointed.

"My name is Strohkirch, Father Strohkirch. I am a priest Oscar. An old weary and jaded priest, but still a priest. Do you know what a priest is Oscar?" asked father Strohkirch.

Oscar's eyes were locked on the wall behind the old priest. Someone there naked but for a loincloth, hanging from a cross and bleeding.

The old priest turned, followed his eyes up the wall.

"Ah yes, that." He turned back.

"Oscar, I know this is all very difficult for you. I know all about you, what has happened to you. I know about the orphanage and what happened there."

Oscar listening now, hearing, seeing. Watching the old priest. The old priest, talking as if to himself, talking to himself, questioning himself. But he wasn't talking to himself, he wasn't, Oscar was listening.

"You know Oscar that orphanage well, sometimes bad people, evil people, hide behind good people, good institutions. The church is a good place Oscar, the orphanage is a good place, but sometimes bad people get into positions of power. It happens in business, in the military and yes even in the church. It happens in life. Do you understand what I am saying Oscar? Maybe not. What I am saying is that this place you have come to, this strange place where you find yourself today, there are bad people here too Oscar. I wish it were not so, but that's the way it is. Some of the men, some of the priests and brothers who work and teach here are good men. They truly do God's work… but others, others have lost their way Oscar. Or maybe never found the way to begin with. These men are not part of the church Oscar, not part of *my* church anyway. They are cruel and they are bitter. But I have said too much now, just an old priest jabbering away."

Father Strohkirch took off his glasses and picked up a white cloth to polish them.

"I guess what I am saying Oscar is that this is not a good place, not a good place for you to be, but here you are and here I am. I will help you whenever I can, but Oscar the best advice I can give you is to accept what has happened to you and to make the most of it."

He put the glasses back on his nose, flicked the wire arms around his ears.

"Yes, that's it Oscar. Try and make the most of it. Now come," he said pushing himself up from the desk, "let's get you settled in."

THE WAY WE WERE

Oscar leaned back in his chair and looked around him, taking a break, a well earned rest, just a quick one, a minute or so but no more. Here in this place, this time, this time and place. Pretending, just pretending to be Oscar Kingman, the old Oscar Kingman. Projected into the space like the old Oscar Kingman. He looked at the other two junior estimators, beavering away, eager to impress, hard at it. He turned away, eyes scanning down the corridor, down to the file room, down to nirvana, then back to the general office, back to the mundane. Oscar floating above it now, floating up there now looking down, coming down, back down now.

Back into this world, this real world of bad attitude and worse manners. Oscar wondered how the world had got like this, wondered maybe was it always like this, him just noticing now, not before. No, he was sure it had been different once, sure people used to care for each other more. He remembered once seeing a man fall shaking, jerking on the pavement and people rushed to help. Epileptic they said, people helping, people caring. Not now, now they'd step on his face to get his spot in the queue, seat on the bus. Kids seemed sweeter back then and had manners. Now it was all *'What the fuck you lookin` at?'* from kids, little kids even.

Seemed there was some hope back then, at least some happy families, some places where there might have been a bit of love, bit of hope. Of course Oscar never had it. It was always *'fuck off!'* for Oscar, except for those thin little threads of happy, little threads of safe that he'd felt when he lived with his Granny Molly. Those little threads like shards of ice, melting away now in his memory, fading fast.

But he'd seen it, knew it was out there. Happiness, hope. He'd seen it from a distance at boarding school, felt it once or twice up close with a kind deed. Seen some hope, some kind of love, some kind of respect, self respect. Fleeting fleeting, just around the corner. Once or twice a little bit of someone else's love, someone else's kindness touched him. Secondhand but still there, still proof it could happen.

If a man wore his trouble too heavy and stood on a ledge back then, people would try to talk him down, everything to live for, everything. Nothing worth dying for, how can we help? Same man on a ledge these days people make book, will he won't he? Jump you bastard, go on. *'Here's your hundred!'*

No, it was different now, Oscar knew. Maybe it was easier for him to see it because he was outside it all, stood on the outfield, could see the whole game from out there.

'And here we are,' he thought, *'here we are at where we are and where we are is all bad. No love, no manners, no respect,'* at least not that Oscar could see. Not from here in this office on level five in the city.

Oscar got to wondering was it just cities, this city. Maybe there was a place somewhere, a place where real people still lived and loved. On an impulse he got up from his desk and went out through the foyer. Went to the lift, pushed the last button, pushed twenty three, one from the top. The lift doors opened and it was all quiet, nobody about, just doors with numbers. He stepped out and tried the fire escape door, it opened into a bare concrete stairwell. He took the stairs up, Oscar Kingman took the stairs up first time ever, new territory. After all these years. He reached the top of the stairway and pulled open the heavy fire door. Weak sunlight flooded into the grim stairwell. He stepped through holding the door open against the automatic closer, tested the outside handle. At his feet was a bit of timber, size of a brick. He kicked it into the gap, let the door close gently on it. Escape assured. For just a second Oscar Kingman had wondered if he'd ever pass through this door again, didn't know why, just a flicker, then the thought flew away and was gone. There had to be a place, had to be.

He looked up at the sky, took a deep breath and turned a full circle, arms spread like in a movie. He wandered over to the edge of the building, close as he could, close as he felt safe. He looked out across the city past the tall buildings, treetops over there, green, breathing. He stepped even closer to the edge. Somewhere out there. In his mind he heard the music, heard the words, heard Judy Garland singing the song. He felt like he could spread his wings and fly. Fly to that place out there, that place over the rainbow. A shudder ran through him and he looked down into the city that swarmed around down below and he felt foolish, like an idiot. Standing on top of a building dreaming about rainbows and flying… still.

He went back from the edge, back through that door, kicking the timber out behind him and down. When the lift opened on his floor it was only five minutes since he'd left. He turned and went toward the toilets, washed his face under the stream from the cold tap, ready to join the battle again. He thought of Edmund Llewellyn, felt the bile rise in his throat, thought he might throw up. He stood perfectly still, then as it passed he looked up and saw himself there in the mirror. Oscar Kingman, totally visible, totally solid around the edges, in perfect focus. He reached into his pocket, felt the panties, magic pink panties, between his fingers. Felt their promise, felt their warmth, felt their magic flow through him. He looked again at the Oscar in the mirror, looked really hard for the first time ever. Nothing to be ashamed about, nothing to apologise for. Just Oscar Kingman there looking back at him that's all. Just Oscar Kingman.

THE JOY OF MARRIAGE REVEALED

There was no honeymoon, no trip to Niagara or Vegas, no time, no money and no reason.

Oscar and Sharon spent the first three weeks of their married life at her parent's house. Her mother, all cold stares, watery coffee, hot buttered resentment and open hostility. Sharon's father, teamster, physical, drunkard, pressed thumb and finger marks into Oscar's soft throat that day in the bathroom.

'Get your own place. Get your own place and take that useless fat cow daughter of mine with you, you little turd.'

Three weeks in hostile territory, three weeks behind enemy lines. Three weeks fighting for space in a single bed in that pink frilly room decorated with cheap dolls and movie posters. Three weeks in that place of torture behind enemy lines. Each night Sharon deciding, Sharon doling out that damp fleshy place like rations. Each night any noise at all bringing angry thumps on the wall, shouts from another place. Easier to sleep on the floor, safer down there below the line of fire.

Three weeks and each night, every night and every morning Sharon whining, Sharon demanding.

"You need to get us out of here Oscar. You need to start looking after me. I need a place of my own. We need a place of our own, can't stay here. Be a man Oscar, go to your boss and get a raise or something. Get us out of here."

So each morning Oscar dragged himself up off the floor, stretched the kinks out best he could and waited until he heard the bathroom was empty, then showered and done, he got the hell out of there. Across the minefield and gone.

Finally Oscar got up the courage to knock on Mr. Alperstein's door. Good kind Mr. Alperstein.

"Young Oscar, come in son, I'm glad you're here. I was going to talk to you later, got some good news for you. Seeing as you're here we'll do it now."

'Good news, good news? Must be some mistake, must think I'm someone else,' thought Oscar.

"I've been keeping an eye on you Oscar. You're a good worker and I think it's time you were rewarded. I'm promoting you to costing clerk," said Mr. Alperstein. "Now it's probably not as much fun as the mailroom, pretty boring to be truthful. But it pays more and it's a good start along the road to *my* job. You keep your head down and work hard Oscar, you'll advance in this company. Mark my words Oscar."

Oscar sat there stunned. Silent, shocked even. His life was so much bad news that he had absolutely no idea how to react to good news. Never happened to him.

Alperstein laughed.

"You okay there Oscar, you look a little shocked?"

Oscar started.

"Oh er, sorry. I'm sorry Mr. Alperstein sir, I'm a bit surprised. That's all, surprised."

He knew what Alperstein was doing, knew he was helping him out. Maybe he'd earned this, maybe he hadn't, but Mr. Alperstein was helping him out. There was that feeling, right there, again. That feeling that he might just have found a place in this harsh world. A place where he was not invisible, a place not drenched in tears, a new future maybe.

"Don't be surprised Oscar, you've earned it. Now what can I do for you? How is married life? How is that new bride of yours?"

"Well actually Mr. Alperstein sir, I came to ask you if ah, well you know, to ask you if a small raise was possible, but now well…. You see we are living with Sharon's parents, in their tiny apartment. I'm afraid it is not working out."

"Of course it's not working out," said Mr. Alperstein. "A young couple starting out need their privacy, a place of their own. As a matter of fact I might be able to help you out with that as well. My brother owns a jewellery store downtown. A little building with two apartments above it. They are very small, just one room with a kitchen and basic bathroom, but something I think you could afford on your new salary."

He beamed at Oscar.

"I know he's just had one of them painted, tenant moved out. Let me call him right away and see if he has a new tenant yet. Now back to it young Oscar and I'll let you know as soon as I have spoken to him."

Oscar returned to the mailroom caught halfway between *'is this really happening?'* and *'this shit never happens to people like me.'* But he dared to dream.

A new job, more money, maybe a place to live. Sharon would be happy, get her off his back and who knows, once they had a place of their own it might even work out between them. Long shot, but who could tell. With a new-found spring in his step, Oscar got through a nervous day, waiting, hoping. Just after 4.00 p.m. Mr. Alperstein put his head round the door of the mailroom.

"Got a minute Oscar?"

Got a minute, got a minute? Sure do.

He calmed himself.

"Yes sir. Yes Mr. Alperstein."

"Well Oscar, it seems it really is your lucky day. My brother has put a card in his shop window just this morning, but the apartment is still vacant. He says he'll hold off until you've had a look at it, you and Sharon."

"We'll take it!" Oscar blurted out. "I mean if you think it's okay, then that's fine with me, with us I mean. Like you said, a place of our own and somewhere to start. Please ask your brother to take the card out of the window, we'll take it."

"Good," said Alperstein. "Good decision Oscar. Decisive, I admire that. I'll call him back and arrange for you and Sharon to have a look tonight, you know, plan out what you might need, when you can move in. No reason why you can't move in straight away he said. All furnished, but of course you'll need your own linen and bits and pieces. Tomorrow I'm interviewing someone new for the mailroom. I'll want you to train the new person. Maybe just take a day or so, but from tomorrow morning you'll be paid as a costing clerk. It's almost a full third more than you earn now. See Mrs. Colby in the morning, she'll sort it all out and organise your desk in the office. So congratulations Oscar, well done lad."

"I don't know what to say Mr. Alperstein. I mean how can I thank you for all this. I mean I never dreamed…"

"You can thank me by applying yourself and living up to the potential that I know you have. You earned this Oscar, you. Now I'm letting you go early, so get off home and tell your new bride the good news."

As the door closed behind Mr. Alperstein, Oscar sat down on his little brown stool. The little brown stool with four legs and castors that had been his office, his world since arriving at Loughrans. Every day he wheeled himself back and forth slotting envelopes, papers, parcels into their correct places, allotted places. Moving around his lonely domain on those four wheels. *Oscar Kingman, costing clerk,* he could hardly believe it. When he stood up off that little stool he felt lighter, he felt taller, he felt more solid and more visible.

Out on the street the city smelt less of shit, dust and garbage and more of cut grass, flowers and promise. Oscar knew that this was all in his mind but it didn't matter. He was looking forward to telling Sharon. *'She'd be so excited, so pleased.'* They'd work it out somehow. *'She'd be so excited.'*

"You what… you actually expect me to live here? In this dump?"

And just like that the best day of Oscar's life to date evaporated, gone in an instant. It was like this super power she had, Sharon had. Open her mouth and the whole world turned grey.

"Jesus it's tiny. And it stinks."

"That's just paint Sharon. It's just been freshly painted. Look it will be fine. I thought you'd be excited. I thought it was what you wanted. I mean it's our own place. Sure it's not much, but we have to start somewhere and with the extra money and all. Mr. Alpenstein said…"

"Mr. Alperstein this, Mr. Alperstein that. Listen to you. Got your… oh forget it. I guess it will have to do. But we're not staying here long, don't think we're staying here long Oscar."

He watched her as she wandered around the place, poking in the cupboards, flushing the toilet, kicking at the edge of the carpet and he felt himself returning to his normal state, euphoria done and dusted, all hope dashed. He felt sick watching her, the weight of a life sentence bearing down on him, grinding, grinding, keeping him down, back in his place. Back down, his feet landing back on the ground.

And so the following weekend they had moved in, struggling up and down the steep narrow stairs with an old television and their life in a few cardboard boxes. They spent their first night together in a double bed. An old sagging mattress, scene of a thousand crimes, on an old double bed. Sharon had drunk too much and groped about on him like some dribbling slathering sweaty thing come out from a bad dream. But she went at him with a purpose, woman on a mission and at some point his hormones kicked in and he got the job done, almost enjoyed it, almost... last little bit.

THE BOARDING SCHOOL

The old priest picked up the little carry bag, handed it to Oscar and ushered him out of the room. Back down the hall, down the three steps and across the big room hung and stood all with strange and scary images. Across the big room and out through double doors on the other side they went, and Oscar found himself on a wide verandah, a type of cloister that ran a great distance directly away from him and a short distance to the right. The cloister bordered a lush green lawn, in the middle of that sat a squat red brick building. Beyond was a large expanse of asphalt all laid out as tennis and basketball courts, all white lines sloping slightly downhill.

The old priest took the bag from Oscar's hand and placed it on the ground by the door.

"Come with me boy. I'll show you where everything is."

Oscar followed him down the long arm of the cloister, while Strohkirch pointed out classrooms to their left, library, stairs to the infirmary and headmaster's office. They turned out onto a wide pathway. A small man dressed like the priest scuffled by head down, ignoring, ignored. Oscar saw what might have been disgust in the old priest's eyes as he passed. They came to a wide set of stairs, at the top of which stood a tall pointy building with a looming glass front.

"This is our church," said Strohkirch. "You'll come here a lot I'm afraid young Oscar," he said walking in through the wide open doors.

Inside was bright and airy, all the seats, all the woodwork pale and new, not like anything Oscar had seen before. Light flooding in through modern stained glass windows and down from the vaulted ceiling. Oscar watched as the old priest dipped his fingers in a small container of water and crossed himself. At the orphanage they had dragged Oscar to what they called a chapel one day and they had punished him for not doing this. The sign of the cross. *In the name of the father and of the son and of the holy ghost.* They had beaten him, beaten him for not knowing. Beaten him and locked him up.

The priest stepped forward and, supporting himself on one of the benches, knelt down briefly on one knee. He stood up and turned to see Oscar watching, confused.

"Don't worry Oscar, you'll soon figure it all out," he said not unkindly.

Mystery, ritual, secret signs, secret handshakes, mystery mystery.

Now they left the church and made their way up onto the big asphalt square. All along one side ran an open fronted shelter, at the far end low modern classrooms. The priest pointed to one of them.

"That will be your classroom Oscar. On Tuesday."

He turned to see Oscar facing away, looking down across the lawn, back at the main building.

"Oscar,"

"Where is everybody?"

"Where is everybody? Well you're the first Oscar. A bit unusual, but your family wanted you here early," replied Strohkirch.

Wanted you gone from them fast, buried, hidden away, out of sight out of mind.

"All the boarders will arrive tomorrow, you're the first. Then on Tuesday all the day boys come. Tuesday is the first day of term."

Oscar trailed along for another half hour while the old priest showed him the dining room, the refectory he called it, then the stairs up to the dormitory rooms above. Thirty steel beds, ex-army cots, laid out in three rows in a big cold lifeless room, each one with a folded tick mattress, a pillow, sheets and two thin grey blankets, each one with a low cold metal locker beside it. Your possessions, your life. Your life in this cold tin box. Two more rooms just like it, all three end to end, end to end to end. Ninety lost children, damned children, invisible children? Who could say?

Strohkirch placed Oscar's bag on a cot.

"This is you Oscar. Everything you need in there," he said pointing at the locker.

"Through that blue curtain is where the brothers sleep. The showers and toilets are at the other end there. You'll need to make up your bed, you know how to do that?"

Oscar nodded. Same as the orphanage, same as the orphanage, same as the orphanage. Same same same.

'You're going to burn in hell, Oscar's going to hell. Already there, already there! Already dead, just not lying down.'

"All right then, well Brother Antonio is around here someplace. I'll let you settle in, maybe get used to it, put your things away. Brother Antonio will tell you when it's time for lunch."

'Brother Antonio, brother Antonio. I don't have a brother. This Antonio is not my brother. I have no brother. I have no brother I have no sister, no father no mother. Everyone I had is gone, has left me. I have only tears. I am Oscar Kingman, I am made only of tears.'

He watched the priest go, stood looking at the space where he'd been for a long time, too long. He cried. Cried for Loretta, cried for Granny Molly, cried for Oscar Kingman. He finally gave a great shudder, looked around him, looked around this long low room with it's three rows of cots. He walked to the window on the other side of the room, could see nothing but fields, fields and a road back over there somewhere, and cows. Hard as he looked he could see no future out there. He went back to his cot, went back to his little tin locker. He folded the hard mattress out flat on the bed then wrapped a blanket around himself and lay down to wait, lay down to die, lay pressed down by the weight of despair, pressed down low, so low he no longer cared. Each tear a little piece of Oscar Kingman, each tear a little less of Oscar Kingman. The mattress soaked, each tear. By morning there would be nothing left of Oscar Kingman but a damp patch on a hard mattress. A damp patch on a hard mattress, painted there by despair, by abandonment, by incomprehensible anguish, by betrayal. Oscar Kingman, boy made of tears.

Two hours Oscar lay there melting away one tear at a time, getting smaller and smaller, until Antonio came for him, brother Antonio came for him.

"You!" heard Oscar, surprised to find himself still there.

"You, get up!"

He opened his eyes and rolled over to see a man looking down at him. A tall man, dark, dressed in black like the others. Another strange accent.

"I am Brother Antonio. You need to make this bed properly and then we will go down for lunch. Yes?"

Oscar looked at this man, this brother Antonio. Deep dark eyes behind heavy black rimmed glasses, bottom half of his face like some comic book villain, shaven but not enough. But it was the eyes, those eyes, those don't-mess-with-me eyes, those I-am-not-your-friend eyes. He kicked the bed.

"I said get up, now!"

Oscar remembered what the old priest Strohkirch had told him, came awake, came alert, wiped his eyes, wiped those bits of him that rested thick on his cheeks, wiped them away.

He set about making the bed. Making the bed the way they had taught him at the orphanage. Hospital corners, hospital corners. Every now and then brother Antonio would cuff him about the head, *'no, like this idiot,'* fix something, straighten something until finally it was done. Then the brother took him roughly by the arm and marched him out and down to the refectory. Down to the refectory where the troops were all gathered. There they were all gathered, discussing, planning and laughing, seemingly oblivious to Oscar's presence. They sat on a raised platform, about twenty of them, two tables, all but one in black and this one in an old tweed suit, not easily recognised as one of them, but one of them just the same.

They sat at two tables raised up closer to their god than the rest of the tables in the room. A step above, *nearer my god to thee*. Finally they noticed him and they watched as the brother called Antonio led him into the room and pointed to a table with four chairs. Just Oscar and three empty chairs. Just Oscar down at this level, the sinner's level. Twenty four tables down there in four neat rows, room for ninety five more sinners, Oscar Kingman and ninety five more sinners. Room at god's table, room in god's house. One table set with just one place, right close-up under the glare of god's chosen people.

Oscar felt them watching now, their eyes on him, felt their scorn, felt their pity and disgust. He kept his head down repentant, not daring to look up until he heard a squeaking noise, saw the wheel of a cart arrive beside his table. A woman, plump and round faced, placed bread on his side plate, ladled some kind of stew onto his large plate, made to smile at him, checked herself and poured weak milky tea from a stainless jug.

Oscar reached for the thick slice of bread.

"Wait Boy!" someone bellowed.

Oscar's heart nearly came out his mouth.

"We say grace here, we give thanks," another voice, softer.

Oscar snatched his hand back, folded it in his lap, head down,

"Bless us O Lord and these your gifts, which we are about to receive from your bounty. Through Christ our Lord. Amen."

"Amen." Many voices now.

Mystery, ritual, secret incantations, secret signs, secret handshakes.

"Well boy?"

"Amen," said Oscar.

"Louder boy."

"Amen!"

Eventually they lost interest in him and he sat eating his food slowly, unsure what to do but look contrite, look repentant. Stupid Oscar Kingman, sinner.

THE BRINGER OF BAD NEWS

Oscar went back to his desk, looked at his watch, hands barely moving, time barely moving now, slowing down making space for him. All around him the office moved in slow motion, stop motion, *tick tick tick tick tick.* He looked down at his hands and felt he could see through them. It was happening, it was coming.

'I am already dead.'

All around him the office moved in slow motion, stop motion, *tick tick tick tick tick* and he sat among them unseen, invisible, a wisp, a faint breeze, a suggestion of the Oscar Kingman that could have been. It was coming, it was happening.

'He is already dead, I am already dead.'

It was happening, it was coming and he could not stop it, nothing could stop it.

Waiting waiting.

He reached into his pocket and took out the panties, Wendy Legget's magic pink panties, right there in his hand. Nobody could see him, see the panties. They all moved so slowly he was invisible, *tick tick tick tick tick.* It was happening. He looked at his watch again, the old watch given him by Granny Molly. He watched the second hand climbing slowly uphill against the pull of gravity, the tug of the universe, against the sense of all reason, *tick tick tick tick tick.* All was silent and still in those final seconds, that final second. That interminable final second hung there in space, one last notch… *tick!*

3 o'clock! *It is now.*

3.00 p.m. and Oscar Kingman switched the magic panties to his left hand. He reached out his now almost invisible right hand

and took the long sharp letter opener from its place on his ordered desk. He slid it up his shirt sleeve, ready, waiting, *'it is now, he is already dead.'* He stood and moved through the office, invisible. Moved through the desks to Edmund Llewellyn's office door. Went in, closed the door behind him.

It is now!

Llewellyn looked up surprised.

"What do you want? You can't just barge in here without knocking,"

Something wrong, something not quite right. Knowing somehow.

'I am already dead.'

Without a word Oscar crossed the floor and moved swiftly, solid now in this room, around Llewellyn's desk. The Welsh knight wide-eyed as he saw the thin silver blade slide from the shirt sleeve, Oscar's shirt sleeve. With silent grace and amazing speed Oscar moved behind him as Llewellyn craned his head around to follow the movement. He tried to stand, but his seat was held hard against the desk. Oscar reached out with his left hand and jammed the panties, the magic pink panties, across Llewellyn's mouth and nose. Llewellyn's foul smart mouth and his nose, buried now in the pink, shiny pink. He tried to suck in a breath, smelt the smell of all those women, his guilt locked there in those panties.

'I am already dead, I am already dead.'

Oscar Kingman's right hand came down swift and true and drove the letter opener, the instrument of news, news of impending death… drove that letter opener through Llewellyn's neck right up to the hilt. He felt the slight jerk and tiny detour as the blade popped through the jugular, bounced off Llewellyn's spinal column and found a clear path onwards, to appear as a sharp obscene but foreign and fascinating protrusion beneath the skin on the other side of the Welsh knight's neck. Oscar saw it there, was fascinated, pulled harder against Llewellyn's face, his struggle, his last breath.

'Bless me father for I have sinned.'

When at last Llewellyn was still, when at last there was breath no more and it was done, Oscar lowered him down, carefully, reverently onto the floor and lay him out behind the desk.

'How have you sinned, what are your sins Oscar Kingman?'

He knelt down and forced Llewellyn's limp body into the footwell of the big mahogany desk, the big important mahogany desk.

'I have killed this man Edmund Llewellyn. I have taken his life.'

He took hold of the handle of the letter opener and pulled, harder than he would have thought necessary, pulled it clean out, and with it came the blood. Pulled it out and wiped it on the panties, the magic pink panties.

'I absolve you in the name of the father and of the son and of the holy ghost.'

There was so much blood. Oscar was surprised there was so much blood.

He stood and pushed the chair in as far as it would go, forced it against the knight, Llewellyn buried there in his own mahogany casket, then he went to the door. He turned the latch and pulled the door closed behind him, locked. Once more all around him the office moved in slow motion, stop motion, *tick tick tick tick tick*. He looked down at his hands, could no longer see through them. It had happened, it was done.

'I am already dead.'

He moved through them quickly back to his desk, the blade, the letter opener, bringer of bad news, concealed once more up his shirt sleeve. He looked at his watch, *tick tick tick*, time speeding up and all around him becoming normal. Nobody looking nobody seeing... normal.

But it wasn't normal, never normal again. Oscar sat there with his heart stopping and starting, thumping in his chest, stopping. Not normal, never normal again. Never the same ever again.

"Where's Mr. Llewellyn?"

Oscar looked up to see one of the sub managers at Llewellyn's door.

"Don't know, gone out I guess," said someone else.

Oscar got up and went to the toilet, threw up, heaved a burning hole in his chest, racked his shoulders. He went out of the cubicle and washed his face in the cold water, rinse and spit, rinse and spit. Not looking in the mirror. Don't look in the mirror, there's a killer there, a murderer. He ran the water hot, then using paper towel, soaped and rinsed the letter opener, soaped and rinsed, dried and cleaned, duty done. He slid it into his pocket and stayed like that, leaning over the sink. Finally his heart stopped stopping, stopped stopping and starting. Finally his heart settled, his pulse slowed and his breathing became normal. In out in out easy, normal. Now he looked up into the mirror, only now. He looked up but, there was no killer, there was no murderer, there was only Oscar Kingman.

THE FIRST DAY

Young Oscar Kingman lay in bed in that big cold bleak dormitory. Each bed empty, each bed filled only with memories and miseries, just one with a boy... Oscar. He lay there in the dark that first night, petrified. Wanting to sleep, maybe to die, anything. Here phantoms played and made their mischief, swooping down on him, skimming over his bed, calling his name.

'Oscar, Oscar.'

He lay there with his eyes clenched tight shut but seeing anyway. Seeing the faces of the phantoms, seeing his mother Loretta. Loretta with the dead eyes and the needle hung from her arm like some plastic leech. The face of Mrs. Garcia pointing, accusing and McKenzie weeping, weeping. The red vicious face of the nun Michael framed all in black and white malevolence. The cane raised above her head, blood pouring now from her eyes. And he saw Granny Molly. He saw her with her head in a bowl speaking, bubbling admonishing.

'Oh Oscar what have you done? What have you done, how have you sinned?'

Oscar, a little boy made of tears, lost in the deepest darkest woods somewhere in the middle of that bleak and lonely dormitory room.

That first night in that bleak dormitory room those phantoms played at his bedside swooping and screaming, crying and groaning until the first light of the false dawn, when they fled, away away, and Oscar fell into a deep and exhausted sleep.

Clap... clap!

Oscar woke to sound of clapping, big hands clapping. He opened his eyes. The room was still dark, just faint light through the windows. He followed the sound and, there beyond the central row of beds, a dark shape glided, clapping, big hands clapping.

"Out of bed, now."

The looming shape of the brother called Antonio came into focus. It was Monday. 5.30 a.m. Monday morning.

"You have ten minutes to be dressed and into the church. Move!"

He arrived in twelve minutes looking ragged and half asleep. He was once more the centre of attention as he was marched into the church by the brother. They stopped at the little bowl of water set on the wooden plinth. The brother made the sign of the cross and by cruelly squeezing Oscar's arm and gesturing, bade him do the same. Next the brother stepped forwards and dropped down onto one knee… dragging Oscar down so forcefully he almost lost his balance.

"Genuflect boy."

Homage paid he marched Oscar down the aisle and pushed him into a seat near the front. All around him there were priests and brothers as well as a scattering of people in normal clothes. Across the aisle from Oscar was the lady who had served his meal the night before. She saw him there looking red eyed and petrified and she smiled. Beside her were three boys of varying ages, one around Oscar's age, the others older. Oscar sat there frightened and clueless, while a priest who he now recognised as Strohkirch conducted some kind of seemingly bizarre ceremony at the altar. The old priest was dressed in strange clothes, stranger still than the black frocks. All creamy white, with gold patterns and trim and a strange black hat. He cried out now and again in a foreign language, intoning responses from those gathered. They stood, they sat, they knelt, each time Oscar dragged into position by the brother at his side until finally it was over. As they left the church the cruel brother with the vise-like grip dragged Oscar over to the young boy that had sat beside the lady from the dining room.

"Bruno, this is Oscar. Take him to breakfast."

Bruno looked at Oscar and smiled a shy smile.

"Come on then. What is your second name?" asked Bruno as they walked.

"Kingman... I am Oscar Kingman."

"Kingman," mused young Bruno, "I have never heard the name Kingman before. I am Simek, Bruno Simek. My family is from Czechoslovakia. We are immigrants."

Oscar had no idea where Czechoslovakia was, nor what an immigrant might be, but he went with Bruno.

"We live in the old house down by the entrance. My father is the groundsman, my mother is the cook. I go to school here with my two older brothers Andrew and Stan. My mother comes up early to cook the breakfast before she goes to the church, so my brothers and I eat up here in the mornings. Where are your mother and father from Oscar Kingman?"

They were in the cloister now.

"I have no parents," said Oscar stopping.

"Everybody has parents," said Bruno laughing.

"Not me," said Oscar. "I don't know who my father is and my mother died a few years ago. They sent me to an orphanage. Then I lived with my Granny Molly but she died too, so they sent me here. I think to punish me because I am a sinner."

"You're a sinner," laughed Bruno. "How old are you Oscar? You're not old enough to be a sinner, you're only my age."

"I am eight," said Oscar, holding back the tears. Not wanting to cry in front of this boy with all the questions.

"Yep, same as me. Come on then," said Bruno.

Oscar found himself seated at the same table in the same seat as the previous night. Right back there in the glare of god's chosen ones. They would keep an eye on this sinner. They would save his soul, yes they would.

At the table with them were Bruno's older brothers Andrew and Stan. They were quiet and they seemed nice; they were nice to Oscar. Stan never said how old he was and Oscar never asked, but he was old, maybe almost an adult. Andrew was eleven and he proceeded to fill Oscar in on the priests and brothers seated above. In a voice barely a whisper he pointed out this one and that one. This one nice, that one violent, this one soft, that one crazy, keep away from that one. That big ugly one with the curly black hair was the headmaster, Dutch and crazy. That one Italian, him too. The one on the end there with the big nose Italian but okay. Irish, Irish and English and so it went until Strohkirch, the old German priest came in, dressed now in his black frock.

"That's father Strohkirch. He's okay. Very kind, but he likes a drink, you know…" and Andrew mimicked taking a swig from a bottle until Stan stopped him.

"That's enough Andrew, shut up and eat your breakfast before you get us all into trouble."

"No talking down there."

"Sorry father," said all three Simek boys together.

Oscar tried to make himself invisible.

THE INCIDENT WITH THE GIN BOTTLE

Over the next few weeks, Sharon managed to take over that tiny apartment in its entirety. She took over the walls, owned them with her cheap kitsch posters and photographs of cats, took over the floor, owned it with her dirty clothes and underwear, drink bottles and take-out containers strewn everywhere. She took over the bed with her garish horrid covers and pillow cases and then she took over all the space and all the air in the apartment, leaving Oscar nowhere to stand, nothing to breathe.

Apart from eating too much, Sharon had taken to drinking. Started off mixing cheap gin with soda then when she wanted to tie one on, mixed it just with itself, straight. Oscar knew the rent was paid because he paid it himself, but he figured most of the housekeeping money went on gin and take-out. Gin and take-out in that order of importance.

Once again Oscar had made himself smaller somehow, he fitted into smaller spaces. Learned to live with less air, less of everything. Anyone watching would have known, would have seen him take that last huge breath before he walked in there each night. The question he asked himself every night at that door was, *'why do I go in, what is wrong with me?'* but he convinced himself this was better than anywhere else, better than nowhere else.

So each night he went home and he ate what was left of her cold pizza, scraps of her burgers and fries and he squeezed himself into a tiny space on a footstool in the corner while she spread across the only couch they owned. Spread herself out there like a great fat pointy headed Cleopatra, covered in crumbs and cigarette ash, stains down her front and sweat down her back. Some nights she fell asleep drunk on the couch, too pissed to make it to the bed and these were blessed nights indeed. Oscar got a good night's sleep alone in that squalid bed under those garish covers. Other nights he watched her stagger to bed, waited till he was sure she was asleep then crept into the room and slid into that bed like some floaty leaf, careful, fearful lest he wake her.

Like a thief in his own house, he crept in each night and crept out each morning stopping for breakfast on the way to work. He enjoyed his work so much back then, a place of refuge. Went out of his apartment each morning like an escapee and arrived for work with a spring in his step. He had no close friends, but not so many enemies either. Things were different back then, people a little kinder, more forgiving. Oscar worked hard and loved it, but he never was that comfortable with people. People, people, difficult things people. Nobody at the office apart from Mr. Alperstein knew too much about his past. He certainly didn't talk about it, but maybe if he had and they had known just a little about him they might have seen things differently, seen *him* differently. Basically Oscar was ill equipped socially, stand-offish, quiet, not so chatty. People took this as attitude, thought he was a snob. But he worked hard and he kept to himself and he certainly never bothered anyone.

By this time, Sharon had stopped working at the deli, claimed she had been retrenched, Oscar not so sure about that. After too many nights standing at his own front door, getting ready for the mess and the thin air, he got resentful. Got so resentful, so worked up that one night he manned up, went in there, switched off the television and demanded she cleaned the place up a bit. He demanded she cook him a meal now and then. He was about halfway through his demanding and explaining how unfair it was that he worked all day while she sat around doing nothing, when she smacked him across the side of his head with a gin bottle.

"Finished?" she asked.

Bam! Down he went, out cold. Lying there growing a lump size of a tennis ball over his left ear, big split now opening up there, cruel red gash. She poked at him with her pudgy little toe then, content he was still breathing, took a tug of the gin, turned the telly back on and draped herself across the lounge.

By the time Oscar regained consciousness she was asleep and dribbling. Asleep snoring and dribbling with the empty gin bottle hugged in her arms like a baby. He opened his eyes and stared into an empty crisp packet, then past it to the thing that was Sharon on the couch. He put his hand to his head, flinched with the size of the lump, felt the warm sticky blood on his fingers. Staggering to his feet he saw the bloodstain on the carpet, lurched into the tiny bathroom and looked at himself in the mirror, knees folding, feet jerking out from under him, letting him down, not working right.

'Something not right, something busted up there,' he could feel it.

The room coming and going with the stabbing pain in his head. He took a towel off the rail, grabbed his suit coat and pulled the door shut behind him, the hospital a long walk away. By the time he made emergency his legs were rubber, his head was volcanic and the towel was soaked. He'd been down three or four times, torn the knees out of his only suit trousers, mashed the heel of his hands, but he'd made it.

Something wrong up there, something not right.

The next morning Sharon woke to find the bloodstain on the carpet, bits of Oscar's scalp, little hairs, flecks of blood on the side of the gin bottle.

'Oh shit, oh shit, oh shit now I've done it. Oh shit!'

It was late that afternoon when she tracked him down in the hospital, stuck on a gurney in the corridor. Gurney in the corridor with a drip, a bag of something hanging from a hook. Extreme blood loss they said. Serious head injury with extreme trauma and blood loss they said. He was on his way back to critical care, looked like shit.

"You know what happened to your husband Mrs. Kingman? Mrs. Kingman?"

Three days later he tried to check himself out. They made him wait for a doctor, a specialist they said, a neurosurgeon.

"Something not quite right," said the specialist after a chat and a few basic tests. "Something not right, some damage done up there Mr. Kingman."

Oscar could sense it too. Like something come loose, wires crossed or fuses blown, something like that. But Oscar wanted out. Couldn't afford the time off from work or the money for fancy tests. Oscar wanted out so Oscar went.

The police had been around to see Sharon. Wasn't Oscar shopped her, Oscar never did it, Oscar never spilled the beans, he was too scared of her. It was Mr. Alperstein. Mr. Alperstein sat there with him one night in that hospital while Oscar writhed around in his sleep saying... 'don't hit me Sharon, please don't hit me Sharon!'

It was Mr. Alperstein that called the cops... not Oscar. But Sharon didn't know that. No matter how much he denied it she wasn't buying him all innocent like. But all this gave Sharon a bit of a fright.

First she gets on a blinder and damn near kills him, plugs him in the head with a bottle, then he calls the cops. She liked to push him around sure, everybody did that, but she didn't want to hurt him bad or kill him or anything. She was smart enough to know where the money came from, who was the golden goose.

"I'll ask you again, do you know what happened to your husband Mrs. Kingman?"

The police knew what she had done and they tried to get Oscar to take out an order on her, restrain her. Oscar said no. He said she'd apologised. Said she'd claimed everything would be different from there on down. Everything better, just rosy, hunky dory, like that. Of course the cops knew better. They knew a hundred like Sharon Kingman and knew that they never changed. Oscar thanked them and showed them the door.

"You know, you grow yourself some cojones wouldn't need for us to be back here next time. Maybe next time she kills you. Think about it," said the uniform.

"I will. I will indeed. Thank you officers," said Oscar one ear bent facing the ground.

When he turned back into the room, Sharon was sitting straight on the couch, white faced and shook up.

"I'm sorry Oscar. I don't know what... well I mean, I was drunk. I didn't mean to hit you like that Oscar, really I didn't. It was the liquor," she whined.

Oscar felt strong right then, more solid, a little strange in the head, but stronger.

"It doesn't matter what caused it or why you did it, next time I'm leaving Sharon."

"But!"

"No buts Sharon. And you need to clean up this place and cook some meals. I come home the place is a trash heap, you're draped across the couch like a jellyfish with a drinking problem and the only thing for me to eat is your scraps and crusts. Sort it out Sharon, I want a meal at least four nights a week. You got that? A decent proper home cooked meal or I'm gone for good and you can live your own selfish life however you please. But remember Sharon, you'll need to find some other sucker, some other patsy to pay the rent and keep you topped up with booze and junk food, because it won't be me, won't be me."

As much as what he said scared her, that nasty little twitch, little tick that started up beside his left eye scared her even more. Maybe the specialist doctor was right. Maybe something had come loose in there.

The next night when he came home from work, Oscar found the little apartment neat and tidy, some kind of meatloaf in the oven and Sharon behaving almost human. She sat him down at the little table and served him up a plate of meatloaf, poured him a drink. They sat there eating and talking just like a real married couple, but all the time Oscar thinking, *'this can't last.'*

FRIENDS

Over the course of the day, the school filled up, came alive. One by one, sometimes in pairs but more often one by one, they arrived. Mid morning found Oscar and Bruno Simek sitting on the balcony of the Simek's house. It was a ramshackle old two storey clapboard place that had seen better days, but it was free, or at least part of the Simek package anyway. The Simek package where Mr. and Mrs. Simek worked their fingers to the bone about sixteen hours each a day, seven days a week for free board and lodging and free education for their three boys, that package.

An old van came up the drive.

"Wolowski, he'll be in our class. Father's a painter, you know houses and stuff, not art. He's in our class," said Bruno.

Oscar nodded.

Black Mercedes. Oscar glimpsed a boy, few years older than himself, in the back seat with an old lady.

"Coogan. Rich kid. Says his father is some kind of actor, who knows? Goes home to his grandmother every weekend."

They looked up as Mrs. Simek pushed out through the old busted screen door with two glasses of cold lemonade.

"You know Oscar Kingman, you shouldn't be down here," she said in a thick accent. "Some of those teachers, if they find you missing… well you know."

"But Ma it's not a school day yet and they won't miss him being that they're busy with all the other boarders arriving," said Bruno.

"Okay then," said Mrs. Simek kindly like. "But you be careful my boy."

Old red truck, busted muffler was next up the drive.

"Kaplin brothers, Trevor and Mick. Good fun. Trevor is in our class and Mick one below. Always happy, don't know why. They come from a farm upstate."

He named a town Oscar had never heard of. Didn't matter.

And so it went for a few hours. Bruno talking, Oscar listening. A role call of who was who and who was new. Bruno talking and Oscar listening. Oscar and Bruno would always get on fine but never be close friends. Oscar so quiet and timid, Bruno so outgoing and all. And so it went on until Mrs. Simek came down the path and chased Oscar off the balcony.

"You need to go boy or you'll miss lunch. Off you go before someone notices you are not there."

So Oscar went up the path to the school and into the refectory. There was nobody sat at the tables, just a line up of boys waiting for a sandwich and a drink. A priest or a brother or something, Oscar couldn't tell them apart, was doling out thick, red jam sandwiches and milk. Oscar moved up with the line, the line getting longer and louder behind him as new boys arrived and tacked on the end. Simpson, Lepke, Brown, Koch, Donovan, McCullough and on and on. New names new faces, but all new to Oscar.

He took his sandwich and milk and followed the trail back out the door and down onto the lawn, where little groups were forming. He knew nobody, knew nothing. He finally picked a bit of lawn and sat down alone. The huge sandwich was as thick as his fist and dry, just some kind of red jam, no butter, nothing. He peeled it apart and took a bite.

"Hey dickhead!"

Someone kicked the sole of his shoe. He peered up into the sun, put his hand up to shield his eyes. Black shape there forming into a boy with a big round face and strange hair.

"You new? First day here?" said the boy with the round face and the strange hair.

"Ah… yes," managed Oscar.

The boy plopped down beside him, nudged him with his shoulder.

"I'm Paul Davenport. What's your name?"

"I'm Oscar."

"Oscar! Be fucked, what kind of name is that?" said Paul Davenport.

He noticed the look on Oscar's face.

"Don't worry, I'm only fucking with you. My first day here too. Don't know anybody either. You and me'll be mates eh Oscar? So what did you do to get sent here?"

"I don't really know," said Oscar. "I've got no family and I'm a sinner, so I guess that's why I'm here."

"A sinner! The fuck you talking about? Who's been feeding you that crap?"

Oscar looked around nervously, hoping nobody could hear them, knowing how bad this could be, how bad it could get. But in spite of himself he smiled. He had never heard anyone swear like this Paul Davenport did. Not Eddie Moran, not his mother, not even some of his mother's visitors as he liked to think of them.

'Who's the kid?'

'Oscar honey wait outside. Mommy's visitor wants to see me alone. Won't be long baby.' Noises, noises, grunting yelling noises, visitor noises.

Oscar looked at Paul Davenport. He had a big round rubbery face, big rubbery mouth and big round smiley eyes. His hair was short in the back and long in the front, brushed sideways just above his eyes, strange.

"Why are you here?" said Oscar.

"I kicked the shit out of the old man, put the fucker in hospital."

"I don't understand, what old man?"

"What? Jesus Oscar don't you know nothing? My old man, my *father* stupid. So my mum died a while back and then it was just me and my little brother living with the old man. He used to get pissed and beat up on mum," said Paul, those big round smiley eyes clouding over now, hooded now. "After mum died he started in on me, but I was pretty quick. Couldn't catch me when he was staggering drunk, but one night he got hold of my brother and started in on him."

He looked at Oscar.

"He was only five, couldn't defend himself, so I got a dining chair and bashed him round the head with it. Got him good, down he went, whammo! Then I got a big glass vase, my mum's favourite and I started bashing and bashing him with it. Course there's all this noise, my little brother screaming and all, so the neighbours came in and pulled me off him. Tell ya Oscar, I'd have killed the fucker if they hadn't pulled me off him," he paused, the pain of it, the remembering of it getting to him.

"It would have been easy to kill him You'd be surprised Oscar, be surprised how fucking easy it would be. Nothing to it."

Tears swelling in those big round eyes. Tears and pain.

"Aw fuck you Oscar you made me cry now, jesus," he said punching Oscar on the arm hard, but laughing now.

Snivelling and laughing at the same time.

"Anyhow here I am just like you. Don't want to have nothing more to do with my old man, so it's just me and my little brother now, just me and him. Smatter Oscar, what the fuck you looking at me like that for?"

"I was just thinking. It's not so bad. At least you've got someone. At least you've got your little brother," said Oscar.

"What! Oh poor old Oscar, got no little brother, got nobody. Poor old Oscar, all alone in the world… boo hoo."

And he jammed his shoulder into Oscar so hard Oscar rolled over on his side, milk everywhere and Paul Davenport on top of him laughing, both of them, Paul Davenport laughing then suddenly both of them laughing. Oscar laughing, Oscar belonging.

"You two. Follow me."

They looked up to see one of the brothers standing there watching them. The one Oscar had passed with the old priest Strohkirch yesterday. Andrew Simek had told him that his name was brother Rinaldo, yes Rinaldo. Said his name was brother Rinaldo and to be careful, watch out for him. Said he was cruel, always angry. He was short with a bony face, all angles. His eyes bulged out behind his glasses, angry, looking for trouble, looking for sinners, found a couple right here on the lawn. He kicked Oscar on the leg.

"I said get up now!"

"Hey! Fucking leave him alone, he didn't do anything. We never did nothing wrong. We're just fooling about," said Paul, getting up now to face the man.

"What did you say to me? Did you just swear at me?" shouted brother Rinaldo, now the centre of attention on the lawn.

"Yeah, fuck off!"

The whole lawn looking the other way now, wanting to be somewhere else, anywhere else.

"Right," said the brother, the little holy man, the little bully and beater of children in god's name.

He reached out and grabbed Paul Davenport by his collar, then bent down and pulled Oscar up off the ground by his arm. He was strong. The two boys struggled but were no match for the wiry little brother Rinaldo. He hauled them across the lawn, down the cloister and into his office.

"There, stand there. You first... hands out."

He took up a thick wide rubber strap and brought it down across Davenport's upturned hand, the noise of it heard way out there on the lawn. Six times the noise rang out, three to a hand and Paul Davenport barely flinched. Oscar watched his face, smiling stubbornly up at the man on the other end of the black rubber strap.

"Right, now you," said the brother pushing Davenport aside.

"What? What did he do? He didn't do anything? Leave him alone you bully."

Paul Davenport. Paul Davenport who he'd just met. Paul Davenport with the big round face, smiley eyes and weird hair, was sticking up for him. Sticking up for Oscar. Standing up to the bully for Oscar.

Oscar stepped in front of Paul Davenport and raised his hands palm up.

Whack! The pain so bad, the pain so fresh on that barely healed hand. The pain so bad he thought he would cry, cry cry cry. But he didn't. He got four, four. Two on each hand and he bit back the pain and tears, teeth clenched so tight it could have busted them. But he made it, made it through. The whole time Paul Davenport's eyes burning defiance at the bully brother Rinaldo.

They went up to the dormitory, to Davenport's bed at the end of the middle row. There were kids everywhere. Clustered around as they sat on Davenport's bed.

"What'd he do to you? Let's have a look."

Returning heroes.

"Wow, look at that. Shoulda heard the noise from outside. What'd he use? Jeez I bet that hurts."

"Nope!" said Davenport, holding out his hands for inspection. Red angry marks, angry red welts.

"Yeah right." The other boys drifted away.

Davenport elbowed Oscar.

"You okay?"

"Yeah, I'm okay. Doesn't hurt at all," replied Oscar.

"Doesn't hurt at all? Bull-fucking shit. Hurts like buggery," said Paul Davenport, licking his hands and blowing on them.

Oscar elbowed him back, laughing.

"Thanks for sticking up for me down there Paul."

"That's what friends are for. You'd do the same for me right? That's what friends are for," said Davenport.

'*Friends*,' thought Oscar. '*Friends.*' Those burning hands a ritual.

And they would be friends.

NEVER GETTING ANY OLDER

Oscar Kingman stood in the bathroom of Loughrans Loss Adjusters on level five and stared at his reflection in the mirror. *'Was it a reflection or was it another Oscar Kingman?'*

He put his right hand up and lay it flat on the mirror. The other Oscar did the same, but with his left hand. *'Was it a reflection, was it another Oscar Kingman? Another Oscar standing there looking back at him, one with tiny blood stains on the front of his shirt, the cuff of his shirt.'* That other Oscar suddenly smiled sending him reeling back against the white tiled wall, same as the reflection. He stood there long seconds watching waiting, something happening up there in his head, something not right, then eventually he stepped up to the mirror and looked down at the bloodstains. He rearranged his tie, rolled up his sleeves. A temporary fix but fine for now. Both Oscars left the room together, but in opposite directions.

He left the bathroom and went straight to the lift, unseen to the lift and pressed for ground. He felt light in the lift, light enough to fly. Stepping out at ground level he checked his shirtfront, held his tie just so, walked out of the building and made his way to the clothing store, in amongst the racks, shirts, tees, ties, jackets, pants and pullovers, Miss Elaine, fifteen years his senior, dark rooted peroxide blond. Her of the lavender soft-on fame, stalking prey, hunting custom.

'She is already dead. I am already dead.'

She was the only one on the floor, only one about. He walked up to her.

"Excuse me?"

She turned, all smiles, all shop smiles and customer service. Customer service and shop smiles fading now as she recognised him.

"Oh it's you. What do you want? Didn't expect to see you back in here," said Miss Elaine.

"Well er yes, well look I'm sorry about this morning, but I was upset and well, well frankly surprised. That sort of thing never happens to me you see," replied Oscar, contrite, shy, penitent, best lamb-to-the-slaughter look he could manage.

Miss Elaine held her ground, frozen.

"But look, I'm sorry. I'm sorry and I need some more things, so I thought I'd come here. I can leave if you want me to."

Miss Elaine thawed a bit round the edges.

"We could start over like this morning never happened," suggested Oscar.

Miss Elaine okay with it now. *She is already dead.*

"Well alright then, first things first. What do you need?"

"I need underwear, you know, boxer shorts and a vest. A couple more shirts, one the same as this, a couple of casual ones and maybe some jeans. Oh and socks. Socks please."

Oscar had never worn jeans in his life, always sports pants, but thought Wendy Legget might like it, might like him in jeans.

"Okay, let's start with the jeans then," said Miss Elaine.

She nodded her head and came at him with a tape measure, all business now. Monkey business. Oscar smiled nervously as she reached around him and measured his waist. Lavender, lavender. He fought the urge to push her away, but she stepped back and, looping the tape around her neck, made an entry on a small notepad. Breathe, breathe. He breathed. She dropped down in front of him, face inches from his crutch.

"Inside leg then," she said sweetly as she pushed her thumb up into his groin.

He looked down at the top of her head, the dark roots striped skunk grey against the yellow of the peroxide white. *'She is already dead.'* Then she popped back up in front of him all business, all customer smiles and service. Miss Elaine itchy between the legs and ready to run the risk. She went to a display rack, same as before and hooked out a pale green shirt, same as before. She checked the size and came back with it.

"If you would like to go to the change room and put this on, I'll be right in with some jeans for you to try." The enigmatic smile on her lips like part of some understanding between them. The enigmatic smile from the Mona Lisa of the menswear department. Man on the hook, reeling him in, reeling him in.

In the change room, Oscar loosened his tie without undoing the knot and slipped it over his head. He hung it on a hook beside him. He unbuttoned his shirt and placed it on the little ledge. He put on the pale green shirt, this one clean, this one new, this one clean and new with no bloodstains, no guilt at all, then he pulled off his pants.

Tap tap.

"Are we decent sir?"

Without waiting for an answer Miss Elaine opened the door, Oscar standing there in his new shirt and old boxers. Without waiting she looked quickly around the store and stepped in with him, closing the door behind her. She dropped a pair of jeans and a couple of polo shirts on the ledge and handed Oscar a slip of note paper. Oscar looked at the numbers, smelt the lavender, cloying now in this small space.

'Breathe breathe, she is already dead.'

"My phone number," she drawled in what she clearly thought was her best sexy, best husky voice. "Tonight. This is just a quick sample, but tonight... well."

Without another word she knelt down and pulled Oscar's penis out the leg of his boxers, stroking, fondling. Then she looked up puzzled, not understanding as Oscar dropped the tie over her head and pulled it tight. Her mouth opened to scream and he jammed the shirt in there, forcing it in with his fingers, huge ball of it. He got back to concentrating on the tie, the easy listening muzak covering the sound of her muted screams, shirted screams weakening now as he pulled up on the tie and pushed down on the knot with all the force a junior estimator could manage. Her legs kicked out wildly, so he stood hard on the back of her calf. He watched her in the mirror as those horrid accusing eyes, those horrid eyes with the purple eye shadow, bulged out further and further like they would pop out and strike the mirror, leave a wet mark, bounce off. Her face was purple now, her only movement just a tiny twitch. A tiny twitch to match the tiny twitch beside Oscar's left eye. *She is already dead.*

When it was done he struggled to loosen the tie, cut so deep into her soft neck, but finally it came and he stuffed it into his pocket. He pulled the label off the jeans and tugged them on, took time to check the new look in the mirror. Not bad, not bad at all. With his old shirt and trousers balled up in his hand, he pulled open the door and was gone from the store. Out through the racks of shirts, trousers, pullovers and gone, through those big glass doors unseen and gone. Miss Elaine gone with him. Miss Elaine never getting any older.

THE TABLE SETTINGS

Monday night after dinner, the boarders were all marched into the church for some kind of service. Oscar understood none of it. He had tried to sit next to Paul Davenport, but the brother called Rinaldo had separated them, dragged Paul off down the front somewhere. When the service ended and they all got up to leave, a priest Oscar had not seen before, told them to sit down. This priest introduced himself as the headmaster, said his name was father Bruist. He started by welcoming the boarders to what he said was one of the finest schools in the city, made it sound like some kind of holiday camp, never want to leave. But as his long talk dragged on and all the boys started shifting around, fidgeting, getting bored, the priest's talk took a turn for the worst.

You will do this, you won't do that, you will be punished, this will not be tolerated, that is not acceptable, you will be punished. If we find anyone engaging in this, or anyone not doing that, you will be punished. You will be punished. *Punished punished punished.* Never rewarded for the good, just punished for the bad, punished for the not so bad, punished for the not really bad at all. *What we do best here is punishment... and so to bed.*

The two brothers Antonio and Rinaldo ran the middle dormitory where Paul and Oscar were housed. Thirty boys. Thirty boys given just fifteen minutes to wash, use the toilets, get pyjamas on and get into bed before the lights went out. Anyone not making that deadline would be punished. Oscar made it, two boys didn't, little boys. Names taken, punishment booked, serious offence this being at the end of a queue business. Serious offence being too small and too timid to defend your place in the line.

The brothers patrolled the corridors, up and down, up and down, up and down. The short brother with the big angular head, Rinaldo, frequently paused to watch the smaller boys undress. The lights went out and the two brothers continued their patrol of the two corridors, up and down up and down, the big one kicking any beds that made a noise, the little one wielding a long T-shaped stick. Like dark riders they drifted through that field of sinners meting out whacks and kicks as required under the code of punishment. Do not talk, do not laugh, do not cry, *do not be a boy*. You will be punished.

Finally after maybe five minutes the dark riders passed through the blue curtain at the bottom end of the dormitory and retired to their own rooms. It was quiet for four or five minutes before Paul Davenport let loose a loud fart. Snickering, giggling admonitions, calls for oxygen then frozen panic as the blue curtain flew back and brother Rinaldo stood staring into the room. He was still standing there when Oscar Kingman finally drifted off into an exhausted sleep.

Tuesday morning wake-up arrived to the slow clap from brother Antonio as he once more took to the patrol.

"Twenty minutes, you have twenty minutes to be gone, to be in church. Everyone showers, everyone makes his own bed. Now get to it," he boomed.

The toilets and showers were at the opposite end to the brother's rooms and consisted of a changing and hanging area, then a big open space with six toilet cubicles along one wall and ten shower heads along the other. The floors were cold hard terrazzo. The little brother with the big angular head, Rinaldo always there, arms folded and leaning against the change room wall facing the shower room. Paul Davenport came into the shower, next to Oscar, all secretive like, laughing and pointing.

"No talking in the showers!" yelled Rinaldo. "Get out of there Kingman. Church in twelve minutes."

Church church church.

As Oscar passed by Rinaldo reached out and clipped him around the head. It hurt. The man was a bully. Davenport was right. Oscar dressed, made his bed and arrived in the church with a minute to spare. Another strange and bewildering service. Costume, chanting, ritual.

Church church church.

After church there would normally have been something called study period before breakfast, but because there was nothing to study yet, study period became a bible reading session. Oscar sat through it like some robot. Information going in, nothing computing. This old testament, a nasty place of revenge and damnation. It didn't figure, not to eight year old Oscar. Eight year old Oscar who had just been marched out of a church where they insisted god was love, god was forgiveness. It didn't figure, it confused him.

Church followed sleep, bible followed church and breakfast followed bible… at least it did on that day.

Everyday was the same, everyday was worse.

The young sinners, those deservers of punishment, filed one behind the other into the refectory, where yet another black frocked person, this one with curly hair and at least smiling, stopped each, asked a name and sent that boy to his allocated table. Oscar found himself at a different table further back, mercifully less under the glare of the chosen ones up on that platform. He was first to that table and so took a seat facing the front. Know your enemy. Streetwise, even at eight, *know your enemy, never let them get around behind you, always keep them in front, where you could see them.* The table was set with four knives, four spoons, four cups, four small plates and four bowls. In the centre was a toast rack and a can of treacle.

The next boy to sit at the table was Trevor Kaplin, big cowlick, sticky-out hair over a wide permanent grin. He bobbed about like a chicken, checking out progress, looking, watching who was where, waving once to somebody behind Oscar, then he settled down and straightened his knife as he looked at Oscar. Oscar already knew he'd like him, already knew he'd like Trevor.

"I'm Trevor Kaplin," he said with that big wide grin.

"I'm Oscar. I saw you arrive in the truck yesterday," offered Oscar.

"Yeah? Jeez I'm surprised we made it. Bloody thing kept breaking down."

"Hi Oscar, hi Trev."

Bruno Simek arrived and took the third seat. He had fine white powder on his shirtfront.

"Flour," he said, looking where Oscar looked and brushing himself down. "Every boy has to help in the kitchen breakfast and dinner. Two for breakfast, three for dinner. There's no roster yet so Andrew and I had to do it today."

"Gerry, Gerry," said Trevor in a loud whisper, grabbing the arm of a boy going past. "Where ya going?"

Oscar looked up to see a dark boy, maybe the same age as him. With piercing eyes that scanned around the table now, not smiling.

"I'm down there," he said to Trevor, pointing a few tables down.

"Go and see him, go on. Brother Hamilton. Go and ask him, he'll change it. Go on."

The boy named Gerry looked at the floor, thought about it a second or two then looked up and nodded. Oscar watched him go. He moved like a tiger, like a big cat. He circled around the tables and came up behind the brother at the entrance, the brother with the curly hair. They watched as he tugged at the brother's sleeve. Gerry got Hamilton's attention. Hamilton shook his head and turned away, Gerry tugged again, spoke again, pointed over to the table where Oscar, Trevor and Bruno sat. Brother Hamilton shook his head and smiled, made a change on his clipboard. Gerry headed back to the table, his table now.

"Hi Bruno,"

He turned to Oscar.

"I'm Gerry Donegan," he said, holding his hand out to Oscar, first time another boy had ever done that to Oscar.

Oscar looked at the hand, hand like a man's hand, strong. He shook his hand and looked up into Gerry's eyes. Deep, piercing eyes.

"I'm Oscar Kingman," he said.

"Attention now. Attention!" This from brother Hamilton, now standing on the platform with all the other priests and brothers.

The talking became whispers, the whispers became murmurs and finally there was just one voice left out there, right out in the open, somewhere down at the back of the room. Brother Rinaldo jumped to his feet, big angular head darting about, searching the room.

'Who can I punish, who is the sinner, who can I punish?'

All quiet now, the look of disappointment painted across Rinaldo's face. He snarled and sat back down.

"Right," said brother Hamilton, moving now behind a wooden lectern and placing his clipboard there. "Good morning boys and welcome to all the old faces."

He scanned around the room making eye contact here and there, smiling.

"And of course welcome to all the new boys who have just joined us for the first time this year. Your places at the tables are now permanent. This is where you will sit for breakfast and dinner. You will not swap places. *Beware the punishment.* You will not move about the room and you will remain seated at the end of meals until you are dismissed. *Beware the punishment.* If you ever need anything, remain seated and raise your hand. Now, while the meal is being served I'll read out the names of the new boys in alphabetical order and when your name is read please stand up, repeat your name, tell us how old you are then sit back down. First the prayer."

He joined his hands in prayer for what he was about to receive.

Mrs. Simek appeared out through the kitchen door with a trolley containing a giant steaming pot of oatmeal and a stainless steel tray stacked high with toast. She moved quickly, ladling a blob of the grey oatmeal into each bowl while, around the room, boys stood up as they were called, nervously repeated their name and stated their age. Behind Mrs. Simek came Andrew Simek pushing a trolley laden with stainless serving jugs. Oscar's table was the fourth to be served and as the trolleys moved away down the room, Oscar's name was called.

"Oscar Kingman," said brother Hamilton.

"Oscar Kingman and I am eight years old," he said.

Oscar sat back down and watched as Trevor levered open the can of treacle and tugged out a thick dark blob of the stuff with his spoon, waiting while it stretched its way down to the hot oatmeal. As it melted, he stirred it in and reached for a slice of toast.

Nobody spoke until the last new boy had been identified, then a low murmur spread around the room to mix with the sounds of metal on china, the slurps of hot tea. Oscar watched what the other boys did, followed suit. He'd had oatmeal and tea before at Granny Molly's house, but it was never like this. The tea was sweet and milky, the oatmeal thick and lumpy like you could cut it with a knife. Trevor watched him.

"Least the toast is okay," he said stuffing another mouthful in.

"Yeah… now," said Bruno.

"Now? What do you mean now?" asked Oscar.

"Well," said Bruno, "One of the kids here, his father owns a bakery. He sells them yesterday's bread cheap. Some of it's a week old before we even get it."

"Then there's the margarine," laughed Trevor. "They buy big blocks of the stuff cheap and melt it in a big tub in there. That way they can paint it on quick with a paintbrush. You'll see for yourself when it's your turn in the kitchen. After a couple of weeks, chucking new stuff in on top, it goes green, rancid green and stinks like dead fish. Only way you can eat your toast then is to keep dipping it in the tea. Ain't that right Bruno?"

"Yeah but it's not my mum's fault. That's all there is, all they give her."

"Who's that?" asked Oscar, pointing up to the platform at the front.

Gerry followed his finger, looked up there.

"That's Mrs. Voss," he said. "She works in the kitchen with Bruno's mum. She looks after the teachers. They don't eat the same as us. They get proper food."

'Teachers. Teachers,' thought Oscar. *'Not brothers, or fathers. Not brothers or priests, teachers.'*

He hadn't really thought about it, but that's what they were supposed to be… teachers.

THE ANNOUNCEMENT

The truce at the Kingman apartment lasted a good six months. In fact it was solid for the first three or four. Oscar slept in his own bed alongside Sharon, sometimes they even made love if you could call it that. They made something at least, some kind of clumsy fumbling that might have passed as nervous pleasure. Sharon nagged him less, belittled, derided and neutered him less. Cooked him a meal every second night. She even lost a bit of weight and a little less Sharon was a good thing. Life was almost normal for a few months. He went off to work and enjoyed the day, felt like he was pretty much getting things together. *It's all coming together, all coming together!* Work was good, his prospects for advancement looked good. *All coming together.* Oscar dared hope.

About four months in Oscar noticed things were slipping a bit. Some of the home cooked meals were re-heated take-out. He kept quiet, kept the peace. He found empty gin and bourbon bottles pushed up under the sink. He kept quiet, kept the peace. For the sake of a quiet life. A*ll coming together!*

It rolled along like this for a couple more months then one night Oscar came home to find Sharon sitting at the table with gin, right out in the open like, next to a container of orange juice. He knew she was drinking again, he'd seen the evidence, but she wasn't drinking in front of him, not while he was at home. She had a strange smile on her face, looked smug.

"Go hang up your coat Oscar, I'll get your dinner," she said.

He came back to find a pizza steaming there on the table, an orange juice poured for him.

"Sit down Oscar," she purred like the cat with the damned cream. "I've got some news."

Oscar sat down, suspicion all over the place while she loaded his plate with pizza slices, *suspicion*. He took a drink of his orange juice, spluttered.

"What's in this, gin?"

"That's right Oscar gin. We're celebrating, so drink up."

"Celebrating?"

"That's what I said Oscar, celebrating. I'm pregnant. I'm having a baby."

Oscar spluttered a little more. Two strange sensations hit him at once, two opposing emotions battled it out in his damaged head, neither side sure of a clear victory. Pulling this way, pulling that.

"Are you sure Sharon?"

"Duh! Yes I'm sure. I went to the doctor. Eight weeks already."

Pulling this way, pulling that, but Oscar was coming round to it. This was good news, a child, a son or a daughter. But at the same time he felt a little breathless, a little trapped now. That bit not going away, not easing up.

"Well that's fantastic Sharon, fantastic! I mean…"

He lifted his glass in a toast.

"I guess this one time can't hurt, the gin I mean. To us Sharon, to us and the baby… wow."

'Of course it means I can't go back to work now and we'll need a bigger place," meowed Sharon.

Suspicion.

"A bigger place, why? I mean there's no rush, not yet anyway. We're doing okay, I've even saved a bit, but I don't know that we can afford a bigger apartment yet," said Oscar downing the last of his gin and orange juice.

"I'm not talking about an apartment Oscar. I'm talking about a house. A house in the suburbs. Just spend a little bit more and we could rent a house in the suburbs. Of course we'd be a way out, but it'd be fine as long as we're near a train or bus or something. What do you think? Please Oscar, pretty please?"

"Well I er. It's all a bit sudden. A bit of a shock really. Let me think about it. There's no rush. I'll look into it and we'll talk about it again soon. I promise Sharon"

Sharon got up and came round and kissed him.

Suspicion.

"That's all I ask Oscar. That's all I ask. My, isn't this exciting. More pizza?"

Truth was Oscar kind of liked the idea of a house in the suburbs. A safe place. A safe place for Oscar in a leafy street in the suburbs. Might be just what the marriage needed. Oscar and the family living in a leafy street out in the suburbs. Yes indeed, he would look into it.

A TURNING POINT

With breakfast done, the boarders were let out of the refectory. Already there were day boys arriving. Cars came and went, depositing boys of all ages, shapes and sizes at the top of the circular drive near the lawn. The boarders were sent back to the dormitory to brush their teeth, get their schoolbags. By the time Oscar came down the stairs there was another stream of boys coming from the other side of the church, where they were being deposited by a cavalcade of buses. Juniors, seniors, short pants, long pants, grey blazers, maroon blazers. In they filed like condemned men. Dumping their bags outside their classrooms and heading up to the big asphalt quadrangle to catch up with old mates, tell lies, swap the first cards of the year, fight and laugh.

"Hey creep, wait up!"

Oscar turned just in time to brace himself as Paul Davenport shoulder charged him.

"Not getting away from me that easy," said his new friend with the weird hair and the big rubbery face.

Together they made their way to their allocated classroom on the other side of the quadrangle. Oscar dropped his bag against the brick wall beside Paul's and followed him out onto the play area, little groups here there and everywhere. Paul, with his hands in his pockets, nudging his way in here and there, talking, laughing, mocking. Paul had told him that he was nine years old. Got held back a year at his last school, didn't say why. As he trailed behind him now he seemed much older, behaved older. He brimmed with cheeky confidence and it somehow rubbed off on Oscar. By the time the siren went for the start of first class they had made a bunch of new friends... and just as many enemies.

The teacher in the first class was Irish, called father Flaherty he said. Red faced, flaky skin not much hair. When he spoke he reminded Oscar of sister Michael at the orphanage. Same accent, same crazy voice, same dangerous beady little rat eyes. Flaherty started by breaking up groups, moving people around. Old enemies were moved up front. *'I'm watching you, yes you.'* Problems were targeted, strategies formed. Oscar watched him, watched the enemy. Watched him take notes during roll call, marking down new targets.

"Brown?"

"Here father,"

"Carmody?"

"Here father."

"Cummings?"

"Here father."

"Jackson?"

"Here father."

"Kingman?"

"Here."

"Kingman?" louder this time.

"Here."

Oscar flinched back in his seat as the rat-eyed Irish priest dashed across the room scattering furniture and small boys like some madman and, grabbing him by the ear, dragged him up out of his seat.

'The ear, always the ear with these Irish people,' thought Oscar, scared now.

"What did you say boy?" spat Flaherty.

"Here. I said here."

"Here *Father* boy. Here Father, you stupid ignoramus boy"

Oscar hung by his ear off the priest's grip, hurting, frightened, but then he saw Davenport. Davenport with his fists clenched, Davenport shaking his head. Davenport's eyes saying, *'don't let him do this. Don't let the fucker do this to you.'*

Oscar was petrified, but he made his choice.

"You are not my father. I have no father."

"What did you say boy? Say that again," he shouted red faced and twisting Oscar's ear even tighter. "What boy?"

"I said you are not my father."

Still holding Oscar's ear with one hand, the rat-eyed Irishman let loose with the other. A vicious flat handed blow caught Oscar across the top of his head.

Whack!

Oscar's brain jolted forward violently in his skull, lucky not to snap off, lucky not to burst open. It all went black and he crumpled to the floor to lie there, his nose bleeding. The priest standing over him breathing spit, knowing he'd gone too far, unable to help himself. Stood there as Oscar Kingman came round, stood there as Oscar got to his hands and his knees then he reached down and pulled him up by the collar, dropped him down in his seat. The priest went back to the front of the class, leaving Oscar concussed and bleeding. With the priest's back turned, the boy to Oscar's right passed a handkerchief, gave him the thumbs up sign, winner! Oscar didn't feel like a winner. He felt sick and he felt alone and he wanted to cry, but he couldn't, not here in front of all these boys. Oscar Kingman, boy of tears.

From the front of the class Flaherty looked around the room. He turned as if to write on the board, then turned back quick as a flash and threw a blackboard duster at Trevor Kaplin, got him on the neck.

"You got a problem Kaplin? You want to be next?"

"No sir father Flaherty," said Trevor all loud and sharp like he was in the army or something.

With things quieted down, the rat-eyed Irish priest called Flaherty began talking again. Oscar saw his lips moving, but now he had a sound like a train in his head, a big engine coming and going coming and going, covering up all other sounds. He felt sick, not quite right, in his head there. He raised his hand slowly. The priest turned to him.

"What now boy?"

"Please sir, father Flaherty. I need to go to the toilet. I don't feel well, I think I'm going to be sick," said Oscar groggily.

The priest stood there with those little rat eyes trained on Oscar. Breathing hard, more spittle forming on his rat lips. He looked around the room, looked at the faces, knew he had to let him go.

"Go on then," he said. "But don't come back in here disrupting my class again boy. Sit on the bench outside and wait for your next lesson."

Oscar stood up holding the desk for support. He made it out the door and weaved his way across the quadrangle to the toilet block. He went into a cubicle and sat with his head in his hands, then span around and threw up, blood from his nose mixing with a string of bile. And then he cried. Cried and cried and cried. Ten minutes he cried, sobbed away in that toilet cubicle, lost and alone. As the sobs eased, his jerking shoulders slowing, he thought about the boy next to him, the one that gave him the handkerchief. He thought about Trevor and Bruno, Gerry even. And he thought about Paul, Paul who stood up for him yesterday, sort of stood up for him again just now, in there. Gave him some strength. Maybe he wasn't alone, maybe he could survive even this.

He went out of the cubicle and looked at his face in the old stained mirror above the basins. He was so small he could only see his head and shoulders there in that old mirror. Red faced, blood snot and vomit. Swollen eyes all gummed up, hair all messed. He looked for a long time, a long time, felt the ache in his head, burning like. Then he washed his face over and over with cold water. Washed a long time, scrubbed away the blood and the snot and the vomit, scrubbed away the guilt, scrubbed away the sins.

'Nothing wrong, I have done nothing wrong.'

But no matter how hard he scrubbed he couldn't scrub away the stains left on him by others, by a cruel world, couldn't manage that. Finally he stopped scrubbing, stopped washing and looked up at his face in that mirror. A little red but clean now, the pain in his ear still stinging, the ache in his head passing now, the nausea with it. He brushed his hair with his fingers, deep breaths, deep breaths, better now, a little better now. The face, the head in the mirror looked back at him more innocent, less innocent, but stronger now. No more tears. Oscar Kingman, boy of tears no more.

THE CONFESSION

On level five at Loughrans Loss Adjusters, Oscar left the lift and went straight to the bathroom. It was mercifully empty. He pushed into a cubicle, threw up, twice now, then he pushed the button, closed the lid and sat down. He looked down at his hands, solid now. Solid now and shaking. *'Oh Jesus Oscar what have you done? What have you done?'*

He remembered the words of his friend Paul Davenport all those years ago. He remembered the words. Came back to him like a blow to the head. *'You'd be surprised Oscar, be surprised how fucking easy it would be. Nothing to it.'* Those words.

He touched his hand to the twitch beside his eye, pushed on it, hard on it, stop it stop it stop it! Wouldn't stop. *Something come undone up there, something not quite right.*

He looked down at the clothes he'd dropped on the floor, picked up the trousers and took out the panties, Wendy's magic pink panties, a bit bloodstained now, and stuffed them in the pocket of his new jeans. Other stuff in there too, loose change and keys, house keys. Keys to the suburban dream. Wife and two kids. House in the suburbs, wife and two kids, station wagon and a dog that greets you every night with your slippers, wife who greets you, that misses you, kisses you and pours you a martini, that dream. Only there was no dog, there was no dog and the car was stolen and trashed by the kids, one of them not even yours.

'And that wife thing... well!'

He put his shaking hand back on the twitch, slid those shaking fingers into the thinning hair over his ear and felt the hard ridge of scar tissue, battle scar. Wife who greets you with a gin bottle to the side of the head. The memory of it now almost as painful as back when it happened. *Something not right, something come undone up there.*

Oscar left the bathroom and went into the lunchroom, pulled out the white plastic bag from the metal locker and stuffed the shirt, tie and trousers on top. Put it back in the locker. He went back through reception, Moira glanced up and smiled as he went through the office and down to the filing room. Wendy Legget looked up as he closed the door behind him, clicked the latch.

"Oscar what?"

"I can't wait. Can't wait till tonight."

He took the panties out of his pocket, held them out in front of him.

"I can't wait Wendy, I can't think of anything but these, but you," he said.

"But we can't Oscar. What about that pig Llewellyn? I mean if he found out, caught us, imagine the trouble. We'd both be fired."

But she could hardly contain herself. Touched herself under the desk.

"He won't find out," cut in Oscar. "He won't find out. He won't cause us any trouble. Never again, never again."

"Well if you're sure…" excited now, ready, no stopping.

"Of course I'm sure," said Oscar as he took her hand and pulled her up from behind the little metal desk all covered with the sticky notes and soft toys and led her behind the tall metal filing shelves. She tore at his clothes, his new jeans down around his ankles, his shirt ripped open, buttons bouncing on the floor, his boxers down and him naked now in front of the woman he loved. The love of his life, Wendy Legget. Right there, right under his nose those last few years. She was fierce, bit his neck to keep from screaming. She was alive, come to life there on the floor of that filing room, behind the tall metal filing shelves, her

Oscar her life. Oscar never knew it could be like this. Never was with his magazines, never was with Sharon. Never knew it could be like that, never been like that before. Never knew it was like that when you loved someone, when you loved Wendy Legget.

They rolled apart and lay on the file room floor gasping for breath, Wendy laughing, Oscar locked still in the mystery of it, watching her laughing.

'I am alive, I am alive, I am finally alive.'

Presently she quieted and rolled on her side.

"Oscar. Oscar what did you mean when you said that Mr. Llewellyn wouldn't find out about this? Wouldn't find out and would never bother us again. What did you mean by that?"

Oscar lay on his back staring up at the ceiling, the acoustic ceiling tiles. *'Little holes, made of little holes like me,'* thought Oscar. He felt his face. No twitch, no tick. He stared at the little holes in the ceiling. Each one same as the other, each one nice hiding place for flies, wasps, for spiders. But where would Oscar hide?

"Because he's dead," he said finally.

Bless me father for I have sinned.

Wendy knelt up suddenly.

"What do you mean he's dead," she whispered, "how do you know?"

"I mean he's dead Wendy. Plain and simple. Dead."

Bless me father for I have sinned.

He turned his head to look up at her.

"I know he's dead because I killed him."

Bless me father for I have broken your sixth commandment.

She looked down. Puzzled. Then she smiled.

"Right… nice one Oscar. Had me going for a minute there. I thought you were serious," she laughed, leaning down and kissing him. "Wish the bastard was dead, the creep."

He reached up and took her by the shoulders. Looked her in the eye, frightened her a bit.

"Wendy I'm not joking. I really did. I killed him. I just did. Just went in there and stabbed him with my letter opener."

Thou shalt not murder.

He grabbed her panties from where they had fallen on the floor.

"Here look. The blood. I held them over his mouth to keep him quiet and I stabbed him through the throat. He's locked in his office, in there now hidden under his desk. I wiped the letter opener on your panties, look," he said stretching them out so she could see the blood, see the last of Edmund Llewellyn.

Wide eyed she took the panties from him, groped around beside her and found her glasses. Looking close at the panties, her panties, her panties almost like a weapon. Learning it, understanding it, knowing it. She thought back to that day when Llewellyn had come to that very room. She had never forgotten it.

Oscar watched her. '*Had he gone too far? Made a mistake. Not killing Llewellyn but telling her. Assumed too much?*' He felt the twitch come back, winced with it.

Slowly she looked up from the panties, the evidence in a murder. Looked up and without expression, straddled him. Taking him in her hand she plunged down on him then stopped... absolutely still. She leant down and whispered in his ear.

"Oscar I have never wanted anyone as much as I want you right now. I love you Oscar."

"But I've killed a man Wendy."

"He was no man, he was a monster."

"But I'm a sinner. I've broken the sixth commandment. Thou shalt not murder."

"You've also broken the seventh commandment Oscar," she said.

"The seventh, I don't think I remember that one. What is it?" he asked, moving gently now. Moving in her.

"Though shalt not commit adultery. And look Oscar," she laughed. "You're doing it again. You don't really believe in all that stuff do you?" she asked.

He fought back against the doubt, the pain and conditioning, the theatre, the costumes, the guilt and the arcane ritual. The cloying smell of incense, the purposeful hypnotic swing of the thurible, the chanting, the begging, the robes, the guilt giving, the asking for forgiveness, the nails, the blame for the nails, the crown of thorns, the blame for the crown of thorns, the cross and that bleeding wound, there on the cross, gaping like the wound on Oscars head, like the wound in Llewellyn's neck. *I will bleed for you, I will swing for you, I will die for you. I am already dead.*

"I... I don't know. I don't think so," replied Oscar.

THE GANG OF FOUR

So Oscar joined an alliance. Oscar joined that little group of rebels who had found a way to survive the hell of that place. Individually they were nothing, individually they were weak. As those first months dragged on, the little alliance of boarders, of those who would survive, grew to include some supporters from the day boys. Many of the day boys looked down on the boarders as if they were some kind of second class kids, charity cases, there on a hand-out because nobody else would have them. A nice comfortable point of view if you went home each night to a family, a warm home, a bit of love. Most of the day boys knew nothing of what went on after class, after they had made their getaway each afternoon, after their parents had collected them in their shiny new cars, after they were loaded on the cavalcade of buses that took them away from that place where such great sadness dwelt. They saw the way the boarders were treated in class and figured they deserved it, steered clear of them did most of the day boys. But some of the day boys knew what was going on. Saw it, heard about it, believed it. Some even experienced it and some of those boys offered their friendship and support.

The alliance of boarders did not include Bruno. He would not compromise his family's future, their precarious position held by the questionable good grace of the priests. The rest understood, Bruno and his brothers were okay. The alliance of boarders included Trevor, Gerry, Paul and of course Oscar. Paul drifted in and out of the group, volatile and explosive, sometimes belonging sometimes not, often too aggressive, too wild and too dangerous. He harboured a secret, a mystery that they never uncovered, never pried out of him, but when his pain became too much for him to bear he was best avoided. Afterwards, they would take him back, always take him back, always he arrived with that big rubbery grin and a punch to the shoulder, never a question they'd take him back. They all had their secrets, some deeper and darker than others.

So that gang of four got tight. The others taught Oscar the tricks, showed him the ropes. Trevor always a bit nervous, a bit hyper with boundless energy and eagerness, always *'yeah let's do it'*. Gerry, quiet and circumspect, always *'well let's just think this through,'* but strong physically. Oscar growing more canny, fast on his feet, quick witted as it turned out, good at thinking, good at strategy. Oscar came to understand what made these two boys different to all the other boys, different even than Paul. He understood that they both shared a keen sense of justice, of what was right and what was wrong and there was plenty wrong in that place.

Oscar listened to them, learned from them. He learned so much from those two boys and their sense of justice grew in him as well. Individually they were weak, just young boys, mere victims. But as a group, the gang of four could survive, might even mete out a little justice of their own on occasion. From the outside this place looked like a well run, charitably founded school. But it had a black heart, a heart so black that not even the good priests and the good brothers would believe it, would accept it. This was no place for children.

LIFE IN THE SUBURBS

Three months after the announcement, Oscar and Sharon had ended their lease on the apartment belonging to Mr. Alperstein's brother and had moved out to the suburbs. They stood in front of the little two bedroom bungalow with the rickety picket fence on the wide leafy street. Sharon had found the place. It was a bit more than Oscar had figured they could afford what with the baby coming and all but well, he was happy. And it was furnished. Maybe they could be content out here in the suburbs. It was a decent walk to the station, but Oscar spent a lot of time sitting down at the office, figured he could maybe use the exercise anyway.

A wife, a child on the way, a house in the suburbs in a nice leafy street.

'It's all coming together, all coming together!'

Of course the bungalow needed a bit of attention, well a lot of attention really, but Oscar didn't mind. *'Something to do on Sundays,'* he thought. He could fix that fence, re-hang the screen door that lay there in the bushes, scrub off the flaking paint on those posts, pick a nice bright new colour. Maybe do the window frames the same. Green maybe, yes dark green.

'All coming together!'

"Well I'm going in," said Sharon. "Our first night. Exciting isn't it?"

"Okay I'll be in shortly."

He watched her go, looking slimmer he noticed, lost a bit of weight. When he went in Sharon was sitting on the bed sorting through her clothes, her bag. She pulled out a dress and Oscar heard the unmistakable sound of two bottles clinking together.

Right there, right there in that bag, right there in that bag with that tiny noise Oscar knew nothing had really changed, not really. He looked at his wife sitting there on the bed.

"What?" she said all innocence and appealing, "What?"

"I… I just thought. Well it doesn't matter."

He shook his head, turned and left the room. Sharon had brought it all with her. Everything she owned *and* all the baggage.

Within a month, just one short month, it was all turning to shit again. Oscar working back, taking the overtime, needing the money. Him coming in late, walking through those dark leafy streets, dark shadows and hollow footsteps from the last train. Her accusing, doing nothing, not cooking, not cleaning, just being Sharon all over again. Him staggering in tired and hungry, too tired to work Sundays on the bungalow. The rickety fence still crooked, paint still flaking and the screen door still down there in the weeds. Down there in the weeds with all Oscar's hopes and dreams of something normal, a normal life. Not much to ask. Not too much to ask.

Oscar took a second job weekends at a hardware store near the station. Selling tools and paint, screws, nails and all manner of fasteners and things to fix stuff. There was nothing could fix Oscars problems, but the money supplemented Sharon's gin habit and caught up the back rent. Oscar even enjoyed it a little, normal people, real people, coming and going. Sharing their problems, sharing their jokes, their jibes.

'Hey Oscar, that's a great shirt, they make one like that for guys?'

He knew they were mocking him, but even so it made him feel a bit more human, bit more part of things. He played along, pretended he was part of the fun, part of their world. Oscar knew he was different, just didn't know why. Maybe too long in the world of women. He didn't much like beer or bars or just drinking, didn't fit in there. Didn't like football or baseball, nothing like that, didn't fit in there. Never made any friends out there in the suburbs or at the hardware store, didn't fit in there. Never got invited to any barbecue, any match any game. He didn't understand any of that. Thought maybe if he'd had a father who taught him this stuff, a father who played ball with him, barbecued in the backyard, drank beers and told bawdy jokes, maybe then he would be different. Maybe fit in. Maybe if he'd had a father who taught him it was okay to lie a bit, okay to do dodgy deals, screw around, gamble and shit… maybe then.

But Oscar never understood the how of it. There were good people in this world and there were bad people in this world. Oscar knew that, of course he did, but he also knew there was a group of grey people right there in the middle. People who could fit in with either of the other groups somehow, hazed the borders, crossed the lines. Those people weren't all bad. They didn't do really bad things themselves, but they were happy to turn a blind eye to really bad. But they would lie, they would cheat and more. They would knowingly lie to each other and cheat on each other and then laugh about it together afterwards, maybe there in the bar. They would lie, cheat and fuck each others husbands and wives, they would effect friendship for gain. They would sell their souls and destroy innocent lives for cash reward and then, having dipped their toes into that bad world, just a toe mind, just a toe into that world of *fuck-you-jack it's all about number one*, they would then dip their toes into that other world, that world where you could pray for redemption and be forgiven, be saved. That one day of the week when they went forth to their churches and synagogs, their mosques and their temples. Where they prayed to their particular god and made their acts of prayer and penitence public, displayed their goodness for all to see on that one day of the week.

The grey people. The grey people who survived and thrived in the clubrooms of the righteous, the houses of the good. This was the bit that Oscar didn't understand. He'd seen the bad, seen all of it, seen too much of it. He knew where it lived, how it lived; that netherworld right below our feet, that darkness right before our eyes, *don't look down, don't look down, never look down.* Murder mayhem sex drugs and slavery. Down there with the cannibals, the unthinkable down in that foul layer of darkness right below our eyes, under our gaze.

Don't look down!

There were two things that Oscar failed to understand, that all the innocent fail to understand until it is too late.

First, it was easy to count the black, easy to know who the black were, where they moved, their feet mired in dark blood and deeds. It was easy to know where to look for them in the shadows and so it was easy to avoid them, mostly. But he underestimated the grey. Just underestimated the numbers, simple as that really, the pure and incredible weight of mathematics. He failed to realise that this was the broad church, this was the great horde, the main tribe. This was how the world functioned, this was how mankind existed, lived, survived, like it or not the world was grey, nearly all grey.

The second thing that he failed to understand, Oscar and those like him failed to understand, was that there was no place for the good, the truly innocent and unaffected. There was no place in this world for any man woman or child who had dwelt in both the world of the good and the bad, the world of darkness and the world of light. For those men women and children knew what others could not. They knew that for them, both paths led to darkness. The bad were as cannibals and they had sequestered the houses of the good. And the good... the good had let down their defences, lowered their shields, their standards painted and re-painted, written and re-written so that they might accommodate the grey, appease the grey.

But it was always so, always cyclic, always moving thus as sure as the phases of the moon, the orbit of the planets. It turned and it turned back, it turned and it turned back and each time it turned back it came round a little diminished. A fraction more chipped off the quaint notions of good manners and fair play, of love thy neighbour or help thy neighbour. A little lighter on conscience, on consequence. So *this* is what Oscar had failed to grasp, Oscar and all those like him. All those men women and children who didn't fit anywhere, who didn't understand why they didn't fit anywhere and why they were different. But it didn't matter, it just did not matter. Because those who did finally come to understand, then had to choose. They had to choose which path, because with the knowing, with finally knowing there came only surrender. With surrender it just remained to take up a white flag and choose a path, one of only two. There were no longer three paths, there were just two. The choice of darkness or light.

But what of those who never came to understand, what of them?

With each passing day week month year, they became more invisible, less visible, less solid. They lived in squalid loneliness hidden behind ever growing piles of old newsprint. They lived in obscene luxury hidden behind ever growing piles of visible wealth. They lived in suburbia, hidden behind manicured lawns and seemingly perfect families. They lived in cities hidden behind cold concrete and tinted glass. They lived in the country hidden behind their desperate dry pastures. They stuffed their faces, their mouths or their veins, with whatever drugs worked, stronger and stronger and when they failed to work, they created more, stronger and stronger, stronger and stronger. Sometimes this worked sometimes it didn't.

Then what of those who didn't yet understand but who would *eventually* understand, what of Oscar?

Oscar was the textbook victim. He was scared of any of those things he might have stuffed in his face, stuffed in his veins to take away the pain. He too became invisible and when he wasn't invisible he walked wide around trouble, flew low under conflict, painted himself into the background. Sometimes it was hard to tell if he was really there.

DEFIANCE

In that first year at the boarding school, Oscar Kingman remained a victim, became more of a victim. In the first year at that boarding school, Oscar Kingman became defiant. From the first day in that first class with the rat-eyed Irish teacher Flaherty, Oscar chose defiance. He came out of that toilet block with his teeth set and his fists balled. He sat on the bench outside the classroom and became an entirely different type of Oscar Kingman. He remembered something Granny Molly had once said to him. He didn't understand it back when she'd said it, but as he sat on that bench and thought about what had just happened, he had suddenly understood what she'd meant.

'Him a kid, just a kid. What did he do so wrong that a grown up would beat him like that... what? Why would he, how could he respect someone like that?'

He thought about the look in Paul Davenport's eyes just before he defied that teacher, Flaherty. Granny Molly had talked about respect. She had said that respect was something to be earned. She said respect didn't matter, was not really important, but that you were no kind of person at all without *self-respect*. Self-respect. What Flaherty did was wrong and he was not deserving of any respect. No god, no robes, no fancy words, nothing would change that. Self-respect was all about standing up for yourself, standing up for others, for what was right. That's what Granny Molly had said.

'These people who push others around, these bullies... they have no self-respect and so they are not worthy of your respect Oscar. Self-respect is about standing up for yourself, standing up for what is right. Living right and knowing you are living right.'

In that first year at boarding school, like all the other boarders, Oscar Kingman was dragged off to church four times a day. But unlike everybody else he was beaten, caned or cuffed three or four times a week. He also did detention two or three times a week while the other boarders were out playing, free at the end of the day before dinner. And there were many times he missed dinner, forced to stand up there at the lectern and read from the bible instead of eating. Often on these occasions he would go to bed hungry, sometimes one of the other guys would smuggle food into the dormitory. Of course if they got caught they got the beating as well. Make no mistake, all this often happened because Oscar made it happen. He brought it on himself, came charging out of the trenches blazing away with both barrels. He was a sitting target, duck in a shooting gallery. If they picked on someone smaller, someone younger than him, he stood up to them. If they picked on one of his friends, one of his gang, he stood up to them. They were always picking on someone, bullying someone.

And so they came for him, came for him at every opportunity. *'He had a big mouth, a smart mouth,'* they said when they came for him.

He called them out, abused them in front of others, in front of the class. He even physically lashed out when they lay their holy hands on him and so they came for him. Of course they came for him, most kids got knocked down they stayed down, not Oscar, not Stupid Oscar, Oscar was alive. Oscar was becoming the very child they were punishing him for being. Oscar was fitting nicely into the role.

He could have shut up, could have said nothing. Could have taken those early beatings and faded away, become invisible, become forgotten. He could have let people fend for themselves. But he knew this was not right. Blame it on Granny Molly, blame it on too many phantom comics, but he knew it was not right, so he went out into battle.

WHO WILL FEED THE CATS?

By 3.45 Oscar was back at his desk looking busy. Nobody had noticed his change of trousers, his new jeans, not even Moira as he'd walked by her earlier, nobody in the general office, not a soul. He was all gloom on the outside but bursting on the inside. He felt invincible. He sat at his desk and slowly, very slowly he returned to reality. He'd killed two people. Two people. He'd murdered them in cold blood. Murdered, stabbed, strangled them. They were dead, really dead.

Mr. Llewellyn would not be going home to his wife again. Mr. Llewellyn would never ever go home to his wife again. Miss Elaine's cats would miss their dinner tonight. Miss Elaine's cats would miss their dinner tonight, but tomorrow they would scamper out between the super's legs when he unlocked her door for the police. Scamper out between his legs and swap their pampered existence at Miss Elaine's for the ever hungry, ever scrounging world of the alleys.

They were dead, both of them. It was all down to lack of respect. Lack of respect and final straw stuff. Oscar hadn't planned to kill them, never planned to kill them. But he had killed them and so now, at the very point where his life might have taken a turn for the better. At the very point where a chance at happiness hung over him, so did these killings. Oscar realised he had to do something to cover his tracks. He scribbled on his desk pad, planning, planning, scheming.

He got up and went to Llewellyn's office door, tapped on it. No response. He knocked louder... nothing. He rattled the handle noisily. He turned back to the office.

"Anybody know where Mr. Llewellyn is?"

One or two people looked up but said nothing, most ignored him.

"Anybody?" he shrugged.

"I dunno, must have gone out."

"Who cares?"

Snickers.

Oscar went out to the reception area.

"Moira, have you seen Mr. Llewellyn? I have a question for him and he's not in his office," he said.

"No," replied Moira. "You sure he's not there, I didn't see him go through here?"

"Yes, his office is locked and the light is off."

"Well you know what he's like. Comes and goes as he pleases, never tells me anything," said Moira.

"Oh! Okay then. Could I ask you to be my witness that I was looking for him. I need to ask him a question. You know... I've got to finish this job and all."

"Okay then Oscar. Nothing else I can help with, like the question?"

"No, thanks anyway Moira," said Oscar wandering back into the general office.

He sat back down at his desk. So far nobody knew anything. Everybody thought Llewellyn was out, maybe gone for the day, door locked and all. He looked at his letter opener. It was standard issue, same as everybody's. Still might be a good idea to switch it with someone else's, another bully maybe. But what about Llewellyn's body. He couldn't risk going back in there. Even if he could risk it he didn't have a key.

Thinking thinking. Scene of the crime, scene of the crime.

'Had he left any evidence in there?' He didn't think so. *'So what now? How long would it be before they found his body?'*

Oscar tried to think it through, was amazed at how calm he was. Llewellyn's wife would miss him for dinner, maybe phone the office looking for him working late. Then probably think he was out drinking somewhere, call the police later or maybe not till the morning when she wakes and finds he's still not home, sheets cold and straight on his side of the bed. *Then* maybe she'd call the police. But around nine o'clock she'd call the office, sometime then. She'd ask was he there, in his office.

'No, bit strange,' they would say.

Then they would hunt up the spare key and open his office. That dark close office with the faint metallic smell would finally yield its secret. Sometime after nine in the morning they would find him. They would find Edmund Llewellyn bloodied and buried down there under his big mahogany desk. Not buried so deep they could miss him.

'And what of Miss Elaine?' thought Oscar.

He was amazed at how calm he felt. He figured they must have already found her. No locked doors, no dark office, just Miss Elaine sitting on the floor in that change room, her desperate eyes bulging out like some frog. Soul climbed right out of her body and left that old dry husk sitting there slumped against the wall. Yes, they would have found her by now. Wouldn't be much of an investigation on Miss Elaine until the morning. That would take a while, customers in and out, could have been anyone. It would take a while before they got organised, started looking for suspects, looking for him, so he figured he had until nine the next morning to be gone, gone from the scene, disappeared.

But he still had one small thing to do, one little chore.

THE PROTAGONIST

During that first year at boarding school, Oscar had turned nine, the occasion pretty much ignored. It came as something of a surprise to Oscar when old Strohkirch called him, Gerry, Paul and Trevor into his office one afternoon right after classes had finished for the day. All the way along the cloister it was *'What now, what'd you do this time Oscar? Me? What about you?'* But when they opened the door, there was the old priest with Mrs. Simek, Bruno and Andrew. All jammed in that little office and all smiling.

"Happy birthday Oscar!" said father Strohkirch.

The others all chimed in with their greetings, Davenport punching him extra hard on the arm.

"Mrs. Simek has been kind enough to make you a little cake," said Strohkirch.

"Yes, happy birthday young man," said Mrs. Simek jostling his hair. "Now I had better leave you to it and get back to the kitchen," she said and squeezed past out the door.

The old priest produced soda, paper plates and cups and they fell upon that little feast with gusto. Presently Paul Davenport cleared his throat.

"Now don't you go getting ideas or nothing," he said, "but I've been staying back after last woodwork class. I made you this. Couldn't think of anything else. Happy Birthday Dickhead."

Whack!

"Sorry father. Shit that hurt."

Whack!

They all fell about laughing. Even the old priest with a smile on his face.

Paul handed Oscar a small wooden box, a bit rough, lid a bit crooked and stuff, but made with love by his mate Paul. Oscar didn't know what to say. Nobody ever made him anything. Of course, Granny Molly had knitted him a sweater, things like that, but that's what grannies did.

"Thanks Paul, it's brilliant."

"Aaww."

"Davenport embarrassed. Never thought I'd see that," said Trevor.

"Piss off Trev."

Whack!

"Ow!"

Eventually they had to wrap it up. They all thanked the old priest and filed out.

"Oscar, I'd like to speak with you please," said Strohkirch.

He pointed to the seat in front of his desk. Oscar sat.

"I've been watching you Oscar and I fear my little talk when you first came here might have fallen on deaf ears, or that you might have misunderstood. Every day I hear Oscar Kingman this and Oscar Kingman that. You're always in trouble and sometimes you get your friends in trouble too. I know it's not always your fault but some of it is and I think now you are purposefully looking for trouble young Oscar. It's fine that you stand up for yourself Oscar and it's admirable that you stand up for others, but you need to be careful. You are a young boy, just a boy. You are no match for these grown men who hide in the church, these men who seem to enjoy bullying children. You can't beat them Oscar. You can't go on like this. You're a smart boy and your grades are good, but you need to settle down."

Oscar sat there nodding, looking at the crucifix behind the priest's head.

"I fear that you are going to get hurt Oscar, both physically and mentally. Do you know what I mean Oscar? And I fear that you will judge the church by the actions of these men. They are not the church Oscar, they are just bad men, like there's bad policemen and there's bad doctors, that sort of thing Oscar. I fear because of these few men you will never know peace, never know the love of our lord."

Oscar just sat there. Finally he looked at the priest.

"I'm sorry father. Thank you for the birthday cake. I will try harder I promise," he lied.

At the end of that first school year, Oscar's grandfather Richard turned up to collect him for the holidays. Oscar was in a panic at the thought of being stuck there all alone in that place with nobody but him for the priests and brothers to pick on. So far he'd spent all his school holidays there including Christmas, but at least then he'd had Bruno and Andrew to hang out with. Christmas was a time of great ritual at the school and for some reason they left him alone, except for church, study periods and cleaning duties. But the summer break was going to be different. It was a long one and Mrs. Simek and the boys were going away to some kind of church holiday camp where Mrs. Simek would work in the kitchen. All those weeks alone and defenceless in that empty school. Oscar had started to think about running away. Maybe run away, see how that worked out.

But he was called to the headmaster's office that last night after dinner and he was told his grandfather was coming for him the next morning, told to pack his things.

"… and Kingman," said the headmaster, "I don't like you Kingman. You are nothing but trouble. Do you understand me Kingman. You come back here with the same attitude and behave the way you have this year I'll expel you, you understand Kingman? I'll expel you and you'll end up in some Boy's Home somewhere. Understand?"

"Yes father Bruist."

A CHILD IS BORN

About a week before Sharon was due to give birth, Oscar arrived home one night to find her sitting in the lounge with a suitcase by her side.

"You took your damned time, my father will be here any minute," she said.

"What's going on Sharon, what's with the suitcase? Are you going somewhere?"

"Yes, I'm going home Oscar. Until after the baby is born."

"But shouldn't we discuss this? I mean it's the first I've heard of it," ventured Oscar.

"What's to discuss. I'm stuck out here miles from anywhere with a loser for a husband, can't even afford a car. How am I supposed to get to the hospital? Tell me that."

"I thought we'd go in a cab."

"We! What we? I don't want you anywhere near the hospital Oscar. You stay away," she said.

"Well when will you be back?"

"Jesus you're thick Oscar. I was going to break it to you gently but, I won't be coming back, understand? I'll send someone for the rest of my things later."

"But this whole thing was your idea. To live out here, this house."

"Don't put this on me Oscar," she spat. "This is all your doing."

Outside on the street a car horn sounded. Oscar watched as she struggled to her feet, tilt this way shift that way.

"Well don't just stand there. Get the suitcase," she puffed, heading for the door.

Oscar followed her out the door, tried to help her down the front steps, but she brushed him off. Her father sat there in the car, never moved to help her. Not happy, he'd thought she was gone for good. She struggled into the passenger seat. Oscar put the suitcase on the back seat.

"Hello Mr. Wilson, look…" he said.

"Fuck off loser," said Sharon's father.

He flicked his cigarette butt at Oscar and it glanced off his shoulder in a shower of sparks.

The car squealed away from the curb, raced down the street and disappeared around the corner. Oscar stood there long after it was gone, then he turned, stamped out the smouldering cigarette butt at his feet and trudged inside.

Every day he'd rung the hospital. He'd tried ringing Sharon at the Wilson's apartment but her father kept hanging up on him, wouldn't tell him anything. So every day he'd rung the hospital, explained that he and his wife were having some problems, nothing serious, she was just a bit highly strung what with the baby coming and all. He explained all this to different people pretty much every day for nine days, over and over, but Sharon wouldn't take the calls and wouldn't see him.

So Oscar just went to work. He ate breakfast on the way, came home late each night and if he hadn't got something at the office, he picked up Indian, Chinese or sometimes ribs from the joints near the station. Weekends he did his hours at the hardware store, counted bolts, stacked shelves, rang up sales. He found he enjoyed being alone at home, enjoyed the peace and quiet, dared to plan a little, dared to hope.

'Well if she really wasn't coming back then...'

But he kept trying. Nine days and always a different person at the hospital, always a different person on the phone there, over and over until on the ninth day the nurse said...

"Oh! Mr. Kingman, I'm glad you called. I understand the problem. You know, we see this sort of thing sometimes Mr. Kingman, I think it's hormonal myself. It's a difficult and stressful time. I'm sure it will all work out now that baby is born. I think you should come in, regardless of what your wife says."

"Born?" said Oscar. "You say the baby has been born?"

"Why yes Mr. Kingman, didn't you even..."

"Boy or girl? I'm sorry is it a boy or girl?" said Oscar interrupting her.

"Why it's a girl Mr. Kingman. A lovely sweet healthy little girl."

"Thank you," said Oscar, the disappointment rising like bile in his throat. "Thank you, I'll come in tomorrow."

The following morning Oscar went in to the office early. He cleared up some paperwork that needed finishing that day, then went to see Mr. Alperstein about taking a few hours off.

"Sure Oscar," said Mr. Alperstein. "But is everything okay with you and Sharon. I worry about you after that last incident. Seems you spend half your life here in the office, don't really want to be at home and all. And you know you've barely spoken about any of this, the baby and all. What's going on Oscar?"

"Well she moved out Mr. Alperstein, Sharon... she moved out. I don't want to worry you with my problems sir, you've been so kind to me. It's just that she started drinking again. Seems I can't do anything right."

"Seems to me you'll never be able to do anything right in a relationship like that Oscar. Seems to me you're better off out of it. Let her go and move on with your life."

He saw the way Oscar was looking at him.

"Look I'm sorry Oscar, I'm speaking out of turn. I should learn to mind my own business. Go and see your new daughter. I'm sure you and Sharon will work this out."

But he didn't really think that and neither did Oscar. Mr. Alperstein was right, he was better off without her. The last few days had confirmed that.

So later that morning Oscar arrived at the hospital with a bunch of flowers for Sharon and a pink rabbit for his new daughter.

At the nurses station they gave him the room number. Four beds. One empty, one asleep, one with a happy couple making plans and one with Sharon. Sharon sitting up there chewing gum and reading a magazine. The anger lit in her eyes as soon as she saw him. He moved closer, behind the half drawn curtain.

"What are you doing here?" she hissed. "I told you not to come here. I told you I didn't want to see you again you thick bastard."

Oscar looked across at the other couple, staring at him like he'd attacked Sharon. It was clear she'd already laid the groundwork for this assault. Clear he was the villain here. He felt the twitch beside his eye, put his hand up there, felt it jump. *Tick tick.*

"Look Sharon," he said, putting the flowers on the bed but hanging onto the rabbit. "If you don't want to see me that's fine, but this is my child too Sharon, my daughter too and I want to see her okay?"

"Over my dead body," she yelled, sweeping the flowers off the bed and waking the sleeping woman on the other side of her. "Go to hell."

Oscar felt the twitch quicken. *Tick tick tick.* He wanted to step up and take her fat neck in his hands and squeeze the life out of her. His face twitching, *tick tick tick tick.* The scar over his ear now throbbing, *thud thud thud thud thud.* He backed away. *Something not right, something come loose up there.*

He turned and went out the door almost colliding with a nurse.

"I'm sorry Mr. Kingman," she said leading him away down the corridor. "I'm the one spoke to you on the phone. I hope you don't think I was eavesdropping but, you know I heard all that and well… look Mr. Kingman if you want to see your daughter I'll take you to her. You can see her at the nursery, through the window."

She took him there and stood by him at the window. On the other side of the glass, another nurse in a full green gown with a hat and mask looked up from what she was doing. Following a short session of pointing and lip reading, the nurse in the green gown nodded and went to a cot in the second row. She took hold of the little bassinet and propped it up at the back.

"There she is," said the kind nurse beside him. "That one. That's your daughter. Isn't she beautiful?"

Oscar stood looking at the tiny thing there in that bassinet behind the glass. His daughter. Then he turned to face the kind nurse, desperation painted across his face.

"Is everything okay Mr. Kingman?" she asked.

"She looks just like her mother, only with no hair."

And he turned and walked away. Walked away along that corridor and down the stairs toward the entrance. In the foyer he paused just long enough to pull the head off the pink rabbit and drop it in a trash can.

THE HOLIDAY HOUSE

The following day Oscar sat in the big foyer, the big room hung all around with strange paintings, stood all around with strange statues. Strange people standing on clouds, arms open, hearts shining on the outside. Near naked, hanging from crosses. He looked around. After being there a year he understood much more of the how of it, but still none of the why of it. Church four times a day. Four times a day, their ideas down his throat. In class all day their ideas down his throat, at meals their ideas down his throat. Oscar sat looking at the statue in the corner, knew now that it was called the sacred heart. The heart out there in front for everyone to see. Burning there with love and forgiveness like some hot shining coal. Oscar understood more of it now. Understood none of it.

These people were the chosen ones, god's chosen people. It said so all around him. All this love, all this forgiveness, all this salvation around him. Every smile benign, arms wide and welcoming. Why then did they treat him like they did? They insisted the children in that other school down the road were damned and would burn in hell? And all those followers of all those other gods, the false gods, they were all damned too and couldn't be saved. How could that be, where was all this love they talked about, all this love of fellow man, all this forgiveness? Oscar tried and tried but it just didn't fit together, made no sense. *He* made no sense of it.

What was wrong with him? Why couldn't he get this faith thing that they always talked about, that they tried to beat into him?

'You need to get on board Kingman.'

After one of his beatings the headmaster had actually used those very words like faith was some bus, some train bound for this heaven of theirs. He'd actually used those words. *'You need to get on board Kingman. You need to get on board or you're going to hell,'* but Oscar was already there.

Along the short corridor an office door opened with a rattle and Oscar looked up to see the man who had brought him here. The man called Richard who said he was his grandfather.

"Hi Oscar, how are you doing son?"

Oscar said nothing. His grandfather shrugged and walked over and stood before him, hands on his hips.

"Okay Oscar, I understand you and I don't really know each other, but your grandmother and I are looking forward to having you with us for the holidays."

Half true thought Richard looking down at the boy. He was looking forward to it, Glenda not so much. Glenda didn't want the boy there, anywhere near her, but Richard had backed her into a corner and as a good christian woman on all those church committees and stuff, she couldn't say no.

Richard bent down and picked up Oscar's bag, Oscar's little world inside.

"All right then, let's get out of here shall we?"

Oscar followed his grandfather out the door and down the stairs. Half of him petrified, half of him excited. It was his first time out of that place since he'd arrived. In the car, Richard turned on the radio. The car crunched off down the gravel drive, his grandfather whistling along with the tune. At the corner, Oscar craned around in his seat, looked back up the driveway past the Simek's old house to that big lonely red brick prison, empty now, almost empty now. Just the priests the brothers and their god.

"So Oscar are you excited son? You must be excited, holidays and all that and…" he said, punching Oscar on the arm a bit like Davenport would, "tomorrow we are off to our beach house. Your grandmother is home now doing the last of the packing. We're off first thing. You'll love it Oscar, I'll teach you to sail. I used to go there when I was your age, spent almost every holiday there since. It'll be fun. You like the beach Oscar?"

Oscar was watching his grandfather talk. He seemed okay. Granny Molly said he was a good man really, just weak she'd said. *'He's scared of that Glenda. She's pretty scary!'* she'd say laughing.

"I asked you if you liked the beach Oscar?"

Oscar looked away, looked out the window then finally spoke.

"I don't know, I've never been."

"You've never been! Well trust me," said Richard. "You're going to love it."

'Trust me,' thought Oscar. *'Another adult saying trust me. Hadn't worked out too good so far. Look where he'd ended up.'*

"If you say so sir," he replied still looking out the window, still escaping.

"Look Oscar," said Richard, "I know this hasn't been easy for you, but we're doing the best we can."

"You don't know," said Oscar turning to him. "You don't know anything. You don't know what it's like in there. You don't know. It's worse than the orphanage, much worse. I get beaten all the time by the priests and the brothers. You don't know!"

And he cracked open. Oscar Kingman cracked open and out it all came. Out it came in a mess of tears and spit and snot. The stories, the hate, the beatings, the loneliness, the desperation, the wanting to be gone, the wanting to be anywhere but there, the wanting to be dead.

Richard pulled the car over, shocked by the violence of the child's outburst.

"Oscar now you stop this. Those are *good* people. Every child gets punished sometimes. You mustn't exaggerate Oscar. You can't say that about the priests."

Oscar getting angry now, yelling, kicking out at the dash, screaming.

"I'm not exaggerating, ask anyone. Ask Trevor or Gerry, ask Paul. You don't know what happens there. You tell me to trust you and you do nothing. You leave me in there with those people. Why didn't you come for me? You told me to call you and I did, but you left me there. You said you would take care of me. Said you wouldn't let anything like that happen to me again but you did. I called you but you just did nothing and left me there."

"Listen Oscar, I have no idea what you're talking about. You never called me."

"Father Strohkirch called you. We're not allowed to use the phone. I asked him to call you and he said he did. He said you wouldn't help, wouldn't come. He said my grandmother told him that."

"Oscar don't shout at me and stop kicking the car. If you behave like this at school it's no wonder they punish you. Now listen. I know nothing about this. I didn't know there was a problem. If the school called I didn't know about it. If they spoke to your grandmother well, she never told me about it. Look I'm sorry Oscar..."

"No you're not. You're not sorry."

"Please Oscar come on. It's the first I've heard of any of this. I'll speak to your grandmother, find out. I'll call father Strohkirch if you want."

Oscar stared at him, looked at him hard through the tears.

"You promise?"

"Yes Oscar, I promise and I mean it. I am sorry. Your grandmother… you know, well you don't know I guess, but your grandmother, she's a strict person. Doesn't know anything about kids. I have to be honest Oscar. She's not really very happy about this arrangement, you coming to stay. But if you promise to behave then I'll speak to her and father Strohkirch and I'll try and get to the bottom of all this. Okay? Okay Oscar?"

The best Oscar could manage was a nod. Just an angry nod; unconvincing, unconvinced.

Oscar stared out the car window until they finally turned into the driveway of a white bungalow in a leafy street.

"Now remember our deal Oscar," said Richard taking Oscar's bag from the back seat.

Oscar was standing in the drive looking down that leafy street. That leafy green street, quiet and safe, safe and quiet. Someone else's safe and quiet.

"Yes sir," he said turning to Richard.

Richard looked down at him, shook his head.

"Okay, follow me."

She was at the door, his grandmother. At the open door like a sentinel deciding whether or not he'd get in. Seemed that way to Oscar at least. She had on blue rubber gloves and an apron and her hair was tied in a scarf. She looked over her glasses at him, judging, sizing him up. She had piercing brown eyes and a stern, sharp jaw, cheekbones brushed pink and bright red lipstick around a puckered mean mouth.

"Glenda, this is Oscar. Oscar... say hello to your grandmother," said Richard all happy families and home beautiful.

"Hello."

"Hello what?"

"Hello er gr..."

"Hello grandmother all right. Not grandma, not granny, grandmother. Look boy It's best you should know that this is not my idea. It's your grandfather's. You misbehave... one problem and it's back to school. You got that? You *got* that?"

Oscar caught the wink from Richard, saw the face he made.

"Yes. Yes grandmother."

She stepped aside point made, rules established, battle lines drawn.

Dinner was alright, quiet but alright. Oscar liked it that way. The food was good, not like the stuff they gave them at boarding school. There was a delicate moment when it came to grace, but Oscar took Richard's lead and joined in with a murmured prayer, Glenda's prayer.

That night Oscar slept in a big soft double bed with crisp sheets. He didn't dream. He felt strangely safe in that big soft bed in that little bungalow out there in the suburbs. He knew he shouldn't have felt safe, wasn't safe. He didn't dream, didn't dare.

The following morning he woke to a set of orders from his grandmother. *'Do this do that, put that in there, no not there stupid boy, here like this. This goes in the car, get those from the garage.'* He did what he was asked, saying nothing, just doing it, taking the flack if he got it wrong until eventually the car was loaded and they pulled away from that little white bungalow in that leafy street in the suburbs and headed for the seaside, Oscar stacked in the back seat alongside the fresh folded linen.

Most of the journey was silent. His grandmother sitting up there in her scarf and sunglasses and his grandfather concentrating on the traffic, getting around the city, out the other side. As the houses turned to fields and the air changed somehow, his grandfather adjusted the rear view mirror and started telling him stories about his summers at the beach. His eyes talking, smiling up there in the mirror.

"This beach house was built by my own grandfather," he said. "I've been coming here every summer since I can remember…"

And so it went until they came into a village perched on the edge of a narrow inlet. There were brightly painted stores and cafes and people everywhere. People poking in and out of shops, eating out on the footpath, fishing off the little finger docks that reached out from the shoreline. On the other side of the town they turned away from the water and drove another ten or fifteen minutes through a swampy forest and then out across a beachgrass plain. Presently Richard turned down a short sandy track and Oscar could see a row of tumbledown shacks dotted around in the sand dunes facing the ocean. Despite himself and his misgivings, Oscar was excited to see the ocean, still and calm, the sun bouncing off it's shimmering surface as it disappeared again behind the dunes.

"Here we are then," said Richard pulling up outside a small white cottage with yellow doors and window frames.

And there they were.

His grandmother went straight to the house, straight into the little screened entry porch, empty handed except for her purse. He watched as she took down a key that was hidden up there somewhere on the frame and used it to open the door. Richard was already rummaging about in the trunk. Oscar walked to the side of the house and looked across the ocean. From where he stood he could see no other houses in any direction. This type of solitude was a new experience for him.

"What do you think?" said Richard, coming up beside him. "Great isn't it? Told you you'd like it young Oscar."

Then it was the reverse of the morning. *'Do this do that, that goes there, no there. Useless boy.'* Until eventually the car was unloaded and the kitchen benches cleared.

His grandmother had made the beds.

"You're in here, next to us," said Richard handing Oscar his bag. "Why don't you put your things away in the drawers and go for a walk on the beach. Be careful and don't be too long though, don't upset your grandmother."

'Don't upset your grandmother. Too late for that,' thought Oscar. *'She's been upset since the day I was born apparently.'*

He looked around the room. Colourful shell patterned wallpaper, white painted single bed, bedside trunk covered with comics and boat magazines, big set of pine drawers with a model sailboat and a shell collection on top, hanging hooks along one wall and a half glass door that opened out onto the front verandah. Oscar unlocked the door and opened it, just the hint of a breeze came in with the scent of the ocean on it. He heard a strange hollow whooshing sound and looking down the path through the gap in the dunes, he saw small waves, just a few inches high, running sideways along the sandy shore. He turned back into the room and grabbed his bag, unpacking his few bits and pieces into the top two drawers. Socks and undies, shorts and shirts and his prized possession, that small wooden box, then he was out the door and gone exploring.

"Oscar!" Glenda called. "Oscar?"

But Oscar was gone along the beach and her calls went unheeded, unheard on the gentle sea breeze.

He went south along the beach away from the inlet, close to the edge, skipping sideways with each new wave that reached out to him. He kicked over rocks and shells, chased seagulls and crabs. He explored in the sand dunes, felt the breeze quicken on his face, turned into it, let it cleanse him. Back on the beach with the wind freshening, the waves licked up even further. He played with them, dared them, got away, dared them, got away again, dared them once more and the ocean beat him. Left him standing there looking down as the foamy water raced over his shoes and socks, climbed up his shins and then fled back down the sand. Oscar felt elated. He put his hands in his pockets and wandered back along the beach counting his footsteps so he'd know how many there were when the ocean cleared them away behind him.

"Where the hell have you been?"

Reality met him on the front verandah in the form of his grandmother, hands on hips and red faced.

"And look at your shoes you…"

She grabbed him and pushed him down into an old cane chair.

"Get them off now. Richard, Richard, where are you?"

His grandfather appeared around the corner of the house and climbed the steps onto the verandah.

"Where were you?"

"I was in the garage cleaning out the boat why?"

"Look at him. He's been on the beach, shoes ruined. What am I supposed to do with them now."

"It's no big deal Glenda, I told him to go for a walk on the beach. Calm down it's only a pair of shoes, they'll dry out."

"Only a pair of shoes, only a pair of shoes? Who do you think paid for those shoes?"

"Well your mother did actually Glenda, it's her trust, her money."

"Don't you smart mouth me Richard. You know what I mean. We'll talk about this later."

And with that she hauled Oscar out of the chair and dragged him into the bedroom. She locked the verandah door and took the key.

"You'll stay in here until dinner time, you hear me you brat?"

She didn't wait for an answer, just slammed the bedroom door behind her and disappeared. Oscar looked up and saw Richard still standing outside the verandah door. His grandfather shrugged, apologising. Oscar went and lay on the bed facing the wall.

He lay there plotting his escape, his getaway. After a while he went to the door, knelt down and put his eye to the big old keyhole. All he could see was the other side of the hallway, all quiet out there except for the odd clang of plates or pots in the kitchen. He'd wait until after dark, take what food he could from the kitchen and he'd be gone. He went back to the bed, grabbed a couple of comics off the trunk and lay down to read. To read and to wait. An hour later his grandmother appeared at the door with a glass of water.

"You need to use the toilet boy?"

Naked undisguised aggression, the jailer now.

He ignored her. She put the glass of water on the pine chest and closed the door. Oscar heard a key go in, heard it turn, heard his escape plan being foiled. He ran to the door and looked through the keyhole, couldn't see out. The big key in the big keyhole. *'Shit! Shit shit shit shit shit!'*

As the day drew to a close and the room grew dim, he heard the key turn in the lock. He looked across his comic as his grandfather came in with a tray. Richard closed the door, switched on the light, came and sat on the bed.

"I'm sorry Oscar but if it's any consolation she's as mad at me as she is at you."

Oscar closed his comic.

"What did I do wrong? You said I could walk on the beach, what did I do wrong? Why does she hate me, why am I locked up in here?"

"Look Oscar, you didn't do anything wrong, you didn't. And she doesn't just hate you, she hates almost everybody."

"Richard!" yelled Glenda from the kitchen.

"I'm sorry Oscar, I'd better go, you know keep the peace."

"No I don't know," said Oscar. "Granny Molly said you were weak. Why are you so weak? Why are you scared of her? Why don't you tell her I did nothing wrong?"

Oscar stared up at his grandfather, saw the look in his eye, the beginnings of anger. He backed off, didn't want another beating. Richard put the tray on the trunk and stood up.

"Okay Oscar. Eat your dinner and go to bed. We'll talk in the morning."

He took Oscar to the bathroom and waited outside, then took him back to his room and locked the door as instructed. Oscar ate a bit of the meal and saved the rest. Potato salad, tomato, cold meat, all loaded in a plastic bag he'd found in a drawer.

He lay there in the dark, hearing the television off in the distance while he plotted his escape. He needed a map. Needed to figure out where he was, how to get back to the city. He thought he could survive there. Then the television fell silent. Doors opened and closed, voices murmuring now. Voices in the next room.

Oscar slid out of bed and put his ear against the wall, against a big wallpaper shell.

"I don't want him here. You need to take him back tomorrow you hear?"

"But Glenda he's just a little boy."

"He's not just a little boy, he's nine years old and he's trouble, just like his mother."

"That's not fair Glenda, Lorrie made one mistake. Just one, and you're going to punish this boy for that?" said Richard.

"One mistake! One mistake. After all I did for her, everything we did for her she went whoring and this happened, this thing next door."

"That's enough Glenda, he'll hear you."

"Do I care if he hears me? Get him out of here first thing in the morning Richard. I want him gone and back to that school before I get out of this bed."

"By the way Glenda, speaking of the school, have you ever had any phone calls from the school?"

"What if I have?" she hissed.

"Jesus Glenda, why didn't you tell me. I promised him…"

"Don't you take the lord's name in vain Richard."

Oscar had heard enough. He turned away from the wall and went back to the bed. He knew what to do, knew how to escape, he'd read how somewhere. He waited an hour or more until the house was quiet, then he got up and went to the bedroom door. He knelt down and put his head to the floor. There was a big gap under the door. *'This might work. This could work.'*

He pulled the centre spread from a magazine and pushed it under the door below the big lock. Pushed it out until only a small section remained on his side of the doorway. *'This might work. This could work.'*

He took down the model sailboat and broke away the thin piece of wood that formed the boom and going to the door, he poked it into the big keyhole. He carefully pushed and jiggled, jiggled and pushed until he felt the key pop out of the lock. It dropped on the floor louder than he expected, but it sounded like it had landed on the magazine pages and not on the bare floorboards. He waited there, not breathing, just waiting for the sound of a door opening, voices questioning, but there was nothing. *'This could work. This might work, could go either way.'*

He put his head against the floor again and looked under the door. There it was. In the gloom he could just make out the key lying near the edge of the paper. *'This is working. I don't believe it but this is working.'*

Oscar Kingman took hold of the pages and slowly drew the key under the door and into the room.

And there it was… freedom.

OSCAR COMES CLEAN

Wendy Legget couldn't concentrate. Nobody could concentrate with a secret like that. It scared her, excited her. What Oscar had done, what he said he'd done. She had gone into the general office careful not to look at Oscar. Avoided Oscar and went and knocked on Llewellyn's door, some file or other in her hand, some question or other needed answering. One of the clerks looked up.

"He's not there, gone home already,"

She looked around the room, nodded to the clerk, eyes swept past Oscar hard at work there, trying to make deadline. Busy busy busy.

"Oh! Okay thanks," she said and went back to the filing room.

Twenty minutes later she looked up from her desk to see Oscar standing there in the doorway.

"You really did it Oscar? He's really in there?" she said.

He nodded, smiling the smile of an assassin, a smiling assassin.

"But that's amazing. I mean I think I believed you but then part of me... well you know. But you did it, you really did it. I could never do that, I'm not strong enough. But you, wow Oscar."

"Wendy, I did it twice," he said ducking his head out to check the corridor.

Nobody about, coast clear.

"I did it twice."

"I don't understand Oscar, how could you kill him twice?" she asked.

"No not Llewellyn," he laughed. "I killed him and then I killed someone else."

"Oh shit Oscar, was it that bastard Marshall, slimy little brown nose got his head halfway up Llewellyn's arse, always trying to get his hand up my dress? Tell me it was him."

"No not him Wendy, it was nobody here. Just some shop assistant. She made fun of me this morning and I just kind of cracked, same as with Llewellyn. I strangled her with my tie and left her there in the change room."

"Jesus Oscar, two people in one day, amazing."

"Well that's why I'm here really. There's one more," he said, watching her closely, watching her eyes.

"One more, what do you mean one more?" said Wendy both surprised and excited.

"I mean I'm going to kill one more person… today, soon."

She got up from her little metal desk and came and stood in front of him.

"Who Oscar, who this time?"

"Nobody special Wendy, just some jogger, the bully that ran into me this morning. Spilt my breakfast all down me, ruined my clothes. Wouldn't apologise, just told me to fuck off."

Oscar felt the little twitch start up beside his eye, *tick tick tick tick*. It was real with the saying of it. It would happen with the saying of it and there it was, *'he's already dead.'*

"I'm leaving now and I won't be back. I'll tell them I have a meeting or something, but I won't be coming back ever. Look

Wendy when I leave I'm going to the bank to take out all my money. Sharon can fend for herself. Tomorrow I'll have to leave the city for good, early. I wanted to ask can I still come to your place tonight? I promise I'll be gone early in the morning. Nobody will connect us and when they question you you'll be fine, just say you don't really know me and well… you know."

"No no no Oscar," said Wendy, "you can't leave now, you can't just leave me here. Not now Oscar, I want to be with you, take me with you."

"Do you mean that Wendy, I mean really mean it?"

"Of course I do you dope. I love you Oscar. I love you and I want to go with you."

He stepped back surprised.

"But Wendy, after what I've done and what I'm about to do. You still want me? And what about the police? It's like you'd be an accomplice…"

"Yes Oscar, I still want you. I don't care about the police and I have lots of money Oscar, I have savings."

Oscar went back into the corridor and paced up and down, thinking, thinking, scheming. He stopped and turned, took her hands in his.

"Okay look Wendy. I love you too but I don't want you tied up in this. Here's what we'll do. I'll go tomorrow, have to, and you can follow me in a few weeks, like you've just quit and moved on. After this all blows over. Okay?"

"But Oscar…"

"No buts Wendy, it's the only way. We'll work out the details tonight."

And without another word he was gone, down the corridor.

He went back to his desk and put everything he wanted in his pockets, not much to show for all those years. Then he took the letter opener, that bringer of bad news, that dispatcher of arseholes, and he carefully poked it down the front of his jeans and under his shirt. Armed and dangerous, he picked up the Chivers file and went out to reception.

"Moira, I've got to go out for a bit, check a couple of details on this Chivers thing," he said holding up the file. "You'll probably be gone when I get back so I'll see you in the morning. If Llewellyn happens to come back tell him where I am and that he'll have the assessment on his desk at 9 o'clock in the morning."

"Okay Mr. Kingman, Oscar. Don't stay too late."

He went to the lunchroom and took the white plastic bag with the clothes from the metal locker. He checked the corridor, got in the lift and was gone. Gone down from level five to the ground.

ESCAPE

Oscar held the big old key in his hand like it was some kind of treasure. He carefully guided it into the lock and gently turned it. The lock gave with a muted click. He tried the door, just an inch then gathered his things together and stuffed everything in his bag. Socks and undies, shorts and shirts, plastic bag with a mess of potato salad tomatoes and cold cuts, then he was out the door. He crept along the hall to the kitchen and helped himself to whatever he could find. Orange juice and a soda from the fridge, bread and cookies from the pantry. He saw Glenda's handbag, sitting right out there in the open, on the countertop right beside Richard's wallet and car keys. He opened Glenda's handbag and took out a small purse. Opening the purse he took out the pile of banknotes and coins, left Richard's wallet untouched. He took the car keys and left through the front door. The car was parked on the lawn beside the house and Oscar unlocked it and climbed in, quiet as he could. In the glove compartment he found what he was looking for, a road map. *'This might work. This could work.'* He also took a torch, then he climbed out leaving the keys on the driver's seat and gently closed the door. He picked up his bag and walked briskly away from the beach house, leaving it there asleep in the night, undisturbed.

Oscar Kingman, nine years old was back on the road again.

ONE FINAL CHORE

Oscar Kingman left the building that housed the offices of Loughrans Loss Adjusters on its fifth level and made his way down the street past the park. He paused outside the glass front office building and looked up. Then he moved into the foyer, pressed the lift button and when it arrived, got in and hit four, Garvie Symmons Stockbrokers. Not believing he was actually doing this, not able to stop doing it. *He is already dead.*

The lift stopped on four, doors opened. He stayed where he was, checking checking, holding the doors open and peering out. Satisfied he was unobserved, he walked straight to the male restroom, into a cubicle to wait, to wait wait wait. Through the gap around the door, Oscar could see the entrance, all shiny white tiled and inviting. It was better than he could have expected. He sat on the seat to wait, more calm, more relaxed than he would have ever thought possible. He looked at his hands. Solid as a rock.

He waited twenty five minutes in that cubicle, poised ready, on hight alert. Three times the door swung open and someone came in. Three times it was a false alarm. Oscar was now getting a little anxious. The jogger had run him down on his way to work that morning, smashed into him dressed in his harlequin fucking shorts. He had seen the green backpack, figured the guys work clothes were in there. Figured the jerk would probably change back into his running gear and jog home, see if he couldn't ruin the day for a few more unsuspecting pedestrians, maybe plough down a pensioner or two.

'So where the hell is he?' thought Oscar, huddled in that cubicle, the letter opener now gripped firmly in his right hand.

Oscar Kingman, armed and dangerous.

And then suddenly he was there. The restroom door swung open and there he was. Oscar waited while the jogger, dressed now in a white shirt and sports pants, checked himself in the mirror. Oscar waited. He waited as the jogger hefted his green backpack onto the vanity shelf. He waited as he unzipped the green backpack and pulled out the red and black checkered running shorts and the red lycra top. Oscar calm now, picking his moment, knowing somehow, somehow knowing the right moment. Watching it all happen there in his mind before it happened. Oscar knew where the letter opener was going and knew when.

He waited while the jogger peeled off his white business shirt, saw his lean back, shoulder blades moving back and forth under the skin saying *stick me stick me*. Oscar waited while the jogger pulled on his red Lycra top, the bright fabric pulling down across his exposed kidney area saying s*tick me stick me*. But Oscar waited until the sports pants were off and the red and black checkered stretchy shorts were on, the whole outfit begging *stick me stick me*.

Now the jogger pulled out his running shoes, kicked off his black leathers and socks. On went the runners over his bare feet. The jogger lifted one foot after the other up to the edge of the vanity to tie the laces, occupied, head down, off balance. Maybe now Oscar, *stick me stick me*. But Oscar waited, seeing it happen before it happened. *He is already dead*. He waited until the jogger dropped his shoes and socks into the backpack then stuffed his white shirt in on top along with his sports pants. As he zipped the backpack, Oscar quietly pulled the latch on the cubicle door, calm, silent, moving now. *He is already dead*. Oscar came out of the cubicle as the jogger hefted the green backpack, the right strap in the crook of his right arm, left arm now bent back behind the left strap. Oscar had seen it, Oscar had waited. *He is already dead*.

Oscar crossed to the jogger in one step. The jogger saw him in the mirror, saw the letter opener, turned, struggling to free his arms. *Those eyes, there we go, those fucking bully eyes.*

"Remember me from this morning? You ruined my day then told me to fuck off."

But there was no hint of recall, no sign of recognition as Oscar stepped forward like a fencing master, the letter opener a foil in his hand. *En Garde!*

One thrust and the bringer of bad news slid up to the hilt in the jogger's right eye. Fluid spilled on Oscar's hand and cuff. He grabbed the twitching jerking jogger, the crazy dancing harlequin jogger and steered him into the cubicle. By the time he had him down on the toilet seat, he was still. One eye staring blankly ahead. Oscar pulled away the tangled backpack and jammed it between the jogger's knees, leaving him there legs parted, firmly planted on the toilet. He held the jogger's forehead and pulled the letter opener out, slightly disgusted with the soft feel and squishy sound of it. He wiped it on Wendy's panties and jammed it in his back pocket. Then he latched the door and waited.

No sound, nothing. Coast clear. He got a leg up on the cistern and climbed into the next cubicle, landing on the toilet seat. He checked his work, hanging there like some peeping tom, looking down on the dead jogger. *All good, it was all good.* The harlequin jogger was dead, justice was served. Oscar went out of the cubicle, bent down and saw the jogger's feet there. He looked at himself in the mirror, solid, totally visible Oscar Kingman. He pulled the letter opener from his back pocket, slid it down the front of his jeans and left.

BOOK THREE

FLIGHT

'Vengeance is Mine, and retribution,

In due time their foot will slip;

For the day of their calamity is near,

And the impending things

are hastening upon them.'

Deuteronomy 32:35

THE HUNTERS

Detective Roger Becker put down the phone and looked around the room, almost empty, the squads out beating the bushes. Just one or two bodies here, writing notes, catching their breath, waiting, waiting.

He'd been with Homicide for four years now and he still looked like a schoolteacher. He had that rare ability to walk out each night and shake off the stains, the sin, the horror. Just something in him. If you imagined your average homicide detective, made up a composite of what you had seen yourself and what you had seen on the television dramas, you might come up with overworked, hard living, hard drinking, chain smoking, badly dressed and teetering on the edge of sanity. All that crap, all that cleaning up after the rest of us, the bodies the blood, the brains up the wall, all of it. Someone had to clean it up, sort it out. Someone had to keep the lid on, but there was a price. You might come up with all that and most of the detectives in the department were some part of that equation, somewhere on that sliding scale. But not Becker, Becker was like some freak. Apparently it all just rolled off him and each night he climbed in his eco-friendly sedan and drove home to his wife and kids like he'd been selling shirts all day.

He looked across at his partner Casey. Gail Casey, thirty six, one bad marriage, one hundred bad relationships and little hope of ever settling down. Casey was classic homicide cop, like she'd studied it from a book. How to look, how to sound, how to grunt and scowl, how to dress bad, how to make the streets with a hangover and still get home each night. Home alone each night. Becker didn't mind, he liked her just the same. She got the job done, together they got the job done.

"Case."

"What?" she said looking up.

"Flowers wants us."

Louis Flowers was their sergeant. He was a career cop whose greatest skill was managing detectives. He also knew how to pick the best team for the job, was pretty good at that. This time there was only Becker and Casey, but he probably would have assigned them to this case anyway.

Becker wandered into Flowers' office and took a seat.

"Lou."

Gail Casey trailed in behind him, scowl on her face, hands in her pockets. She dropped into the seat next to Becker. Flowers looked at her, shook his head.

"Okay I've got a strange one here and with most everybody else out running round the jungle," he said waving his arms in the direction of the squad room, "you're it!"

He pushed a paper across his desk, Becker took it and read what Flowers was saying, as he said it.

"Woman named Elaine Benny, mid to late fifties found dead in the change room in the menswear department of a clothing store… you've got all the details there and you know the drill. Looks like she was strangled. There's two uniforms there and the Medical Examiner is on his way."

They arrived at the scene to find a uniformed officer at the entrance to the store, talking with a middle aged man. Casey flashed her badge and went inside while Becker stopped and spoke to the uniform.

"So, what do we know?"

"This is Mr. Bannister. He's the assistant manager here," said the uniform.

"Well er, it seems a customer complained to the cashier that there was nobody on duty in menswear. The cashier went looking for the sales assistant, she'd seen her on the floor just a few minutes before and figured she was around somewhere. She found Mrs. Benny in the change room. At first she thought she might have been unconscious, had a stroke or heart attack or something. She called me and well, I noticed the mark on her neck... and the smell. So anyway I called the police," said Mr. Bannister.

"Okay, thank you sir. We'll need to talk with you again shortly and with the cashier who found the deceased, so can I ask you to get everybody together in the staff room or somewhere? Is this the only entrance?"

"There's a delivery door," said Bannister, "but it's locked. I checked."

"Okay well until we tape this off I'd suggest you shut these doors and put some kind of sign up saying you're closed. You're to make sure nobody gets in or out unless they are with the police department, okay." Not a question, an order.

Becker made his way through the racks of clothing, right back to the change room. The other uniform stepped aside to let him in close. Casey was standing there holding the change room door open, the back end of the Medical Examiner down there on the floor, leaning over a body propped up against the wall. Casey stepped aside a bit for Becker to stick his head in there, the strong smell of piss wafted up to greet him. The ME turned and looked up at him.

"Hi Rog, what's happening?"

"You tell me Pete," said Becker, taking out his notebook.

"Well, pretty straight forward I think," said the ME standing up. "Been dead less than an hour I'd say. Strangled. If I had to make an initial guess I'd say whoever did this used a necktie, but used it like a hangman's noose, pulled up on the ends and pushed down on the knot. There's trauma on the neck here," he leant down, pushed the victims hair aside. "See here. Looks like the loose skin was pinched up, you know, caught in the knot. Pretty angry person did this," he said pointing lower down around the neck. "Lots of force needed to leave those kind of marks."

"Okay thanks," said Becker. "When will I get your report?"

"How long's a piece of string Rog, how long? Soon as I can obviously, but you know we're backing up in there. City's gone crazy."

"Okay," said Becker straightening up and moving aside so the ME could get out.

"Patience is a virtue Rog, patience is a virtue," said the Medical Examiner. "I'm done, she's all yours."

Becker and Casey spent the next ten minutes bending, crouching, twisting and holding their breaths. They picked through the scene, picked through the change room. A hair here, thread there. Label, shirt, gathered it all, tagged it all. Moved Elaine Benny this way and that to check under and around, around and under.

"What do you think Case?" asked Becker finally, straightening up.

"Well the way I see it... she's dead and she stinks," said Casey.

She said that because that's what a wisecracking hard-arse detective would say on television.

"Okay, sorry I asked. Let's go see if there's any security footage and talk to the staff."

• • •

It was 7.45 a.m. at police headquarters and the calls were coming thick and fast, coming from phones all over the city, coming from desks all over the city, other stations, other departments. Missing persons, runaways, assault and battery, domestic violence, murder, robbery, vice, bashing, rape. They came and they came thick and fast just like every other day of the week because, this is what was normal now, this was normal, this was the new world. Thick and fast, more and more.

Sometime between 7.45 and 10 o'clock in the morning, three calls came into missing persons. Lots of calls came into missing persons, but these three... these three. Two wives, one girlfriend.

"Yes Mrs. Llewellyn, how may I help you? And you've checked with his office?"

"Kingman you say. When was the last time you saw him Mrs. Kingman?"

"Please calm down Miss. I'm sorry, what do you prefer Miss or Ms? Right so he works at Garvie Symmons Stockbrokers?"

There was no call from Elaine Benny's apartment, just the whine of hungry cats, but no call.

DOWN FOR THE HOLIDAYS

While the morning briefings got underway at police headquarters, Oscar Kingman lay on his side in Wendy Legget's single bed. He watched her dress, he watched her tease him, loved it.

"Right," he said dropping onto his back as she zipped up her skirt, "you know what you're going to say if they ask you any questions about me, like we discussed last night?"

"Oscar, don't worry. Why would they ask me any more questions than they would ask anybody else? Nobody knows anything about us. I mean I can't believe it myself. I went to work yesterday and suddenly my whole life is upside down, everything changed. I can't believe this is happening."

She came and sat on the edge of the bed, reached under the covers.

"Wendy stop it," he laughed, pulling her hand away, wishing he hadn't, wishing she didn't have to go, wishing he didn't have to leave. "You know I have to go. Straight away I'll be a suspect and if they questioned me I'd crack into about a thousand pieces. I couldn't hold out Wendy. What I did well, that was some kind of raw energy. That's not me. They put any pressure on me and I'd just crack open, I feel it. If I go now, this morning, I'll be long gone before they find Llewellyn and he's the only one they can connect with me straight away. The others well, I guess they'll figure it out pretty quick. But I'll be long gone. People like me Wendy, we don't stand out, we're almost invisible. If I go now I'm sure I can get away with this."

"But where will you go?" asked Wendy grabbing his face.

"Best you don't know Wendy. It's just a few weeks and then when it has all died down you just resign, tell them you are

227

going travelling, tell them you have a new job, whatever. I'll contact you and then we can be together. It's best this way, the only way. Now go to work."

"I'm scared Oscar," she said in a tiny voice.

"Wendy, there's nothing to be scared of, you haven't done anything wrong."

"No not that," she said. "I'm scared that you won't call, scared you'll forget me and leave me here."

"Wendy… as long as I live and breathe, I swear I'm going to call you. Wendy, I love you."

After Wendy left Oscar got up and took a shower. As he stood under the warm water he tried to get his head around some kind of plan. The more he thought, the harder it got. Slowly realisation started to set in. He realised he had killed three people, murdered three people on impulse, in cold blood and now what? All this talk of running, resettling, phoning Wendy, telling her to join him. Oh the romance of it all, like some b-grade movie. Where would he go, how could he go? Not as Oscar Kingman that much was certain. All this realisation came a little late. He couldn't go anywhere as Oscar Kingman, too easily traced. Couldn't leave the country, there were records. Easily traced. Couldn't work, couldn't get social services if he stayed in the country. There were records. Easily traced. He was panicked, getting paranoid.

'Need to think it through.'

Of course the answer was obvious, he needed to *not* be Oscar Kingman anymore. Needed to be anyone but Oscar Kingman, but how? He was an impulsive murderer, not a career criminal. He couldn't just rock up to a downtown bar, pass through a side door and enlist the help of someone called 'Lefty' or 'Fingers' to help him get a new identity. There was no side door. There was no Lefty or Fingers. There probably was, but not amongst Oscar Kingman's circle of acquaintances. For that matter Oscar Kingman didn't even have a circle of acquaintances.

He got out of the shower and dried off, then sat on the bed and counted out the money from the two accounts he had closed the day before. Just under fourteen thousand dollars. Not much to show, not much to show. He went to Wendy's closet and found a small travel bag. He jammed in the money and his meagre belongings and then he checked Wendy's apartment, using a handkerchief to wipe down handles and things he had touched. Seen that done on television, remove the evidence, wipe the prints. He had no idea if this worked or not but it seemed sensible.

He took the travel bag and walked a few blocks to the bus stop, waited, waited. He sat on the bus, his money on his knees in the bag. He was close to tears, feeling desperate and lonely. As much alone as ever he had been, moving away from all that was suddenly good in his life. He looked at the bag, everything he owned now in that bag. In that little bag. Here he was again, life gone full circle. Everything he owned in that little travel bag. It was just like the last time he'd run away. The time he'd run away from his grandfather's beach house. Oscar Kingman thought about that time and suddenly, without even knowing how it happened there was his answer. He was running again, only this time he was running towards his grandfather's beach house.

He changed buses and headed for SouthPark Mall. On the way, he made a list. He shopped quickly and frugally, starting with a larger travel bag. An hour later he was in a cab headed down South Boulevard with some new clothes and enough supplies to last him a couple of days. The cab dropped him at a car dealership and he bought a beat up old silver Toyota for cash. The dealer handed him all the usual shit but Oscar didn't care. It was the most nondescript car on the lot and after being assured by the salesman that it would get him across the country to California with no problems, he headed west, then south, then east. *'Cover your tracks, cover your tracks.'* Then Oscar Kingman turned south east, almost invisible out there in his almost invisible car. Five hours later he came over that last little rise before the inlet. It had been many years since he was last there, so he had no idea what to expect. As he approached the coast, the whole place seemed to be golf courses. Resorts and country clubs nestled proudly in the green. Big money.

When he got to the village it had spread further inland and down along the inlet, but around the water's edge it seemed the same, preserved somehow. After a series of false starts and dead ends, he finally found the road out of town, the road his grandfather had driven all those years ago. It was wider now and paved, lined first with shops and small businesses and finally with houses. He stopped at a convenience store and bought more supplies including fresh eggs, bread, milk and fruit. Back in the car the panic returned, little things started popping into his head. Little things started poking him in the chest.

'This close, so close. What if the beach house was gone? What if he couldn't recognise it? What if his grandparents had sold it?' Then it hit him. They were probably dead now and if they were alive they'd be in their late eighties. *'What if someone else lived there now? What was he thinking?'*

He leant his head on the steering wheel, his forehead against the fake leather, his thoughts in turmoil. Suddenly he sat back up and slammed his palm against the wheel. *'No point hanging around here. Go find out. Stupid Oscar!'*

The forest he remembered was all but gone, but the marram grass plain was still there. Big signboards advertised land for sale, large houses dotted here and there around the beachgrass expanse, coloured bunting marking out the beachside dreams. He found the turnoff, which was now a hard gravel road instead of the old sand track. There were more houses now along the dunes, bigger houses, but Oscar could see some of the old shacks still there in the dune grass. He drove along the track toward the end and there it was, the old white shack with yellow doors and window frames. There was a gate across the driveway now. Some trees had been planted along the road front and there was a new garage in the yard, painted white with yellow trim to match the house. Oscar parked the car, opened the gate and wandered down the drive.

He walked up to the door, knocked.

"Anyone home? Hello, anybody home?"

Nothing stirred in the beach house, the only sound the buzz of insects and the gentle growl of the ocean. He walked around to the front and climbed the steps to the verandah, peered in the windows, in through the half glass bedroom door. The memory struck him like a blow. There he was. There he was in there on that bed, young Oscar Kingman looking straight at him. He felt dizzy, saw his own reflection shimmer and form on the glass. Shaken, he dropped into a metal chair, the old cane one gone now, a thing of the past. He calmed down, looked out at the ocean. The dunes smaller, the beach closer. The house too seemed much smaller than he remembered, shrunken with time. Finally he rose and went back to the front door. He reached up and felt around the top of the porch frame, fingers scrabbling back and forth like some crab, fingers finding the prize, fingers finding the key.

Oscar looked at the key, it was clean. He unlocked the door, called again.

"Hello, anybody home?"

Quieter still now, inside. Just a fly in there somewhere and the waves way off. The house smelled musky, was a little dusty and damp in places. Oscar started in the kitchen, checked the cupboards, the drawers. The refrigerator was held open with a broomstick. Hard to say, stuff looked familiar, old, unchanged. *'Do I remember this plate?'* The lounge room had sheets thrown over the furniture. He lifted the covers. *'Do I remember this sofa, do I remember this seat?'* He checked every room but one. Went past that door about three times, saw the big old key poking out of that big lock. He wanted to go in, but didn't want to go in. Didn't want to see that frightened boy in there on that bed. The future looked tough enough, the past was just too painful.

Slowly he put the pieces together. The electricity was on. There were photos, a photo of his grandfather and some fishing buddies. His grandfather older but still recognisable, standing there laughing with his mates and the catch. There was mail open on the kitchen table addressed to Richard Kingman. It felt strange to Oscar, strange and somehow sad to see that name there, Richard Kingman. Kingman, his name, his grandfather, his family. What might have been. In a frame by the bedside in the main bedroom there was a picture of Glenda, his hateful grandmother, and slid in the edge of the frame, a holy card, a liturgy to that sainted woman, dead now twelve years according to the date on the card. The wardrobe held only a man's clothes, an old man's clothes. The house slowly came alive and spoke of his grandfather and Oscar realised that his grandfather was still alive, still came here sometimes. He went back along the hall and stood at that bedroom door, just stood and stared. And then he did it. He reached down and turned the handle. The bedroom was exactly the same as he remembered. Just the old single bed, the old pine drawers, the model boat, all of it and no ghosts. No sign of young Oscar Kingman, gone now, run away. He sat on the bed, at peace. At peace... a rare thing for Oscar Kingman.

Oscar Kingman, down for the holidays.

He sat there a long time. Shadows crept across the floor, light dimmed. He made his decision. It was not really a difficult decision, not really a choice at all. There was no place else that

Oscar could think of to go. It was more than twenty seven years since he'd had any contact with his family. This would do, would have to do. He went outside and brought the car down, parked it behind the new shed and closed the gate. Tomorrow he'd look in the shed, but for now he'd get inside, have something to eat and make up a bed. He turned on the refrigerator and put some of his food in.

Oscar Kingman, down for the holidays.

Oscar wasn't much of a cook really, but after a meal of baked beans on toast he felt a little better. He opened Richard's drink cabinet, poured himself a drop of Macallans, then went into the bedroom and lay on the bed. He was asleep before the single malt had finished warming his body.

DISCOVERIES

Moira arrived at work at 8.15, first through the door at Loughrans Loss Adjusters. She got busy turning on lights, copiers and computers, filling the coffee machine, checking the answering machine. By 8.45 everybody was at their desk but Oscar Kingman and Edmund Llewellyn. She hoped Oscar made it in before Llewellyn, didn't want to see a repeat of what had happened the day before.

At precisely 8.50 a.m. the phone rang.

"Loughrans Loss Adjusters how may I direct your call."

"Hello Moira is that you?"

"Yes Mrs. Llewellyn. How are you this morning?"

"Ah yes hi, sorry Moira, look is Edmund there?"

"No he hasn't come in yet Mrs. Llewellyn," said Moira. "Is there a problem?"

"Well ah… I don't know," said Mrs. Llewellyn sounding quite lost and confused. "It's just that he didn't come home last night. I've reported him missing. It's not like him you know."

"Gosh I'm sure there's a reason Mrs. Llewellyn. I'm sure he'll turn up here any minute. I'll get him to call you as soon as he comes in okay?" said Moira.

"Well, okay I guess," replied Mrs. Llewellyn and hung up.

Moira looked up to see Wendy Legget standing there.

"Oh hi Wendy."

"Hi Moira," said Wendy brandishing a file. "Do you know when Mr. Llewellyn will be in? He wanted this file yesterday, said it was urgent, but then he left early."

"No," replied Moira seemingly lost in thought. "That was Mrs. Llewellyn. She was looking for him too. Seems he never went home last night."

She pulled out a key on a chain and unlocked the key cabinet below the counter. She took out a key on a green tag, Llewellyn's office spare.

"Guess I'd better go check his office," she said to Wendy.

"Okay well I'll just leave this on his desk," said Wendy following Moira across the general office.

"Mr. Kingman's not here either," said Moira. "I hope he gets here before Llewellyn shows up."

Moira turned the lock in the key and opened the office door. She flicked on the light. Wendy could barely contain herself.

"Oh dear, bit woofy in here. Give me that file and I'll just leave it on his desk," said Moira fanning her hand under her nose as she went around the desk. She pulled on the chair, went to sit down and check her boss's diary. Something in the way, something under the desk. Llewellyn's leg, Llewellyn's body, jammed in down there. The floor black with blood.

"Oh shit! Oh shit shit shit!" screamed Moira. "It's Mr. Llewellyn. He's here. Oh shit! Shit shit. Christ Wendy, I think he's dead. Quick, go get Carver."

"What! Are you sure?" said Wendy all innocent like and moving around the desk. "Oh my God," she screamed convincingly, looking down at Llewellyn's body.

All hell broke loose as the rest of the staff piled into Llewellyn's office to gawk and muse, muse and gawk. The Welsh knight was definitely well and truly dead.

"What the fuck!"

"Don't touch him."

"Anybody called the police?"

"What's going on here?" said Ron Carver, Assistant Manager, elbowing his way through the gawkers.

By 9.30 a.m. the office was a designated crime scene.

• • •

A little later that morning, a block and a half away, Detective Eric Cotton was sat in the foyer of Garvie Symmons Stockbrokers finishing up the interview with the cleaner and the maintenance man who had found the body sitting propped on a toilet in the men's room. He looked up as Detective Jack Gill came into the foyer.

"Whatya got Gillie, anything?" he said getting up and going over to his partner.

"Well maybe," said Gill. "When Mrs.... Sutton? Right. When Mrs. Sutton here came to clean, the cubicle door was locked. She called Leonard here and he had to force to door open. Whoever killed this guy couldn't fit under the door so, after they locked it from the inside, he or she must have climbed over into the next cubicle. There's a barely visible shoe print, a mans I think, on the top of the cistern and if the perp wasn't wearing gloves there could be fingerprints around the top of the dividing wall. Dunno though, seems pretty cool and coldblooded, sorta planned out."

"Why's that Sherlock?" asked Cotton.

"Well the staff said the dead guy jogs to work and home again in that lycra outfit, jeez. So he normally goes in there to change before heading home. He did that last night and that's the last anyone saw of him. I'd say he was put in the cubicle after he got popped."

The cleaner looked up, upset, not amused.

"Sorry... murdered. He got put in there after he was murdered. He still had his pants up. So we'll get 'em to do the whole room for prints."

"Okay well, there's Malik," said Cotton, looking over his partner's shoulder. "You go and see him and I'll wrap it up here."

Gill turned to see the Medical Examiner, Peter Malik heading from the lift to the restroom, where a uniformed officer opened the door for him. He gave his partner the thumbs up and headed back out to the restroom.

"Hiya Pete."

Malik looked up to see Detective Jack Gill come through the door. He liked Gill. Thought he was a strait shooter who told it like it was even when that upset people, which was pretty often. But he knew Gill had a sharp mind and scored high on hunches.

"Hi Jack, what we got here?" said Malik stepping aside to let the photographer out of the cubicle.

Gill pulled out his notepad.

"One dead male, Daniel Mills, twenty six years old with shit dress sense. I couldn't find any damage or wounds anywhere but the right eye. Bit of blood and stuff weeping out there, but a lot of contusion in the surrounding area. Reckon he was stabbed out here, right in the eye, then placed in there all propped up like he's taking a dump. Whoever did it locked him in and probably went over the top into the next stall. I'm guessing revenge killing. Wanted to look this guy in the eye, right up close then bingo! Ten bucks on it."

Pete Malik laughed.

"Yeah sure, when was the last time you were wrong?" he said. "All right, let's take a look."

The ME went into the stall and Gill watched from the door. He spent a lot of time at the right eye, poking prodding, swabbing and gathering. That eye past all seeing now.

"We need to lose this backpack, give me a hand Jack, careful," he said. "Okay now help me tilt him forward."

They pushed the harlequin jogger backwards and forwards, left and right, lifted him up and placed him down again until Malik was satisfied.

"Okay, the forensic boys can have the body now," he said as they backed out of the cubicle.

Eric Cotton was standing there holding the restroom door open. The ME closed his bag and all three went out into the foyer.

"Well was I right or was I right?" asked Gill.

"It's my job to determine the cause of death Jack. Your job to fill in the gaps," he laughed. "But on a serious note, you boys might have a bit of a problem with this one."

"How so?" asked Eric Cotton.

"Well I might be wrong, but that wound. He was stabbed in the eye, but the eyeball is intact. The wound is in the socket behind the eyeball so the weapon must have pushed the eyeball aside. There's blood and traces of clear fluid down his cheek, my guess is that it's cerebrospinal fluid. The blade probably passed right through the lateral ventricle or the third ventricle and back into the brain. Thing is it's a very narrow wound, narrow and long. Had to be to get back that far."

"What you mean something like a needle, knitting needle maybe?" said Cotton.

"Yeah, but flat, the wound is slightly flat."

"Okay," said Gill, "we've got a long thin flat weapon, through the eye socket into the brain. So apart from having to find the weapon and the guy who stuck it in there, why do we have a problem?"

"Because," said Malik pausing for effect, "I've just seen the same type of wound in the neck of a victim right around the corner."

"Oh shit," drawled Cotton. "You mean the insurance office, Torres and Brosa?"

"That's the one yes."

"But hang on, surely there's lots of long thin flat sharp weapons out there?" offered Jack Gill.

"Sure there is," replied Malik. "But who said anything about sharp. This weapon wasn't sharp. If it had been it probably would have pierced the eyeball. The other victim was stabbed in the throat, went right through and hit the skin on the other side but didn't break through. Lots of haemorrhaging right there under the skin but no puncture. Must have pushed the skin well out, but wasn't sharp enough to break through. No point on the thing at all maybe."

"Screwdriver?" ventured Gill.

"It's possible yes," said Malik, "but it would still have to be pretty old and blunt."

"Okay," mused Gill, "we got two victims couple of blocks apart, both of them killed sometime yesterday afternoon or evening right?"

Pete Malik nodded.

"Both," continued Jack Gill, "killed yesterday afternoon or evening and both with a similar long flat thin blunt weapon."

"Looks like it at this stage, but let's not get ahead of ourselves here," said Malik.

"Right," said Gill. "But I think we can assume they both got popped by the same person. I'm going to anyway."

THE VISITORS

Oscar woke in a sweat. It took him a little while to get sorted, to figure out where he was, then it all came rushing back. Llewellyn, Miss Elaine, the jogger, Wendy… all of it came back. He was at the beach, his grandfather's house.

There was someone there, someone in the house with him. He felt it. He felt the hairs rise on his neck, the sweat bead and trickle across his soft stomach. There was somebody there, somebody in the house. He waited for courage, frozen in fear. He waited for courage.

'Get up and look, get up and look pussy!'

He lay there still as death and listened to the sounds of the house. The tick of the old tin roof cooling in the night. *Tick.* The timber frame trading back the heat of the day. *Tick.* He waited.

The next noise, *'the next noise and I'm up,'* he told himself. *'Maybe the one after this.'*

Tick!

And he was up off the bed, moving in the dull half light. Voices now, voices. There was someone in the house, someone talking. Moving now through the door and into the hall, his feet catching on something on the floor. He stooped down and picked up whatever it was, feeling it warm and shiny in his fingers, peering at it not knowing. The voices now louder, laughing, grunting, coming from the other bedroom. The light on and shining out under the door. Something else there, something else in the glow there, something pink. He moved closer, wanting to but not wanting to… saw what it was. He knelt down and took the pink panties in both hands and buried his face in them, in Wendy. Wendy's pink panties there in his hand along with the red and black lycra running shorts… now he saw them. Now he knew. He rose up from the floor and listened at the door, the grunting and the laughing. He turned the handle slowly and there was Wendy laughing on the bed, on her back in his grandfather's double bed. Laughing as the jogger grunted over her, crashed into her, hump backed like some demon dog and, as Oscar watched, she turned to face him, stared straight at him defiant, each grunt a blow to the heart, each laugh a betrayal. Then suddenly the jogger was off Wendy and on him, stabbing, thrusting with the letter opener.

"But you're dead. You're dead, I killed you," screamed Oscar, clutching his bloodied gut, his life escaping between his fingers.

Oscar woke gasping, terrified. He leapt from the bed and switched on the light, breath coming in great desperate gasps, heart pounding. A dream, a dream. It was just a dream. He sat back on the edge of the bed, pulled up his t-shirt, felt his stomach, nothing. Nothing there… a nightmare.

The house was quiet, the only noise the distant sound of small waves pushing relentlessly against the sand. He sat and calmed himself, his mouth dry and his throat parched. He stood and walked to the door, still nervy. Opening the door, he peered out along the hallway. All quiet, just the waves.

'Idiot,' he said to himself, shaking off the last shred of fear.

He went to the kitchen, turned on the light, got himself a glass of water and leant against the kitchen sink while he drank it. He thought of Wendy, then thought of her making it in there on his grandfather's bed. Making it with the jogger.

'Fucking nightmares, weird shit.'

Oscar flicked off the kitchen light and went down the hall to the bedroom. *'Get some sleep,'* he told himself.

He pulled the bedroom door closed behind him and turned just in time to see Edmund Llewellyn lunge across the room at him. Lunge at him eyes all crazy and the letter opener still stuck through his throat. He turned and pulled the door open but Llewellyn slammed the flat of his hand against it banging it closed. He was trapped, Llewellyn's arm across his shoulder, his face just inches away. Oscar smelt pickles. Pickles and something else, realised he had pissed himself.

"Thought you could kill me that easy you miserable little fuck," spat Llewellyn. "Thought I was dead did you Kingman?"

Oscar turned his head away, jammed his eyes shut. *'How could this be happening?'*

"Look at me Kingman," screamed Llewellyn, his hand coming off the door and clutching Oscar's throat, squeezing. "Look at me!"

Oscar opened his eyes, tried not to, didn't want to, but opened them anyway.

"Your turn now Oscar," said Llewellyn right up close.

Then he pushed back and held Oscar against the door with his left arm extended, while he reached up with his right hand and pulled on the letter opener that was still jammed in his neck. Bit tight at first, but then easy, slid out easy. Oscar tried not to look, not to see it. Couldn't not see it. Saw it draw out and finally saw that little slit, the trickle of blood there as the letter opener, the bringer of bad news, came away. Llewellyn placed the tip against Oscar's throat.

"Your turn now Kingman."

Oscar screamed a scream like would wake a city. He shot upright in bed, clutching his throat, choking gasping, crying now. He staggered out of bed and turned on the light. No Llewellyn, no letter opener. *No no no no no!* Choking, gasping, struggling to breath, heart going like a damned jackhammer. A dream. *A dream a dream a dream!* Another dream, nightmare, maybe the same one. Hard to tell, hard to tell. He slumped onto the floor, his back against the door, tried to calm himself, shaking, shuddering. Still unsure, still scared and shivering. Not cold, just shivering. After a long time he pushed himself up and stood looking around the room. Then he opened the bedroom door, put his hand out, out there in that darkness where demons dwelt, and groped around for the key. *'Be calm, be calm.'*

He pulled the key out of the lock and gently closed the door again.

'No sudden noises Oscar, gently Oscar gently, don't stir anything up.'

He locked the door. Locked himself in. Knew it was a nightmare but was scared witless anyway. With the door locked and the key grasped firmly in his hand he went back to the bed, leaving the light on.

'That's it Oscar, leave the light on. They can't get you with the light on. They can't exist with the light on, can't get you.'

In gradual stages he lay down. Bit by bit he eased down until he was lying on his back, light on, eyes wide and alert. He tried to laugh at himself, failed. Lay there feeling like a fool and a coward, like a loser.

At some point in those early hours of the morning before dawn, his eyes closed. He couldn't fight it anymore. His eyes closed and he slept. He slept a peaceful sleep with no dreams or nightmares. Oscar Kingman exhausted after one of the hardest days of his life. Oscar Kingman needing a break, a holiday, sleeping like a baby there on that soft safe bed in that beach house. The waves on the shore keeping time with his deep breathing.

Oscar woke not long after sunrise. The light and warmth of it creeping around the edge of the drapes. He lay on his side, eyes closed for a few minutes, unsure where he was, trying to figure it out. He opened his eyes and saw the shell wallpaper and it all came back to him. The nightmares came back to him. But he'd made it. The sun was out and he had made it through the night. He rolled onto his back and looked up at the light, still on up there. Now he could laugh at himself, now the sun was out and all. He was hungry.

'Right,' he said to himself, *'up!'*

He threw back the blanket and there she was.

Miss Elaine was slumped down on the floor, her back against the wall, her face sick purple, her eyes more purple still and bulging out like she was some cartoon character. Her face purple and her hands clutching like claws. Oscar screamed, threw up. Hard to say what happened first. He dived back under the covers.

Oscar woke not long after sunrise. The light and warmth of it creeping around the edge of the drapes. He lay on his side eyes closed for a few minutes, unsure where he was, trying to figure it. He opened his eyes and saw the shell wallpaper and it all came back to him. Was she there? Was Miss Elaine there?

'Am I awake, am I asleep?'

He could no longer tell, felt like he was awake but could he be sure? Was she there? He rolled onto his back and looked up at the light, still on up there. He closed his eyes and rolled onto his other side, opened them slowly. Nobody there. No Miss Elaine slumped there, no Edmund Llewellyn stood there, nothing, nobody. He realised he was hungry.

'Right,' he said to himself with forced bravado, *'up!'*

He threw back the blanket and went to the door, shook his head when he found it locked, but couldn't do it yet, couldn't unlock that damned door yet. He went to the verandah door, drew back the curtains and light flooded into the room. Light heat and life. He held his hand up against the glare of the sun out on the water and peered across the ocean with one eye. He turned back into the room, looking for confirmation, proof he was really awake. He went to the model boat there on the old pine chest of drawers, the stick that formed the boom, his instrument of escape repaired, glued back together. All those years ago.

Oscar shook his head, shrugged off the doubt, went to the door and unlocked it. In the kitchen he made a quick breakfast of cereal and coffee, took it to the lounge room and turned on the television. He cycled through the channels, all the news, found nothing, nothing nothing nothing until… there it was!

"Shop assistant Elaine Benny was found strangled at her workplace blah blah blah. Police are searching for these people seen leaving the store shortly after Miss Benny was last seen alive. Police are today reviewing footage from other security cameras in the area and are hopeful of an early arrest, blah blah blah."

A woman with a stroller, two men in suits, chatting as they walked out, a man in a shirt and jeans carrying something rolled up in one hand. Oscar felt the air go out of the room, sucked harder at it. There he was, right there on the tv screen. Of course it was a fuzzy, heavily pixilated black and white image and it was impossible to identify him, but they were looking for footage from other cameras, that's what they had said. Cameras cameras, *'what the hell is the matter with me, cameras!'*

Maybe they would find more footage, maybe clear enough to show someone who looked like Oscar Kingman, so he needed not to look like Oscar Kingman and as soon as possible. He decided not to watch any more, not to follow it down. It would

just distract him. Best just assume the worst, get on with it and sort out a disguise.

'Stay calm Oscar. Apart from the clerk at the convenience store, nobody down here has laid eyes on you.'

LET'S NOT GET AHEAD OF OURSELVES

It was early morning the day after the discovery of the bodies at Loughrans Loss Adjusters and Garvie Symmons Stockbrokers. The squad room was already buzzing. Captain Henry Worrell stood at the front of the room, deep in conversation with two of his sergeants. Agreement reached, plans made, orders given, heads nodding. Worrell turned to face the room.

"Okay, drop what you are doing and listen up."

Bit by bit the buzz died off, Worrell waited.

"Right. We have the medical examiners preliminary reports on the Llewellyn and Mills murders. The full autopsy reports will take a few days. The only thing we know for certain today that we didn't know yesterday, is the cause of death. Single stab wound in both cases, no other wounds evident. So we've got two murders with very similar MOs."

He went to the board and pointed at the photos.

"Edmund Llewellyn, caucasian male thirty three years old, stab wound to the neck, body concealed under his desk at his place of work. The ME suggests that his nose and mouth were held closed and or he was smothered while he bled out. The angle of entry of the weapon suggests that whoever killed him came around behind his chair, held something over his face and stabbed down like so, before he had a chance to stand or defend himself."

He mimed the action.

"The fact his mouth was covered would also explain why people sitting at their desks just twenty feet away didn't hear a thing. Our other victim, Daniel Mills, was also a caucasian male.

He was twenty six years old and died of a stab wound that passed through the right eye socket and lodged in his brain. His body was concealed in a toilet cubicle at his place of work. Nobody heard anything and nobody saw anything suspicious.

We have one person of interest connected with the first victim, but at this stage we can establish no link between our person of interest and the second victim. Nor can we establish any connection between the victims. The Medical Examiner suggests a very high probability that the same weapon was used in both murders. If we assume that this is the work of one person or one group of persons, that doesn't necessarily suggest that we have a serial killer scenario but, we need to be alert to the possibility.

The media have already got onto our suspect and his face is all over the tv and newspapers, so that horse has bolted. I personally don't think we've got a serial killer, I think maybe we've got one nut job who killed two people. That's likely the end of it, but we don't want the media screaming serial killer and causing a panic. I don't have to tell you what that's like. It brings the crazies out of the woodwork and we waste valuable time and resources trying to sort real leads from bogus leads. We are a bit thin on the ground at the moment, so here's how we are going to work it. We're going to stick with the two teams who are already individually assigned to these two cases, but I want those teams working as one unit. Detective Cotton will take point with Gill, Brosa and Torres. Cotton will report to Sergeant Flowers. If we need more manpower your sergeant will try and arrange it."

He turned back to the board and tapped on the second row of photos.

"I want the rest of you to take a good look at these photos, think about the MO. You come across anything like this on your own cases, however remote, bring it to your sergeant's attention immediately. I'll leave you with Sergeant Flowers who'll fill in the details."

"So," said Flowers as Worrell left the room, "this person of interest then. We've had to officially release details to the press of one Oscar Kingman, employee at Loughrans Loss Adjusters where our first victim, Edmund Llewellyn, was the manager. At this stage he's posted as missing and wanted for questioning. Detective Brosa has provided us with a potential motive in the first murder. Apparently this Edmund Llewellyn liked to push his weight around, he was a bully. There is a long history of trouble between him and our suspect Kingman. On the day of his murder, Llewellyn had publicly humiliated Oscar Kingman in front of the rest of the staff. Maybe Kingman finally snapped, which seems pretty plausible, but as the captain said, we've got nothing connecting Kingman with the second victim. If we assume Kingman is up for both murders, there must be a link. Jack, I want you and Eric to run down that connection while Torres and Brosa find this Oscar Kingman. I know you interviewed Kingman's wife yesterday, but do it again and push a bit harder. Then get back to Loughrans and interview all the staff."

"But sarge there's over fifty of them," complained Torres.

"What about yesterday? Who did you interview yesterday?" asked Flowers.

Torres flipped open his notebook.

"Four of them," he replied. "The two women who found the body, the assistant manager and let's see, one other person, a clerk named Adrian Bygreaves."

"Okay, well there's nothing else for it. It's going to be a long day, so get to it," said Sergeant Flowers.

A VISIT FROM GRANDFATHER.

Oscar finished his coffee and went outside. He was relieved to find that there were still no other buildings overlooking his grandfather's beach house. From the front verandah he could just make out the roof of the closest house which was nestled in the dunes, back along the road. He went inside and took down the set of keys he had seen hanging inside the pantry. Five minutes later he had the side door to the garage open. It was gloomy in there, just a small window with mesh curtains to supply natural light. He searched around by the door and found a switch. There was a little sailboat on a trailer and some old furniture. The walls were all neatly hung about with fishing rods and life preservers, hiking gear, tools, ropes, hoses and all sorts of crap that his grandfather must have figured was worth keeping. Everything in its place and a place for everything. Oscar opened the big front door and moved the little boat back to make room for his Toyota.

Back inside the house he went to the bathroom and stood looking at himself in the mirror searching for clues how not to look like Oscar Kingman. Maybe shave the hair off, what was left of it, or maybe dye it and style it. He could try not shaving, grow a beard. Shit, hair grew faster on his chin than on his head anyway, so that was an option. Maybe find some glasses. He'd search the whole house, see what he could find, how long he could last without going to a shop, going out in the open.

An hour later he sat looking at the pile of stuff he had found. The pantry had yielded a decent supply of dried and canned food, powdered milk and snacks. He figured he had enough to last maybe two weeks. That should be long enough. He stacked all the food away. Knew what he had now, knew where it all was. Maybe in a few weeks he could contact Wendy. He sat there thinking about Wendy, Wendy Legget, love of his life. Wendy Legget, gangster's moll, soon to join him on the run.

He picked up the glasses he had found in his grandfather's bedside cabinet, put them on. They were a little strong, hard for his eyes to manage, but he went to the bathroom and checked himself out. *'This could work. No time like the present, let's get it done.'*

He'd found lather and a razor, so he dug these out now and got to work shaving his scalp. He towelled off and stood looking at the new Oscar in the mirror. He put the glasses on and was startled at how different he looked. A beard and a different style of clothing and he figured he'd hardly recognise himself. Trendy Oscar. *'This could work!'*

The other thing he had found was a pile of sleeping tablets. These might get him through the night, send him deep, too deep for the demons to find him.

He heard a motor, looked out the kitchen window to see a small truck go past southwards. He heard it stop not far away, squeak of brakes, engine switched off. He remembered from his walk all those years ago that there had been only one old house down that way, a long way away, so where did that truck go. He went out and looked along the road but could see nothing, so he went down onto the beach and walked south. The dunes were a bit higher here, so he clambered up and sat in the marram grass, listening. Nothing. He stood up and wandered along the top of the dunes, his city shoes filled with sand and then he saw it. A building site. Just a house frame, that's all, no problems. A guy unloading lumber. Oscar waited until the truck left, then he went through the site and walked to the very end of the road. Here and there an access had been carved in, house sites cleared. Here and there a construction shed, pegs in the ground, progress coming. The old place at the end of the road was gone, replaced now by a modern two storey house that crested the dunes. There was a blue sedan in the drive and Oscar ducked off the road into the scrub as he saw a woman planting something beside the driveway.

He clambered back over the dunes and down to the beach, then turned north and wandered right past his grandfather's house to the next property, the roof he could see from the verandah. It was a big house, sat bold on top of the dunes. The doors out onto the front deck were open and he could hear music coming from inside. Stairs from the deck joined a long boardwalk that came across the dunes to the beach.

Oscar turned and made his way back down the beach. It was getting late, the sun hanging low and he was hungry. He would cheer himself up with a good meal. *Everything would work out, everything would be okay.*

After he had eaten he went through the bookshelves. There were books here, good books. He ran his finger along the spines, some fresh and new, some old and torn, but all there waiting. From those very early days in boarding school, Oscar had escaped into that magic world of fantasy between the pages. He'd ridden with Jesse James, fought in the Spanish Civil War with Ernest Hemingway, travelled in the asteroid belt with Isaac Asimov. Books had been his saviour. He had been a voracious reader, devouring whatever he could lay his hands on. Western, sci-fi, thriller, mystery and then on through the astounding world of the classics to poetry, non fiction, history and bio. He'd suffered many a beating when he was caught reading with a torch under the bedclothes after lights out. Then when he escaped that hell, when he finished school, it all stopped, the reading all stopped. With that escape there was no more need for escapism. Pretty much the only thing he ever read after that were cereal boxes and girlie mags.

When Sharon had walked out on him, when she left to go live with her parents and the first of the harpies was born, he'd started reading again. He'd had the time. Not to escape but to learn, to enjoy. But she came back. She came back and took away his time, took away his peace and quiet, took away his very air. But there were books here, good books and Oscar had all the time, all the peace and quiet and all the air he needed.

His finger came to a rest on a beat up old red spine, the gold leaf title almost rubbed away, but still just visible. Tom Sawyer, he would start with Tom Sawyer. He took it down and pressed it to his nose. It smelt musty, it smelt of the ocean, it smelt like adventure. He went through the bedroom, out onto the verandah and was soon off with Tom on his adventures. After an hour or so he was slouched snoring in that chair with the book forgotten on his lap and his mouth open. Oscar had had a rough night, he was catching up.

. . .

The second night at the beach house was just like the first, one sleeping tablet just not enough. They all came to haunt him, to terrify him, all the phantoms, accusing, screaming, taunting. Frightened, alone and scared to close his eyes, he finally gave up and got out of bed. For the next two nights he sat up with every light in the place burning brightly. He jumped at every sound, his heart seemed to stop and start with every creak of the old house. He read, listened to the radio and watched television, avoiding all the news breaks. He prayed for the sun to rise, for the light to wrest him from his armageddon. Sometime around dawn each day he fell into a deep exhausted slumber as the sun burst through the drapes and crept across the lounge room floor.

. . .

He came awake to a noise, not sure at first what it was. A telephone. A telephone was ringing, in the house. He pushed himself up, shook out the kink in his neck and followed the noise through to the kitchen. The culprit was fixed on the wall by the fridge. Ringing ringing ringing. Oscar stood looking at the thing, who, what? Then it stopped. It stopped so suddenly that it startled him. The ringing gone now from the room but still there in his head.

'Who, what? Couldn't be anything to do with him, just somebody looking for his grandfather, had to be.'

He went back to his book, but an hour later it rang again and an hour after that and an hour after that. And an hour after that Oscar sat at the table watching it, waiting, but it never rang again.

Oscar read until the sun went down, then he closed all the drapes and checked for gaps. He switched on the kitchen and the bedroom lights then went outside and walked around the house checking. All dark, all good. He settled in at the kitchen table and read until late, just him and Tom there in that house, staying up late making the night shorter. Less time for demons. At around eleven o'clock he made himself an omelet and some toast, then he took two sleeping tablets and went to bed to read himself to sleep.

Oscar woke. He woke knowing there was someone there, heard the breathing. They were back to taunt him. *'Was this how it would always be, every night, every damned night? Was this his punishment?'* He slowly raised one eyelid. Nothing there, just a sense in the darkness, but gradually he could make out a faint patch where the pine drawers would be. Something slightly darker than the darkness itself.

'Just a dream, just a nightmare, just a dream. Ignore it. Just a nightmare.'

He lay there petrified, trying to wake up. Petrified and watching as the shape grew even more dark against the darkness, separated and moved now across the room. Oscar was frozen in fear, he wanted to scream, to cry. Oscar petrified. Suddenly the room was flooded with light and there stood his grandfather, arm outstretched, fingers on the light switch. The horror of it. The nightmare of it.

The horror of it cracked him and he screamed, closed his eyes and screamed.

"Leave me alone, leave me alone. You're not real, leave me alone."

But he felt the hands on him, clutching, his name called out too, somewhere beyond those clenched closed eyelids.

"Oscar!"

He fought to escape those hands, those old claws grabbing at him.

"Leave me alone!"

Hands now pushing, scrabbling, fighting. Like real flesh, real clothing. *It's only a dream, only a nightmare.*

"Oscar. Oscar stop it. It's me. It's your grandfather. Calm down Oscar."

Real flesh and bone, real clothes clutched now in his hand. Oscar opened his eyes.

"Oscar, it's me, Richard. Your grandfather. Calm down now. I'm not going to hurt you."

Oscar lay there eyes wide staring up at Richard. Not a ghost, not a phantom, just a frail old man looking down at him, holding his wrists. As he watched the old man, his grandfather, let go his wrists.

"Oscar please, you're hurting me."

You're hurting me. And Oscar finally knew him.

Oscar released his grip on the old man's shirt and watched as his grandfather stood up and straightened his clothing, breathing heavy. He watched as the old man got his breath back.

"What are you doing here, what time is it?" said Oscar, his voice crackling in a dry throat.

The old man looked at him for what seemed a long time, then he turned towards the door.

"I'm here because it's my house son. It's about four o'clock in the morning. Get dressed Oscar. Get dressed and come out to the kitchen. I think we need to talk," said Richard from the doorway.

Oscar got out of bed, sat there listening as the old man turned on a tap, filled a kettle. He got up and pulled on his jeans and a sweater he'd found in Richard's closet. His grandfather was in the kitchen making coffee. He took a seat at the table and waited, watching the old man. Finally Richard turned and placed two steaming coffees on the table. He went to the cupboard and took out the bottle of scotch and two glasses and placed them in the centre of the table.

"So," he said, lowering himself into a chair, "where do we start then?"

"I... er I," Oscar stammered.

"Okay son, let's just start with the big questions shall we, you okay with that?"

Oscar just nodded, not sure where this was going, still half asleep, the tablets still tugging on him, pulling him back towards sleep.

Richard took the top off the whisky and poured a finger in each glass. He pushed one towards Oscar, then slid a coffee cup in there as well. He picked up his own glass and took a drink.

"Did you kill those people Oscar? Did you kill your boss and that woman in the store?"

Oscar felt the blood rush to his head. Blood and blackness, thought he was going to faint, thought he was going to throw up.

"What?" All he could manage.

"Look Oscar," said Richard. "I'm not here to judge you. Okay, *I'll* start at the beginning then. Yesterday morning there was a television news story about a woman strangled in a clothing store. They had video footage and stuff, but I thought nothing of it. Just another murder in this godforsaken world. Just one of many right across the land I guess. But then I was in the garden pottering around, I still live in the same house you know. Of course your grandmother's dead now but... Sorry, I'm rambling a bit. Anyway like I was saying, I was in the garden pottering and I had the radio on. I heard your name. Another murder and your name. Said they wanted to speak to you, to Oscar Kingman. I didn't catch all of it. So I went inside and turned on the television while I made my lunch. And when the news finally came on there you were Oscar, your photograph. They said your name of course, but I still recognised you, remembered you. They said they wanted to speak to you, were looking for you, in connection with the murder of your boss. There was also an unconfirmed report that you might be connected with the murder of that shop assistant."

Oscar sat there looking at his grandfather. He saw the spots on his temples, the back of his hands cracked like dry parchment, saw the tremor of his hand as he lifted his coffee cup, took a sip. *'He is a good man but weak,'* said granny Molly to him now from somewhere in the distant past. *'A good man.'*

"I telephoned here yesterday. I called here three or four times," continued Richard. "I thought you might be here."

"You thought I might be here. Why would you think that? I don't understand," said Oscar. "Was it a hunch... what? I mean."

"Well no," said Richard. "It was more than a hunch. Well, call it what…"

"I did it," blurted out Oscar. "I killed them. I did it! But I don't understand why you thought I'd be here. Why would you think that? I mean I haven't seen you since I ran away from here, all those years ago."

Richard finished his whisky. He looked down, toyed with his empty glass, thick frown lines across his forehead, maybe a small tear in the corner of his eye. He spoke without looking up.

"No that's right Oscar. You haven't seen me. You haven't seen me since that horrible night here in this house, but I've seen you. This will sound strange Oscar, but I've watched you grow up, tried to help whenever I could. You told me once that your granny Molly, your great-grandmother that is, told you I was weak. You called me weak. You were right Oscar, I was weak. I was weak and I was selfish and I was scared of making waves, so I went along with it. For the sake of an easy life I went along with whatever your grandmother wanted, whatever she told me to do. But in my own pathetic way I tried to help. I organised your job for you, at Loughrans. That was me. I asked Father Strohkirch to play along, say it was him that organised it. I came to the school on occasion and I watched you with your friends. I know you were always in trouble and I finally believed you about the cruelty and the beatings, but I was also somehow kind of proud when you stood up, when you fought back. You did what I couldn't do, what I was too weak to do. You stood up for others, you stood up for yourself.

There were so many times I wanted to speak to you but I felt that would only make things worse. My wife Glenda, your grandmother, well she could be cruel and nasty. I fought with her a lot about you Oscar. In fact the only time we ever really fought, it was about you. I mean she picked at me and nagged me the whole time but, god help me Oscar, I loved her and I miss her. I miss her everyday and in a way son she was a victim too, just like you and I. It has taken me all my life to understand that the more stupid we are, the less capacity we have to understand that. In fact the more stupid we are, the smarter we think we are."

Richard thumbed a tear out the corner of his eye and took a deep breath. Oscar picked up his coffee and took just a small sip. He pushed it away and drained his whisky glass, waiting, waiting. Waiting on an old man lost in his sweet and sour memories.

"I'm not here to turn you in or anything son. I've come to do whatever I can to help you. What I should have done all those years ago, listen to you and help you if I can... really help you, because I think you need help Oscar."

He reached for the scotch and poured just a small drop in each glass.

"Tell me what happened Oscar, tell me the whole story, all of it and then tell me what I can do to at least try and make it up to you."

"Make it up to me?" blubbered Oscar. "Do you really think you can make it up to me, what you did to me, what you all did. You're just here to salve your own conscience, that's all. Just like a fucking catholic, tell me your sins and beg for absolution. That's all you're here for. You talk about stupid, do you really grasp how fucking stupid you are, how stupid this whole thing is? You people, you see what's going on in the world, all the injustice, all the disasters, all the war and the starvation and then you ask yourself why your god lets this happen. I'll tell you why you stupid old man, it's because there is no god. You're morally derelict, fucking lazy. Blame this god of yours and that means you don't have to act."

He stood up from the table and flung his chair across the room.

"You're a lying fucking hypocrite," he screamed, fists balled, wanting to strike the helpless old man before him. "Why don't you just fuck off and leave me alone. You're not my grandfather, you're a total stranger. Go before I throttle you, you miserable shit. Get out of my sight, I never want to lay eyes on you again you hypocrite!"

Richard slowly got to his feet.

"All right Oscar, I'll go," he said sadly, softly. "But you can't survive here indefinitely. At least let me bring you food, supplies, that sort of thing. At least let me do that."

Oscar watched the old man and saw his grief, saw his need. He felt the rage fall off him and he suddenly realised he didn't want to be alone anymore.

"Sit down," said Oscar, as he went across the room and picked up the dining chair from where it lay. "Sit down and I'll tell you everything."

AND ELAINE MAKES THREE

After Flowers dismissed the room, Detective Roger Becker went back to his desk and pulled out the file on the murder of Elaine Benny.

"Case, what did you come up with on this video camera thing?" he said to Gail Casey.

"Well the store has only got two cameras so far. The one inside the front entrance and one over the loading bay door. This is pretty new technology Rog and there's not another camera anywhere around the area except inside a few stores, but hell, look at the image," she said holding up the still frame taken off the video feed. "It's rubbish!"

Becker's phone rang and he reached forward to pick it up.

"Becker. Okay, put her through." He held up a hand to Casey.

A woman's voice on the other end of the line.

"Detective Becker? This is Enid Taylor."

"Yes, this is Detective Becker Mrs. Taylor. How can I help?"

"When we spoke yesterday at the store, you asked us to call you if we thought of anything else that might help."

Becker waited.

"Well that man in the photograph. On the television there was a photograph of a man. That man you are looking for in relation to another case," she said.

Becker sat forward.

"Yes okay. Oscar Kingman. I think you mean Oscar Kingman right?" said Becker.

"Ah yes I think that was the name. A stabbing or something."

"That's right," prompted Becker. "What about him Mrs. Taylor?"

"Well he was here in the store, I'm sure it was him. Elaine served him…" Upset now, choking back a tear. "I'm sorry, Elaine had served him and he came to me to pay."

"Okay thank you Mrs. Taylor. We're going to need to come and see you. We'll be there shortly."

He put down the phone, looked at Gail Casey who was taking all this in but hadn't yet fit the pieces together.

"Come on," he said to Casey. "We need to see Flowers."

Sergeant Flowers looked up from his paperwork.

"What do you want Becker?"

"I just took a call on the Oscar Kingman photo…"

Flowers cut him off.

"Jesus Becker, we got at least fifty of those so far and most of them will be duds."

"No no. This one's different," said Becker.

"Okay, I'm listening, why is this one different?" asked Flowers.

"Well it came in on *our* case. I just took a call from Mrs. Enid Taylor, the cashier at the store where Elaine Benny was killed. Mrs. Taylor recognised Kingman from the photo on the television. She says she is sure that Kingman was in the store the day Elaine Benny was murdered."

"So what are you doing hanging around here then?" said Flowers. "Go!"

Casey and Becker headed for the door.

"Wait a minute," said Sergeant Flowers. "Remember what I said out there about serial killers and the media. Keep it low profile. If Kingman turns out to be the murderer in all three cases, then it's a triple homicide okay. Not a serial killing, understand?"

Enid Taylor had come off the shop floor and was sitting in the manager's office. As they walked in, Casey pointed at the manager and thumbed over her shoulder. The manager was confused. Becker spoke up.

"I think what Detective Casey means is that we'd like some privacy. We need to interview Mrs. Taylor on her own. We can find somewhere else if that's a problem."

"No that's okay," said the manager. "I'll get out of your way."

When he was gone Becker pulled up a chair next to Enid Taylor while Casey propped herself on the edge of the desk.

"In your own time then Mrs. Taylor, Enid, tell us what you know," said Becker.

"Well like I said on the phone, that man, the man in the photo on the television, he was here in the store," she said.

Becker and Casey waited.

"It was the day Elaine was killed. That man, he was here. It must have been early, right after we opened. I think he was my first sale."

"And what else do you remember about him?" asked Casey.

"Well that's the thing Detective. I remember because he seemed strange, kind of agitated. And Elaine, well Elaine could be a bit blunt sometimes and…"

"Okay, let's just take a step back," interrupted Becker. "How did Elaine come into it?"

"Well Elaine was looking after him, on the shop floor that is. After the man left she was swearing about him being, being… I'm sorry, I don't swear."

"That's okay Enid. We're police. We need to know what Elaine said after the man left," said Becker.

"Well she said…" Enid sucked in some air, put her hand to her mouth.

"She said, well she said he was a limp-dicked cheapskate faggot. Yes that was it. A limp dicked-cheapskate faggot," said Enid, carefully forming each word. "Sorry."

"And you've no idea why she might have said that?" asked Casey snickering.

"No. No I don't," she replied looking at Casey. "I don't know what happened. I'd seen her take him some shirts, but that's all I saw."

"Okay, then what?" asked Becker.

"So this man comes out of the change rooms and comes to the cashiers counter. He was still wearing the shirt and tie he had tried on. He asked for a bag to put his old clothes in. I think it was a shirt, tie and a suit coat. He seemed pretty agitated and I remember he mumbled something about spilling his breakfast on his clothes. And then he just paid, took the bag of old clothes and left."

"So that's it. You can't remember anything else? Can you give us a description of what he bought, what he was wearing?" asked Becker.

"What he bought, the shirt and tie? Well there should be a docket to confirm, but it was a pale green business shirt and a brown tie. I can show you if you like."

They followed Enid Taylor to the shop floor and she took a shirt from a circular rack, then picked through a tie rack until she found the tie.

"This shirt and this tie," she said holding them up.

"We'll need to take these with us," said Casey. "And then we'll need you to come downtown and make a formal statement."

"Oh. I'll just have to find the manager," said Enid Taylor looking like she might break in half at any time.

THE SUM OF ALL GUILT

Richard Kingman reached for the bottle of Macallans and poured himself another drink. He took his glass and the bottle and sat on the old sofa in the lounge room. Outside the first light of dawn peered over the horizon, waking the gulls. Richard waited.

"You know, I've always loved this time of the morning down here. I like to go down to the beach, walk for an hour or so and watch the sun come up across the ocean. It's as if you are the only person on the planet, so peaceful."

Oscar finally went and sat in the old armchair opposite his grandfather. For a long time he remained silent, staring at the worn carpet, the threadbare track that led from the kitchen door to the old lounge, tracks of his grandfather's life. *'I am guilty but he is to blame. He is to blame but I am guilty.'* Slowly, slowly slowly, still looking down he started speaking.

"Do you know what it is like to be alone?"

His grandfather remained silent.

"I'm not talking about loneliness, I'm talking about being completely utterly and desperately alone. Having absolutely nobody in the world. In the whole world, nobody to turn to, to love or to love you back, to help you, talk to about your problems, your hurt, nobody to hold you and keep you safe. You say you are my grandfather…"

He now looked up at Richard.

"Can you just imagine what it is like to be a young child standing completely alone in a barren and never ending wasteland, not a living soul as far as the eye can see and beyond, forever and ever? Can you imagine that *grandfather*?" The last word spat bitter into the space between them.

"Can you imagine what it would be like to be three years old and torn from the place that you thought was your home? To be dragged out of there and have to fend for yourself on the street. Three years old! Three fucking years old and forced to steal whatever I could to survive while I watched my mother... your daughter, let men use her for a few lousy bucks just so we could eat. To watch her lie around in squalor and jam whatever she could into her body to try and ease the pain. The pain of what *you* did to her. *You* and her mother. Can you imagine that? Can you imagine what it was like to find her there, my mother, dead in a pool of her own waste with the needle still there in her arm? You getting it yet grandfather?"

Oscar looked down at Richard's hands. Old spotted papery claws, but clenched tight. *'I am guilty but he is to blame.'*

"I was six... *six*, when I watched them zip what was left of my mother into a bag, hardly anything left of her anyway. Just another dead junkie hooker. That's what someone said there. I was in the back of the police car and I heard someone say that. *'Just another dead junkie hooker.'* That bag, it looked like just any other trash bag and for a minute I thought they were going to throw it out there with the rest of the trash in the alley. I remember the lights and the people, like some sideshow.

I remember I sat in a police station while they told me they were contacting my grandparents, contracting you. I didn't really know who you were but, they told me everything would be all right, that you would come and get me, take care of me. But you didn't come get me did you? You threw me out, like you threw my mother out, both of us just trash."

'I am guilty but he is to blame.'

Oscar paused and watched his grandfather, older now and smaller. The old sofa seeming to grow around him.

"And then when Granny Molly died," he continued slowly, "you let them take me and put me in that place, *guilty guilty guilty*. The last people on earth, the last family I had and you put me in *that* place! Every single person I thought I could trust, gone or turned their back. How can you expect a child to grow up normal, whatever that means? How could you expect that, when every single person charged with the care of that child either turns their back, or turns into a predator? Who protects us from the protectors?"

Suddenly he was on his feet in front of his grandfather. Richard pressed back into the sofa, afraid, *guilty*.

"Eight years old, eight fucking years old and they beat me until I bled. Look at these hands you fucking pathetic old man. Look… you did this!"

But Richard turned his head away, closed his eyes. Oscar shook a fist in front of the old man's face, but held himself in check, straightened up.

"That's right, ignore it. Close your fucking eyes and it will all go away. But it didn't did it? It didn't go away. It's right here in front of you, I'm right here in front of you. Open your eyes grandfather, open your fucking eyes."

He kicked out at his grandfather's foot and slowly Richard turned back to face him, *guilty guilty guilty*. Oscar dropped back in the armchair, *deep breaths deep breaths*, calmer now, calmer. The room fell silent but for the big old clock on the wall.

Tick, tock, tick, tock.

Oscar matched his breathing to the rhythm, and the mantra, that corny mantra that had run through his mind in Llewellyn's office, now came back to him and fell into step with the tick of that clock.

'Every doggy has his day, every doggy has his day, live to fight another day, every doggy has his day. Tick, tock, tick, tock.'

Richard jumped as Oscar broke the silence. *Guilty guilty guilty.*

"But you weren't finished with me yet, were you old man? You actually managed to find somewhere worse. Somewhere worse than the street, worse than that orphanage. You found that boarding school and you threw me in there. It was like, how many times do we have to take out this fucking trash, how many times do I have to scrape this shit off my shoe?" his voice raised now. "Will we ever be rid of the stench of that fucking kid, that bastard Oscar Kingman, that bastard son of our dead junkie hooker daughter? That *fucking* girl... after all we did for her!"

He quieted down and when he spoke again it was low and with menace.

"Well I didn't go away did I? I'm still here and everything that's happened since is your fault."

'I am guilty but he is to blame. He is to blame but I am guilty.'

Finally Richard spoke. His voice cracked and broken, his soul in tatters.

"Oscar. Oscar son I'm..."

"Don't do that!" Oscar yelled. "Don't you tell me you're sorry. Don't tell me you understand, you fucking hypocrite. I'm not finished. There's so much more to this story isn't there grandfather? I mean we haven't even got to the juicy bits yet have we?"

Richard closed his eyes and lay his head back on the couch.

"So, that boarding school. That place run by those priests and brothers, sure, maybe some were okay, a few. But those few were like you grandfather. They knew what was happening and they let it happen, just turned away. There was evil there. Evil in the name of some god; actually not just some god... your god. Do you know what happened in there in the name of your god? Would you believe me even now if I told you what it was like? What it was like to be the only boy in the world, lost and alone and to be beaten on the hands until they bled, until your fingers broke, to be beaten around the head until you fainted or threw up. Can you imagine what it's like for a scrawny eleven year old boy to have a china cup busted across the side of his head by an adult well over six foot tall? Didn't even see him coming, came from behind. And in the emergency department at the hospital, the doctor pulling out pieces of the cup, stitching the gash, while the fucker that did it sits right there smiling and telling the doctor how it happened while I was fooling around in the kitchen with some other kids. *'Kids doctor, what are they like eh?'* And all of this for no reason. All for no reason except I was a sinner. A sinner right? I must have been a sinner, after all I *was* the bastard son of a junkie whore, so bad that even her own family threw her out and disowned her, disowned her unborn child.

You getting it grandfather, you understanding yet? You understand what it was like to lie there in the dark and hear the whimper of other boys behind that blue curtain? You know what it's like to watch a priest beat a twelve year old boy around the head and shoulders with a ship's rope as thick as your arm. That twelve year old boy who brought a girly magazine to school, shared it with his friends. Can you imagine that grandfather? A girly magazine, shit, the nude photos didn't even have genitals in those days. But what a sin, what a heinous sin that was. I watched that boy beaten around the head by a man three times his size and age. I saw the blood coming from his ears grandfather. I watched him pass out and collapse on the ground, not moving. We heard the rumours that he never moved again, maybe just rumours, but we never saw that boy again. Up until then I believed them when they told me I was a sinner, I tried to understand their faith thing, figured I deserved the beatings. I must have been a sinner if their god... your god, said I was.

But on that day I finally understood. I had done nothing wrong. I was no sinner, I was a victim in a nest of bullies. And as that boy Danny, a friend of mine, as he sank unconscious to the ground I tried to go and help him, to stop it, but I was too late."

Oscar stood and got himself a whisky, sat back down, calmer now.

"I'm telling you this because it's important. But it's more important to understand *why* I'm telling you all this. I'm not telling you all this to suggest that it's an excuse for what I have done, or to seek anyone's forgiveness. It's bigger than all that, much bigger. I am guilty, you are guilty, the world is guilty. The world we live in is a world of bullies and bullying. Call it oppression, call it suggestion, call it faith, it doesn't matter.

It started for me in that first school where Granny Molly sent me. I was picked on because I was different. I was bullied, called 'Stupid Oscar' even by the teachers. Then that orphanage, those nuns. What those hateful people did in the name of their god was sickening. And that school, that boarding school where I arrived believing I was guilty, believing I was a sinner. Bullies can do that you know grandfather. Bullies can easily convince a person that they are guilty, make you think it's your fault. Ever wonder why women, or even men for that matter, stay in an abusive relationship? I'll tell you why. It's because they think it's their own fault. Guilt by difference, guilt by silence, guilt by innocence."

I am guilty but you are to blame. You are to blame but I am guilty.

"Teachers, thieves, rapists, child abusers, wife beaters, husband beaters, nuns, priests, bosses, neighbours and colleagues, not just the kid in the schoolyard who smacks you in the face. At least he's upfront. Look at me I'm a bully; at least he's honest about it. But at that school and on that day I finally realised I wasn't guilty of anything. I wasn't a sinner. I had done nothing wrong. My only sin was being born into this family and that was no sin at all. That was fate and I was a victim. But that was my last day as a victim, for a while at least. From the very next day I went out and earned those beatings. My target was the bullies. I realised that being a nun or a priest or one of those brother things meant nothing, they just hid behind those costumes and that's all they are... costumes. If there was a god of love and justice then this shit couldn't happen. These people were just bullies who should have been dealt with, who should garner no respect. But who would deal with them?

There were a few of us stood up to them, and so the last years at that school were a blur of beatings, violence and vengeance. I have broken bones that were never attended, I have scars and stitches on my head and body that were put there in god's name, but in the end we sort of won. Finally somebody listened, somebody did something. But it was all just window dressing, nobody really did anything about those priests and brothers, just shipped them off to another school, someone else's problem. There was no justice, never any justice.

When I left there I was alone again, my school friends gone, scattered all over. When I started my job, the job you say you organised, everything seemed better. I was alone but at least I had a job, I had some money and while people left me alone I was okay. Then I met Sharon. Well I didn't really meet her, I just stumbled into her trap. She told me she was pregnant and that I had to marry her. I found out it was a lie of course, but I was worn down somehow and I just let it happen, thought it would get better. It didn't, she was manipulative and divisive, another bully. I have two daughters, the second one is not even mine, no idea whose it is, but Sharon even turned *them* against me."

He looked over at Richard, sunk deep now in that sofa.

"I did what you did. Went along for the sake of an easy life and that was okay for a while then, when my boss Mr. Alperstein retired, it all went bad again. I'd worked hard as a junior estimator and Mr. Alperstein had told me I would soon be promoted to a more senior position, but after Alperstein left I was cheated out of my job by a younger man. A lazy deceitful person whose only real skill was sucking up to his bosses and bad mouthing me."

"Edmund Llewellyn," said Richard realising.

"Yes," replied Oscar, "Edmund Llewellyn. He started rumours, he stole my work and he sucked up to our new boss. Once he became senior to me his bullying became worse and worse. I had no friends, I had a dreadful marriage and my earlier confidence was gone. I was laughed at and derided by most of the staff. I became the butt of their jokes, Stupid Oscar all over again. Then just recently I met a wonderful woman at the office and I fell in love with her. She told me how Llewellyn had practically raped her. How he kept her back one night and forced himself on her. That's the sort of person he was."

"So you decided to kill him," said Richard nodding his head and tilting a little sideways on the sofa.

"No you stupid old fool," shouted Oscar, "of course I didn't! The thought never entered my head. It was later. I never planned it, I just snapped, later."

He stood and went to the window, the sun now lighting the top of the dunes. Oscar listened to the sound of the waves, wondering, thinking about exactly when he had made that decision.

'I am guilty but he is to blame. He is to blame but I am guilty.'

He heard a noise behind him, slippered feet trudging back along that threadbare track to the kitchen and beyond. He stayed there staring out the window, waiting until finally he heard his grandfather come back into the room. He heard the kitchen faucet running, Richard getting himself a glass of water. Heard the soft swallows, heard the glass go down on the countertop.

He turned to see Richard standing there, a photograph in one hand, something unseen clutched in the other. Richard held up the photo. It was the one of Oscar's grandmother from beside the bed. The holy card slipped from the edge of the frame and fluttered to the floor.

"I'm sorry Oscar, I am so very very sorry. I should have done something, but I loved her," he said through the tears, looking down at the card.

He seemed to falter, sat heavily on a kitchen chair and then toppled sideways onto the floor. A small bottle rolled from his open hand as his eyes closed. Oscar went to him feeling nothing, bent down, picked up the bottle and read the label, *Potassium Cyanide - Poison.* Oscar felt nothing, nothing at all.

WHERE'S OSCAR?

It was late, there were seven of them. Becker, Casey, Gill, Cotton, Torres, Brosa and of course Sergeant Louis Flowers. It was nine days since the murders and the trail had gone cold.

"Okay," said Flowers. "Give me that again, but more slowly this time."

"Right," said Becker, "so the Medical Examiner says that Edmund Llewellyn was probably killed first. I say probably because the bodies of Llewellyn and Mills were not discovered until the next day and while it is impossible to be precise, the ME thinks they died within four to six hours of each other. Llewellyn was last seen alive when he returned from lunch at around 1.30 and went into his office. Daniel Mills was last seen at approximately 5.30 when he left his office to change in the restroom. Mills was a fitness fanatic who used to jog to and from his office."

Becker went to the white board and wrote Llewellyn's name with an arrow underneath pointing to Mills' name.

"According to what we now know, Oscar Kingman's day started bad and just got worse. His wife stated that he'd rung to tell her his car had been stolen and to call the police and report it. It turned out the car was taken by one or both of Kingman's daughters, who had crashed it while joyriding. Next, the staff at Loughrans tell us that Llewellyn publicly hauled Kingman over the coals for being late. Kingman claimed he was late because his car had been stolen and a jogger had run into him and spilt his breakfast all over him. We know all this is true. We know from Enid Taylor's statement that Kingman went into the store where Elaine Benny was killed and bought a new shirt and tie, which he wore out of the shop. We also know from Taylor's statement that there was some kind of argument or altercation between Kingman and Benny. After Kingman left, Benny told Enid Taylor that Kingman was a..." He consulted his notes.

"Here it is, Kingman was, and I quote, 'a limp-dicked cheapskate faggot.' So we have Kingman run into by a jogger whom we shall assume was Daniel Mills, then involved in an altercation of some sort with Elaine Benny, then arriving at his office to be publicly abused by Llewellyn."

Becker sketched out the timeline on the white board.

"The girl that looks after the front desk at lunchtime, remembered seeing Kingman go out for lunch sometime around 12.45. He came back into the office at around 1.15 or 1.20 at the latest. We have two positive sightings of him sitting on a bench just inside the park, during the period he was out of the office. One from a stranger he sat next to on a park bench. This girl recognised him from the photo because he freaked her out, she said he seemed very agitated and was talking to himself. Then there was a workmate who spoke to him in the park sometime just after 1.00 o'clock. We also know that the jogger was in the park at the same time, although we can't establish any contact between the two."

He tapped a photo on the board, a photo of the jogger propped on the toilet in his running gear.

"It was hard to miss this guy considering his outfit. Mills by the way, was also pretty unpopular around the office. Bit of a bully it seems."

"Okay okay," interrupted Flowers. "Let's pick up the pace a bit. Where you going with all this Becker?"

"A simple scenario sarge?"

"Please," breathed Flowers. "Simpler the better."

"Kingman, already off to a bad start, gets knocked down by Mills and ends up with his breakfast all down him. He goes to buy new clothes and has some sort of argument with Elaine Benny. He gets nailed by Llewellyn for being late, then he goes into the park at lunchtime and maybe, just maybe, has another run in with Mills. Unconfirmed sure, but they were both in the park at the same time and we've confirmed Mills was dressed in his strange jogging outfit, so he would be instantly recognisable.

Kingman comes back from lunch, only to be needled again by Llewellyn. He finally cracks and somehow gets into Llewellyn's office, stabs him in the throat, then gets out of there unseen. Revved up now he goes back to the store where he gets Elaine Benny into a change room and throttles her with something, ME says most likely a tie. He goes back to the office and everything appears normal. Around 5.00 p.m. he leaves Loughrans, telling the receptionist he has a meeting out of the office. We found no evidence of any such meeting. He goes to Garvie Symmons and hides in a toilet cubicle. He gambles that Mills will change out of his working clothes to jog home. He waits for his moment and when Mills comes in, he confronts him and stabs him in the eye. That's it."

"Just like that?" says Torres.

"Just like that," agrees Becker. "We know Llewellyn was a bully who picked on Kingman regularly. We're told Mills was also a bully who liked to push people around. Finally Enid Taylor stated that Elaine Benny, whilst not strictly a bully, could be pretty rude and blunt."

"I got all that," said Flowers, "but I'm still not quite there."

"Look sarge…" said Casey.

"That's Sergeant to you Detective Casey," snapped Flowers.

"Right right, whatever Sergeant. Look, Kingman was a class 'A' victim. Everyone pushed him around starting with his wife.

Jeez I can't believe he didn't begin the day by popping her, the way she spoke about him. She told me and I quote, 'the little dweeb is too much of a snivelling coward to even stand up for himself, let alone murder anyone'. I'd say that slob has been hanging it on him daily all their married life. My guess, he's been pushed around and pissed on his whole life and finally he just snapped. Once he'd done his boss, he got all worked up and went after the other two." She stopped talking, stood up and took a bow.

"Sit down Casey," said Flowers. "Anyone else agree with Detective Casey's logic? Everyone... okay then strange as it may seem, having heard the facts, so do I. So where is he then, this Kingman? Anyone?"

"Well," said Brosa, "we can be ninety nine percent certain he hasn't left the country. We got the watch on airports train and bus stations and borders pretty quickly. Too quick for him to get false documents. Unless of course all of this was planned out well in advance and he already had papers. If that was the case he could be lying on the beach in Acapulco by now."

"Nope, I don't think he planned it."

This from Detective Eric Cotton.

"Why Eric?"

"Well... what Casey said. This guy has topped a few people who pushed him around. Shit his boss was on his case pretty regular, but there's absolutely no evidence to suggest that he had even met the other two before the day he killed them. His wife, well she probably pushed him around every day of his miserable life. The receptionist at Loughrans said he hated her, was maybe ready to walk out on her. I agree with Casey. If he planned any of this, planned to start killing people, his wife would have been on top of his list surely," said Cotton.

"All right," said Flowers, "we've got a whole lot of assumptions to work with here and not much else, but this character does fit the profile. So he snapped. He snapped and he killed three people in the heat of the moment, so where did he run to? Friends, family?"

"Well he doesn't really have any friends," offered Torres, "and he only has one surviving relative outside his wife and two daughters. He has a grandfather. One Richard Alvin Kingman, but we've been unable to locate him yet."

He checked his notes.

"Yeah, Kingman's wife said, that to her knowledge, he hadn't seen his grandfather since he was a kid, maybe nine or ten years old."

"Well," said Flowers, "find the grandfather. Talk to them all again, the wife and daughters, the staff at his office. Someone must have liked him or at least felt sorry for him. He can't just disappear off the face of the earth."

ALONE IN THE DUNES

Oscar sat there for a long time, sat for a long time on that kitchen seat his grandfather had just vacated. He looked down at the body of his last known blood relative, trying to feel something, anything. Prodded the old man's leg with his toe, trying to feel something. But he felt nothing, not disgust, not pity, not sadness… nothing. Richard Kingman free now from his guilt and torment.

I am guilty but he was to blame. He was to blame but I am guilty. Richard Kingman, victim.

Finally Oscar gave up his fruitless search for feelings and went to the countertop. He rinsed the glass, washed away the residue and removed the evidence. Then he wiped the glass and the little bottle and wrapped them in a hand towel. He took Richard's car keys and parked his grandfather's car in between the shed and the house where it couldn't be seen from the road. In the shed he found a plastic tarpaulin and he brought it inside and wrapped his grandfather's body in it, tying off both ends with twine. He went back to the shed and found a shovel hanging amongst the tools neatly arranged on the wall, then found a nice secluded spot in the dunes away from the house and started digging. It was hard work, the sand spilling back in on itself, but a couple of hours later he stood stripped to the waist and belly deep in a hole big enough to house Richard Kingman. After the sun set, he dragged the body up into the dunes and slid it into the grave, dropping the hand towel, with the bottle and glass, on top of his grandfather. Filling it in was much quicker work and soon he was done. Richard Kingman was laid to rest. Still Oscar felt nothing, wished that he could, stood there in the dark leaning on that shovel, sad only that he wasn't sad, nothing more.

Oscar went inside and washed, made himself a nice dinner and got back to his adventure with Tom Sawyer.

That night he slept soundly. That night and every night thereafter. Sure he dreamed sometimes, sometimes crazy dreams, but mostly nice dreams, sometimes dreams with Wendy in.

After two weeks he realised he was running out of supplies. He would have to leave the house to buy food. He stood in front of the mirror studying the Oscar that looked back out at him. Shiny bald head, thick glasses and the start of a reasonable beard. He looked harder, searching in there for the old Oscar, hard to find. *'This might work.'* He had switched on the television the previous night and had found nothing about him or the murders, on any of the news broadcasts. News that was two weeks old was old news these days.

At about eight o'clock the next morning, he drove through town and headed further up the coast. He found a small supermarket in a little coastal hamlet and was able to tick most things off his shopping list. Nobody took any notice of him. At a nearby gas station he filled the car and bought a couple of newspapers. He wandered down to the fishing dock that was tucked around the corner in the inlet. Two or three fishing boats clung to the dock and scavenging gulls wheeled above screeching and brawling. This part of the coast was flat and featureless, but Oscar didn't care. He strolled around taking in the sights like a tourist, glad to be out and about for a change. Before heading back to his car he bought fish from a local vendor. Everything was normal.

'This might work, this could work.'

That night after dinner he went through the newspapers, pieced the story together, figured the odds. He found the story in both city papers, but only one carried his photograph. That old Oscar Kingman, that photo taken maybe four years back at a work function. Oscar in a short sleeve business shirt, tie askew.

Oscar with that soft look, the wispy hair. Oscar the loser. He went to the bathroom and held up the picture, stood staring at the mirror, the picture, the mirror, the picture.

'Not the same, not the same at all,' he thought.

There was no mention of anyone other than Oscar. All roads lead to Oscar Kingman. Oscar Kingman had allegedly stabbed two people to death and strangled a third in cold blood. Oscar Kingman, the alleged triple murderer had absconded and had not been seen since, but police were confident of an arrest in the very near future. He dropped the papers in the waste basket and took his car keys off the countertop. It was time. He could wait no longer. He would call Wendy, but not from the beach house.

He drove into the town and found a phone booth outside a gas station. Never hesitated, just went straight in and dialled the number. When he heard her voice he thought he would die.

"Hello Wendy speaking."

"Wendy. Wendy it's me Oscar."

"Oh my god Oscar. Oh shit Oscar I've missed you so much."

"I've missed you too Wendy, more than you can imagine."

"God, where are you Oscar?"

"I'm out on the coast Wendy. I have a safe place. Safe for the moment anyway, but what about you? Did they question you, does anybody suspect anything?"

"No I don't think so. I was only questioned twice, once the day they found Llewellyn and again a few days ago. But they interviewed everyone again. They say they have linked you to all three killings. They say they have firm evidence."

"I know, I read the papers today, first time. I think I'm safe for now but I really want to see you. It's four or five hours out here by bus from the city. I thought maybe this weekend... you know, we could plan what happens next."

"Where exactly are you Oscar? I'm coming, what do I do?" Wendy said, overcome with the emotion of it.

A landslide of questions unearthed a landslide of emotions. Oscar was forced to consider the questions carefully. All the old insecurities came back, pecked at him, taunted him. Was it a trap, would Wendy turn him in? Why would she want him, why would she love him? He had to decide. Choose life, choose death it didn't matter, they were both the same. He gave her the details. He put his life in her hands and if he was wrong then that was okay. If he didn't have Wendy he didn't want life, not anymore.

Finally it was agreed that Wendy would try and get off early. She didn't think it would be a problem. Oscar would meet her at the bus station in town. When they hung up, Oscar leant against the side of the call box panting, ecstatic. Wendy Legget still loved him.

LITTLE BY LITTLE BIT BY BIT.

Detective Dale Torres stood on the front verandah of Richard Kingman's bungalow. He peered in through the half open blinds, knocked again.

"Mr. Kingman, you home sir?"

Silence.

'I should have called first,' he thought as he wandered back down the path and checked up and down the tree lined street.

The whole scene was quiet green and smelt of fresh cut grass and suburban contentment. The letterbox by the gate had a couple of envelopes sticking out of it and Torres absent-mindedly pulled these out to look at them. Just a couple of bills and a catalogue. He stuffed them back into the box and turned for one last look at the house.

Over the next two days he called Richard Kingman's number a few times but there was no answer. Finally he decided to swing by and check the place out again. Once more there was no response to his loud knock. He came down off the verandah and circled around to the back of the house, looking for anything unusual. Finding nothing, he went back and checked the letterbox. The same mail was still there along with a couple of new items. Torres went back to the front door and tore a blank page from his notebook. He wrote a brief note telling Richard Kingman to contact him urgently and slipped this and his card under the door. Then he went to the closest neighbours house.

"No, he hasn't been here for a week or so," said the neighbour. "He's probably at his beach house, although usually he lets me know when he's going away."

"So do you know where his beach house is Mr…?"

"Hancock, Kel Hancock. No, never been. All I know is he has a house on the beach somewhere that belonged to his parents. He's been pretty quiet since his wife died a few years back. Don't see so much of him these days, keeps to himself in there, except as I say, he generally tells me if he's going away."

Back in the office, Detective Dale Torres got Brosa to run a county by county search for any house or land titles in Richard Kingman's name. Kingman was the only one they hadn't been able to interview and his disappearance in the middle of a triple murder investigation involving his grandson, seemed just a little odd. Becker agreed, in fact Becker went even further and postulated that Richard Kingman might be involved somehow, might even be a target, so locating the beach house became a matter of priority.

• • •

Sergeant Louis Flowers came into the squad room and dropped a file on the small table by the white board.

"Okay, listen up," he said waving a slip of paper at the assembled crew. "We've got a new lead here. A used car salesman out on South Boulevard claims he sold a car to Oscar Kingman the day after the murders. Salesman said he'd been away on a fishing trip and had missed all the news. Got back yesterday and says he recognised Kingman straight away when he saw his picture in the newspaper. He said Kingman arrived by cab, all loaded up with shopping bags and just seemed to buy the first car he came to."

Flowers wrote the vehicle details on the white board.

"Silver Toyota hatch, plate number JLT 1542. The guy said Kingman was in a hurry, never even took the car for a test drive. Loaded his bags in, paid cash and headed for California."

"California?" said Jack Gill.

"Yes," said Flowers shrugging. "California. Guy said the only thing Kingman wanted to know was if the car would get him to California."

"You said a house on the beach Dale. You didn't say that beach might be on the West coast. So should I be looking for his grandfather's beach house somewhere in California?" asked Brosa.

"No," replied Torres. "The neighbour said the old guy sometimes went to his beach house for just a few days at a time. Shit, it would take you five or six days to drive to California from here."

"Hang on, we're just assuming that Kingman might be at his grandfather's beach house, wherever the hell that is," offered Gail Casey. "Maybe he really did head to California."

"Maybe," said Roger Becker slowly, thinking, pondering. "We know that there was no love lost between Kingman and his grandfather. After his mother and great grandmother died, Richard Kingman and his wife wouldn't have anything to do with him. He was what, nine years old or something? The idea that Richard Kingman would be protecting him now well... I don't know, seems like a long shot to me."

"Okay okay," said Flowers. "Becker, get these car details to the California boys. We've already got it out here both sides of the border. And speaking of borders, I take it you're checking titles both sides of the border Brosa?"

"I am now," replied Brosa, holding an imaginary gun up to his head and pulling the trigger. "Sorry sergeant, I've kinda googled myself to a standstill."

"You've googled yourself to a standstill? Jesus Brosa, act like a detective. Let someone else do the googling. Pick up the phone to every county and get them doing the records search. I know the internet is clever people, but let's not disregard the old tried and proven methods please. This guy's not hiding in the internet, he's hiding in the real world, so that's where you have to look for him," he said shaking his head.

"And of course we've got a bulletin out on Richard Kingman's vehicle right?" asked Flowers.

"Last two days," said Torres.

THAT'S JUST THE WAY IT IS

Oscar parked by the roadside across the street from the bus depot. He'd arrived early, almost beside himself with anticipation. He'd spent most of the day rearranging and cleaning the house, getting things just right for Wendy's arrival, even found himself whistling while he worked. He was amused when he realised he was doing it, saw himself in some kind of documentary of his own life.

Oscar Kingman... happy homemaker and triple murderer.

He had moved his things into the big bedroom, stripped off the existing sheets and made up the bed with clean linen that he found in a cupboard. After dinner, he had taken all the photos and memorabilia from the room and dumped them in the top of the closet. When he was sure everything was in order for Wendy's arrival, he had left for the bus station.

The sun had set at around 8.00 p.m. and now it was just after 9.30. He looked at his watch, checked his rear view mirror over and over until finally, he got out of the car and walked toward the depot. The office was closed and the only light burned in a open front phone booth, a dull yellow glow on graffiti and a handful of suicide bugs. On the wall of the depot, a dirty glass cabinet held the timetables and advertisements for the local taxi services, guest houses and resorts; more trapped bugs in there, past seeing, past escaping. He checked his watch again and peered off down the road into the darkness. Two cars arrived, drifted in slow and parked close by. Then a resort mini bus pulled into the vacant lot beside the depot. Oscar wandered back to his car and sat in the dark as another car arrived, then a taxi. He watched them come, one by one, quietly, like birds of prey creeping in on the soon to be dead; more each time he turned back.

'Each car holds its own story, its own secrets,' thought Oscar. *'Each car its own love story, its own tragedy.'*

He caught the glare of the headlights in his rear view mirror as the Greyhound bus rolled down the street, like some ghost ship bringing home the souls of the departed. Bringing the other half of scattered stories, the missing parts, back to this flat featureless town on this flat featureless coastline. As the bus rolled past, Oscar looked into the soft framed glow and saw the faces. Faces searching, happy, sad, scared, tired faces. The bus wheeled into the vacant lot and as it did, lights flicked on in some of the cars. Cab signs lit up, *pick me pick me*! The depot remained in darkness as the first passengers stepped down and waited for the driver to open the luggage hold. Oscar got out of the car, stood there excited, waiting for Wendy, waiting for his life to begin.

And suddenly there she was. She looked different, smarter, dressed different. Oscar went nearer to her, as she stood glancing around but not seeing him. The white light from the luggage compartment glowed around her. She had on jeans and a smart yellow hiking jacket, flash red hiking boots. He watched as she stepped forward, motioned to the driver as he handed her a backpack. She hoisted it over one shoulder and looked around again, heading out to the street.

"Wendy," he called from the shadow of a tree.

She turned and peered in his direction, as he stepped out into the pale light of the half moon. She peered harder.

"Oscar... Oscar is that really you?" coming towards him now. "Oscar, I can hardly recognise you."

In his arms then, the pair of them clutching and groping.

There was barely any traffic at that time of night and on the way back to the beach house, Oscar drove faster than he had ever driven in his life. Wendy chattered on incessantly about what was happening at the office, about the police and their progress, about how much she had missed him. At the house he took Wendy's pack from the rear seat and unlocked the house. He directed her to the bedroom and went to put the Toyota in the garage. When he came back into the house, Wendy was lying naked on the bed. Oscar drank her in, circling around the bed as he unbuttoned his shirt.

"Christ Oscar it's been weeks... come here!" she said reaching up to grab his belt buckle and pull him onto the bed.

Afterwards, they lay there talking, laughing, Oscar almost embarrassed by the ferocity of it all, his jeans bunched around his ankles, his shoes and socks still on his feet. Wendy crawled down to the end of the bed and slowly removed his shoes and socks, pulled off his jeans, then slid her body back over his until she was leaning over him, kissing him, moving more slowly this time.

Oscar slept the sleep of the dead. He woke at around 5.30 a.m. with his bladder demanding attention and slipped quietly out of bed to head for the bathroom. There was still an hour until sunrise, but already the early glow of dawn sent a soft grey light into the room. When he returned, Wendy was waiting for him. Her hand went between her legs and Oscar felt himself responding, weakening.

"This can't be real," he said as he fell on top of her. "I must be dreaming."

Later, after they had showered, Wendy sat at the kitchen table while Oscar made toast and sliced up fresh fruit for breakfast. He slid the coffee pot onto the table and sat down facing her.

"That's a lot of toast and fruit," said Wendy looking at the pile on the table between them.

"Are you kidding? You and I have made love what, four times in the past three weeks and three of those times in one night... last night. That's three times more than I've managed the whole previous year. I need to keep my strength up, get in shape," he laughed, flexing his biceps.

"Actually Oscar, you look pretty good. I mean apart from the shaved head, which actually suits you, you've lost a bit of weight, firmed up a bit."

"Well," replied Oscar blushing a little. "I guess I'm getting more exercise, you know, walking on the beach instead of sitting around in the office. And I'm choosing my own food instead of eating the crap that Sharon served up. Most of the time she..."

He stopped talking, realising he hadn't thought of Sharon in weeks, didn't care. That first few days he had thought about her a lot, malicious thoughts all. He had thought about going back there to the house that he paid for, the house that he slaved for. He'd thought about going back and finishing her off, her and those fucking girls. But then the anger fell away, washed off him day by day, bit by bit. It wasn't really her fault. Sure, she was a stupid conniving cow, but he realised that all this had started long before she came into his life.

He looked up at Wendy.

"I'm sorry. I shouldn't have mentioned her."

"That's okay. You don't love her do you? I figured you hated her so much that you know, you might have..."

"No, I don't love her. I never loved her. I met her at some dance and tried to screw her. I was just a kid, a virgin, all raging hormones. Next thing I wake up hungover in an alley. Couple of weeks later she says she's pregnant and I have to marry her. I was so dumb, I knew nothing. Funny thing, drunk as I was, I don't think I really had sex with her at all that night. Of course it turned out there was no baby, she wasn't pregnant, but by then it was too late. And then when she did get pregnant, after we were married and my first daughter was born, there seemed no way out. The second girl isn't even mine. Don't know whose it is, but it's not mine," he said chewing on a slice of toast.

"I did think about it, killing her, but then I figured she wasn't worth the effort, the trouble."

"Moira told us that your wife attacked you once. I didn't know that," said Wendy. "She said one of the older guys at work told her about it. When the police came to the office the second time they asked Moira about it. She said she'd heard that you were seriously injured and ended up in hospital. She remembered the guy who told her the story, saying you were different when you came back to work afterwards."

Oscar felt the twitch. *Tick tick tick tick tick.*

"She hit me with a gin bottle," he said from somewhere far away. "She was drunk most nights when I got home, house filthy, nothing to eat. I told her I'd had enough. Told her it had to stop and bang, she just hit me around the head with a gin bottle. I sure wasn't expecting that. The specialist said I had brain damage, that I needed more tests, said it was serious."

Something broken up there, something come loose, something not quite right.

He shook it off.

"Sometimes I seem to get crossed up," he said touching his temple. "Sometimes I feel the rage come on and it's like, I don't know, it's like I'm not me. I kind of see my life, my childhood from outside somehow. When I get like that it all seems so unfair and the rage knots me up. I remember one time I clenched my fists so hard I actually cut into my palms with my own fingernails, was bleeding."

Tick tick tick tick tick.

Wendy got up and came around the table. She held his head in her arms, tugged him close, felt the trembling, felt the tears on her arm, heard the muffled sobs.

He pushed back a little and looked up at her. Clawed away the tears. The twitch gone.

"This time... the murders I mean, it didn't go away. This time I felt something snap up here," he said tapping his head. "Then everything was so clear. I hadn't planned any of it, it just happened and I knew without any doubt what I would do. It was all so clear Wendy, so clear. And on that same day you came into my life. It all happened on that one day and I'm not sorry it happened Wendy, not sorry at all. I'm not sorry that I killed those people and I'm not sorry that I found you. It was the best day of my life. The best ever day in my horrible life."

He took her hands from around his neck and pushed back his chair. He stood up and leaned on the sink, embarrassed.

"Shit, I'm sorry. I don't know why I'm telling you all this. I don't know why I'm snivelling. I promised myself years ago I'd never do that again but well, I just can't believe what has happened. I can't believe you're actually here."

They were silent for a while, each lost in their own thoughts, until finally Oscar went back to the table and sat down.

"I know nothing about you Wendy and I want to know everything. Like your clothes," he laughed. "I was quite surprised last night when you got off the bus. I mean I've only ever seen you in work clothes. I really know nothing about your life."

"So where do you want me to start?" she said reaching across and taking his hand.

"Well I don't know. Why not start with the clothes. Are you into hiking, camping, that sort of stuff?"

They sat there for three hours while Wendy told Oscar about her childhood. Told him how as a kid she had spent her weekends and holidays hiking with her dad. How she came to love the peace and quiet, the solitude, and how she still escaped whenever she could to hike the mountain trails on the outskirts of the city. She told him that her mother and father weren't really close and that she had spent more time with her dad. He'd died a few years back and she still missed him terribly. She said her mother and father were a mismatch, her mother hated the outdoors, couldn't go a week without having her nails done, hair fixed. Couldn't stand to be more than walking distance from a supermarket. Theirs was an unhappy marriage, but Wendy's childhood had still been a happy one spent mostly in the company of her loving dad. She felt her mother had been jealous of her relationship with her father and, over time, had become bitter toward her. The last time she had seen or spoken to her mother was at her father's funeral. Her father had left her a big chunk of money and that seemed to upset her mother even more, so she'd moved out of the house and rented the little apartment in the city. Almost immediately she had got the job at Loughrans and had been there ever since.

"That's really all there is to me Oscar, pretty simple and boring really. I'm not very good with people. I guess I just never developed the right social skills," she said. "But what about you, your childhood, all that?"

So Oscar told Wendy the whole story. The story of his mother and how she died, about granny Molly and the orphanage. He told her about the boarding school and the cruelty. Not because he wanted sympathy, but because he'd never had anyone he wanted to talk about this with before, certainly nobody who would understand or care. And then he told her about his grandmother and grandfather. How this was his grandfather's house and how Richard had come to the house just days ago. Oscar told her how his grandfather had killed himself, poisoned himself, and how he had buried him outside in the dunes.

When he finished speaking Wendy rose from the table, took his face in her hands and kissed him. She shook her head.

"It makes me so mad the way people judge us, people like you and me I mean. Just because I don't like noisy places like bars and things, because I don't socialise with my work colleagues, people think I'm weird. Most of them are morons anyway. I'm just not interested," she said. "And you wow, I mean if people knew what you had been through in your life they'd see things differently."

"It wouldn't make any difference Wendy. Even if they knew all that about me, it would change nothing. I'm different so I'm weird. That's just the way it is, always will be."

They talked for hours until hunger told them it was lunchtime. They made sandwiches together, laughing and fooling about like a couple of teenagers, then took the food out onto the front verandah to eat. The wind was light from the south and pushed little wavelets north along the hard sand with a hollow ringing sound.

"Oh Oscar, it's beautiful here. Perfect. I can't wait to see the beach."

"Well," said Oscar, "after lunch why don't we take a long walk, unless there is something else you'd like to do?"

A FISHING TRIP

Detective Victor Brosa put down the phone and swivelled round in his chair.

"Yes, got it!"

"Really? You can probably get some sort of cream to put on it,"

"Yeah thanks for your help Casey. Of course you'd know."

"Where?"

This from Becker.

"Tyrells Inlet," said Brosa getting up and crossing to the map on the wall. "Here!"

"Okay," said Becker, "let's get the local county guys to do a couple of drive-bys. See if either of the vehicles are down there, lights on at night, that sort of thing. But stress that it's a drive-by, nothing more, and absolutely no press involvement. If he's there we don't want to spook him."

Becker went back to his desk, opened Google maps and copied in the address. He watched as the map zoomed in and dropped a little red pointer on Ocean Beach Drive. He hit the 'earth' button and the map transformed into a satellite shot of a dirty green ocean bounded by expansive sand dunes. He zoomed in as close as he could, took it all in, then dragged the pointer back and forth to check out the surrounding area.

"Okay, take a look at this," he said.

They gathered around.

"Here's the grandfather's house. It looks like one of the originals. It's pretty remote, the closest house is this one here, the big joint. There's a house at the end of the road and then if we head back north, here comes suburbia."

On the screen they could see a solid row of large houses built on the dunes.

"What are these things?" asked Casey, tapping the screen.

"I think they're boardwalks, you know, so that the rich people don't get sand in their feet on the way down to the beach."

"So let me get this straight, each house has its own private boardwalk from the house to the beach. Shit, I'm in the wrong job," mused Casey.

"Been telling you that for years," said Cotton.

Becker zoomed the map out even further.

"Okay kids, minds back on the job. So if Kingman is at this house, there's only one road in and out, and it's a dead end. Of course someone could escape along the beach on foot or hide out in these dunes, but either way, thanks to the geography with the inlet running back here and all, it looks like we could seal off the whole area right here," said Becker, tapping the screen.

"Yeah, that's assuming he's down there at all, and not off sunning himself in California," said Brosa.

• • •

It was just after 8.15 a.m. the following morning and the squad room was pretty quiet, when the call came through from the county police. By 8.45 Flowers had the whole team on deck for a briefing.

"Right, the local boys at Tyrells Inlet have confirmed there were lights on in Richard Kingman's house on Ocean Beach Drive. That drive past was at 10.20 last night and, when they returned a little after midnight, the place was in darkness. We've been asked if we want them to investigate further. They feel they can set up a surveillance point pretty easily, given the house is very private and surrounded mainly by grassy dunes. Oscar Kingman's photo could also be spread around the town, supermarkets, gas stations, that type of thing. What do you think of the idea Roger?" asked Flowers.

"Don't think so sarge. This guy's done a pretty good job of avoiding us so far, if he is in the house I wouldn't want him getting out of there. If it is him, we've got him pinned down. No, I think we should get down there ourselves, set up surveillance and get the local guys to seal off a wider area further back, if and when we get a positive sighting."

"Okay, take whoever you need. I suggest you and Casey, Brosa and Torres. Okay with you? Good. The captain will talk to the local chief direct. I think you're right, the fewer people know about this the better. Also, Captain Worrell says you won't get a warrant to search without a positive sighting."

"Is sighting Richard Kingman, his grandfather, enough for a warrant?" asked Becker.

"Unfortunately not, it's his house and he has every right to be there no question. Has to be Oscar Kingman or no warrant. Now," said Flowers, "the ME says he thinks he may have zeroed in on the weapon that killed Edmund Llewellyn and Daniel Mills. He thinks it was one of these, or one something like it. Ninety nine percent certain."

He held up a long silver letter opener.

"They're not as common as they used to be once, but let's find out if Kingman had one of these and if it's still in his office somewhere. If it is, get it to forensics, if not then find it. So Becker, keep me posted on how you intend to play this thing, but don't hang about. If the press get hold of it he'll be long gone, so let's get on it."

"Yes sergeant. Jack, you and Eric get over to Loughrans and chase down this letter opener. The rest of you clear your social calendars. We're going to the beach for a few days. Casey, find us a creditable cover and suitable accommodation. It's a little town, let's try not to stand out."

"Surf fishing," said Brosa. "You know... fishing off the beach. It's perfect. It's a legitimate reason to be there and it also let's us cover the beach access without looking suspicious."

"You know how to do that, fishing I mean? Enough to make the rest of us look like we also know what we're doing?" asked Becker.

"Sure. I try and go a couple of times a year when I can get away. In fact I've probably fished that very beach."

"Okay then that's perfect, surf fishing it is. Victor, can you arrange with Sergeant Flowers that we get all the gear we need to look legit. Casey, you sort the accommodation for four fishermen, fisherpersons. You know what I mean."

He saw the look on her face.

"Okay then make it three fisherman and one obnoxious wife or girlfriend. That work better for you? And just one other thing," said Becker, "we can't turn up in department sedans. I'll take my pickup and how about your Cherokee Vic?"

"Fine with me," said Brosa. "You put the gas in it, that's fine."

"Right, let's make it happen!" exclaimed Becker.

• • •

Two hours later Detectives Cotton and Gill arrived back from Loughrans with the news that Oscar Kingman did indeed have an old style letter opener. A few of the older staff had them and they were all branded with the Loughrans name and logo on the flat handle section. Gill passed around the photo on his cell phone.

"They were given to clients about fifteen years ago, and some of the staff back then scored the leftovers. We figure that there are probably seven still in existence in that office and we could only account for six. Kingman's is not on his desk or anywhere else that he might have left it. The guy who sat next to him said it was always sticking out of a red plastic cup on his desk. Cup's there but not the letter opener," said Gill. "I borrowed one the same and we dropped it in to Malik for him to compare and confirm."

Right then Victor Brosa walked into the room. He was wearing bright orange shorts that reached down to his knees, black and white flip flops and a dirty white t-shirt under a camouflage fishing vest. On his head was a sorely beat-up Hornets baseball cap. He carried a couple of long surf rods in his right hand and a tackle box in his left. He did a quick pirouette for his audience, the rods collecting some paperwork and a coffee cup as they went.

"Oops! Well, whatcha think?"

"I think you need a new fucking hat," laughed Casey.

"You never knock a fisherman's hat, that's the first thing. Second thing is this hat was my old man's. He was a big fan."

• • •

Just after 5 o'clock in the afternoon, a silver Cherokee made its way slowly along Ocean Beach Drive.

"This is it coming up on the left Vic," said Dale Torres.

As they passed the house Torres took it all in, the driveway, the garage, front of the house. Brosa just took one quick casual glance. Just a couple of fishermen looking for a beach access. The house slid out of view behind the garage and Torres strained around to look back.

"The grandfather's car is blue right?" asked Torres.

"Ah… yeah. Blue Focus sedan, why?"

"Well it was hard to say what it was, but there's something blue behind the garage. I just got a little glimpse. Pull over here."

"What, why?" asked Brosa.

"You carry on down to the beach with the gear and I'll double back through the dunes, take a closer look. Then I'll find you on the beach."

"But Becker said…"

"I know what Becker said," replied Torres cutting him off. "But Becker's not here and I am, and I say we need to take a closer look."

"Okay, it's your neck," said Brosa pulling off the road into a small sandy parking area.

Brosa unclipped the rods from the roof rack and pulled a tackle box and buckets from the back of the wagon. Torres hung his binoculars around his neck, jammed on an old fishing hat and disappeared into the low sand dunes. Brosa watched him go, then headed down a boardwalk towards the beach.

Torres stayed low in the dunes and tried to figure how far he had come back toward the house. As he moved slowly forward he saw the roof of the beach house appear through the marram grass ahead. He dropped to his knees and crawled closer until he could see the south side of the house, a couple of windows there with the curtains closed. He got down on his stomach, dragged himself closer to the house and there it was, a blue Ford Focus. He lifted the binoculars to his eyes, tried to make out the license plate through the grass, but it was concealed behind a pile of lumber. Still, not much doubt whose car it was. He pushed himself back down the low dune and crawled closer to the road, coming up behind the garage. He could see a small window, but there was at least fifteen to twenty paces of open ground to cross. Torres weighed up the odds of being seen from the house.

'Gotta get a look in that window, gotta know if Oscar Kingman's car is in there.'

He took the gamble, crawling on his stomach and cursing the sand until he reached the open ground. He leapt up and sprinted across the space in one swift movement, stood beside the garage window listening for any sound other than his own rapid breathing. After waiting a full minute, he edged closer to the window and used his shirt sleeve to wipe at the salt rime on the glass. Then he cupped his hands around his face and peered into the dark interior. As his eyes slowly adjusted, the dark gave way to gloom and the big shape in the garage morphed into an old silver Toyota.

Torres allowed himself a smile. *'Got you, you bastard!'* He turned and darted back into the dunes.

I WANT TO WAKE UP IN A CITY THAT NEVER SLEEPS

Wendy and Oscar lay panting side by side in the sand dunes, their clothes spread about where they had torn them off. Oscar wasn't sure if he could ever get the grin off his face, wasn't sure he wanted to.

"Jesus Oscar, you're like a tiger," cooed Wendy.

She sat up and looked along the beach. To the north, she guessed somewhere near the house, she could make out a couple of people playing at the water's edge. Just a couple of tiny black spots. Other than that, the beach was deserted.

Suddenly she leapt up.

"Last one in is a rotten egg!"

Oscar watched her run down to the water naked, then he jumped up and ran after her. Oscar Kingman skinny dipper, alive at last, all his worries forgotten in this moment of contented bliss. He ran into her arms and they crashed sideways into the water laughing and spluttering.

After their swim they pulled their clothes on over their wet sandy bodies and headed back along the beach. They had been gone for hours and it was getting late. Coming up the track from the beach, they were almost at the house when Oscar heard a car on the road. He pulled Wendy sideways off the track into the longer grass and watched as a Jeep Cherokee drove past the gate. There were fishing rods on the roof and he could make out two people inside. The driver was wearing a blue baseball cap and glanced at the house as he passed.

"Sorry, they're gone now. Just some fishermen I think, but we can't be too careful," said Oscar as they stepped back onto the track.

But as they went in the door, Oscar heard the car stop not too far along the road. He told Wendy to get dressed and stay away from the windows, then he went straight into the bathroom and, closing the door behind him, adjusted the curtains so he could look out without being seen himself. He watched the low dunes on the south side of the house and with his face up closer to the glass, he could just see the strip of open ground behind the garage. He stood silently for some time and was about to chide himself for being so jumpy, when he saw what he thought was someone in the dunes. He saw movement as a man raised binoculars to his eyes. He remained perfectly still as the watcher withdrew into the dunes again. Then he caught movement as the man dashed out of the dunes toward the back of the garage. Oscar felt the first icy tendrils of fear grip his chest. Cops, they knew he was here. Suddenly the man reappeared as he fled back into the dunes. Oscar watched his head bobbing up and down as he hurried away from the house. He flung open the bathroom door.

"Quick Wendy," he called, "grab your bag, we've got to get out of here. I think it's the police. Make sure you've got everything, nobody can know you've been here."

He ran into the bedroom, pulled on his clothes, unsure what else to take, then he went to the closet and took out the bag with his money and stuffed in the letter opener and Wendy's pink panties. That was all he needed. Wendy had thrown her belongings into her backpack and was out the door before him. He opened the garage while Wendy went up to open the front gate, then he ran down the track to the beach.

He stopped at the edge of the dunes and staying well hidden, looked south along the beach. There was a fisherman, just one. It was hard to tell given the distance, but he thought the man was wearing a blue cap. He hadn't been there ten minutes ago when they had walked along the beach, but where was the other one. *'There should be two, there should be two.'* As if on cue, the other guy burst out onto the beach further along and headed straight for the fisherman at a run. There was only one way out and Oscar realised that if they had seen his car in the garage, they could cut off his escape route. Time to go!

When he got to the garage, Wendy had the car out on the drive and was closing the garage door. He jumped into the driver's seat.

"How many?" she said as they sped away.

"Two that I could see. I don't think they know I've spotted them, but this is the only way out through town and I'd guess they will be setting up some kind of roadblock real soon."

He reached over and took her hand.

"It's fine, we'll be okay as long as we get through now," said Oscar, as much to try and convince himself. "We've got to get you back to the city, you can't get caught up in this."

"But I…"

"No buts Wendy. We'll go with the original plan. Just another couple of weeks, I'll find us someplace."

She looked across at him. He was like a different person, somehow harder, more in charge. He pushed his foot flat to the floor and the little Toyota scrubbed its way through the bend.

• • •

Becker and Casey were in the convenience store picking up supplies for what looked like being a long night, when Torres called.

"He's there, both cars are there," Torres panted, running now across the beach.

"What are you talking about Torres, how… the local boys said there were no cars visible."

"They're not visible. One's hidden behind the garage and one's inside it."

"How the hell would you know that Dale, I told you to keep well clear?"

"Yeah fuck you Becker. You do it your way I'll do it mine and let's see who's getting results!"

"Okay we'll talk about this later. We're on our way. We'll call the local boys. Meantime you and Brosa cover the beach access and Torres… stay out of sight," said Becker as the phone went dead.

Becker motioned Casey outside and filled her in on the development.

"Get onto the local PD. I want two officers back-up right now and two cars for a roadblock there," he said pointing south along the road. "Tell them we'll wait for them but tell them to get here now. I'll get Flowers working on a warrant just in case."

They climbed in the pickup and moved off down the road, pulling onto the verge at the start of the straight that headed across the marram grass plain. Both on their phones, both busy. Casey struggled to hear over Becker's conversation, so she got out of the pickup. As she did, she heard a squeal of tyres off in the distance and looked along the road just in time to see a small silver car drifting around the corner and coming fast. She banged on the hood to get Becker's attention, then ran down the middle of the road and drew her gun. Becker saw the car coming fast, saw Casey sighting down her right arm and holding up her left hand, palm out.

"Case, get out of there," he screamed, jumping out and running towards her.

But he was too late. Detective Gail Casey got off the last two shots of her life, before the silver Toyota slammed into her and pitched her spinning into the air like some cheap flimsy rag doll. She was dead before she hit the ground. Becker found her broken in the marram grass back along the roadside.

Inside the Toyota Wendy saw it happen all slow and pared down step by step. All the details, the woman on the road ahead, her hand up, the other arm pointing towards them, the gun, *'she's got a gun Oscar,'* the loud snap as the windscreen fractured, fist sized hole like an Aztec sun, Oscar flinching as another bullet slammed into the windscreen pillar on his side. And then the woman, the woman wide-eyed and knowing, *'oh fuck, those eyes.'* The impact, there one moment gone the next, all arms and legs up and away.

Wendy looked at Oscar then twisted around to look back. A guy in jeans and a t-shirt running up the other side of the road, then they were gone around the next bend.

"Christ Oscar they were cops weren't they? What the hell just happened?"

"I... I thought it was just a breakdown, then I saw the gun. Shit, I thought she'd move but..." He thumped the steering wheel. "Shit shit shit! I didn't mean to hit her, but she didn't move and then the gunshots and I guess I just panicked."

"It's okay Oscar, it's okay. Like you say, she didn't move. But what do we do now?"

Oscar calmed himself down. He took one hand off the wheel and gripped Wendy's leg.

"Look, I figure we've got just enough time to get through town before there's cops climbing all over the place. There'll be roadblocks. You've got to get out, get to the bus station and go home. Nobody knows you are here. You're like, just another backpacker right?"

He was calmer now, putting it together.

"I'll drop you somewhere on the other side of town, soon as I can safely, then you get to the bus station okay?"

"But I want to stay with you," she begged.

"No, listen to me Wendy. We have to do it this way. It's safer this way. You go home just like we planned and I'll be fine. I'll ditch the car and sort it out. It will be fine, you'll see."

They made the junction in under two minutes. Right towards the town centre, left towards the west and freedom. Oscar went left and headed out of town on the wide avenue.

"Sirens!" said Wendy.

Now he heard them too. He checked the rear view mirror, still clear, so he pulled off into the parking lot beside a small supermarket, slotting the Toyota in between two other cars. He reached across and kissed Wendy clumsily on the lips.

"This is it, it's not safe to go any further."

She looked at him and shook her head.

"Oh Oscar…"

"Please Wendy, you've got to go. Don't worry about me, I'll be fine. Let's just stick with the plan and I'll call you as soon as I can, now go!"

She reached into her jacket and pulled out a bulky envelope.

"It's for you, there's over twenty thousand dollars in there."

"But Wendy, I have money."

"Just take it Oscar, you never know."

"Okay… but it's for us, for when you come."

He kissed her once more, reached across her and opened her door. Then he climbed out and took his bag and her backpack from the back seat. He helped her shuck the pack on then, without another word, he took his bag and disappeared around the supermarket. From behind a garbage skip he watched her go. She paused and looked back, sensing he was watching. He felt his heart breaking, wanted to go to her, but finally she turned and strode off back the way they had come.

Oscar went west on foot, staying off the avenue where possible. He occasionally heard sirens, and at one point took shelter in the front garden of a funeral home, while a police car sped by, sirens blaring and lights flashing. A few minutes later he came to a ramshackle auto repair shop. According to the faded sign that hung a little askew on the awning, it was 'Chucks Personal Auto Service'. There were a few cars parked under a pine tree on the far side of the entrance. He kept walking and glanced into the workshop as he passed, an old guy in there with his head up under a car on a lift. Clear of the entrance he ducked in between the cars and tried the door handle on a grey Ford Taurus. It was unlocked. Looking around to make sure it was all clear, he pulled the door open, checking for the keys. There was nothing in the ignition, but when he pulled on the visor, they dropped down and bounced off the steering wheel. You could always trust a mechanic. He checked around again, then threw his bag across onto the passenger seat and climbed in. Oscar Kingman, invisible man, on the run again. *'Where to hide, where to hide?'* Instinct told him to go north. He could get lost in a city of eight or nine million people. Oscar Kingman, just one more invisible man in a city of millions.

Two hours later as the road blocks closed in behind him, he joined Interstate 95 and less than eight hours after that, in the early dawn, he came up out of the Holland Tunnel and ditched the Taurus in a parking garage on Hudson Street in Greenwich Village. Oscar had been to New York twice before, once on a disastrous holiday with Sharon and once on a training seminar.

He knew the general layout of the city, but would need more information to find somewhere to stay. He wandered around the Village until he found a twenty-four hour cafe and stuffed himself on coffee, omelet and waffles as the city came awake around him. On 8th Avenue he found a magazine and newspaper store where he bought a good map of the city. The person that sold him the map was very friendly and they got to chatting. Oscar told him he was looking for a cheap apartment. The guy gave him the name of an agent in Brooklyn and told him that if he paid in advance, there were places he could rent without references or employment history.

"I'd try Brooklyn first," he said, "it's probably the easiest… and cheapest."

So Oscar did try Brooklyn, and he found a good cheap place in Greenpoint, furnished and ready to move in. Of course he paid too much for it and he had to pay six months in advance no questions asked, but after spending three nights at the Ramada on the Eastside, Oscar Kingman, now calling himself Walter Johnson, moved into an apartment above a grocery store in Greenpoint.

THE SECRET OF THE SAND DUNES

Detective Roger Becker sat on the running board of his pickup and watched Gail Casey's body loaded into the back of the Coroner's van. The road was lined with police cars, lights flashing, doors open.

"It's not your fault Rog," said Victor Brosa. "It could have been any one of us."

"But it wasn't just any one of us was it? It was Casey wasn't it!"

Not a question.

"And it was my fault Vic. It was my fault for trusting you and Torres to do your job properly. To follow my instructions."

"Look I'm sorry Roger. I tried to tell him, but you know what he's like. He's always right, always gotta do things *his* way," said Brosa.

"Yeah right," said Becker bitterly, "and look where *his* way has got us now. Casey zipped up in a fucking body bag and Kingman gone. Jesus Vic, we had him!"

He stood up.

"Where is he anyway, Torres?"

"He's still at the house," replied Brosa.

"Right, so he's still out there doing things his own way, like trampling round on any evidence. Get the local forensic guys out to the house immediately."

He climbed into his pickup and accelerated away, spewing a hail of gravel over the nearest cruiser. Brosa shielded his eyes with his hand.

"Shit!"

Brosa called to the nearest uniform to get the forensics team out to the beach house, then ran to his Jeep and took off after Becker. By the time he got to the house, Becker had Dale Torres by the throat hard up against the kitchen wall.

"Roger, come on, this is not like you… this isn't the way," he said, placing a hand on Becker's arm. Becker turned and looked at him, then back at Torres.

"You're right, this piece of shit just isn't worth it."

He pulled Torres off the wall and slammed him into the refrigerator door, where he dropped stunned to the floor.

"This is not over Torres, you're on report. Get him out of here Vic!"

Brosa helped Torres up off the floor and took him outside. He was back in five minutes.

"I've sent him back to the motel in my car. Look I'm really sorry Roger, I should have tried harder to stop him, you know, called you or something but well…"

"It's okay, it's not your fault," said Becker. "It's done now. Let's get on with finding Kingman. That's all we can do for Casey now."

"Right, so the local CSI should be here soon, but what exactly are we looking for?" asked Vic Brosa.

"There was a girl. A girl, a woman, in the car with Kingman. There was a woman in the car with him and that means she was here with him in this house. I want to know who she is. There's got to be clues here. Something that we can use to identify her. Find her and maybe we'll find Kingman."

"Roger, are you sure it was a woman in the car? You sure it wasn't the old guy, you know Kingman's grandfather? His car is still here, but there's no sign of him anywhere."

"No," replied Becker. "It was definitely a woman."

"Then where's the old man?" asked Brosa.

The CSI team arrived and while two of them went inside, the team leader went straight to Becker and introduced himself.

"Look Detective, I should get back to the crash scene, so I'll leave those two with you, but if there's no crime scene here then what are we doing, I mean what are we looking for?" he asked.

"I know it's a bit unusual, but I need your help here. There's an old man, the killer's grandfather. This is his house, that's his car there and he seems to be missing. Because it's his house it will be full of his stuff, so I guess we're looking for any signs of struggle or foul play, that kind of thing. Also we think the killer had a woman here with him. We're looking for anything that might help identify her and so lead us to him, prints, clothing, anything unusual. We'll take a look around out here," said Becker.

The CSI team leader shrugged and went into the house.

Becker and Brosa went to look at the old man's car, careful not to touch anything. Then Becker turned toward the shed, the side door open.

"This where Kingman's car was?" he asked Brosa.

"That's what Torres said, yes," replied Brosa.

Becker found a light switch and used the tip of his pen to turn it on. He stood there in the middle of the empty concrete floor. Brosa watched him as he turned a full circle. Becker, doing what Becker was famous for.

"What are you looking for Rog?" asked Brosa.

"I don't know but, I know whatever it is, it's around here somewhere," he replied, going to the front of the garage and carefully inspecting whatever he saw.

Now and again he poked at some tool or coil of rope, or flipped the lid off some box with his pen. He moved intently to the opposite wall, just a quick glance at the little boat. Brosa watched carefully as he moved quickly past a rack of fishing rods and stopped in front of a hanging collection of garden tools. One hook empty, one tool missing. Becker cast about the garage till he found what he was looking for. He looked up at Brosa.

"The old man is still here," he said quietly.

"Where? I mean how do you know?" asked Brosa.

"I don't think he was harbouring Kingman at all," said Becker. "I think the old man suspected Kingman was down here and came looking for him. That's why he left without telling the neighbour the way he normally would."

"You're guessing right?"

"Sure I'm guessing, but if Oscar Kingman ever came here then obviously his grandfather would know and his grandfather might figure this was one of the places he might disappear to... and he was right."

"So where is the old guy then?"

"My best guess is not too far away, in a shallow grave."

Becker pointed to the shovel that was leaning against the wall, then motioned to the gap between the other tools.

"The old guy was clearly a stickler for neatness. He wouldn't have left that shovel there against the wall, he'd have hung it back where it belonged all neat and tidy like. And look carefully at it. Every other tool has a fine coating of surface rust from the salt air environment. Not the shovel, look at that bright edge. Somebody has used it recently to dig something and I'm betting it wasn't the old man… like I say, he'd have put it back in its allotted place."

Becker took one last look around the garage then headed back outside.

"Tell the CSI boys to photograph this area and tell 'em about the shovel. They might find prints that match the ones we took from Kingman's home and office. Also I think the local guys have a K9 squad or something, so see if you can get some dogs down here. Tell them we're looking for a fresh grave and victim number five. I've got to call Flowers."

• • •

Becker waited for Sergeant Louis Flowers to come on the line. He wasn't expecting this call to go well.

"Flowers. That you Detective Becker? I was wondering when you would get around to calling me."

"Yes I'm sorry sergeant but…"

"Don't tell me you're sorry Becker, just explain to me how this thing went so wrong. I've got the captain busting my balls about Detective Casey and the whole thing is all over the news here. We've got a press conference in less than an hour and I need to know what the hell is going on."

Flowers wasn't exactly shouting, but he was just one notch down. Becker held the phone out and looked at it.

"Look I'm sorry sergeant, I'll take full responsibility for what happened. It was my fault."

"That's not the way I heard it Roger. I heard that Torres failed to follow procedure and ignored your specific instruction."

"Well yes but…"

"Yes but nothing Roger. Look I'm as much to blame as you are. I sent him down there with you knowing the sort of crap he pulls sometimes. It was a poor judgement call on my part, but we didn't even know for sure Kingman was down there. The damn lights could have been on a timer or something," said Flowers. "Listen Roger, we've got to get on this guy, the media are going to town on it. That's four dead now and one of them a police officer."

"Five."

"What?"

"I said five… five dead. I think Kingman might have murdered his grandfather."

"So this just gets better and better," said Flowers.

They spent the next five minutes talking plans and resources, then Becker provided some background for the press conference. He looked up to see Brosa standing there.

"I've got to go sergeant, things are happening here," said Becker.

"Okay, keep me across this Roger and send Torres back here now. You need anyone else to wrap it up down there just let me know. Oh and Roger."

"Yes sergeant?"

"I'm sorry about Casey. She had a quick mouth on her, but she was a good cop."

Becker hung up and turned to Brosa.

"Tell me!"

"The K9 squad is on its way from Wilmington along with a couple of recovery guys, they'll be here in ten or fifteen minutes. The boys inside have got fresh prints and they found a pair of lady's hiking boots in the main closet, almost new but very common. A few other things like a lip pencil, whatever that is, in the bathroom trash and makeup smudges on the pillow slips along with long hairs. So you were right again, there was definitely a woman here with him. Also they found Kingman's car in a supermarket car park in town. No sign of Kingman of course. The car will go to the Wilmington impound okay?"

"So where the hell would he go and how does this woman fit in the picture?" mused Becker.

Ten minutes later a white 4x4 arrived with a handler and a Belgian Shepherd named Devil. The officer consulted with Becker, who left them waiting outside and went into the house. Keeping clear of the forensic unit, he rifled the closet for items that clearly belonged to an older man. He found an old sweater and an oilskin as well as a couple of old hats. He took the lot outside to the K9 officer, then stepped back and watched as the officer did his thing, talked to the dog, held up each of the items.

"Okay," said the handler. "We'll start by circling the house in ever widening circles. If the old guy is here, Devil will find him. You stay back here, I'll call you if we find anything."

Becker walked to the front of the garage and watched as the dog and handler disappeared around the side of the house and down the track that led to the beach. Almost immediately the dog backtracked, dragging his partner along with him. He poked about in the marram grass occasionally emitting a kind of sneezing noise, then raised his head and sniffed the air before heading off down the track again. The same thing happened on the second circuit of the house, only further into the dunes. On the third circuit, the dog took his partner still deeper into the dunes. After thoroughly picking over a clear area between the clumps of grass, he looked up at his partner and started digging.

The handler called Becker into the dunes, where he watched the officer give a quiet instruction to the dog. Devil looked up at his partner and then just dropped down and lay where he'd been digging. The officer nodded to Becker who returned the nod with thanks. He went back towards the house in time to see a white van arriving with the recovery team. The CSI team had moved into the garage while Brosa stood at the door taking notes. Becker stuck his head in.

"Unfortunately it looks like we might have found you fellas a real crime scene. I think we're going to need you outside for a bit."

He led them and the recovery team into the low dunes beside the house.

"Here," said Becker to them, "but carefully please."

Once the K9 pair had moved aside, the CSI team went to work photographing the site.

"You want this area taped off?" asked Becker.

"Bit late for that really detective but okay, run a wide perimeter from here and here," he said pointing further into the dunes, "and back to the side of the house. We can comb it later if we need to. What exactly *are* we expecting to find?"

"An old man. Richard Kingman."

Becker stood to one side with Devil and the K9 officer while the CSI guys directed the recovery team to commence carefully digging. They shovelled away, pausing often to force thin spikes down into the sand. Gradually they cleared away the sand until one of the spikes struck a solid object. Now they proceeded more carefully using small trowels until a green plastic tarpaulin started to appear at the bottom of the collapsing sand pit. One of the CSI men took photographs as more of the sinister parcel was exposed. The officers shifted position, straddled the hole and shovelled more sand from the sides of the pit with steady efficient strokes.

"What's that?" said Becker. "Something red, by your foot there."

The officer leaned down and carefully swept away the sand with his hands, uncovering a small red and white towel. He motioned the CSI photographer in, then took hold of it carefully and gently shook the sand off.

"There's something in there detective, something hard," he said as he handed it up.

Becker followed as the CSI man stepped back from the pit and placed the towel on the ground. Devil strained at his leash and pulled his partner closer. His nose went to the package on the ground and he looked up as if confused, a kind of *beats me* look on his face. He turned and went back to watch the activity in the pit.

The CSI man took the edges of the towel and carefully opened it out. Inside he found a glass and a small bottle. He tore off his old gloves and pulled on a new pair, then he carefully lifted the glass to his nose, nothing. He held the bottle up before his eyes and read the label. There was a tiny amount of residual fluid. He bagged the items for the lab and stepped back to the sand pit as the recovery team each took an end of the tarpaulin and carefully hefted it up out of the grave. The package bent in the middle causing the two men to struggle with their footing.

"If this is your guy, he's been dead at least a couple of days," said one of the men. "No postmortem rigidity."

Becker helped them get the body clear of the hole, then looked at the CSI team expectantly.

"Go for it," said one handing Becker a pair of gloves, while the other one moved in with the camera. "It was your call, and a pretty good one I'd say."

Becker pulled on the gloves, then knelt beside the tarpaulin and untied the twine at one end. He pulled and folded it back until the side of a man's head appeared. Tugging the tarpaulin back even further, he uncovered Richard Kingman's face. The old man wore a rictus leer as if caught halfway through an exaggerated sarcastic smile. Not quite the same as the file photo, but no doubt. Becker looked up and nodded.

"That's him."

At five o'clock that same afternoon, a local real estate agent arrived to collect his car from Chuck's Personal Auto Service.

EVIL BY DEGREES

Oscar spent the afternoon on the streets of Greenpoint shopping for groceries and whatever essentials he'd need in his new apartment. He discovered that he liked Greenpoint. It had a nice old-fashioned community feel to it and most everything a man might need could be found in the eclectic mix of shops along Manhattan Avenue. A couple of blocks back from the East River, amid the trendy new bars, he came across a couple of nice old original joints, where a fugitive might lose himself in a dark corner. And that's what he was, Oscar Kingman, fugitive.

Oscar had never been much of a drinker, but in his days at the beach house, he had gone to work on his grandfather's supply of whisky. After the old guy had pulled his stunt with the potassium cyanide, he'd picked up the pace even more. He found it helped him sleep, kept the demons at bay so to speak. It also triggered bouts of self analysis and now he sat at his little kitchen table staring at a bottle of Johnny Walker. There were new demons to assuage, or even exorcise completely. Up until now he had argued justification for his killings. Those people were bullies, they had bullied him. Of course if his life had been different, those people may well be alive today, bullies or not. Oscar saw it as some kind of ledger system. All of his life they had drawn down on him, sucked the life out of him, stripped away his ego one day at a time. They were like a tribe, or a single seething mass, that constantly reached out their tendrils and sucked him into the dark pit of fear and doubt that had become his life.

Individually of course, they were evil by degrees, but to Oscar they were one entity. What he had done was strike back at that entity and for that he felt no regret. When he killed Edmund

Llewelyn he was killing those nuns, that one fucking nun. When he drove the letter opener into the jogger's eye, he was just starting to balance the ledger with all those priests and brothers. Those self proclaimed holy men who professed a belief in the afterlife and queued up for their dubiously conceived paradise. If there *was* a hell, the jogger certainly knew about it now.

'Even a dead jogger is smarter than a live priest.'

And then there was the shop assistant, just like Sharon, tugging on the dicks of the disadvantaged and vulnerable, sex as a weapon, sex as fate. He hated the shop assistant for that, but he hated her even more for the fact that he had been tempted. Tempted by some crazy slapper old enough to be his mother. He hated her most because she had made him hate himself for what he had become.

So he'd drawn back on the ledger, made a start at balancing the books and with it had come Wendy, had come love. He thought of those first tender moments in the file room and afterwards, when he felt his heart would burst with the joy of it. Oscar Kingman on the threshold of a new life. If the violence and killing had ended there, so would have ended his guilt, but it didn't... it didn't because now he had killed an innocent person. Just someone doing their job.

He screwed the top off the whisky, poured a generous shot into a coffee mug and took a pull at it. He felt the twitch beside his eye, *tick tick tick tick*. That policewoman, *'shit, why didn't she move?'* She just stood there firing, and all Oscar saw was his life with Wendy slipping away. That's all he saw until that final second before she hit the hood. Her eyes wide enough to take in all the horrors of the universe, as well as that one final mistake. Those eyes wide with understanding and pleading, then gone.

Her and those fucking pleading eyes, up and over the roof of the car to land somewhere in another place entirely.

Of course he knew she was a policewoman and she might have been guilty of lots of things, but did she deserve to die? *Tick tick tick.* They would come for him now. Oscar knew they would come for him. Eventually they would find him, *he was already dead.* They would never stop now. He drained the cup and filled it again, then took it to the window that looked out onto the street below. Out there people going about their day, happy, sad, confused, excited. He turned away and slumped down on the tattered old lounge, thinking of Wendy, wondering where she was, if she was safe. It had all been so close and now he cursed himself for putting her in so much danger.

He pulled the little table and chair closer to the window, closer to the life that existed out there. Closer to the warmth of normal, the everyday world that happened just beyond that grimy window. Shadows climbed the wall opposite and the street lights and apartments lit up one by one. Here and there a face at a window, here and there eye contact, those faces frozen in the moment like some bug in an ice cube.

He fell asleep by the window on that first night in the apartment, his head down on the table, his mouth slack and dribbling, the empty bottle clutched in his right hand. While he slept, the demons arrived at his window, found him there in Greenpoint and waited out there calling low and mean. *'Come out and play Oscar, there's more fun to be had. We're just getting started.'* Just there in the greasy half dark, beyond the window at the edge of the real world.

At some point in the early morning he released his grip on the bottle. It bounced hard but whole on the cold linoleum floor, then skidded away to rest gently against the skirting. Oscar woke

sweating and afraid in that cold place. He staggered away to his bedroom avoiding the window, *'don't look, don't look'* and collapsed on the bed while that part of the earth where he slept, slowly turned its face away from the dark and started back towards the sun.

It was after 11.00 a.m. when he finally woke. He lay there quietly with his eyes closed as if stillness might stem the nausea that welled up in him. A sharp pain drove in behind his eyes like a steel spike and he winced as he carefully fluttered one gummy eyelid partly open. He rolled onto his back, immediately rank acid rose in his throat and he dived off the bed and raced to the bathroom retching and gagging. Afterwards he hung face down in the toilet, eyes watering and stringy bile hanging from his nose and mouth. He dropped back and slumped against the wall, where he sat regaining his strength and wishing he'd thought to buy aspirin and mouthwash.

Pulling himself up by the basin, Oscar stood in front of the mirror. Considering all things, he wasn't altogether too unhappy with the image that stared back at him. Sure, the Oscar in the mirror was profoundly hung-over, had red-rimmed rheumy eyes, a sick pallor and needed a shave, but even that Oscar looked harder and meaner, like someone to avoid. He unbuttoned his shirt, yesterday's clothes filthy now and stinking. He looked at his naked torso. The healthy diet and beach walks had done some magic, the soft round edges a little tighter now. He flicked on the cold tap and stuck his mouth under the stream, noisily sucking in great gulps, then climbed into the shower and let the steaming water massage the back of his neck. Still unshaven but clean and dressed, he went off in search of something to fill his fluttering belly.

Lunch was a burger and black coffee, shovelled down between bouts of queasiness and then, feeling a little more alive, Oscar set out to explore more of the surrounding area. On Meserole Avenue he stumbled across a tattoo parlour and stood at the window staring at the designs for a long time before finally getting up the courage to go inside. There was a guy leaning on the counter reading a magazine of some kind. Half his face was tattooed with what Oscar assumed were some kind of tribal markings. He had huge black discs fitted into his stretched earlobes and three metal studs clipped through his right eyebrow. Oscar fought the urge to turn and leave, but the guy looked up and smiled.

"Hi, I'm Lex, how can I help you sir?"

Oscar didn't know what he was expecting, but he was surprised to hear a cultured accent matched with a polite demeanour.

"Oh hi, well I was just wondering about a tattoo," said Oscar.

"Well that's what we do here, so what were you thinking of?"

"Ah… a name, just a name here," said Oscar touching his right bicep. "Wendy, I'd like the name Wendy right here. When could you do that and you know, how long does it take?"

"Is this your first tattoo?" asked Lex.

Oscar just nodded.

"Right, once we pick a typeface and colours… let's see, Wendy… about an hour I guess. It's quiet at the moment, I could do it right now."

"Okay then," said Oscar, pushing ahead before he changed his mind, "Let's do it. There's a typestyle in the window that I like."

A little over an hour later he emerged with Wendy's sweet face fixed in his mind and her name inked on his arm.

'How the hell will I survive until I see her again?'

But survive he did and, with his new name and his new found confidence, Oscar Kingman set about carving himself a slice of normal life among the good folk of Greenpoint. He grew a close-cropped beard and wore almost nothing but denim jeans and black t-shirts. For the first time in his life he went into a gym, tried the circuit thing and found he enjoyed the introspection of doing weights. *'Oscar Kingman pumping iron, who would have thought?'* Wendy's name grew bigger on his arm each week and after just a month he could barley recognise himself in the mirror.

He found work at an old fashioned hardware store on Manhattan Avenue and here the customers laughed with him, not at him. It wasn't just that he needed to pay the rent and hang onto his and Wendy's cash, it was that he needed to belong. The owner of the store was a nice old guy named Harvey Bennet and Oscar liked him. For his part, Harvey couldn't believe his luck when Oscar walked in. He figured he'd found the perfect employee.

There were parts of Brooklyn that had resisted the creep of urban trend and nearby, Oscar found an old-school local's bar full of cheap drinks and bad jokes. In a few short weeks he had become a regular for the football broadcasts, but almost every night he stopped in after work for the company and a drink or two.

BECKER.

As usual Detective Roger Becker woke before the alarm. He reached out and switched it off so that his wife could sleep on. It was 5.30 a.m. and he lay listening to the sound of his wife's breathing. Somewhere off in the distance a dog barked just the once, a lonely desperate sound. His mind went to Oscar Kingman, also out there somewhere in the half light. *'Was he lonely, was he scared?'* It was almost four weeks since Kingman had slipped through the net. Almost four weeks since Kingman had ploughed into Gail Casey, ending her short life. Becker had the time to go over that day again and again, frame by frame. *'Why didn't Torres follow orders, why didn't Casey jump clear, why didn't Kingman swerve to miss her? Why didn't he swerve to miss her?'* This one the most interesting question of all.

Becker lay in his bed replaying those few seconds over and over again. He heard the bang on the hood and saw Casey run down the road and draw her gun. He saw the silver Toyota coming at them fast and he saw Casey take aim and raise her left hand. His own shout of warning was lost in the noise and panic of the moment, as he reached out to her, all so slow, too slow.

He heard those two shots and he saw the look on Kingman's face. Not intent, not resolve… panic. His attention on Kingman, the other person in the car, a woman, barely glimpsed. Then he heard that sickening thud, saw Casey spinning in the air like some circus acrobat and the Toyota was gone.

Becker thought he understood that look of panic. Kingman hadn't meant to kill Casey, hadn't wanted to. He had panicked when she started shooting, but almost anyone would. When Becker married this thought with all the information they had gathered on Kingman, a picture emerged. Kingman was a victim first and a killer second. Becker now knew all about Kingman's past and while it changed nothing, it led to an understanding of why the guy snapped and killed three people in the one day. Sure, none of those people were saints and it was hard to find anyone with a kind word to say about any of them, but that didn't mean they deserved to die. There were still a few mysteries to solve. Becker looked across at his wife, beautiful asleep, kind and supportive awake. He'd met Kingman's wife and she was such a piece of work it was all he could do not to reach out and strangle her himself. He'd suggested she might need police protection from her husband, but she'd been so dismissive and rude, that he left not really caring and now he hated himself for that.

His wife stirred next to him, stretched, yawned and rolled over to face him, her eyes opening. She reached out under the covers and took his hand in hers.

"What's the time honey, did I miss the alarm?"

"No it's just after 5.30, go back to sleep," he replied softly.

"What are you doing awake? Want to share?"

"Oh it's nothing, I was just thinking about this Kingman case. There are so many unanswered questions."

"You mean like where he is?" she drawled, snuggling closer.

"Well yeah that, but there's other things."

"Like?"

"Like who the hell was the woman in the car with him, the woman who had been at the beach house with him? And why would he kill his grandfather, poison him? It makes no sense."

He turned to her, but she had drifted off to sleep again. Becker smiled, swung his legs out of bed and went to the shower.

When he arrived at the office, Captain Worrell and Sergeant Flowers were waiting for him in Flowers' office.

"How are you doing Detective Becker?" asked Worrell motioning for him to sit. "I mean the Casey thing. It's been a few weeks, but the sergeant tells me that you're still wearing it a bit hard. That's not like you Roger, are you sure you don't need a few days off?"

"Look I'm sorry captain, but is this necessary? I mean I've been cleared by the shrink."

Worrell stared hard at him for a long ten seconds, then nodded slowly and stood up.

"Okay... I'm going to leave that call to Sergeant Flowers here, but you need to shake this off and get back on your game Roger. It's nearly six weeks and we've gotten nowhere on this Kingman thing."

He turned to Flowers.

"Louis, you need to get on this, the commissioner is all over me," said Worrell as he turned and left the room.

"Okay Roger well... you heard him."

"I'm fine Louis, really. Of course I was shaken by Gail's death and sure I blamed myself, but that's not the problem. The problem is this guy has just disappeared. I mean he's not a criminal. Well you know, at least he wasn't a criminal, so he's an unknown. There's no news on the street because nobody's ever heard of the guy. We've got nothing. It's like he's invisible."

There was a knock at the door and they both looked up to see a grinning Brosa standing there holding a slip of paper like it was a winning race ticket.

"Sorry to interrupt but we've located the stolen Taurus."

Becker was on his feet now.

"Where?"

"New Jersey. It's in a private impound yard in Newark, been there a few weeks. Seems it was abandoned in a car park in Greenwich Village. It sat there a few days before it was towed out to the yard in Newark. The yard waited seven days, but when there was no claim they reported it to the Newark Police Department. It finally got somebody's attention yesterday. I've got the Newark PD running prints for me and I'm waiting on video from the car park in the Village."

Becker turned back to Louis Flowers.

"I'm going to need you to pull some strings with the NYPD sergeant," he said.

"No," said Flowers bluntly.

"But sergeant..."

"I said *no* Becker. You know the procedure. We have no jurisdiction. It's down to the local authorities. I can prosecute an interstate arrest warrant. In fact there's good cause to seek a national warrant, but you're staying right here unless they send you a gilt-edged invite, you got that? So get out there and set up the necessary liaison."

He paused, then turned to Brosa.

"If that's all, you can leave us Detective Brosa," said Flowers.

Brosa nodded and left the room, the door closed behind him.

"Of course," said Flowers pensively, "you heard the captain. If Roger Becker private citizen, wanted to take a few days off somewhere, say like Florida, then I guess I'd have to approve your leave. I mean I can't tell you where you can and can't go on your days off. But Roger... by the book right. It's New York's show and if I'm asked I'll say you told me you were going to Florida for a couple of days. You'll be on your own."

LOST IN AMERICA

"So Wally, what do you do?"

It was after 3.00 p.m. on a Wednesday afternoon and the bar was quiet, just Oscar and the barman named Woody.

"Walter,"

"Say what?"

"Walter," said Oscar, "my name is Walter not Wally."

"Yeah yeah sure," said Woody. "Sorry no offence okay."

"None taken, just saying is all. I don't like Wally, don't like shortening names down," said Oscar.

"Yeah," laughed Woody, "that's easy for you to say. You didn't get lumbered with Woodrow. Woodrow Wilson for christ sakes. Can you believe it? My parents named me after a fucking president, must have hated me."

"Well yes I guess I see your point," mused Oscar. "Woody it is then."

He pointed to Oscar's glass. Oscar nodded and Woody poured another generous double. The barman was bored, he hated these mid-week afternoons when the joint was like a morgue.

"I work at H&M Hardware over on Manhattan," said Oscar finally.

"Hardware? You shitting me! Look at this," said the barman motioning Oscar around the end of the bar.

"Reckon you got anything like this?" he asked pointing down at a broken latch on the under-bar refrigerator.

"I'm not sure, it's pretty old, but who knows. The basement at the store is full of old stock that should have been tossed out years ago, maybe there's something there that will fit. You just need to line up the screw holes. If you take that broken one off and bring it in, I can have a hunt around for you," said Oscar going back to his stool.

"Great, thanks, I'll do that. Damned thing's driving me crazy. Won't stay shut. So where ya from then Walter?"

Oscar looked at him over the rim of his glass, unsure whether to engage with him or not. They hadn't talked much, but he thought the guy seemed okay, kind of felt he knew him. Some barmen were like that, but he was always alert to his situation. He decided to trot out his prepared story. The barman must have seen the hesitation in his eyes.

"Sorry Walter, I go a bit stir crazy days like this. I'll just leave you to it."

"No no, that's okay," replied Oscar. "Atlanta. I'm from Atlanta Georgia originally. I was in the hardware business down there, but my wife died a year or so back and I felt like a change of scenery. I travelled around a bit and ended up here."

"Any kids?" asked Woody.

"No, no kids. What about you, wife, kids?"

"No not me. Well I say no but, I've probably got kids all over the east coast," said Woody laughing.

"I don't understand," said Oscar. "I thought you were a local."

"I am. Brooklyn born and bred," said the barman, "but I was what we used to call a travelling salesman. I sold copiers, you know, photocopy and fax machines. Worked for a wholesale supplier here in Brooklyn. There's lots of jokes about travelling salesmen and most of them are true. I had this technique see, where I could pick out the lonely girls in the small towns. Bank tellers, waitresses. They all wanted out, all wanted to head for the bright lights. I just told them what they wanted to hear. Man it was easy, like taking candy from a baby. I must have slept with hundreds of them over the years. Of course as I got older, so did the women. Then, with the coming of the digital age, the market for copy machines dried up and I got retrenched when I was fifty nine. This joint had always been my local, so when the owner wanted to retire I applied for the manager's job and here I am."

Oscar felt the tick come to life beside his eye. *Tick tick tick.* This guy was just like his father, the man he didn't know, the man who promised his mother everything then hightailed it out of town with Loretta just another notch on his gun… just another gullible conquest. There must be thousands of men just like him out there preying on the weak. He found himself starting to dislike this Woody guy, but he buried his feelings.

"So you covered the whole east coast. That's a big area," said Oscar.

"Sure did, all the way to Florida. I'd be out for weeks on end, take the orders, phone 'em in and get back on the road. Business was good back then and so was all that pussy."

Woody saw the strange look on Oscar's face.

"No need to worry though Walter, only been through Atlanta a few times, so I'm probably not *your* father," he said reaching across and slapping Oscar on the shoulder like he was his best buddy.

Oscar felt it, felt something with that one touch. It went through him like an electric shock. Woody saw the look on his face.

"Sorry Walter, just fucking with ya."

Oscar took a pull of his drink and tried to recover his composure, *'this could be my father, is this man is my father?'* He felt something happening, smelt the damp sheets and the rotting garbage over the tang of stale beer. Felt time slowing down while he looked harder at the barman, his nose, eyes, hairline, maybe saw a younger Oscar in there. *'It was impossible, couldn't be.'* Fate twisted the gears and the tumblers clicked one by one. All of this in a split second. He got his breathing under control. *'Now you're just being stupid Oscar, thinking this guy could be your father.'*

"You okay there Walter?"

Oscar was going there. Without knowing why, he was going there. He didn't know what or why, but something was pushing him onwards.

"Yes, just went down the wrong way is all," he coughed. "Tell me more about the girls. Man I wish I'd been a travelling salesman, I mean you hear all the stories of course, but I had no idea they were true."

"Well they weren't true for everyone, I mean you had to have certain skills. You had to know how to pick the loner, then convince her you had fallen for her and wanted to marry her. Sometimes it took a couple of visits but in the end... bingo!"

Tick tick tick.

"You had to know how to manipulate 'em I guess," said the barman leering, remembering.

"So were they the same everywhere you went? I mean the girls in Miami, were they you know, hot like we hear?" asked Oscar.

"Well I guess they were," said Woody. "My favourite pick-up places were always the interstate diners. But you don't want to hear all this shit," he said wiping the bar.

"Yes I do. I'm just trying to imagine what it must have been like. A different girl every night."

"Jesus Walter, don't get too excited. You need to get yourself a girlfriend," laughed Woody.

"Oh I've got a girlfriend," offered Oscar. "She'll be moving here now I'm settled in, got a place and a job and that. Any day now," he said watching Woody carefully. "She's from Charlotte. I don't know about Miami but some of the girls in Charlotte are pretty stunning."

Playing the hunch.

Oscar watched as the barman carried on wiping down along the bar. *No reaction.* He tried again.

"You had any girls from Charlotte Woody?"

That got his attention. He threw the cloth in the sink and looked up at the ceiling like the answer was written up there somewhere.

"Charlotte, Charlotte. You know, now you mention it there was this one girl. Not from Charlotte exactly, but right near there. Place called Huntersville I think, yeah Huntersville."

Oscar felt light-headed. He clutched the bar. *'Don't say it, don't say it. Do not be my father, do not be that man.'*

"She was a stunner. Linda or Lorraine or something. Wow, long time ago. I'd forgotten about her. Loretta! That's it Loretta."

Oscar felt the planet turning on its axis, heard the creak of the shifting stone deep down in the earth below his feet, below this floor, in this bar in this city… in this life. Things unseen were shifting, tumblers falling into place. His head hurting. *Tick tick tick.*

'He is already dead. I am already dead.'

Oscar was aware that Woody was still talking, could hear him kind of muffled through the thickness of the atmosphere in that little bar where life began and life ended.

"… yeah she was kind of different. I remember I took off and left her asleep. I remember sitting in my car and thinking I liked her, nearly went back inside…"

Oscar stood up shakily.

"I've got to go," he said turning away.

"You okay? Shit man you look fucking green," said Woody. "Oh, I'll try and come by tomorrow with that latch okay… okay Walter?"

But Oscar Kingman was gone. Out into the streets of Greenpoint where there was still no air to breathe.

NEEDLE IN A HAYSTACK

Becker took a room in a small hotel on West 11th street in the Village. He had no idea where to start, but he had to start somewhere. Kingman had dumped his stolen car in the Village, so that was as good as any place to begin his search.

Flowers had organised the arrest warrant and Becker himself had provided a pretty solid briefing along with files, case notes and pictures to the homicide squad in New York. Becker had offered his services as a consultant to the NYPD, but the department had no interest in an out-of-towner getting underfoot in the Big Apple. Kingman hadn't murdered anyone in New York, so he clearly wouldn't be a priority. Becker figured the only way the NYPD might arrest Kingman is if he walked in and surrendered himself. So while Becker was ostensibly sunning himself in Miami, he was actually sitting in a cheap hotel in New York looking at the pictures spread on the bed cover, of Oscar Kingman and his various victims.

They had determined that Kingman had been to New York at least twice before, but there was a big difference between being a tourist and being a murderer on the run. Every big city had its underbelly and New York was no exception. Becker prodded at the photoshopped pictures of what Kingman might look like now if he had altered his appearance. Kingman with a beard, Kingman with a moustache, Kingman with a shaved head, Kingman with long hair, wigs, different colours... any of these. He could be any of these. He took a selection of photos and jammed them in his inside coat pocket. To find Kingman he would have to become Kingman.

Becker knew from the car park video what time Kingman had left there and in which direction he had headed, but that was all he knew. He started his search at 5.00 a.m. the following morning, outside the garage on Hudson where Kingman had abandoned the car. He wandered aimlessly like he imagined Kingman might have done, gradually coming to understand that he needed food and shelter. Working in a widening grid pattern, he stopped at every cafe or newsstand that was open, showing the photographs, repeating the spiel. By 5 o'clock that night he had covered over forty blocks between Hudson Street and 5th Avenue. He found a grill, had a steak and a couple of beers, went back to his hotel where he rang his wife, then collapsed on the bed.

The following morning Becker set out in the dark to cover the area west of Hudson Street and up into Chelsea, stopping only briefly for a quick breakfast and lunch on the go. But New York was a big place and by the end of the second day, Becker was beginning to appreciate the scope and futility of the task he had set himself. He was a cop and a good one, knew that even in today's modern world, you could still get results from beating the pavement. Day three was a later start and Becker lay staring at the ceiling for a while, before finally throwing back the covers and going to the window. A lone car passed below him, pushing a long shadow ahead of it as the first sharp rays from a rising sun raced down along the tree lined street. As he watched, the street came alive with more cars and cabs. It would be a nice day.

Becker was showered and out on the street by 7.30. Once more, he set off towards the car park with a plan to stay on Hudson Street until it became 8th Avenue, and then to continue on through Chelsea right up to Times Square. No turn-offs, no diversions. By 8.30 he had worked his way up to Bleecker Street and come across a busy little magazine store. He was about to pass it by when he noticed the sign over the door that listed maps for sale. Inside, he waited until the clerk was free, then stepped up to the counter and held up a photo of Oscar.

"Good morning. Wonder if you could help me. I'm trying to track down my friend… this guy, Oscar. He moved here a few weeks back and nobody has heard from him since."

The guy looked at Becker, then at the photo.

"You a cop?" he asked.

"No no," laughed Becker digging out his North Carolina driving license and holding it out. "No, like I say he's just a friend from back home and we're all a bit worried about him, he gets, you know, depressed."

"Well he does look kind of familiar. There was a guy in here a few weeks back looked a bit like that, but if I remember right he was completely bald."

"Bald? Oh sorry," said Becker, " That's an old photo I showed you."

He shuffled through his shots.

"Here's a more recent one."

"Yeah well that might be the guy. He was looking for a cheap apartment. I gave him the name of an agent in Brooklyn that could maybe help him out," said the clerk.

"That's great. If you give me the name of the agent I might be able to track him down. Man I've been searching for days and was about to give up and go home," said Becker.

The clerk looked him up and down again, then jotted down a name on a piece of paper.

"This is the agent," he said handing it to Becker. "Good luck."

Then he reached past Becker to serve a waiting customer.

Out on the street Becker stared at the slip of paper. He could hardly believe his luck. He had a name, a lead. He went into the nearest coffee shop, bought breakfast and called Louis Flowers. It really was turning into a good day.

"You want me to feed this information to NYPD Roger?" said Flowers on the other end of the line.

"No not yet," said Becker. "I don't want to do anything to frighten him off again. I want to track him down. Find out exactly where he is. He's never seen me, doesn't know who I am. I should be able to get pretty close once I find him."

"And then?" asked Flowers.

"And then I'll call you with information for the NYPD," replied Becker.

"Okay, but remember you've got no authority and no jurisdiction there. You're a tourist right?"

"Right sergeant."

"Well be careful Roger. We don't know what this guy might do if he's cornered."

Becker hung up and finished his coffee. He walked back to his hotel and googled the estate agent.

• • •

The agent's office was situated in an old building on India Street. Becker was dressed in his suit and carried a briefcase as he stood across the street watching the tiny shopfront. Through the office window he could see an overweight middle-aged man in a shirt and tie and a young girl sitting behind a computer at a desk by the entrance. He moved off up the street and waited. Twenty minutes later the agent came out of the office and drove off in a black Honda. Becker crossed the street and went in. The young girl looked up and smiled.

"Good morning, how can I help you?"

"Hi," said Becker holding up his badge with his fingers across the state ID. "I'm Detective Roger Becker."

The girl's eyes widened.

"No need to worry, just a routine check is all. I just need to see your rental records for the past four weeks. We come by all the agents at least once a year," he lied.

"Well I don't know, maybe you should wait for my boss, he just left. Or I could call him."

"Look, I wouldn't bother disturbing him. Nobody is in trouble, we just cross check these records against our missing persons files, that sort of thing. It's all pretty boring stuff really. If you could just give me a print-out of anyone that has rented from you in the last four weeks, simple."

"Okay, well I suppose that would be all right," she said punching at the keyboard. "Here they are. Let me separate the last month's new entries. There we go, just eleven."

She sent the document to print and turned to collect the sheet of paper from the machine behind her.

"That's great, thanks for your help," said Becker taking the paper from her and putting it into his briefcase. "Bye now."

It took a while, but he finally found a cab and headed back to his hotel. It was getting late and he was tired and sore. Tired and sore but elated. He felt close, he had a list. Just eleven names and maybe one of them might be his man.

THE HAND OF FATE

Oscar stood at his window watching the world go by but seeing none of it.

'How could it be? How?'

He believed in fate. Up until recently he'd accepted it and everything it dished out to him.

'Strange' he thought, *'but when I finally chose not to simply accept my fate, when finally I said enough and killed those people, turns out that was fate too. Fate that brought me here, brought me face to face with my own father.'*

He tried to imagine, to calculate the odds of him ending up in Brooklyn and stumbling across the man who had run out on him nine months before he was even born. He figured there wouldn't be a mathematician in the world who would accept the probability and yet here they were, all neatly pinned down and crossed up at that time and place where fate had steered them.

That night the demons came again. They visited him first one by one in an endless passing parade of truths and horrors, relentless. The stinking drunk that attacked his mother, tearing at her clothes while little Oscar pulled at his leg. The drunk rearing up and turning on him, his mother terrified, legs spread and eyes wide pleading. Oscar felt again the blinding pain as the brute smashed him across the head with a closed fist. Oscar collapsing, his eyes swimming in his head as he woke screaming and sweating. His heart thumping so bad it might burst right out of his chest. When he finally calmed down and drifted back to sleep they came at him not one at a time now, but all at once. All those foul nuns and priests, the jogger and the shop assistant stinking of lavender, Edmund Llewellyn eyes wider, still with the letter opened buried in his neck up to the handle. They raged around his head, around his room spitting blood and vile blackness from their soundless mouths until finally, together they reached down for something on the floor at the end of Oscar's bed. They came up swinging a limp body at him, a young woman with a gun... a cop. She cartwheeled across the room and landed on him, at once a tangle of torn flesh and broken bones. He struggled to push her away, to get out of bed, and suddenly they were gone, almost all gone. In the gloom he sensed one more shape, as his grandfather stepped forward holding out a glass.

'Drink this Oscar. Drink this and it's all over'

The old man shrugged, laughed and tipped the drink down his own throat, then melted to the floor looking up at Oscar.

'All that pussy,' he said, *'all that pussy, like taking candy from a baby Walter, candy from a baby.'*

Oscar had pissed the bed. When they finally left him he sat up in the sharp stink of it and hugged his knees to his chest. He stayed like that, rocking back and forth and weeping uncontrollably for hours. When the sun rose he was still there, silent now except for the great hacking sobs that convulsed through his exhausted body, causing his chin to flap and his teeth to chatter. He pitched forward and lay shivering for a long time, his jaw aching, his body racked, until eventually all noise and movement ceased as Oscar Kingman fell into a deep sleep.

When he woke, he lay watching the dust motes float and swirl in the light that peeked through his broken blinds. He felt like he'd been hit by a bus, then he remembered that Harvey was having the morning off to see a doctor about his arthritis. He had trusted Oscar with the keys to the store and asked him to open up. Harvey reminded Oscar of old Mr. Alperstein, so he would not abuse his trust by letting him down. He staggered into the shower and stood under the steaming hot water for fully fifteen minutes, finally emerging from the bathroom a little less stiff and a little more awake. The store was just a ten minute walk from his apartment so, on the way, Oscar stopped for a quick breakfast and still arrived with almost an hour to spare.

It felt good. It felt good to unlock the security grate and the front door. It felt good to turn on the lights and to turn off the alarm system. It felt good to belong and that's how Oscar dared to feel… like he might belong. But last night's events played on his mind. He went about getting ready for the day's trade. Twenty minutes before opening he took a delivery of fasteners and plumbing supplies from a truck that was double parked out front. Oscar went down through the basement and opened the cellar hatch in the pavement. The delivery driver handed him down the heavy cartons and he stood on the middle rung of the ladder and slid them into the shelving beside him. The whole time he worked, his mind was on the events of the previous night. It seemed inconceivable to him that he should come face to face with the man who was his father. There was no way he could be one hundred percent certain that this was his father but, if he was, then he was responsible for everything that had ever happened to Oscar. His mother had been part of a respectable middle class family and this man had taken all that away. One night of pleasure traded off for a lifetime of hell.

He had never found it in him to blame his mother for his own situation, with such a long list of other culprits it hardly seemed to matter. But this guy, this Woodrow the travelling salesman, he was the first point on the map. He was the wellspring from which all of Oscar's problems had flowed. He would learn of the consequences, he would meet his son. *He was already dead.*

With the last carton stored and the truck driver gone, Oscar closed the hatch and checked the time. He still had almost ten minutes so he sorted the cartons into their correct storage places in the long narrow cellar, then took the consignment note and headed back up the stairs to open the store. He was fine while he was serving people but, in between customers, he was having mild panic attacks.

'What if I am wrong? What if it was just coincidence and this man isn't my father at all?'

But with righteous logic he discovered he could reconcile that problem. Even if this Woodrow wasn't his father, he was certainly the same miserable excuse for a human being as his father had been, and so could reasonably be visited with the same fate.

But Oscar perceived that the biggest problem was his future, or more correctly Walter Johnson's future. It was weeks since he had fled North Carolina and come to New York. Here he had established a new personality, started building a new life. Oscar Kingman dared to hope that he had made a getaway. Here there was no Oscar Kingman, there was just Walter Johnson and maybe, just maybe, Walter Johnson had a future. He felt that soon he would be in a position to call Wendy, not yet but soon. First he would have to deal with this new development. Oscar felt the twitch beside his eye. *Tick tick tick tick tick.* Woodrow Wilson would pay for his sins, would be strung aloft on the crucifix of consequence, but Oscar had to be very careful. This thing would require lots of planning. He would not jeopardise the future that he and Wendy would have together.

The decision had cheered him up. Resolution was always a good thing. It would happen at some point in the future. It would be planned with precision but, right now, Oscar had a hardware store to run.

Later in the morning Oscar had his head down updating stock sheets when he heard the door alert.

"Good morning Walter."

He looked up to see Harvey Bennet standing there.

"Oh Harvey, how'd it go with the doctor?" he asked.

"More of the same I'm afraid Walter. He says it's not going to get any better. He wants to try a new anti-inflammatory treatment, but he says I really need to retire, like that's going to happen. It's a good thing you're here now to do the heavy lifting. I struggle with those cellar stairs something terrible."

"Listen Harvey. I know I've only been here a few weeks, but I've got lots of experience and I'd be more than happy to come in earlier and open the place up, take the deliveries, that kind of thing. That way you don't need to get up so early. You just concentrate on the customers and I could manage the stock and ordering for you. I can serve customers when it gets busy and I can lock up at night so it's not such a long day for you."

"Well that would be great Walter, but I just can't afford to pay you any more than I do now," said Harvey.

"That's fine," replied Oscar. "I've been looking at areas where I think I can improve things, maybe tighten up on stock control, that type of thing. I've also got some ideas for some new lines that we had in my last place. I think some of them would go well here, they kind of suit the city handyman thing. If you're happy to give it a try and I can improve the store turnover, then we can talk about a pay rise later on. But let me see if I can do it first… and if you're happy for me to try."

Harvey Bennet seemed to hesitate, so Oscar backed off.

"Okay I'm sorry Harvey. You're right. It's only been a few weeks, so it's probably a bit soon for me to take on a bigger role in running the store. I know I've got no references or anything, but I've told you why I left my last job, the business with finding out my children aren't really my children and all. It was a miserable marriage right from the start and I just had to get out, that's all. I don't want anybody knowing where I am. I just want to make a fresh start."

"No, *I'm* sorry Walter. I don't want to seem ungrateful. It's a very generous offer and it really... well it's just my wife Marjorie. She's not a very trusting person I'm afraid," said Harvey appearing embarrassed. "She was against me hiring you to begin with, what with at your age and with you having no references."

"I understand Harvey. It's no big deal," said Oscar.

"When she met you the other day she nagged me for hours. She said she felt uncomfortable around you."

He took the stock sheets off the counter in front of Oscar and looked them over.

"Oh hell Walter. Let's just do it. There's not enough trust in the world these days. You let me worry about Marjorie. I'll make us a coffee and you can tell me about some of these new lines."

Sometime around 2.30 in the afternoon, Oscar found Harvey sound asleep at his desk. He decided to let the old guy sleep, but he woke up when the next customer tripped the door alert.

"Sorry about that Walter," he said when the customer was gone. "I'm not getting any sleep at night with this back problem and all."

"Why don't you head home and rest up a bit? There's nothing here I can't manage. I'll ring you when I lock up, to let you know everything is okay," said Oscar.

"There's no need for that," said Harvey. "We've got ourselves a deal, so I'll trust you."

He pulled a big bunch of keys out of his pocket and took off the big old fashioned safe key. He handed it to Oscar and slapped him on the shoulder.

"For the days takings," he said. "Just put any cash in the safe and I'll bank it twice a week like always."

He saw the strange look on Oscar's face.

"Don't look at me like that Walter. You can't *half* trust a man can you? I'll see you sometime in the morning."

ON FOOT IN BROOKLYN

Becker had been a little disconcerted to find that the realtor's records were pretty short on information. There was no indication of any of the customer's ages and in only one case did it mention a couple. The video from the car park showed Kingman on his own, but it was still possible Kingman had the woman with him, had dropped her off before dumping the car. He figured he had to check out the couple on the list, but that didn't mean that either Kingman or the mystery woman hadn't gone to the agent alone. There was also an Alex Hannaford on the list, with no indication whether it was a male or a female. That meant Becker had to investigate all eleven names and addresses. He would start with the couple.

There was a light rain falling when Becker woke the following morning. Straight after an early breakfast, he left his hotel in the Village, dressed in a pea jacket and knit cap. He got a cab to the first address on his list, which was a basement apartment in a dreary four storey walkup on the edge of Fort Greene Park. He pulled the cap low on his head and turned up his jacket collar. Hunched against the drizzle, he passed by the entrance to the apartment and took in as much as he was able with surreptitious glances, then he crossed the street and went into the park. There was a path leading up a gentle slope to some kind of monument and from there, Becker was able to keep a watch on the apartment through the trees. After almost an hour he had begun to feel a bit conspicuous, as well as cold and wet. He figured whoever lived in the apartment had most likely already left for the day. He would have to return at another time, so under the dubious shelter of a tree, he pulled out his list to check the next address. It was time to move on, so he made his way back down the path. He was almost directly opposite the building when the basement door opened.

Becker fumbled for the digital camera in his jacket pocket. He got it turned on just in time to capture a man and woman come up the steps to the pavement. They were both rugged up against the rain, making it impossible for Becker to see either face at that distance. He kept shooting as the man and woman kissed and headed off in separate directions. Becker went out through the park entrance and followed the man, while he switched the camera to view mode and zoomed in tight on the best of the images. It wasn't Kingman. They were too young, the man maybe twenty six to twenty eight years old with sharp features and long blond hair… not Kingman.

And then there were ten.

Becker spent the rest of that day scoping out three other addresses. The first two were easily crossed off his list, one was a Chinese student and the other a gentleman well into his eighties. The last one, Alex Hannaford, was a woman, no doubt about that. Her studio apartment was at the top of a building on Metropolitan Avenue in East Williamsburg. Becker had followed someone into the building and then risked climbing the stairs. There was only one apartment on the top floor. He had listened at the door for a minute or so before turning to leave… and walked straight into her.

"Can I help you?"

"Jesus you scared the crap out of me!" said Becker thinking on his feet.

He clutched his chest.

"Sorry, I'm looking for an apartment. Someone said this one was for rent."

"Not any more, I've just moved in… John!" she called over her shoulder.

Becker heard the footsteps on the stairs and a man appeared behind her.

"Is there a problem Honey?"

"No no," cut in Becker. "I was told this apartment was available, but clearly it's been rented. I'll just get out of your way. I'm sorry to bother you."

He squeezed past the couple, headed down the stairs and out onto the street. The rain was heavier now and Becker got a cab back to his hotel where he copied out the remaining names and addresses onto seven individual slips of paper from his notebook, then jammed them under the mirror frame. He spent the next half hour or so looking at them, taking them down one at a time and saying the names out loud. It didn't help. He checked and re-checked the addresses against his map and planned a route for the next day, then he went out in search of something for dinner.

The following morning Becker woke to the sound of traffic under his window. An hour later he was in Greenpoint on Manhattan Avenue. The apartment he was watching was situated over a grocery store in an old red clapboard building. It had been rented in the name of Walter Johnson. That name could be real or could be fake. Any of them could be fake, Becker had no way of knowing. The entrance opened directly onto the sidewalk and he could see there were four apartments up there. Walter Johnson had rented 3A. He stayed put until around 9.30 a.m. and the entrance door opened only twice. Once when an old lady came out pulling a shopping cart and another time when a man came out and placed some cartons on the kerbside. Each time Becker made to leave something drew him back. *'Walter Johnson, Walter Johnson. Who are you Walter Johnson?'* But finally at around 10 o'clock he dragged himself away.

He set out to walk the twelve blocks to the next address on his list. This one was rented by someone calling himself Darrell

Thompson. On the way, Becker decided to risk a new tactic for finding out if the apartments were actually occupied, or if he was wasting his time standing around outside empty buildings. On arrival he pushed the buzzer and was surprised to get an answer immediately. It was a mature male voice.

"Yes it's Fedex Mr. Thompson. I've got a delivery for you, but I'm double parked around the corner and I'll need you to come right down and sign for it," said Becker.

"A parcel? Oh okay, I'm on my way."

Becker crossed the street and waited. In a few minutes the door opened and an old man, a short old man who wasn't Oscar Kingman, came out onto the top step. He was still there looking up and down the street scratching his head, as Becker walked away to find the next apartment on his list. Becker used the Fedex ruse on all the remaining apartments and by 4 o'clock he had ticked two more off his list. Now he felt he was getting somewhere, just four apartments left. He figured if those apartments were empty during the day, he'd have to stake them out at night.

He was on Flatbush Avenue, so he grabbed a sandwich and sat in Prospect Park while he called the office. He got through to Victor Brosa and filled him in on his progress. Brosa told him that Flowers had received a fairly serious bawling-out from the captain, who was screaming for answers and wanted to know why Becker wasn't back in the office.

"You need to speak to the sergeant Roger. All hell's gonna break loose if you don't call in. He's been ranting about you not answering your phone."

"I can't talk to him yet Vic. Listen I know I'm close. If I phone him or answer his calls he'll order me back. I'll call him as soon as I've got something to tell him," replied Becker.

"All right then, I hope you know what you're doing."

Becker hung up and got a cab straight back to Greenpoint. He was working on a hunch. *'Walter Johnson.'* Working against the clock and working on a hunch. *'Christ, could it get any worse?'*

The cab dropped him around the corner from Walter Johnson's apartment and after carefully checking the area he went straight to the door and pressed the buzzer... nothing. He went into the grocery store, just an old lady behind the counter and a woman buying milk. He waited for the customer to leave.

"Hi, I'm looking for my friend Walter Johnson. I think he lives upstairs, but he's not home. I don't suppose you'd know where I'd find him," said Becker, brandishing the photo.

The old lady barely glanced at the picture.

"Walter. Sure, I know Walter. Such a nice polite young man. He works at a hardware store. Let me see, I think it's HM Hardware or something like that, maybe fifteen twenty blocks down on Manhattan Avenue, left hand side," she said pointing south. "About ten minutes walk, old place, been there for years, you can't miss it."

Becker checked his watch.

"Thank you so much for your help."

The old lady was still giving him directions as he went out the door.

Walter Johnson, Walter Johnson. Hardware store.

Becker remembered that Oscar Kingman had worked part-time in a hardware store. It was on his file.

As he headed down Manhattan Avenue, Becker called Victor Brosa again.

"Rog, what now?"

"Look Vic, things are moving quickly. So here's what I know. I've got a guy works in a bookshop in the Village who identified Oscar Kingman from a photograph. Kingman was asking about apartments, so he referred him to a dodgy realtor in Brooklyn. I went to the realtor and got the rent list for the past month. There were eleven names on the list, but I've worked through it and I've tracked down a person calling himself Walter Johnson. What? No you don't need to know how I got that list. So, this Walter Johnson moved into an apartment in Greenpoint just a few days after the stolen car was dumped in the Village. But here's the thing… he's got himself a job in a hardware store here in the neighbourhood."

"What neighbourhood?" asked Brosa.

"Greenpoint Brooklyn Vic, where I am. I'm on my way to the hardware store right now."

"Jesus Becker, to do what?"

"It's okay Vic, I know the drill. I'll be careful. Once I've identified him I'll phone it in to NYPD and I'll call Flowers."

Becker hung up the phone as he saw a blue shopfront come into view on the other side of the road. H&M Hardware. He checked the pavement ahead and continued on until he was directly opposite the store, but he could see no activity inside. He needed to be closer, so he crossed the road.

NOBODY'S GETTING OUT OF HERE ALIVE

Harvey Bennet left for the day and Oscar got back to work sorting stock down in the basement. After coming up to serve customers four or five times in a half hour, he decided to leave the stock until Harvey was back the next day. He shut the basement trapdoor at the rear of the store and went into the lunchroom to make himself a coffee. The kettle was boiling when he heard the door alert and he stepped out to find Woodrow Wilson standing there with a plastic bag in his hand. Oscar was a little shaken to see him and struggled to recover his composure.

"Woodrow... sorry, Woody, what are you doing here?"

"Well I told you I'd be coming in with the latch."

"Latch?"

"Yeah the latch, the broken latch remember?" said Woody laughing. "But then you left so quick I wasn't sure you heard me. You okay now?"

"Oh yes, nothing serious. I remember now," said Oscar, "the broken latch off the freezer."

"Right," said Woody, pulling the latch out of the plastic bag. "I've taped the door shut, so I sure hope you can find something."

Oscar felt lightheaded. He felt the twitch beside his eye, *tick tick tick tick tick,* little pain there. Suddenly he saw it all laid out before him, saw it all happening, down there in the basement, the boiler room... everything. Fate had delivered Woodrow Wilson right into his hands. He looked at the man now and thought he looked older, more frail. Oscar realised that this was the first time he had seen him out from behind the bar. He looked down at the creased and baggy pants and the worn runners with the toe broken through. This man, his father, once a predator, now little more than a pathetic bum. He felt disgust. Then he sensed Woody's eyes on him, looked up to see the barman watching him carefully. He was looking at him warily.

'What was he seeing?'

"Look, if it's a bad time."

"No no," said Oscar. "Right, well if we have anything it will be down in the basement. There's piles of stuff down there."

He reached back into the lunchroom and took a sign saying, 'back in five minutes' and hung it on the front door, sliding the latch closed. He came back past Woody and opened the trapdoor to the cellar.

"If you wouldn't mind waiting a second I'll go down and turn on the lights. I don't want you tripping over something and hurting yourself," he said as he disappeared down the steps.

He switched on the lights and slowly turned a full circle, reminding himself of the location of those things he might need. He would have to move fast. Satisfied, he poked his head up out of the trapdoor and called to Woody, who was hanging around suspiciously near the battery display.

"You need batteries too?" he asked innocently.

"Er, no, just looking," answered the barman, a guilty flush on his face.

"Okay then," said Oscar. "You could come down and give me a hand if you don't mind. Be quicker with the two of us looking. Bring the latch,"

Oscar stood by the foot of the steps as Woody came down.

"Try in there behind that divider," he said pointing further into the basement. "There's lots of little boxes of locks and hinges and stuff there. It's as good a place as any to start."

Woody went off in the direction Oscar had pointed, checking his surrounds as he went, maybe looking for something to steal when Walter wasn't looking. Oscar was three paces behind him, and as the barman went around the divider, he reached down and took hold of a nice shiny new shovel. Two more paces, he swung it back like a baseball bat and stepped up fast just as Woody stopped and turned around. The barman saw it coming, but could do nothing as the flat of the blade struck him a sickening thud across the side of his face. The shovel jarred in Oscar's hands and rang out like some cheap gong. Woodrow Wilson collapsed on the basement floor and lay there on his back, legs scraping back and forth looking for purchase. He reminded Oscar of a cockroach whacked with a shoe and trying to flip over, find his legs. He was staring up at Oscar with a look of total confusion on his face. Oscar noticed the strange shape of Woody's cheekbone and the thin stream of blood that flowed from his bright red ear. The barman tried to say something, tried to raise his head but Oscar brought the shovel down again with all his weight, this time flat across his face and everything went quiet in the basement. The cockroach's legs stopped moving. Oscar waited, listened, then stood the tool against the divider and knelt down with his ear to the barman's bloodied face. He was breathing, but the blood from his smashed nose and mouth was pooling in his throat, creating an obscene gurgling sound now as Woody started choking, drowning in his own fluids. He coughed out a gout of blood and a few teeth, which stuck to his chin.

Oscar rolled him onto his side and watched as the blood drained from his mouth and the gurgling noise lessened. Quickly he went to the shelves and gathered together a packet of zip ties, duct tape and a coil of nylon rope. It took him no more than five minutes to secure and immobilise the unconscious barman. With his mouth securely taped up and his feet taped and zip tied,

Oscar dragged him to the back of the basement and into the boiler room. He rolled him onto his stomach and taped and tied his hands together behind his back. Content that the barman was secure, Oscar gave him a hefty kick in the ribs, then went out, locking the boiler room door behind him.

Upstairs, Oscar checked himself in the washroom mirror and then went to the front, unlocked the shop door and removed the sign. It was barely ten minutes since Woodrow Wilson had entered the store and provided Oscar with the unplanned opportunity to exact revenge on him, this man who was his father. This man who had preyed upon hundreds of vulnerable young girls. Back in the lunchroom, Oscar flicked the kettle on again and sat down at the table, pulling in deep breaths, blowing them out.

Each time he had engaged violence, he was amazed to discover how focused he became. How he acted with cool resolve and got the job done quickly and cleanly. He was able to think on his feet and react to circumstances with quick decisions, always the right decisions. Today was no different, but as he sat at that table, his hands began to shake uncontrollably and the twitch beside his eye came back stronger, *tick tick bang bang bang*, firing sharp jolts into his brain and causing him to wince with the pain of it. He felt the bile rise in his throat and he stumbled to the washroom. Clutching his head he dropped to his knees at the toilet bowl and threw up. He was still there ten minutes later, shaking uncontrollably when he heard the door alert.

"Just a second. I'll be right there," he called, pushing himself up and checking himself in the mirror.

He splashed water on his face and dried himself with his sleeve, then content he was at least presentable, he went out into the shop.

In the course of the next half hour and in between customers, Oscar went down to the boiler room twice. The first time he looked there was no sign of life from the barman. The second time, as he opened the door and flicked on the light, the barman turned his mangled face toward him, his chin scraping on the rough concrete floor as he strained to look up at his attacker. Thick ropey streams of blood trailed from his face to the floor and Oscar could see that one eye was totally dislocated from its socket and faced into another place. Woodrow Wilson's shoulder twitched as he tried to blink away the blood from his one remaining eye. All the big questions were evident there in that one eye, that one bloodied swollen eye, no more than a crude slit.

Why?

Oscar looked at his watch, then turned off the light and locked the door. It was almost an hour until closing time and then he would answer those questions. He went back up to the shop and stood behind the counter, very still and staring straight ahead. A great sense of calm came over him, as he felt somehow nearer to the end of a long and exhausting journey. He realised that the journey might end with his own death, but the thought did not concern him. If that was to be his fate then he had no control over it.

'Fate, fatalistic, fatal.'

Funny how he'd never connected the word *fate* with *fatal*, so obvious, but now he finally saw how it all fitted together. Life and death all mapped out and driven by fate. He smiled as he remembered the words from a novel he'd once read… *'Nobody's getting out of here alive, we're all going to die. Just some sooner than others.'* It had stuck in his head back then and now he saw how beautifully and succinctly it summed it all up. *'Just accept it and get on with your life, there is nothing you can do about it. You did what you did, you made your decisions.'* It was all just part of the process.

So now Oscar pushed on. *'Just accept it and get on with your life.'* He considered how he might succeed at this, how he might dispose of Woodrow Wilson's body before Harvey Bennet arrived in the morning. How he might get away with it, how he might call Wendy and together they might live here in New York. Oscar understood that this might just as easily be the path that fate had mapped out for him. Happy ever after or dead, it was all the same now to Oscar Kingman.

The last few customers straggled in, bought fly spray, glue, nails and paint. Oscar smiled, chatted and bade them a good evening. He went through the till and tallied up the takings then, took the key and opened the safe. Oscar had never been in the safe before, it had been Harvey Bennet's last gesture of trust to give him the key. It sucked open with a faintly oily scent. Besides the old metal cashbox there were neat stacks of paper, invoices, records, all bundled with string. On the bottom shelf there was something wrapped in a cloth. Oscar took it out, the oily smell stronger now and adding clues, along with the weight and shape, to what was inside the bundle. He unwrapped it carefully and stared down at the handgun that lay in the cloth draped over his hand. The imprint on the top of the pistol grip read 'Made in Austria - Glock' and the slide was pulled back. He knew very little about handguns, but he soon found the button on the grip to eject and check the magazine. He popped out the rounds until the magazine was empty... four bullets. He studied the action, figured out how to get a round in the barrel once the magazine was inserted and how the strange trigger lock worked. Then he jammed the magazine back in the pistol and it made a satisfying metal click as it locked home. He pulled back on the slide and sent a round into the chamber. He was a bit scared of the thing and had no way of knowing if he'd got it right, but then he didn't expect to actually use it.

With ten minutes left to closing, he went to the lunchroom, jammed the gun in his pocket and carried an old wooden chair down to the basement. He unlocked the boiler room door and turned on the light. Woody had pushed himself into a corner and got himself somehow half propped up against the wall. Oscar was amazed at how swollen Wilson's head was. His left eye hung bloodied on his cheek, the socket split wide and gaping toward his temple. His right eye was no more than a slit, that side of his face now swollen beyond recognition and his nose was grotesquely trashed and flattened against his big watermelon head. He flinched as Oscar stepped closer to him and, through the slit, Oscar saw a tiny movement of that tortured eye. He stepped back and pointed to the chair.

"I'll be closing the shop soon and when I've done that I'll be back to answer your questions. But before I go and close up, I want you to think about something. You should know that I have killed many people, they deserved it, but I killed all of them quickly. You... you are going to die slowly. I'm going to tie you to this chair and take your life one tiny bit at a time then, when you are just about to die and only then, I will tell you why."

He locked the boiler room and went along to the divider near the front of the basement, picked up the pieces of Woody's broken latch and inspected the shovel closely for blood. It would need cleaning. He turned to go to the stairs, then froze.

He heard the creak of the wooden floorboards above him, then gentle footfalls. Someone was in the store.

'Why didn't I hear them come in?'

THE BASEMENT

Trying not to look too suspicious, Becker crossed the road and leaned against the front of the store next to H&M Hardware. He edged along past the display window until he could see in through the door. The store was long and narrow, with a counter close to the entrance on the right hand side. It appeared to be just one long corridor lined with busy shelves disappearing away to the back where, a white door marked 'private' stood beside a display of bulk rope and chain spools.

Becker still didn't know if Oscar Kingman might recognise him. He had avoided any media coverage or press conferences concerning the case. He knew his name had been used but was unsure if any media outlets had picked up a file photo of him to go with the story. Then there was the day Casey had been killed. *'Had Kingman got a good look at him?'* He tried to figure the odds of being recognised, if in fact Kingman was in there. And that was the decider, that was the problem... was Kingman actually in there? He still had nothing for NYPD or Flowers. Of course, he could simply watch the door from the other side of the street. The place would close soon. But Becker had always worked on hunches and he was going to do that now. He stepped up to the door and leaned in, immediately seeing the infrared customer alert mounted on the base of the shelf just inside. It was around knee height and Becker figured if he was careful he could step over it. It might give him an advantage if he could get in unannounced.

His right foot came down carefully on the other side of the beam and he lifted the left one over and clear. The floor was covered in some kind of multi-coloured rubber tiles, but as he took his first step it gave a little creak. He paused briefly then moved further into the store past the thermos flasks and lightbulbs, where he encountered his first problem. Amid the general cluster of the store, he hadn't been able to tell that the store opened out into three aisles at this point. Nuts, bolts and nails to the left, electrical and gardening to the right. He realised Kingman could be working in either of these aisles. He made a decision.

"Hello, anybody there, can I get some help here please?" he said as he stepped through and looked up the lefthand aisle. Empty.

"Hello, anybody?"

He checked the right aisle, also empty. He walked quickly to the rear of the store. Behind the rope and chain spools was a small window. Becker could make out a desk with a computer and a couple of old wooden filing cabinets. He could see the room was empty. He tapped on the white door marked 'private' and pushed it open.

"Hello!"

He stepped into the space beyond, something willing him on. The right hand side was lined with metal racking and the left hand side consisted of three small rooms, the first being the office. The door to the second room was open and Becker could see it was a lunchroom. The third door was slightly ajar and he pushed it open to reveal a toilet and washroom.

'Where the hell is everybody,' thought Becker.

Then he noticed the trapdoor against the right hand wall, partly concealed by the racking and piles of cartons. It was open, but it was in darkness down there and so Becker called again.

"Hello, is anybody here… can someone help me please?"

But there came no response from the basement.

Becker tried to think it through. *'Was this a trap and if so, then how could Kingman have known he was coming, him or anyone else for that matter? There was still the question of*

*whether Walter Johnson was Oscar Kingman and if he was, did
he work here? Had the old lady in the grocery store got it right?
Was this the right hardware store?'* There were just too many
variables, too many questions. Becker needed answers. He
needed something solid.

He went back out into the store and took a torch from the
display, slipped in some batteries and checked that it worked.
Then he took a small pinch bar from the tools section and went
back to the basement trapdoor.

He shone the torch down the stairs. They were steep with
open metal treads. He started down and as his foot touched the
third step, something clutched him around the ankle, catching
him completely off balance, then pulled back and pitched him
headfirst down into the darkness. He heard the rattle of the torch
as it bounced down the stairs and broke apart, the pinch bar
hitting the concrete floor below. His head struck something solid
and Becker felt the sickening rush of blood to his skull. He
struggled to stay conscious, but the blackness took him.

When Becker came to, he felt the ropes around his legs and
chest. His head throbbed and there was a serious pain in his left
arm which, along with his right arm, was bound to his sides. His
mouth was taped over and he could taste blood. He could hear
movement close to him and he pretended that he was still
unconscious, opening one eye just a fraction. It was dark, but
there was light spilling under a door and Becker could see that
he was tied to a chair. Right in front of him, he could make out a
pair of legs bound with duct tape and zip ties. He opened his
eyes wider and saw a man propped at an awkward angle against
the wall. The man appeared to have a head injury and as
Becker's eyes became more accustomed to the gloom, he could
see lots of blood and an eyeball hanging in strings of gore and
fibre on the man's cheek. It was hard to tell with all the blood
and swelling, but Becker did not think this was Oscar Kingman.
If it wasn't Oscar Kingman, then who the hell was it? The man

was trying to kick Becker's feet and he started grunting through his taped mouth to get his attention.

Becker opened his eyes completely and grunted back, nodding his head, the tape pulling at his hair, as he realised it went all the way round. The man was shrugging, his swollen eye moving rapidly beneath the slit, when they both heard someone at the door. Becker strained to look around as the light was switched on and he stared straight into the grinning face of Oscar Kingman. In one hand he held a pistol, in the other, Becker's wallet and shield.

"Good evening Detective Becker. My, but you're a long way from home."

I WAS YOUR SON

Roger Becker watched as Oscar Kingman turned and left the boiler room. He heard him shifting some gear around out in the basement, then he reappeared with a wooden crate, which he placed in the doorway and sat on.

"Right then," he said all smiles, "where do we start?"

He held up his hands palms out and shrugged. He was enjoying himself.

"Nobody? Well okay then, I'll start the ball rolling with some introductions shall I? So, I'm Oscar Kingman, although the gentleman on the floor knows me as Walter Johnson. The gentleman on the floor is of course, Woodrow Wilson, but he figures his parents made a poor choice naming him after America's twenty-eighth president, so he prefers to go by the name Woody. I don't like that name much and I sure don't like shortening down perfectly good names, so I am going to stick with Woodrow okay? No objections? Then Woodrow it is.

Now as Woodrow no doubt already heard, our new friend on the chair here is Detective Roger Becker, one of North Carolina's finest.

But where's my manners?"

He stood up, put down the gun, took out a box cutter and leant over Woodrow Wilson.

"Let's get these tapes off shall we."

He sliced straight through the tape and deep into Woodrow's cheek with it, leaving an obscene gash that quickly welled with blood. Wilson emitted a long shrill groan as the blood flowed down his cheek and soaked his shirt collar.

"Oh dear, silly me, how careless, I seem to have nicked you slightly there Woodrow. Never mind," he laughed.

He reached down, gripped the edge of the wound and tore the tape off Wilson's mouth, opening his cheek to the bone.

Woodrow unleashed a deep muted horrific sound as Oscar turned towards Roger Becker.

"Oh by the way, feel free to make as much noise as you like gentlemen. The shop is closed and so is the trapdoor. So there's nobody can hear you down here."

Becker's eyes widened as Oscar pulled his head forward and gripped the back of the tape. He sliced it through carefully, then just as carefully pulled it off Becker's mouth.

"Don't look so surprised Detective, I mean you no harm. I will kill you, but I have no reason to hurt you in the meantime. I promise I'll make it quick when the time comes."

He sat back on the box, picked up the gun and waved it at Becker.

"So that's the introductions done. Would anybody like to take a guess at why we're here? Of course Detective Becker you weren't invited but, now that you're here, you might as well join in."

Becker looked at him. He'd seen this before. He could tell Kingman was running on the adrenaline that coursed through his body like speed, and kept him flying.

'He might make a mistake, they almost always do.'

"I'm happy to join in," said Becker. "But you're wrong when you say I'm uninvited Oscar. You invited me in when you stuck that letter opener through your boss's neck."

Becker saw just the tiniest little flinch, as Kingman's left hand went up and touched his temple. *Right there, right there.* A reaction.

"Ah yes that," said Oscar. "You see Woodrow, what Detective Becker is referring to is the day I killed my boss."

"And a few others besides," added Becker.

"Let's not jump ahead now detective, why don't you tell me why I killed my boss. By the way Woodrow, just for the record my boss's name was Edmund Llewellyn. Please carry on detective."

"From what I know, I think you must have harboured a serious grudge against him. It seems he outmanoeuvred you for a promotion and once he became the manager, he treated you badly," said Becker.

He saw the look of anger that crossed Kingman's face like the shadow of a fast moving cloud.

"He treated everybody badly detective, he just picked on me more than he picked on anyone else. He got his promotions by sucking up to the morons at head office... and cheating. It wasn't beyond him to steal my work and claim credit for it as his own. And are you aware that he abused some of the women in the office Becker?" he spat. "He forced them to have sex with him. He couldn't help himself. He pushed people around, nearly everybody in the place was scared of him, scared of what he would do."

"Were you scared of him Oscar?" asked Becker, maintaining solid eye contact with him.

Oscar held his stare, then his hand went to his temple again and Becker saw the tiny flinch. He looked away and when he answered his voice held less conviction

"I was scared of him," said Oscar, the memory of it tweaking that spot in his head. *Something not right up there.*

"So you murdered him just because he was a bully?" said Becker.

"And there it is detective, right there in that one word... bully. I murdered him because he was a bully and that's reason enough. Have you taken a good hard look at the world lately? You of all people should understand. You're the poor bastard who gets sent out to sweep up the shit. It's gotten so you can't walk the streets safely. You look at someone sideways and they're likely to shoot you, or stick a knife in you. If they get caught, some fucking low-life defence lawyer gets them off on a technicality. You know the drill detective, something like inadmissible evidence or 'they had a deprived childhood, were temporarily insane, drunk or high on drugs.' I don't fucking care about all that shit detective, it's all just excuses. And then if by some twist of fate they do get sent to prison they generally serve only a fraction of their time. You got gangs marauding around our cities raping and pillaging, murdering innocent people and nobody seems to give a damn."

He was wide eyed and ranting now, all over the place, losing it.

"The streets are full of garbage, everything's covered in graffiti and the do-gooders tell us it's a legitimate art form. Tell me Becker, is it a legitimate art form when somebody paints 'Fuck the Pigs' across the front wall of your house? No it isn't, and every generation just accepts more and more and more of this shit as normal and, with every generation, we're too far gone to claw our way back to civilisation."

Oscar was distracted from his tirade by a loud groan from Woodrow Wilson. He was trying to speak, but his mouth was now so swollen that whatever he was saying came out garbled. He gave up and quieted down, exhausted.

"You do know he's dying don't you Oscar?" said Becker.

"Well you know I'm counting on it detective, that's the desired outcome sure enough."

"Who is he? What the hell did he do to you to deserve this, to die slowly? That's what you're doing isn't it? You're going to let him bleed to death. Why for christ sakes?"

"We'll get to that soon enough, but I got distracted. Where was I? That's right I was about to say the streets are a jungle. Sure it's an old cliche, but the world is on fire and everyday it's getting worse and worse. Common sense has been replaced by so-called political correctness. Hold a door for a lady, you're likely to get abused."

Ranting again, one rant spilling into the next.

"Just take a look what passes for entertainment these days. Look at the television shows, the movies. And don't get me started on this reality television shit. It's just not right."

Oscar suddenly stopped talking and looked at the gash on Woody's cheek. The blood had congealed and all but stopped flowing. The front of his shirt was a deep red stain. His breathing was shallow and raspy. Oscar tried to estimate how long he had left. He got up and kicked him hard in the side of the head. Woodrow let out a muffled bellow. Becker shuddered at the sound. It reminded him of a camping trip he'd been on as a kid with his father. They were on the shore of a shallow bay and during the day you could see cattle, standing well out in the water, just their heads visible. At night their bellows echoed up out of the dark like they were some kind of banshees. Little Roger Becker had been petrified and he remembered pulling his sleeping bag over his head and sticking his fingers in his ears to try and block out the unearthly noise. But here there was no sleeping bag. Here, there was just a killer and a man dying in horrific pain.

"And of course, there's all sorts of bullies," continued Oscar in a pleasant conversational tone. "There's your politicians, your banks and your government bureaucrats that play god with peoples lives. Even your lot detective, plenty of bullies in the department I'll wager. Then there's the religions. All those different holier-than-thou bastards that set themselves up as our moral guardians. Each claiming to worship the one true god and each one as bad as the rest. They're fucking bullies detective. Put your money on the plate or you'll burn in hell. Sure some of these people might be genuine, might be deluded enough to genuinely believe it all, but many of them are the lowest of the low and they prey on the poor and the innocent. They play the eternal damnation card to force their will on others. Bullies detective, just bullies."

"And what are you Oscar?" said Becker. "Here you are forcing your will on me, on this person here. You're exactly the same... exactly. Maybe worse. Here you are lecturing me about all these bullies and you're going around killing people. Hasn't it occurred to you that making people dead is another way of forcing your will on them. And what about their families Oscar, what about the pain you cause every time you kill one of these so-called bullies of yours? You are right Oscar, they are bullies and the world is a fucking mess, but you're a part of that mess. You're swilling around in it like the rest of us. What's going to happen to my family when you kill me? What's going to happen to this poor bastard's family..."

Oscar was on his feet in a flash, the muzzle of the Glock pressed hard against Becker's forehead, his other hand pushed into his own temple. His whole body was jerking and Becker thought he might be crying.

"That's enough! Shut the fuck up, you don't understand!" he screamed.

There was a long silence.

"No I don't," said Becker quietly. "I don't understand Oscar. So you can kill me and add me to your tally, or you can tell me what's really going on here. I might even be able to help you. So tell me, help me to understand what's going on. "

"Is this the bit where you feed me a line about getting the charges reduced if I surrender? North Carolina still has the death penalty detective, remember. Is this where you tell me if I cooperate you'll see to it I just get life in prison instead ending up on death row?"

"No," said Becker looking up at him. "You traded away any chance of clemency when you killed Elaine Benny and Daniel Mills."

"Who?" said Oscar looking down.

"Elaine Benny…"

"Yeah yeah not her, Daniel Mills. Was that the joggers name?" asked Oscar.

"The jogger?"

"Yes the guy in the fucking lycra who spilt my breakfast all over me. Just bowled me over, no apologies no nothing. Made me late and next thing Llewellyn is abusing me and I…"

He stopped talking. The tears were streaming down his face now and Becker thought he might have pushed him too far, or maybe not far enough.

'Go for broke Becker,' he thought, *'take a chance, there's nothing to lose.'*

"Let me get this straight. You killed all those people because you were having a bad day. Are you seriously telling me you didn't even know who Daniel Mills was?"

Oscar jammed the Glock harder into Becker's forehead. Becker felt the tremble down through the barrel as it pushed through the thin layer of flesh and ground against the bone. He imagined the fierce red circle pressed there, the nose of the bullet up in its burrow like some deadly rat, waiting waiting. He swivelled his eyes to look up and he could see Oscar Kingman's teeth bared and gritted, as he fought to control his temper. Becker was looking to force a mistake not to get shot, so he backed off.

"I'm sorry Oscar okay… I guess that was out of line. I'm sure there was a lot more to it."

His head jerked forward as Oscar suddenly pulled the gun away. He stood there for a second or two watching Becker, then sat back down on the crate. Still holding the gun he wiped at his eyes with the back of his hand. Becker saw the tears. He tried to free his right arm, but it was bound too tight. His left arm was probably broken and was just a dull ache. He could see no way to escape, no way to overpower Oscar Kingman and to save himself and Woodrow Wilson. Then he realised Kingman was talking, almost a whisper.

"You're wrong about me detective. I'm not like those others. Well at least I wasn't. All my life I've never hurt a fly, never broken any law. I just kept my head down and worked hard. Tried to live a decent life, but around every corner… well anyway, I guess now I *am* like them."

He looked up and smiled a humourless smile, flinching with the pain in his head.

"I guess now I finally fit in."

He placed the Glock on the ground between his feet. Becker was careful not to break eye contact with him.

"I told you we'd come back to this person here, this Woodrow Wilson. He's the reason for all this," said Oscar.

Woodrow was in bad shape. He mouthed something…

"Teeelllp nee," he uttered.

"Help you?" asked Oscar.

"No, n no no. Tel nee, tell nee," he gurgled, his swollen tongue protruding through his bloodied lips.

"Right, got it. You want me to tell you," said Oscar getting up and taking hold of Woodrow's hair. "I'll tell you then. You see Becker this person, this Woody as he likes to call himself, used to be a traveling salesman. He bragged to me about his conquests all up and down the east coast. He bragged how for years he preyed on innocent young women, just girls really. He'd pick out the most vulnerable then, after he slept with them, used them, he just ran out on them, disappeared. Hundreds he said, bragged there were hundreds. He thought it was funny, funny mind you, funny that he might have kids all over the place. He just didn't give a damn what it did to those girls, or those kids, how many lives he destroyed."

Woodrow tried to spit on Oscar, but his fat bloodied tongue got in the way. He probed around with it until a tooth popped out and stuck on his chest in a clot of red slime.

"Show hot, show shucking hot. Hot's itch to ju. Shore jus, jus shucking shellas."

Oscar's shoulders slumped. He let go of Woodrow's hair and dropped down onto the crate. He shook his head, looked at Becker and then back to Woody.

"Jealous? I'll tell you what it is to me. One of those girls… in Huntersville. One of those girls was called Loretta. Remember Loretta Woodrow? You told me about Loretta. Well that was Loretta Kingman. My mother."

The room went totally quiet, then a strange buzzing sound rose up and turned into a low moan. It was coming from Woodrow Wilson. Oscar Kingman watched with a glassy-eyed stare as what was left of his father's face registered the understanding of it. Oscar's stare turned into a sneer. He swallowed and turned to Becker.

"This stinking pile of shit is my father. He destroyed my mother's life. Left her pregnant and alone in some two-bit motel. Her parents disowned her and she ended up on the streets selling her body for drugs and booze. I was there too, I saw it all. I was there every time she got beaten up by some pimp or john, every time she got used, and I was there when she died. I was six years old, fucking six, and she was sitting there on the floor with that needle sticking out of her arm while I tried to wake her up. He did that," he said pointing to Woodrow Wilson. "He did that…"

His voice died away and Becker realised that Oscar was crying again. Woodrow Wilson's feet were scraping back and forth on the dirty floor. He was trying to speak, trying to get something out, still trying when Oscar reached down, picked up the Glock and put two shots through his head.

"I was your son," he said.

BOOK FOUR

THE MEASURE OF THE MAN

'Judge not that you be not judged.

For with the judgement you pronounce

you will be judged, and with the measure

you use it will be measured to you.'

Matthew 7:1-2

THE JUDGEMENT OF OSCAR KINGMAN

The noise of the gunshots in that small brick room were sharp percussive shocks. Not like on television. There was no reverb, no echo, just two loud snaps and the rattle of the ejected shells as they bounced around on the concrete floor. The sound lasted longer in the memory than it did in that tight space.

Becker watched it happen but could do nothing. He saw Oscar Kingman screw up his face and wince, one hand went to his head as he leaned forward. Becker's eyes followed the gun in Kingman's hand as he half stood and moved closer to his father. That first shot punched a neat little hole in the bridge of Woodrow Wilson's nose. Becker closed his eyes against the percussion and heard the next shot maybe a second later, his ears ringing with pain, a high pitched noise that was in his head but not in the room. When he opened his eyes, apart from that neat little hole, Wilson looked the same as he had just seconds before, but the wall behind his head was now splattered and glistening. One less bully, no more pain for the girls of the east coast run and no more pain for Woodrow Wilson.

The smell of gunpowder hung close in the air along with the quiet. Two men left and neither man spoke. Becker thought about his wife and children. He saw their faces right there in that little room and he needed to be with them, needed to stay alive. Oscar Kingman was looking at the gun in his hand like it had gone and killed Woodrow Wilson all of its own accord. He turned to look at Becker, puzzled.

Becker's ears were still popping and ringing and when Oscar spoke it was like he was far away, muffled.

"I don't feel anything," he said. "I thought I would, but I don't feel anything. One minute I was getting ready to cut him again, make him bleed some more, suffer some more, then all of a sudden I just wanted it over. My whole life has been leading up to this one point and I was sure something would happen. I don't know what, but something. I thought when I told him who I was that I would feel something, some kind of release Becker. That I would at least enjoy his pain. But I didn't, then suddenly I felt sorry for him. I don't know, it's like he wasn't my father, I never knew him, he meant nothing to me, just something broken and suffering... so I ended it."

"Oscar!"

"I'm not saying I'm sorry to see him dead because I'm not. It's strange, I felt some kind of elation with the others I killed but nothing, nothing at all here."

He was starting to sound a little panicked. Flinching again and getting irritated.

"Oscar listen to me!" said Becker.

Oscar slowly put the gun on the floor. He took a couple of very deep breaths then turned to face Becker.

Becker was working without a net. He couldn't gauge if Oscar Kingman was more dangerous now than when he'd been waving the gun around. He played his hunch.

"Oscar listen, he was dying. I think in the end you did the right thing, you ended his suffering," he said quietly. "I think that means you are sorry. I think that means that you're human after all. Believe me Oscar, it's a good thing."

Oscar held his gaze then Becker saw a slight nodding of his head. He took another big breath and exhaled noisily.

"So now what detective, what happens now? I don't want to kill you but it seems I've painted myself into a corner."

"You could let me go Oscar. I really just want to go home to my wife and kids. Or you could leave me here and just go yourself. By the time anybody finds me down here you could be long gone," said Becker.

"So how long before they catch up with me? A week a month? They are going to catch up with me aren't they detective? Or are they already here? Is the shop surrounded by half New York's finest already?"

"No Oscar, nobody knows I'm here. There is no cavalry outside, there's just me," said Becker still working on instinct. "But yes, they are going to catch you. There's no telling how long it will take, but they are going to get you."

"But you often hear about cold cases you know, where they never find out who did it, never catch the person."

"Sure," agreed Becker, "but they already know you did it Oscar. Most of those cases go unsolved because there's no name or face. They know you did it Oscar, they won't rest until they have you."

Becker watched him as he digested this information. He was silent for a long time. Becker used his shoulders to put pressure on his bonds again. He tried to move his left arm, but a severe pain forced a scream out of him. The scream seemed to bring Oscar Kingman back to reality.

"It's your arm Detective Becker, you broke it in the fall."

"I didn't fall Oscar, you pulled my legs out from under me," said Becker.

Oscar held up his hands in mock surrender.

"Guilty as charged detective. And speaking of guilt, I've made a decision," he said. "I want a trial."

"Well of course you'll get a trial. This is America, everybody gets a trial."

"No I don't think you understand Roger. You don't mind if I call you Roger do you? It's just that it's one of my conditions. You see I want my trial now... here."

"You're right, I don't understand. How can we have a trial here? What's the point?"

"I'll tell you the point Roger. You find me innocent and I'll let you go and give myself up. You find me guilty," he leant down and picked up the Glock, "I'll kill you and then I'll shoot myself. You understand? I'll carry out the death sentence myself. There's two bullets left."

"You'll shoot me then yourself, are you serious?"

"Of course I'm serious. What kind of question is that? This is a serious situation we have right here."

"Okay then, why me, why now?" asked Becker.

"Fair question. Look Detective, you said a while ago that I did the right thing, ending my father's suffering. You said that it made me human after all. Now I know I've got you tied up here and all but, even so, you've talked to me the whole time like I *am* a human being. You know, in all my life I can count on one hand the people who treated me like a human being. Like just now, you could have lied, said the shop was surrounded. Most people would have done that in your situation. No, you'll be fair. I don't know why, but I trust you and I'd rather trust my fate to you than to a judge and jury that see me as some kind of freak right from the start," he paused, "or I can just shoot you now and get out of here. But like you say, they're going to catch me, especially if I kill you."

"But don't we have a problem here? I mean what makes you think I won't just go through with all this and no matter what I think, tell you I find you innocent just so you let me go?" said Becker.

"I don't think you're that person Roger. I think you have principles and believe me, I've seen enough in my life to know an honest man when I see one. They stand out you see. No... I'll take my chances with you. So I mentioned conditions. The first condition is we work on a first name basis, the next condition is I want a straight one-word answer to a simple question right now, before we actually start the trial. Tell me Roger, and remember one word only, do you think I am innocent or guilty?"

"Guilty," said Becker without even a pause.

"There you go then," said Oscar, "a no-bullshit answer. I think I'm right about you Roger. Third condition. There's a woman. Her name is Wendy, she works at Loughrans. We are in love. I've never loved anyone before, certainly not the woman I'm married to. Wendy and I figured to run away together, but I guess that's not happening now. Somehow Roger, just to know that you're loved by someone is enough," he laughed. "I guess in my case it'll have to be enough. Anyway my condition is I want her left out of all this. She didn't know about the murders until they were all over. In fact we'd barely spoken until that day. I won't lie Roger, once she knew what I'd done she said she didn't care, but that doesn't make her guilty does it?"

"It probably makes her an accessory after the fact. Is that the woman who was with you at your grandfather's beach house?"

"Yes, but like I said she had no part in any of this. She's innocent."

He rolled up his sleeve and showed Becker the tattoo.

"I guess this might raise some questions, somebody might join the dots. I'm sure you can come up with some cover story. You can say I told you about some other woman named Wendy that I once knew, something like that. So anyway, I want you to talk to her. If you find me innocent and I let you go, I won't contact her again, I won't risk her safety. But I want you to see her for me and to tell her how much I love her, how much she means to me. Will you do that Roger?"

"They already know there was a woman down there with you, but I think I can figure something out. Swear to me that she had nothing to do with any of the killings."

"I swear, but you have to talk to her, right?"

He seemed to be getting agitated and quickly. *Tick tick tick tick tick.* Becker watched as his hand went to his temple, he grimaced.

"This is important right!" he screamed. "Look Becker how do I know you're not conning me here."

Becker took a while to answer. When he did he was more cop. He was well off script here and not sure how to respond.

"Look, this is your idea Mr. Kingman. You asked me and you can either believe me or not. You'll just have to decide."

Oscar stood up and kicked the crate away. He pointed the Glock straight at Becker.

"Mr. Kingman… Mr. Kingman, where did that come from?" he was shaking, his finger was on the trigger. "Oscar, my name is Oscar, fuck!"

Becker thought it was all over. He raised his eyes above the barrel and looked Oscar in the eye. The hairs on the back of his neck were up and he felt the cool trickle of sweat down the inside of his right arm.

'I will die here,' he thought. *'This is where I will die.'*

"If you're going to shoot me because I'm being straight with you then go ahead, but I thought you wanted an honest man. You want to be called Oscar fine, Oscar it is. But you give me a condition like that and I need to think it through, make sure I can deliver on the promise before I say yes. If I just said yes straight up without thinking it through, that wouldn't be honest would it Oscar?"

Becker felt sick, lightheaded with the strain. Not fear but sadness and regret. He could count the seconds that he was looking into the barrel of that Glock and then suddenly it fell away from his vision as Oscar dropped his arm to his side. Becker felt the tension ease in his body, but he fought the urge to look away.

"You're right, you're right of course. I'm just, well I guess I'm just a bit touchy is all," he said blinking hard. "I've got this pain in my head, not a headache but something else. Sometimes feels like my head is going to explode."

He recovered the crate, pulled it closer to Becker and sat back down.

"So… yes or no Roger?"

"Yes," replied Becker. "I'll work it out. I'll keep her out of it and I'll talk to her."

Becker pictured the situation in reverse, pictured Oscar Kingman knocking on his door and saying to his wife, *'You know he really loved you Mrs. Becker.'*

He shuddered, came back to where he was, back to reality, back to this tiny little room in a basement in Brooklyn, where he was about to sit judgement on a mass murderer.

"So how do we do this Oscar? How do we start?"

"Start anywhere you like Roger. Just ask me questions."

Becker tried to line it up in his head. There were plenty of questions and they all carried weight, but he decided to start with the dead man on the floor.

"Okay, okay then, maybe I'll get the order all wrong, but let's start with all this… today."

Oscar Kingman nodded.

"You say this man is… was your father, but you say your mother never saw or heard from him after that one night in the motel. But she knew his name right?"

"No, not his actual name. She told my great grandmother that all she knew was a nickname. My great grandmother couldn't remember it, didn't really care, but thought it was something to do with wood or forests or something."

He laughed.

"Woody?" said Becker.

"Turns out," said Oscar.

"So you've been searching for him all this time, all your life?"

"No again, I've never searched for him."

Smiling this time.

"All right," said Becker. "It might save time if you tell me how you found him."

"Yes it might. Well it was fate plain and simple Roger. When I arrived here of course I didn't know anybody. I've never had any friends really, just the odd one or two, but I figured with my new life and new identity I might change that. I don't know why, but after what had happened in Charlotte I felt different, sort of more empowered somehow. I just kind of felt that I didn't want to be left out any more. So anyway I got this job here…"

"Can I just stop you there Oscar? You mentioned this job. I've got to ask you something that's been on my mind. You've only worked here a few weeks and you're here alone right? You can't have had any references, so it doesn't make sense that you're here alone. Well not to me anyway."

"C'mon Roger just ask me the question."

"Well the manager or the owner, your boss, he's not down here in a box somewhere is he Oscar?"

Oscar nodded his head.

"Great question Roger. No he's not. He's a nice old guy. Harvey is his name and he's home safe and sound with his wife Marjorie. He's just not well, old age and back trouble and he trusted me to look after things for him. Even gave me the safe key, that's where this came from, I found it in the safe," he said pointing at the Glock. "I mentioned before about a handful of people in this life who have treated me as a human well, Harvey Bennet is one of them, okay."

"I believe you."

"Thank you Roger."

"So back to your father. You were saying about the job here."

"Right, well I didn't want to sit in my apartment all alone until it was safe to call Wendy. People seemed to like the new Walter Johnson more than they ever liked Oscar Kingman, so I started venturing out. I went into a few bars but they were full of trendies. I think they call them 'hipsters' here. Just shallow people, selfish people. They don't care about anyone but themselves and their trendy clothes and shiny new phones. So anyway I found this little old fashioned bar, mostly old timers and long-time Greenpoint residents. It was a 'no hipsters allowed' kind of place. I liked it. I met good people there, went in most nights for company, you know, watch the game and stuff."

He paused and pointed down at the mangled lifeless form of Woodrow Wilson.

"He was the barkeep."

"Wilson was the barkeep?"

"That's right Roger, I told you it was fate. I didn't know who he was and had barely spoken to him. He seemed okay. I finished up early one afternoon and called in for a quick drink. The place was empty and we got chatting. Like I said before, he started bragging about all those girls he slept with when he was a salesman. It's funny but little pieces started to drop into place like a jigsaw puzzle. I started to notice he looked a bit like me and somehow we got onto Charlotte and he told me about this one girl in Huntersville. I thought my head was going to explode right there, but I still wasn't sure. Then we got onto the name Loretta, my mother's name. I swear Roger, I never spent a single day in my life looking for my father. Maybe I wondered about who he was once or twice, but no more than that. It was just fate Roger."

"But Oscar are you sure he was your father, I mean one hundred percent certain?"

Oscar seemed to ponder this question carefully before he answered.

"No," he replied eventually, "not one hundred percent no, not without blood tests or something, but that's him," he said gesturing at the lifeless form of Woodrow Wilson.

"Okay, so once you figured he was your father, you plotted to kill him, maybe get him in here?"

"Wrong again Roger. He just walked in here this afternoon looking to buy a handle or a latch or something. I didn't plan this, it just happened, fate put him here, fate caught up with him. You know it's funny," said Oscar getting up and pulling at

Wilson's trouser pockets. "He wasn't in the shop a minute before he felt he had to steal something."

He pulled a couple of blister packs of batteries from Wilson's pocket and dropped them in front of Becker.

"He came down here into the basement and was still looking around to steal something even while I was serving him. He didn't know who I was. I just couldn't help myself, my head. Couldn't help myself. I was disgusted by him, so I picked up a shovel and I whacked him. He was lying on the floor out there, scratching around and I couldn't help thinking he looked like a cockroach, so I whacked him again. Turns out that's all he was Roger, just a stinking cockroach."

Becker let this sink in while they both sat in silence. Finally Becker spoke.

"So I'd like to understand all of this better. You mentioned how your mother's parents threw her out, why? Why would they do that?"

"They were catholics, that's what they did in those days. They took unmarried mothers and hid them away somewhere or they just disowned them."

"Surely they didn't all do that?" said Becker.

"No not all of them, just the worst of them, the holier-than-thou ones. They were more concerned what the neighbours might think, what the person sitting next to them in church might think. But you know all this Roger. You know what went on, probably still goes on."

Roger nodded. Over the years he'd scraped up plenty of the victims of this kind of attitude.

"So," continued Oscar, "my great grandmother Molly, she took my mother in and that's where I lived after I was born. She was wonderful, but my mother never got over the way her parents treated her. She became very bitter and she fought with Granny Molly a lot. She started drinking and I guess taking drugs, until finally she took me and left. We lived on the streets and she got worse and worse. I can barely remember the beginning of it all, but she got more and more sick. There was no money, mostly nothing to eat, so I had to go out and steal food for her."

He looked up at Becker, just holding back the tears, his eyes watery with the memory.

"Can you imagine it Roger. Can you imagine at five or six living under bridges or in alleys. Occasionally a cheap room somewhere. Men would come and use her. Sometimes they'd throw me out, but mostly they wouldn't bother, like I was invisible. And then one day I came back and found her dead, just sitting up against a wall dead…"

He told Becker about the day they took him back to Granny Molly's house and how she'd looked after him, loved him. Then he told Becker about how Molly died and he'd ended up in the orphanage. He showed Becker the scars on his hand and Becker sank lower and lower as this man Oscar Kingman poured out this story that stepped from one tragedy to the next. Becker had seen plenty, and he knew this was not an uncommon story, but he'd never sat like this and watched a man bleed from the soul. It made him think of his own childhood, happy enough in the suburbs, while all around him these arcane torments pretended by like normal lives. Oscar Kingman's voice became a low drone somewhere behind his thoughts. He had to force himself back into that little room and back to reality.

Oscar was talking about his wife Sharon, how she had trapped him into marrying her how she had finally put him in hospital with a head injury.

"I saw that in your file, it was serious wasn't it? They suspected brain damage but you didn't go through with the tests."

"I don't know how serious it was Roger, but I started getting these headaches. Not really headaches, but like this pressure comes on. Mostly I can get over it, it just passes but then it started getting worse and more frequent."

Becker watched him carefully as his fingers played over his temple.

"I get this twitch here and it's like tick tick tick. I feel it coming and it grows into this pain. On the morning I killed Llewellyn it just got worse and worse then it stopped; stopped so sudden it was like, I don't know, coming into a safe quiet room from a screaming hurricane or something. All of a sudden I felt great calm and everything was crystal clear. I knew he had to die. But look Roger, this is not an excuse. I already told you how I feel about people committing crimes and then claiming some kind of sickness or memory loss or something. Doesn't matter whether they're sick or not, on drugs or whatever, they still did the crime... still guilty. So you've got to ignore that when you make your decision. If you find me innocent it can't be for any of those reasons. If I get out of here and end up in a real court room, a real trial, I'm not going to mention it."

He laughed again in that mirthless way he had.

"We'll just call it inadmissible evidence okay. I've got to live and die by my own rules, my own code, otherwise what's the point?"

Becker felt the first seeds of something like an understanding of the man opposite him, the man who had him hog tied to a chair and would most likely kill him before the night was out.

"So that day then, tell me how it all started."

Oscar started with the stolen car, then the jogger and how this had set in motion the series of events. He told Becker how he had gone to the clothing store and how the assistant had grabbed him right there in the change room, had treated him like shit when he rebuffed her.

"I mean christ Becker, she was old enough to be my mother. I mean I was tempted and then I smelt the lavender, her perfume."

"Lavender, I don't understand," said Becker.

"Lavender. It was the lavender that stopped me, brought me to my senses. Granny Molly used to have these little bags of lavender around the house. You know, in the drawers, places like that."

"So you went back later and killed her because she molested you and then mocked you, bullied you?" suggested Becker.

"No, that's not the whole reason, not at all Roger," said Oscar looking up at the low ceiling. "That's not the whole reason at all."

He took a deep breath then faced Roger again.

"I've thought about this a lot. Sure she was a bully, but if I'm to be completely honest, I think I killed her because I was disgusted... in myself okay. I was also disgusted by her, but I think I really killed her because I was just too weak to kill myself. I had sunk that low."

Becker left this sit for a while.

"But I killed Llewellyn first, for no other reason than he was a cheat, a liar and a bully. It started with the car being stolen, then the jogger ran into me and spilt my breakfast, scalding coffee and a bagel, all over me without even a glance backwards. The selfish bastard just kept running. Then I'm standing there covered in shit and some little fucker steals my briefcase and runs off before I can do anything. My clothes are ruined, so I have to go buy clothes and I meet that Elaine woman. What was her last name?"

"Benny."

"Benny, Elaine Benny. Like some fucking harridan trapping her victims in the change cubicle. Anyway when I get to the office late, Edmund Llewellyn is waiting for me. It was his favourite thing to get all the staff together so he could pick on someone, most often me, but not always. He was good at it. He knew how to make you feel about two inches tall. Up until that day I had just taken it. It was just like the rest of my life, I was pretty much invisible so what did it matter. That day he went too far and I saw the look of doubt in his eyes. He knew he'd gone too far and once I saw that look I knew him to be a coward as well as a bully. That day the tick got worse, the pain came harder with each of those little incidents. Oh and yes I know they were just little incidents Roger, but they just built up. And then that moment of quiet clarity when I just decided to end it, to stop him.

I took the letter opener. I didn't plan it that way, I just saw it there and picked it up and went into his office. I killed him and I stuffed him down in the footwell of his desk. You know Roger, I went in there and I killed him. I came out again and nobody even saw me, room full of people and nobody even noticed me. That's how fucking invisible I'd become.

So after Llewellyn, I had bloodstains on my clothes. I went back to the store and it was a repeat of the morning's episode. That crone, she started on me again, so I throttled her with my tie. It was so easy. Then I just went back to the office. Remember I talked about fate Roger? Fate fate fate. You know it's fate that this Daniel Mills, the jogger is dead? It really never occurred to me that I might kill him. I didn't even know who he was, or where he was from, then right on cue fate steps in. I rarely left the office at lunchtime, normally ate at my desk, but that day I guess I was pretty hyped after Llewellyn and all, so I went out for lunch. I went into the park and just like that, there he was. I spoke to him, told him what he'd done that morning and do you know what he said to me Roger? Of course you do. He told me to fuck off. *Fuck off!* So I followed him and found out where he worked. I went back in the afternoon. Just a little bit of thought was all it took. I figured if he jogged to work in the morning, he would most likely jog home at night, so I waited and well, you know the rest."

Becker thought he would keep talking but he didn't. He just shrugged as if to say, *'That's it.'*

"Okay so then you went to your grandfather and he hid you at his beach house right!"

"Wrong. I went there on my own. I knew about the place because they took me there one summer. He came and got me out of boarding school and they took me there. But my grandmother didn't want me around. She was a horrible woman and she was going to send me back to that school, so I ran away. Things down there had changed a bit over the years, but I found the place easily enough. I hadn't seen my grandfather in all those years, but he must have figured it out, or at least suspected I was there and he just turned up. He told me he'd seen me on the television and all."

"So why did you kill him? Why poison him and where did the poison come from?" asked Becker.

"Is that what you think, the police? Do the police think I poisoned him?"

"Didn't you?"

"No I didn't. I swear to you Roger, we had a long talk and he told me how sorry he was about what had happened, about what he had allowed to happen to me and my mum, his daughter.

He said he was scared of my grandmother and that she was very dominant, that she was cruel and nasty but that he loved her anyway. Can you imagine that Becker? He was crying and apologising. He went and got a glass of water. One minute there he was blubbering away and the next he's fallen to the floor. I thought maybe a heart attack, but then I found the potassium cyanide bottle. He'd come there for my forgiveness and when he didn't get that he killed himself. He'd come there prepared Roger."

"I understand Oscar,"

"Do you? I mean do you understand, do you really believe me?"

"I believe you Oscar."

Again Oscar Kingman nodded slowly.

"You must be thirsty Roger. I'll get you a glass of water," said Oscar getting up and leaving the room.

He came back in almost immediately with a small tarpaulin and draped it over the body of Woodrow Wilson, then he was gone again.

Becker heard him go up the stairs and he tried to work on his bonds, but it was useless, he was bound too tight. His left arm was now blessedly numb. All he could do was wait. He thought about the odds of rescue, tried to remember what he had told Victor Brosa during that last telephone call. He remembered mentioning a hardware store in Greenpoint, but that was all. He figured if Brosa hadn't heard from him by morning maybe he might think something was up, but not before then. For now at least, Becker figured he was on his own.

It was hard for him to get a handle on Oscar Kingman. He found himself swinging backwards and forwards from pity to revulsion. Kingman's story was pretty torrid and Becker could figure he had left out a lot of the painful details, but it wasn't enough. *'It couldn't be enough could it?'* Not to justify what Kingman had done. All of a sudden Becker had an old song from the sixties playing in his head.

'Walk a mile in my shoes, walk a mile in my shoes and before you abuse criticise and accuse, walk a mile in my shoes.'

Round and round it went, round and round over and over, just that chorus. Becker was forced to admit that he couldn't say for certain how he would have reacted if it had happened to him. Of course none of that made it right, but Becker was beginning to understand.

Oscar was gone quite a while, but finally Becker heard him on the stairs.

"So here you go Roger," he said almost cheerfully as he came back into the boiler room carrying a glass of water.

He went to hold it up to Becker's lips, then paused.

"Oh! I suppose you might want me to take a drink of this first Roger? I don't want you to think I might be poisoning you."

He raised his eyebrows, questioning.

"That won't be necessary Oscar," replied Becker.

Oscar nodded tentatively then held the glass up to Becker's mouth so he could drink.

"So where were we up to then?" asked Oscar.

"I think there's just the matter of Detective Gail Casey. You know Oscar, bearing in mind everything you have told me, that's the one that doesn't fit…"

"I panicked!"

"Sorry?"

"I panicked. I was scared and I was going too fast, and well she just stepped out onto the road. I didn't know how to react. It was all so quick. I mean she was shooting at us and I panicked. I was worried what might happen to Wendy. I didn't aim the car at her or anything, she just didn't move. I swear Roger it was an accident. That is the one thing I am truly sorry about. I mean it, I am so sorry."

"She was my partner," said Becker quietly, remembering. "She was young and she was a bit of a hot head, but she was a good person Oscar, a good person..."

His voiced trailed off. Oscar waited.

"That's it," said Becker. "I guess I'm done. Now what?"

"Well," said Oscar, "It's time that in my defence, I deliver my summation. I mean otherwise we could be here all night right!"

He kicked Rogers foot.

"That was a joke Roger, here all night. Okay I guess this is not really the time for levity, so," he clapped his hands, "I will list the charges by event.

My client... that's me of course, is charged with killing Edmund Llewellyn, Elaine Benny, Daniel... yes Daniel Mills and of course Mr. Woodrow Wilson here."

He almost seemed to be enjoying himself and Becker thought he knew what that meant.

"I am further charged," he continued, "with causing the deaths of Detective Gail Casey and Richard Kingman. Regarding the death of Gail Casey I would plead manslaughter by misadventure, if there is such a charge. I would also offer my most sincere and heartfelt apologies for her demise. I certainly meant her no harm.

In the case of my grandfather Richard Kingman, I would plead innocence. He died by his own hand as a direct result of being unable to live any longer with his own guilty conscience. However in the case of the other four people, I place myself at the mercy of this court.

I would contend that each and every one of these people deserved their fate and the world is certainly a better place without them in it. I killed Edmund Llewellyn, Elaine Benny and Daniel Mills. Each one in cold blood and with no regrets. As for this man here, my father, I would contend that every son is entitled to the death of his father and not the other way around. Beyond that, I would refer to the nature of my upbringing and to the possible existence of a medical condition occasioned by a serious head wound at some point in the past. As I have previously stated I offer these facts only to assist in understanding how I came to that fateful day, not as an actual defence. And finally, before sentence is passed I should like to name my accomplices in these crimes, for of these there are many."

He turned to Becker and Becker saw a look of such bleak sadness, such emptiness as to catch his own breath in his throat.

"I name my accomplices as this man, Walter Woodrow, and I name all those like him both male and female who contrive to force their will upon others either by force or for a few desperate dollars. I name every parent or grandparent that does not or will not love their offspring unconditionally and to the fullest extent of their ability. I name every man and every woman that mocks or belittles or strikes another without provocation, and every man or woman that sees this happen and does not move to prevent it. I name all those organised religions whose members beleaguer the young, the lonely and the helpless. All those that would steal the innocence of a child. And I name the priests, the bishops, the archbishops and the cardinals. Those self appointed guardians of morality who hide within their fine disguises, feign ignorance or worse.

I name those that purport to entertain us but instead deliver chaos, anarchy and bloodlust as the new normal.

And finally I name the politicians and the lawmakers that refuse to act and I name those in the judiciary that are wrought of steel not flesh.

We are all of us to be held accountable together, for this is our doing."

He sat back down on the crate, his head hung low in contrition.

Roger Becker was stunned with the eloquence of it. Oscar Kingman was no fool and Becker wondered how long he had been preparing this speech, because that's what it sounded like, a speech from the dock. He would struggle to dispute it, any of it. He was lost in thought and questioning his own role on the planet, when Oscar Kingman spoke.

"I guess it's time then Roger."

"Time?"

"Time to deliver your verdict Roger."

He took the box cutter and placed it under Roger's seat then sat back and nodded. Roger Becker tried to shake off the feeling that he was being conned, refused to believe it because he didn't want to believe it. There could be no condoning what Kingman had done, society had boundaries and Oscar Kingman had stepped outside those boundaries.

"I understand everything you have said and I struggle to argue with any of it, but you aspire to a perfect world. You paint a picture of a world that just cannot be. I understand you and I understand, even sympathise with, almost everything you have said but, I still don't grasp why we have done this, the trial I mean. What does it achieve?"

"That all depends on your judgement Roger, please."

Roger Becker now found himself between the proverbial rock and a hard place. He was playing for his life here, but he already knew the answer.

"Before I answer you I have a request," said Becker.

"Go on I'm listening."

"I told you if I find you innocent, I agree to speak to Wendy Legget, to protect her, but I want something similar from you. If I find you guilty I want you to let me use my phone to call my wife. I... I want to say goodbye to her."

"No tricks?"

"What tricks, you'll have hold of the phone and you can hang up any time. Besides even if I shouted the address nobody could possibly find us before you could shoot me."

"That would be a sad phone call Roger... devastating. Of course I will let you make the call if need be. But it remains your choice."

Becker took a deep breath and signed his own death warrant.

"Guilty. You're guilty then, plain and simple.

I accept that you didn't kill your grandfather and I accept, as hard as it is for me personally, that Detective Gail Casey's death was an accident. It was a combination of your desperate panic and her reckless actions. As to the other deaths well, you've confessed to the murder of Edmund Llewellyn, Elaine Benny and Daniel Mills and we also have physical evidence of your presence at all three murder scenes. Lastly we come to Woodrow Wilson. I witnessed you shoot him," said Becker fixing a stare on Oscar. "I'm sorry Oscar but I doubt if there is a court in the land that would find otherwise."

The expression on Oscar Kingman's face was unreadable but Becker tried anyway. Was it fear, was it rage or was it resignation? Very slowly and deliberately, he picked up the Glock from between his feet. Becker fixed the image of his wife and children in his mind. Flooding doubt caused him to regret what he had just done. Now he would die and for what, a principle?

'I will die here, this is where it happens.'

He tried to speak but for a brief moment nothing came. When it did come it sounded like somebody else's voice.

"Can I have my phone call now please? I wish to speak to my wife."

"No!"

"Oscar you promised. You gave me your word."

"Roger, your phone is on the desk up in the office."

He lifted the gun.

"Close your eyes Roger."

"No I won't close my eyes. I want to see the man who shoots me. I want to look into your eyes," said Becker with more conviction than he felt. "I want to see the man who lied to me."

"I did lie to you Roger, but not about the phone call. I lied about killing you. I never had any intention of shooting you regardless of the outcome. I am not that person. I wanted you to close your eyes while I carry out *my* execution. I'd untie you now but I know you would try to stop me. Afterwards with a bit of effort you can reach the box cutter and free yourself. Then you are at liberty to phone your wife or whoever else you choose," he said.

"Then why," asked Becker, "why did we do all this, what was it all about?"

"I think you are a good policeman Roger and an even better man. With the world plummeting into chaos the way it is, there will be more and more like me. The disenfranchised are on the march like some hellish army and nobody seems to notice, or if they notice, they don't know why it is happening or how to stop it. It's a scary world full of nasty people, but the scariest thing is that nobody wants to do anything about it. Somewhere back there we simply abandoned the idea of consequences and the notion of respect. Half the world lives its life at the extreme limit of fear and pain. Our cities are full of drooling madmen flailing about on some kind of chemical that burns the soul worse than that narrow strip of sunlight overhead burns their eyes. Nobody dares help them anymore.

I said nasty people, not evil people, because it's not evil Roger. Evil implies some inexplicable unknown cause, some kind of pre-existence. We know the reasons, we know why this is happening. These people are manufactured Roger. They are simply products of this new world of ours, like me. I am simply a product of a selfish and uncaring world where cruelty and violence are the new normal and nobody cares. Ask yourself how many people have been bullied, abused, cheated, scammed, raped or murdered in this country, in the world even, just since we've been down here in this basement.

God's not coming Roger.

Don't you think that if there was a benevolent god and he was coming to save mankind he'd have done so by now? It's up to you and people like you Roger."

He sat there looking down at the bundle that had been Woodrow Wilson, had most probably been his father, his eyes lost and blinking slowly like some blind cat.

"Faith can be a disease Roger. Any man who clings fast to a savage faith will know only fear and superstition. These are not the weapons that can save us," he said almost to himself.

In the quiet that followed, Roger Becker was so alert, his senses so heightened that he could swear he felt the earth rolling under him. He leant against the spin as far as his bonds would allow. When Oscar Kingman spoke again his voice was normal.

"What I've done was wrong, no mistake, but if I can turn it around, then some small seed might grow from it. If this helps you understand what's going on out there, to actually feel it, then you will be an even better man and a better policeman. If there were more like you this might never have happened. You need to find a way Roger, please don't waste my life."

He stopped talking and pulled a bulky envelope from his back pocket.

"You don't have to do this Oscar."

"Yes I do Roger. I became one of them, but I won't die one of them. Would you please give this to Wendy for me," he said dropping the envelope on the floor beside the box cutter.

He put the barrel of the glock in his mouth and pointed it upwards, then quickly pulled it out, looking frightened, suddenly unsure. He took another few breaths, deep in deep out, then picked up the box cutter and sliced away some of the bonds holding Roger Becker's right arm so that Becker had movement from the elbow down.

"It seems I have one last favour to ask of you Roger," he said as he slid his crate over to Roger's right hand side. "Will you please hold my hand otherwise I'll, I…"

"Of course," said Becker.

Oscar smiled and in one movement he reached out his left hand and took hold of Becker's and at the same time jammed the gun back in his mouth and pulled the trigger.

The shot knocked him off the crate and his body twisted around in Becker's firm grip to lie on the floor beside the chair. Becker held his hand white-knuckle tight as those final twitches pulsed through his body and he lay still.

Oscar Kingman was finally at peace.

EPILOGUE

Detective Roger Becker sat in his car outside a three storey apartment complex on the north side of the city. The small windows and drab grey cladding lent it the look of a prison. It was 6.30 in the evening and he waited there rather than seeing her in the office. He had promised Oscar Kingman that he would keep her out of it and it was a promise he intended to keep. She was an accessory after the fact to three murders and had been in the car that had struck and killed Gail Casey. Becker had read her file, made more enquiries and had understood that she was not unlike Oscar Kingman. Wendy Legget was almost invisible like Oscar. She was mousey, quiet and unremarkable, old fashioned even, but if Oscar was right she was really guilty of nothing more than loving him. He could think of nothing to be gained by involving her. She needed kindness and understanding. Becker wondered what might have happened if Oscar had met her earlier. Maybe things would have been different. It was impossible to know.

It was five weeks since he had freed himself from the basement in Greenpoint and the case was now officially closed. Oscar Kingman gone down in history as a dangerous psychotic killer, Becker gone down in history as the hero that had almost died at the killer's hand. Becker knew different, Becker now understood that at no time was he ever in danger of being killed by Oscar Kingman. He had gone with Louis Flowers to speak to Sharon Kingman and for one brief moment he had felt himself in Oscar's shoes, while this disgusting woman cursed her late husband to hell. The two daughters sat there playing with their phones and Becker felt he wanted to reach out and slap all three of them back to reality.

As they left Sharon Kingman was in the doorway screaming after them.

"What about me? What's going to happen to me now?" she had demanded.

When they got in the car, Flowers had shaken his head.

"I can't believe she wasn't the first," he had said.

A woman was coming down the sidewalk. Becker sat up straight and peered through the window at her... not Wendy Legget, but as she got closer he checked the photo he held and looked again. It was Wendy Legget. She looked different.

"Wendy, Wendy Legget," he said getting out of the car as she passed.

He held up his shield, clumsy with his arm in the cast. She stopped and turned back, uncertain.

"Wendy I'm Detective Roger Becker. Can I talk to you?"

"I remember you," she said. "I know who you are. What do you want with me?"

"I needed to see you privately. I have a message from Oscar."

She hardened.

"Oscar? You mean Oscar Kingman? What's that got to do with me?" she countered, uncertain.

"Wendy, I was with him at the end. I know all about you and Oscar. He made me promise to keep you out of this, to protect you. He asked me to come and see you. Can we go inside and talk please?" he said looking around. "It's a bit public out here."

"Okay, okay," she nodded. "It's this way."

The apartment was tiny but modern and very neat. Becker was surprised to see her take out two glasses and a bottle of single malt.

"Would you like a drink or are you on duty?"

"No I'm not on duty Wendy and yes please, I'd like a drink."

She poured two measures and pointed to a chair, sat down opposite him, suspicion lurking right there just below the surface. Becker took a sip and studied her over the rim of his glass. This was not the same girl he had interviewed just weeks before at Loughrans. Well it was the same girl, he could see that now but, she had make-up on, her glasses were more trendy and her clothes more fashionable. But there was something else. Becker put his glass down and took the envelope from his coat pocket.

"Like I said Wendy, this is not official business. In fact if the department knew I was here I'd be on report and if they knew why I was here you would be arrested."

"So why are you here detective?"

He pushed the crumpled envelope across the table. She stared down at it.

"What's this?" she asked.

"Oscar gave it to me before he... I'm sorry Wendy, before he killed himself. He asked me to tell you how much he loved you. How he had never loved anybody like he loved you. He showed me where he had a tattoo of your name... here," he said touching his bicep.

She put down her glass and picked up the envelope, squeezing it between her fingers, then she tore the end off. From inside she pulled out a pink cloth bundle held together with rubber bands. Becker saw the look of surprise on her face as her eyes flickered briefly to his. She reddened slightly, then pulled the bundle apart. It was a pair of women's panties and inside was a wad of cash. She pushed it to one side then reached into the envelope and took out a single sheet of paper. He watched her lips moving as she read, saw the tears well in her eyes. She took off her glasses and clawed away the tears then looked up.

"Would you like to know what it says Detective Becker?" she asked.

"That's up to you."

She put her glasses back on and started reading.

My dearest Wendy. I can never express how much I love you. Those few days we had together made up for all of the pain in my whole miserable life. Maybe if we had found each other before I killed those people things might have been different, but we will never know. I tried so hard Wendy and I'm sorry but there was no other way. You need to know that I loved you. I have missed you and have thought about you every second of every day.

I spent my last hours with Roger Becker and he will tell you what happened. I hope he will also tell you that I died happy knowing you loved me. Roger Becker is a good and fair man Wendy, do not be afraid to ask him for help if you need it.

I will love you forever - Oscar.

"That's it Mr. Becker. That's all there is. Will you tell me what happened?" she asked.

So Becker told her everything that had transpired in that basement in Greenpoint Brooklyn and when he finished she sat there looking at him, then reached out and poured him another drink.

"You know I used to drink wine before Oscar came into my life, always too much of it and always alone. Now every night I have a little drink of whisky. I still don't like the taste, but I guess I'm getting more used to it. Oscar introduced me to it at that beach house, so every night I drink a little toast to Oscar and not just because I loved him, but because he made me human. After Oscar died I went up on the roof of our office building and I stood there on the edge. I was going to throw myself off. I saw no point in going on. Without Oscar I had nothing to live for. I was so close, so close and suddenly I realised I did have something to live for. Oscar Kingman gave me a life, he made me human. Do you understand that detective?"

"Yes," said Becker, "yes I do."